The Best Summer - UBETCHA

Jim Stout

AuthorHouse™
1663 Liberty Drive
Bloomington, IN 47403
www.authorhouse.com
Phone: 1-800-839-8640

First published by AuthorHouse 11/24/2009

ISBN: 978-1-4490-4989-8 (e)
ISBN: 978-1-4490-4993-5 (sc)

Printed in the United States of America
Bloomington, Indiana

This book is printed on acid-free paper.

Chapter 1

"Private Short, the Captain wants to see you and Fred today SURE," the first sergeant said at lunch on Friday. "I suggest you'd better see him first thing after lunch ... he has to go for some dental work at three, and he might not be in such a happy mood later."

"We'll be there, Sarge. I think Corporal Harris went to the PX, but I'll catch him before we take up class this afternoon. Then we'll give this bunch their test grades and send them back to California. They all passed, by the way, even if one guy isn't too good at loading the tanks. I'll have the letter ready for you about this class when we come in."

The Captain was talking with the recently arrived Second Lieutenant Sumovitch, and Fred and Jan faced the Captain and both saluted. Taking in the lieutenant's physical appearance, they later compared notes and agreed that he was "overweight, overdressed, and over twenty-five". His dark flabby jowls and thinning black hair gave the impression that he was over forty, but they knew there was a low cut- off age for OCS entry. His upside-down build was more like a woman's, with narrow sloping shoulders and broad hips. His tailored uniform jacket was smartly creased, and unadorned with any ribbons or patches, yet was a style an officer would choose for a parade, the full-length suit style rather than the GI's preferred Eisenhower jacket.

Captain Ross returned the salute, as did the Lieutenant. Captain Ross looked at Harris, and said, "Men, we have a tough task for you. Harris, have you been to Yakima?" Fred nodded in the affirmative. "Well," the Captain continued, "the wheels in the Pentagon want us to take these semi-tractors over there for a two-day cold soak at zero or below, and the forecast for the firing range is below zero next week. Then we'll see if they can pull the tanks back over the Cascades. Corporal, I think you'll need a pretty big support convoy...I'd suggest a mechanic or two, a couple cooks, a medic, and probably three or four six-by-six trucks. You'll want to carry extra fuel for every vehicle, and it'll be cold as hell, so you'll want a lot of kerosene for the cook stoves and tent heaters. Get your suggested personnel and logistics list to Lieutenant Sumovitch as soon as you can

We've canceled your class for next week, so you might as well go out on Tuesday morning. Harris, see if Sergeant Martin in Supply can find you some arctic gear. Any break-down out there at minus twenty could be dangerous without the right clothing."

Lt. Sumovitch sat in on their afternoon class session, and as Fred and Jan explained the answers that had been missed on the final test, he interrupted several times with questions that showed them he knew very little about heavy duty vehicles. Jan was relieved to hear the bus honking outside the classroom to take the graduating drivers to their train south. As soon as the group of drivers left, Jan and Fred sat down with a notebook, with the lieutenant looking over their shoulders.

"One day over, one day back, two days cold soak, one extra day in case of breakdowns ... better plan on rations for five days," Corporal Harris said. Lt. Sumovitch interrupted:

"What breakdowns are you talking about? Four days rations are enough. You know if you take rations for an extra day and we don't need them, they'll just be thrown away. Besides, if we need more, we can just phone and have them bring them out."

"Sir, perhaps you don't understand ... we need to be self-sufficient at Yakima. The firing range is across the Cascade Mountains, and sometimes it snows so much this time of year the road can be closed for days. There aren't any troops over there in the winter, just some civilian guards. And no barracks. We'll have to put up big tents. Besides, it's a six-hour drive at best," Fred said. "Probably ten for the tank haulers."

The lieutenant grunted. "Well, how many vehicles and men will we need?"

Harris continued, "Jan, don't you think a six-by for the cooks, pulling a 400-gallon kerosene trailer, will do for the meals? Then another six-by for the tents, and it can pull another 400- gallon unit for gasoline for the trucks. Another six-by can take the water jerry cans and duffel, and pull another tank trailer for diesel fuel. Is that enough?"

Jan added, "We'd better take an ambulance with a medic, and a wrecker with a mechanic. Sir, will you want to drive a jeep?"

"Of course I want a jeep, Private. I'm not going to freeze my butt in a damn six-by-six."

Jan was writing on his sheet. "Looks like one officer, two cooks, three six-by drivers, two medics, one mechanic who'll drive the wrecker, and you and me, Fred. Does that cover it?"

"How about my jeep driver?" Sumovitch snorted. "And we'll need six or eight men for KP and guard duty, too."

"Sir, the six-by drivers will be happy to pull KP if we're only feeding twelve men, since they'll be in a warm mess tent all day," Fred suggested. "We could add two or three men for guard duty; they could ride in the front of the six-bys, but I'm not sure what they'll be guarding in that wilderness. They can do four-on and four-off during the night and sleep all day."

Tuesday morning at 0400 the men assembled in the mess hall for a hearty breakfast. The Captain had reviewed Jan's list and the Lieutenant's, and had cut the eight extra men Sumovitch had wanted for guard duty to three.

When they were ready to leave, Sumovitch called a meeting. "Now everybody keep up, and keep this convoy tight. I don't want to see any straggling vehicles on this trip. I'm going to follow the agreed routing at forty-five, and I want to see a tight unit."

Jan was about to speak, but Sergeant Bob Herndon, the chief mechanic, who had volunteered to be the wrecker driver, spoke up.

"Sir, I followed those haulers to Seattle and back, and they can't no way run that fast, especially up them grades to Snoqualmie. Hell, they'll probably be cogged down to 5 miles an hour and gruntin'."

"Sergeant, are you telling me that these vehicles aren't capable of running forty-five?" Sumovitch retorted, showing redness in his face.

"Lieutenant, I don't reckon I can tell you nothin'," Herndon chuckled. "You run forty-five, and we'll all get there by late supper time."

As the convoy moved up the steep mountain road toward the pass in the Cascades, Jan and Fred were finding the climbing very slow in their heavily-loaded tractor-trailer rigs with tanks aboard. They were placed late in the convoy, just in front of the ambulance and the big wrecker. Jan was driving the lead tank hauler, and was falling far behind the other trucks in the convoy as he ground up the steep mountain grades on the two-lane road; he was losing ground on the down-grades as well, since it was necessary to go downgrade in a lower gear as well. Even so, Fred was losing ground behind Jan, since his truck didn't seem to have quite as much power.

...Jan noted the scenery as he climbed. The valley narrowed into a twisting, V-shaped cut, with the highway dug out of what appeared to be solid rock in many places. The vegetation was mostly tall evergreens. There were large patches of bare rock where the wind had blown away the fresh snow cover. As he climbed, the plowed snow got deeper, and some-times on what he guessed to be the north slope, he was driving over fresh snow hiding what seemed to be ice with some sand spread over it. In the bitter cold the snow was as dry as bits of confetti, and the wind carried it from place to place, building drifts such as Jan had never imagined.

When Fred's truck had not appeared in his mirror for a few minutes, he looked for a place to pull off and wait. Topping the grade he was pulling, he found a place where the snow plows had cleared a wide shoulder long enough for both rigs to park. In a few minutes Fred ground up the grade and parked behind Jan. The ambulance and wrecker drivers looked at the minimum space left by Fred's trailer, pulled barely off the road against a forty-foot snowbank, and decided to drive farther to find a better place to pull off. Jan buttoned his field jacket to the neck as he walked back to talk to Fred. "Do you know how many more hard climbs we have, bud? I'll need more fuel if we're not over the hump soon." "Jan, I think we'll be going downhill pretty soon, and it'll be down-grade most of the way to Yakima. I remember this flat spot we're on from last summer. We'll be passing several strange 'A-frame' houses in a couple miles, if we can see them. This is called Snoqualmie Pass ... I guess that's probably an Indian name. ... How come you got the faster tractor? I can't keep up with you on the upgrades, and I'm smokin' my brakes trying to catch up on the down slopes."

"I dunno, Fred. I'm driving as hard as I feel safe. I wonder how far ahead of us the rest of the convoy is. Lootenant Sonovabitch is probably ready to crap in his sharply creased britches since we can't keep up with the six by's." The lieutenant's jeep was leading the convoy, far ahead of the laboring tank transports. The "six-by-six" trucks had no problem keeping up with the under-powered jeep. Even the one that was carrying the tents and pulling the tank trailer with fuel for the two tractors wasn't falling behind often."Yeah, he doesn't have a clue about how slow these beasts are on the grades ... hell, they're slow as cold West Virginia molasses on the flat, for that matter." Fred couldn't miss a chance to razz Jan about his home state; and Jan frequently returned the favor with some crack about Kansas.

"Fred have you noticed some of the snow piles? Those big blowers must throw the snow over a hundred feet." They heard a jeep whining toward them. Fred threw his cigarette toward the snowbank and both of them climbed back into their tractors. Before they could pull out, the jeep rolled up and turned behind them, and pulled up in the eastbound lane, blocking traffic.

The lieutenant bellowed at Jan: "Private, if you can't keep up, I'm gonna find some drivers who can ... dammit; NO stopping again until we stop for lunch, do you hear? That's an order!"

"We'll try, sir," Fred said, "but no matter what we're driving, we have to stop for a piss every couple hours." As Lt. Sumovitch turned away, Fred muttered, "Try driving one of these things yourself, dammit. They're nothin' but slow, and both of us would be delighted if someone else could drive them." He recalled that they had trained two back-up drivers, but Pfc Ketcham broke a leg when he fell off a tank, and the other trainee reupped so he could get a transfer to Belvoir to be nearer home. Who could blame him, Fred thought. Maybe I'll ask for a transfer, too. Maybe they'd send me back to Ft. Riley, near home ..."

The lieutenant drove off with a grimace when the traffic he was blocking started a persistent blowing of horns. Jan pulled out when the traffic opened up enough for both rigs to get out on the road again. He wondered, what else is this green shavetail gonna pull on this trip? I don't like the smell of his attitude. They had actually reached the summit, and for the next hour most of the highway was down-grade. The terrain opened up into more level ground, still with lots of pine trees, Jan noted, but he was also seeing cactus and other dry-land species. They finally caught up with the rest of the convoy, when they stopped near a small town, so they could have their lunch of C-rations.

When the two tank haulers finally pulled into the assembly area of the firing range, followed by the ambulance and Sgt. Herndon in the wrecker, they saw chaos. The lieutenant had ordered one of the six-by drivers to beat down the three and four foot snow drifts with his truck so they would have a cleared space for the tents. The truck had become stuck during the first pass through the drifts, and was in danger of tipping over on a hidden stream bank. Another truck had been called into place to try to rescue it with a winch cable, but the winch had just pulled the second truck into a precarious position as well. Jan and Fred talked with Herndon, and they decided to unload Jan's tank to pull the trucks to safety, and also to use the tank to pack down the snow for the tenting ground. Jan's tank engine was soon roaring, and he leveled the area chosen for the tents in a few minutes; then Fred drove the tank to the stranded trucks with Sgt. Herndon riding in the tower, and pulled both of them to safety easily with a chain. In just over an hour the tents were all erected, the tent heaters and cots set up, and the cooks were banging a pan to call everybody in for a meal of hot beef stew, apple dumplings, and lots of coffee, served in a drafty mess tent with the cold air carrying the acrid smell of burnt kerosene. The temperature hovered at five below zero that evening, and the soldiers were dressed in three or four layers to keep warm. They had all been issued arctic parkas from supply before they left, and after an hour spent shivering in his dress topcoat, even the lieutenant relented and donned a parka.

Jan and Fred, Herndon, the medic, and two cooks had bunked together in a twelve-man tent with a kerosene heater that barely kept the temperature above freezing, but had made a mess of the uncovered snow on the ground. Fred had insisted that they bring two extra blankets for each man, so in addition to their "mummy" sleeping bags, each had two Army- issue blankets, heavy wool that held body heat well. One of these they used in a triple layer between their cots and sleeping bags, and the other in a double layer on top, so they could sleep warmly, even at fifteen below zero the second night. Fred said he had seen the lieutenant moving his cot to the back of the ambulance; Lt. Sumovitch had told Fred that, since he was Officer of the Guard, he wanted to be where the night guards could find him. The off-duty guards had to move their cots to the other sleeping tent. During the daytime, Jan and Fred had no official duties, but Sumovitch wanted to spend the morning trying to master the technology of the tank haulers, so he ordered Jan and Fred to teach him the details from their lesson plans. He could not grasp many facets of the air brake and the hydraulic systems, and he complained that their instructions lacked thoroughness. That afternoon they spent gathering firewood in a big pile, "just in case", Jan told Fred, but his purpose was to be clear of the Lieutenant.

Wednesday night after supper, Fred and Jan resumed their talk of the night before, when Fred had noticed Jan's moody silence and correctly guessed his thoughts. "Friend JANUS, keeper of the gates. You're still mooning over that fickle chick, aren't you?"No reply. "Jan, you're just gonna have to get over Mona, or Dee, or whatever the hell her name is. You've been moping around for a month. She's gone, can't you under-stand? Once a girl tells you she's engaged, it's official, man, and she isn't ever going to change her mind except in the movies. That diamond on her finger is the end of it for you."

"Fred, I keep hoping I'll get another letter that says 'I made a big mistake, please take me back!' I told her I would, in a heartbeat, in the letter I wrote her." Jan sighed and shook his head. "I guess I can just forget about that happening. Fred, you don't know how much it hurts. I just can't get her out of my mind. Everywhere I look I see her face ... in the clouds, or in a lake ... hell, even in the galloping pine bushes along the road. It hurts, damn it! You don't know how much."

"Well, maybe I do know, buddy. Have I ever told you about Ronnie?"

"No," Jan answered, "you haven't, Fred. Where does Veronica fit in your history? You still have all those pictures and letters ... she must have meant something to you once."

"Oh man, she was everything. We were in high school together ... she was a beauty, home-coming queen and all that; her folks were split, her dad was in California, and she lived with her mom and grandparents. We dated all through high school, and we sat together and cried all night after Dad's wheat crop got hailed down two years in a row. In the middle of our senior year she thought she was pregnant, and we really sweated that one out. Man, we really had some good times together. We were going to get married as soon as we got a good wheat crop, but the third year there was drought -- we barely got our seed back. Dad couldn't make the payments, and I joined the Army just to make some money to send home so he wouldn't lose that pretty Kansas farm. Veronica even rode a bus to Fort Riley to spend a weekend with me when I finished basic. I promised to marry her just as soon as I could get Dad out of trouble.

But then I was sent here from Fort Riley, and I met Shirley at a USO dance. She came on to me really strong ... this gal isn't the least bit shy! I guess I wasn't used to that kind of stuff from a girl. A couple dates and we were in bed ... and I had such a mixed-up head I couldn't think straight. We shacked up every weekend, and I got such a guilty conscience I couldn't write to Veronica at all. I finally had to do something, so I did something stupid: I sent her a Dear John letter with a bunch of crap about re-enlisting so I could make enough money to save the farm, and she should just find somebody else, because I wasn't going to get out of debt for ten years, and I knew she couldn't wait that long. I cried a lot of nights about that. I even woke up crying at Shirley's, and I called Shirley Ronnie more than once. Boy, did I ever make a big mistake." He shook his head sadly.

"Well, Fred ... it sounds to me like you still love her. Did you ever think about writing to Veronica to ask if maybe she'd take you back? Or have you given up on her completely?"

"Jan, I don't know. Mom keeps telling me that she's in college and gonna be a teacher, and she isn't dating anybody, and she keeps asking about me. Dammit, Shirley keeps bugging me about getting married ... I don't really want to marry her. Frankly, I'm kinda tired of her hangin' all over me and bossing me around like she owns me. But would Ronnie forgive me if I went back there and got down on my knees and begged? She was only eighteen when I done her wrong." Jan thought to himself – eighteen! Dee and I are only 19. I wonder how much she was shocked when I sent her the letter saying I was going to stay out here for college? That offer of 30 hours work plus TE paying my college tuition was just too much to turn down – but was that good or bad news to her? Her "Dear John" letter had asked isn't that GOOD news for you but BAD news for ME?"

What a lucky break when I thought of that special resistor to give the V2 box a higher operating temperature range...that had been rewarded with a raise and the offer of a full time job with tuition after he was free of the army. What a change in their product he had made.

The next day they were scheduled to start up the tank haulers and head for home. After breakfast at 0600, with the temperature at minus fifteen, Jan tried to start his tractor, and the starter just barely turned the engine over. He pulled out the oil dipstick and discovered that the oil looked like heavy, cold molasses. He took off the fuel tank caps and peered down at the diesel fuel; it looked much thicker than normal, the fuel tank in both tractors, and the tank trailer with the extra diesel fuel: were all the same. For a while Jan was stymied.

Then he remembered something a bulldozer operator back home, old Cleaver' had said about working in Alaska with a diesel bulldozer in the bitter cold: "Sometimes you have to build up a fire under the damn things to thin the motor oil, and heat up the fuel so it will go through the filters. Sometimes you don't even shut them down for a month at a time except to check the oil and add more... And we found out that iff'n you add about ten per cent warm kerosene, the fuel will still flow, down to minus fifteen or so."Jan and Fred conferred with Herndon, and they decided to move the sleeping tents over the tractors so they could heat the engines with the tent heaters. Lieutenant Sumovitch was in a dither, thinking they had gone crazy. He shouted irrelevant and conflicting orders that slowed down the work. They started the gasoline-powered wrecker and both tanks, and after they had unloaded the tanks, they pulled the trailers away from the tractors. Then they could move the tents to enclose the tractors.

By noon they were able to crank the engines, and they ran, but without much power, as if they were starved for fuel. They shut them off, and Jan pulled off the fuel filters. The paper elements looked like they were full of paraffin. After another conference, Jan suggested that they ask the cooks to heat a large flat pan full of water; a smaller pan holding kerosene was placed in the heated water to warm the filter elements laying on their side, immersed. After a few minutes, the gel dissolved, and the engines ran normally when the filters were replaced.

The lieutenant called a meeting. He asked Fred: "Well, Corporal, can you get those damn things running well enough to crawl back over the pass, or do we just leave them here until summer? It's after noon now, so I guess it's too late to start over the pass today, but we're leaving at seven a.m. tomorrow, with or without the damn things. I'll drive the jeep to town and call the Captain. You guys get those things back together and loaded up, and the tents ready for sleeping again." He climbed into the jeep, and headed off toward town, throwing a shower of snow as he spun the wheels. The tents were moved back to their original spots, and the tractors were left running after the trailers were hooked up and the tanks loaded again. Fred's unit was more exposed to the wind, and when they walked out of the chow tent after supper it had stopped running. Jan went back to set up the makeshift "double boiler", while Fred and Herndon ran to remove the filter again. When they brought it into the mess tent in a small bucket, Fred was holding his hands wrapped in a towel. Herndon dropped the filter into the warm kerosene, and asked Jan to get the medic; he thought Fred's hands might be frostbitten. While the young medic had Fred soaking his hands in a pan of cool water to warm them slowly, Herndon and Jan replaced the filter. Jan had heated five gallons of the kerosene, and he poured this into the fuel tank of Fred's tractor. When he had started it again, he heated five more gallons to pour into the his tank.

It was a dark night, so Sgt. Herndon had driven the wrecker into position to shine the lights on the tractor. Sumovitch drove his jeep in just as Jan was pouring the warm kerosene into the fuel tank. He walked over and asked if Jan was topping off his tank. Then he smelled the kerosene and he exploded, his speech slurred, "Why're you pouring kerosene into that tank, Private? That's for diesel fuel only, *DAMMIT* ... it says so right there. Can't you read? Short, your insubordinate attitude will not be tolerated! I'm going to court-martial your ass when we get back to Fort Lewis!" With that he stumbled off toward the ambulance, but stopped after a few steps and threw up.

Sgt. Herndon muttered, "Jan, he's been drinkin' -- I could smell liquor on his breath. Our Lieutenant Sonofabitch is drunk as a skunk! What an asshole. He prob'ly won't remember a thing he said come mornin'. And if he does, I'll tell the Captain what went on here tonight."

"Sarge, I sure hope so. His attitude scares me, sometimes. Can you imagine being in combat with an officer like that in charge? I'm going to ask for a transfer if I have to work for that jerk."

Jan found the return trip to Ft. Lewis easier than the laborious trip to the Yakima range had been. The grade up the Cascades from the east is gentler, so the convoy speed was faster. Even with the slightly reduced BTU available from the mixed fuel, the tractors climbed the grades like horses turned back toward the barn at the end of a day in the field. While Jan was coasting down the western side in a low gear to keep from over-speeding, enjoying the much warmer temperatures of the western slope, he knew his partner Fred was having a troubling trip with his hand. Fred had shown his left hand with a badly frostbitten finger to the medic corporal, who could only suggest wearing a glove to avoid chafing the most severely injured digit, the smallest finger. During their lunch break Fred admitted to Jan that he was having really severe pain in his hand. They talked to the medic, Corporal Art Glover, who gave Fred three more apc pills to swallow ... the Army version of aspirin ... and advised them to get Fred back to base quickly. Jan talked with Sgt. Herndon, who could drive anything, and suggested that he drive Fred's rig back to camp, and let Fred ride in the ambulance. Herndon agreed, and suggested to the Lieutenant that the ambulance should leave the convoy and rush Fred back to base for treatment as quickly as possible. Lieutenant Sumovitch objected, but Cpl. Glover and Sgt. Herndon finally convinced him that a delay might endanger Fred's entire hand, since the one finger was now turning dark.

The ambulance sped away and arrived at the hospital an hour before the convoy reached the fort. Fred was rushed into intensive care, and quickly moved to the operating room where a surgeon arrived a few minutes later.

It was after four p.m. when the convoy finally ground to a halt in the motor pool compound. Lieutenant Sumovitch strode to Jan's rig with a smirk on his face. "I didn't forget, Short," he shouted. "I'll see that you both pay for breaking my orders. We'll have a full debriefing in the orderly room in fifteen minutes." With that he stomped off toward the orderly room.

The medic, Corporal Glover had driven directly from the hospital to the motor pool and advised the first sergeant and Captain Ross of all that had happened. When the Lieutenant stormed in, he was offered a cup of coffee, and told the Captain would return in a few minutes to conduct a debriefing. The Captain was aware that Lieutenant Sumovitch had threatened Jan and Fred with a court martial over the kerosene incident, so he had gone to the maintenance building when the guard at the gate reported the convoy returning to the base. He was able to meet briefly with Sergeant Herndon and Jan before he returned to the orderly room. He thanked Herndon and Jan, and asked Jan to write a brief report on the problems they had had starting the diesel engines when they were cold. Then he looked directly at Jan: "Pfc Short, I want you to write that report in the Day Room, and bring it to the first sergeant. Then I want you to pick up a pass he has for you, and get your mail, and I don't want to see your butt in this compound for three days. Do you understand?"

Fred woke up in an all-white hospital room, and quickly discovered his left hand was heavily bandaged and supported in a sling. The Army nurse watching him, a pretty lieutenant in a white uniform, smiled as he opened his eyes. "You're waking up right on time, Corporal. How do you feel?"

"Pretty groggy, sir ... or do I call you 'ma'am'?"

"I like 'ma'am' better, Corporal. Do you have any feeling in your hand?"

"No, everything's numb. But I really need to go to the bathroom. Can I get up and walk?"

"I'll help you, Fred, and the sooner you can walk the better. The chart says they anesthetized you with sodium pentathol, so you'll come out of it quicker if we walk around a bit. Let me put these slippers on your feet, and I'll help you out of bed. ... By the way, the motor pool called and said they would send a sedan to pick you up in the morning so you can go on leave."

"What leave? Hell, man ... oh, pardon me, maam ... I'm not planning any leave."

"Corporal, you *ARE* going on leave ... it's one of the few benefits of losing a finger. What kind of work could you do with that arm in a sling for a week? You won't be charged for this time off, it's called a medical leave. Wouldn't you like to spend a week in Kansas with your family and your girl friend?"

"What! They took my *damn* finger off?" Fred exclaimed. "Oh ...," he groaned, "I'm sorry, Lieutenant. I was just sorta surprised." His voice was still slightly slurred, his movements slow.

"You're just lucky the surgeon on call this afternoon had a lot of experience with frostbite in Alaska ... he took one look and said we either took off one today or three tomorrow."

"Wow. Well, one's better than three. .. Ma'am, I think I can walk in there by myself ...," Fred said as the nurse helped him to his feet.

"Soldier, I'd be the laughing stock of the nurse corps if I let you fall in the john. Now just lean on me, and we'll walk you right in there. When we get back I'll call Pvt. Short at Takoma Elektroniks ... he said he had picked up your mail and wanted to bring it to you."

"Hey, Fred ... how are you, buddy?" Jan asked when he found Fred sitting on the side of the bed nursing his bandaged hand.

"Damned if I know, Jan, " Fred answered. "I'm so dopey. Did you know they took my finger off? How the hell can I hold my teacup properly with my li'l pinkie gone?"

"Yeah, they told me. Tough luck, Fred. .... Hey, maybe you'll get a Purple Heart. You were wounded in action at the Battle of Snoqualmie. That was some action, wasn't it? I'll tell you what, friend ... I hope that's the last battle I have to face under the leadership of THAT officer."

"Amen to that. Didja bring me any mail, Jan? Not that I expect much. My folks aren't much to write. Maybe I'd hear from Mom if she knew I got wounded in action, though."

"I did bring you a piece of mail. And I brought my valentine along to show you. You know, we spent Valentine's Day up there in the snow. Kinda nice to come back to this ...," and he gave Fred a pink envelope that carried the familiar scent of lilacs, and another addressed to Jan.

As he looked at the mail, his face registered astonishment. "Oh, my God, Jan ... I got a valentine, too. It's from Ronnie." There was a quaint picture of a feminine hand with a string tied around one finger. Inside the card the message read, "I'll never forget." And the signature, written in bright red, was "Veronica"

."No kidding! Well, Fred ... there's you answer. I guess Ronnie still has feelings for you."

"I haven't gotten a valentine since I was ten," Fred said in a husky voice. "What a sweet kid she is." Then he chuckled. "Hey, Jan...- now I'm confused. I've got two girls! You've had lots of experience with women, buddy. How would you handle this big problem?"

Jan's valentine was from Alpha Lee, a friend he had made in high school. 'You are just my cup of tea,' was the hand-printed message inside. On the front of the card was a picture, done in colored pencil, of a cup of tea with a face reflected in the surface ... Jan's own face, copied, he knew, from the charcoal portrait she had done last year at High School. The edge of the teacup had a smudge of pink lipstick, and on the saucer was a heart-shaped cookie with one bite out of it. "Hey, Jan, your new girlfriend's an artist," Fred said with a grin, handing the card back to Jan. "Yes she is, Fred. She has real talent, my Alpha Lee."

Jan finally found time to write to Alpha Lee:"

Ft Lewis Feb 20 "Dear Alpha Lee,"Sorry it has taken so long to write. I got your letter on the eleventh, just as we were packing to go out in the field for four days. Your cute valentine was waiting when we got back, just when I needed a smile. Thanks, sweetie! Would you believe Fred got a valentine, too, from his high school galfriend in Kansas? He was pretty excited about that.

"Fred and I drove the tank haulers all the way to Yakima, to an army firing range. Man, that was some drive, over the Cascades and through

Snoqualmie Pass. (Look that up on the map, Alpha Lee ... Snoqualmie is northeast of the Fort, east of Seattle.) The snow was piled up 40 feet deep along the roads. They don't plow that snow, there's way too much ... they move it with huge blowers mounted on big trucks, and I guess they must be able to throw it 50 yards, as high as it was piled up. We saw houses with extreme pitch roofs (they call them A frames, and that's what they look like from the front: the letter A) surrounded with snow maybe 30 feet deep, and tunnels dug to the front door.

Anyway, we got there ok, and then when we thought we were ready to come back, we couldn't get the tractors started and we were there in that frigid cold another whole day. Alpha Lee, I've had enough cold to last me the rest of my life. We slept in tents with big kerosene heaters, so we were pretty warm in our mummy-type sleeping bags and a couple of blankets, the color of the drab olive, like everything else is. And we needed them, because the wind was blowing through at 50 miles an hour part of the time. We had a devil of a time getting the trucks started after two days below zero, and once we did get them started we didn't shut them off at all. At those temperatures, Alpha Lee, the diesel fuel gelled up ... believe it or not! ... and it wouldn't flow through the fuel filter.

"I know the Germans used diesel fuel during the war, and we sure as hell need to find out how they did it on the Russian front and at the Battle of the Bulge, or we're not going to be able to fight a war in the winter with these diesel trucks. Finally, I remembered a trick one of the guys I worked with last summer told me about. He had worked on the Alaskan Highway project, running a bulldozer. So I did what he said he'd done: we heated a couple gallons of kerosene in hot water (like in double boiler pans) and poured the warm kerosene into the diesel tanks. Our damfool new lieutenant saw me pouring the kerosene into the fuel tank and he threatened to court martial me for using an unauthorized fuel! I was afraid maybe I'll spend the rest of my life in the brig, Alpha Lee. *But* we made it back over the mountains ok. Well, almost ok. Fred got his hand frostbitten and he had to be taken to the hospital right away ... he couldn't even drive all the way back, it was hurting him so much. They had to amputate his little finger.

"Fred and I had plenty of time on our hands while we waited for the desired two days of "cold soak.". He got sick of me moping around about Mona, and he told me about his own woman problems. He said he had been in love with his HS sweetheart back in Kansas. They had "played house" for nearly a year before he enlisted, and they had big plans together; but when the Army sent him to Ft. Lewis, he met Shirley and couldn't resist the temptation... he really wanted to marry the girl from home, but he said he was so ashamed, he couldn't bring himself to tell her what he had done and ask her to forgive him and try for a new start. Can an 18-year-old woman forgive *THAT*? Sad story! He still has her letters and pictures, and he still has strong feelings for her."So guess what, Alpha Lee? When we got back from our mission, there was a valentine from Veronica for Fred! Was he ever surprised. Wonder what will come of that? Will she eventually 'be his Valentine'? Stay tuned!

"When we got back, Fred and I both were going to ask to be taken off the project. The Captain met us in the big garage and said not to worry about any charges being filed, and he pointed to a waste basket. He asked me to write a report on the problems of cold weather starting, and he said he'd send it to the Pentagon and try to find out how the Germans got diesels to run in the winter. He said 'Bring me that report and then take a 3-day pass and try to thaw out.' I heard that the next day Lieutenant Sumovitch (the guys call him Sonovabitch) had orders sending him to Japan.

"I left on the 17th, right after mail call, and came to TE, and I've been working a bunch of hours. They let me sleep in the shipping room. Thank goodness they have a shower here. I eat my meals at a little 'greasy spoon' diner near the TE plant, and then I go back and work some more. I have a nice little savings account in the bank here.

"I could go on and on, Alpha Lee, but I'm so tired, and it's late.

I hope your date with Mark is a lot of fun. I wish I could see you in your formal gown. How about sending me a picture? And I'm happy for you for going to All-State Chorus, too. Why wouldn't you be chosen to go? Your voice is as rich as cream. You know, honey, when I get out of this rat race, you and I are gonna have a *LOT* to talk about. I look forward to that day. "Love, Jan"

Fred stepped off the bus from Portland, and Jan noted that his arm was no longer in a sling. He walked over to shake Fred's hand and get his duffel bag. "Welcome back, Fred. Hey, it looks like you got rid of the sling. How was the vacation?"

"Great, Jan, just great. Yeah, my hand barely hurts now, with this metal shield over the place where my pinkie used to be. See ... don'tcha think that looks sexy?" He showed Jan the shiny steel shield. "I have a long story to tell you. Thanks for coming down to get me, by the way."

"Hey, no problem ... what else was I doing on a Sunday night at ten? I guess your train must have been right on time in Portland, since you're on this bus. ... So just what happened in Kansas? That happy smile on your homely face can't be because you're glad to be back."

"Jan, you won't believe what happened. My dad's old worn out pickup ... same beat-up old Chevy he was drivin' when I left wouldn't start when it was time to come after me. Mom called Ronnie, and *she* drove her Grandpa Stone's car the thirty miles to pick me up! No kiddin'! When I got off the train, there she was, standing there looking so pretty, with a look on her face that said 'Hug me, Fred', so I did! A long time, Jan.

"When Fred stepped off the train, the first thing he saw was Veronica, standing beside her grandfather's car, her long blonde hair tied back in a pony tail. She was wearing a Navy pea coat and dark plaid slacks, and she smiled at him and waved. He hurried to meet her, and for just a second they both hesitated; then she was in his arms, and he could feel her tears on his cheek. Her slim body felt so familiar, so sweet. "Welcome home, soldier," she said softly in his ear, and Fred felt as if he truly were home.

"I didn't know what to think, Jan, but we had a long time to talk on the way home, and she got really serious. I told her I had cheated on her with another woman, and said I was sorry. We both had tears in our eyes, and she said she needed to stop for a minute to collect herself. We found an all-night diner and stopped for coffee. I asked her if she could forgive me, and take me back. I promised to go straight. She wasn't even mad at me ... just glad I came back. It was two in the morning when we got to her Grandpa Stone's place, and snowing like the devil ...

there was already three or four inches on the ground ... so I called Mom, and I just slept there on the couch. Ronnie woke me up with kisses at breakfast, and then she drove me on out to Dad's. Wowee, what a hot and heavy three days." Fred recalled the final moments they were together. Ronnie had asked him if he wanted to drive back to the train station in Hays. It felt good to be behind the wheel again; the missing finger didn't interfere with his driving at all. Sooner than he wished, they arrived at the train station, and it was time to go. Fred held her close, memorizing the feel of her body against him. She stroked his face with gentle fingers, and he saw tears in her eyes.

"Goodbye, Fred. I love you so much. Seeing you again was more than I could have dreamed of. It's almost like you've never been gone. When will I see you again?"

"Honey, I won't be gone from you like that, ever again. We'll be together soon, for good ... believe me. Bye, Ronnie," and he kissed her again, hating to let go ..."God, Jan. I hated to catch that train for another day and a half ride back out here. That's some trip ... three days out and back on the train just to get three days in heaven. But I wouldn't have missed it for anything."

"It sounds like it, Fred. I'm glad you and Ronnie got back together again. Looks to me like that amputated finger had a pretty good payoff! But now you've got a problem ... how to dump a gal in Tacoma who isn't gonna like it much. So what are you gonna do, bring Ronnie out here?" "As soon as I can, buddy. She's taking some college classes at a Junior College, and come spring ... at the end of the semester, she'll come out and see if she can find some kind of a job. She wants to finish enough college so she can be a teacher. And we're gonna get married, Jan, just as soon as possible... Hey, Jan, what happened to your court martial? Is that dumb bastard still making waves?"

"No, man, we don't have a problem with Lt. Sonovabitch any more ... he's gone -- transferred to Japan as a platoon leader in a rifle company. I feel sorry for those unlucky guys! Captain Ross said Herndon would be our supervisor, and if we need anything, we can just see him or the first soldier. Herndon will be good to work with. We did have a class this week, by the way. Sarge helped, and Captain Ross sat in an hour the second day. He was real cool, and really interested. He said we'll have at least six more classes to teach ... one every other week."I have some other news, too, Fred. I made an offer to rent a cabin down on the sound, just a couple miles from Takoma Elektronics. Naomi, the secretary at TE -- her grandfather had this pretty little log fishing lodge on the sound, with a private pier, even. She wants to sell it, but she and her husband may rent it to me furnished. Thing is, it doesn't have a water heater, and just a wood cook stove in the kitchen with a coil to heat water for the shower."

"Wow, that is news. How are things at TE, Jan? Are they still going strong? Do you think Ronnie could get a job over there in May or June?"

"Fred, unless somebody makes a horrible mistake, I think they'll still be going strong ten years from now. If Ronnie is good with her hands, she could fit in and do well over there. Some of the new products they are working on in that lab are really exciting ... some of them could be bigger than the V2 box. Well, here's good old Easy Company. I'll let you out by the orderly room so you can sign in, and I'll drag your bag in."

Chapter 2

Alpha Lee sniffled into her pillow, unable to fall asleep even though she had heard the clock downstairs strike half past twelve. The pain deep in her abdomen had diminished to a dull cramping, much like the monthly pain that sometimes forced her to leave school early. She felt miserable; the physical pain, bad as it was, was less than the emotional pain and anger that kept her awake and tearful in spite of her weariness. Her romance with Mark was over; she would never go out with him again ... and she knew he would never ask.

Their first date had been the Valentine Dance at the college, ten miles away; that had been wonderful, and she had felt excited and thrilled, (if somewhat frightened) by Mark's attentions. She had made a gown to wear to the All-State Chorus in April, but she wore it first to the dance. She had chosen taffeta in a shade of orchid pink, with a swirling skirt that rustled when she moved, and a snugly fitted bodice with demure short cap sleeves.

The "sweetheart" neckline, however, was not demure; it was cut deeply to show just a bit of cleavage, so the total effect was what she had wanted: a look of tempting innocence. (She hoped her mother would see only the innocent part.) She wore a string of tiny pearls around her neck centered with a small enameled orchid; she had chosen the fabric to match the color of the orchid. Alpha Lee had been pleased with her reflection in the mirror; she had lost the fifteen pounds she promised herself almost a year ago, and the dress flattered her new slimmer waist.

They had done a double date with Ben and Susan, both living in Brick City. The McAllisters were glad for Susan to begin at last to enjoy the kind of experiences that were normal for a girl of eighteen, and they liked and trusted Ben, son of a local Veterinarian, now in college, so the relationship had developed steadily. Ben was very busy with school and the couple were together only on weekends. Ben had no car; he was able to borrow his father's car sometimes, but he commuted to college with Mark and three others.

Alpha Lee was glad to be with Susan and Ben for the dance, since she didn't know Mark very well, and she knew only a few others who were attending Wesleyan; she saw only a few students at the dance that she knew. The gymnasium was decorated with hearts and balloons in a valentine theme. Alpha Lee wondered if Jan had received the card she had made for him .... She wished it were Jan she was dancing with, instead of this tall stranger. Mark was over six feet tall, so he towered over Alpha Lee. Even in high heels (which hurt her feet), she had to tilt her head back to look up at him. She wondered how old he was; he had served in the Air Corps in England during the war, so she knew he was several years older than she. He was very good-looking, with dark hair and blue eyes, slim and well-dressed, and a good dancer. He held her very close as they danced, and they moved gracefully together. Ben danced with her a few times, and she felt more relaxed with him; theywere long-time-friends.

It was after eleven o'clock when Mark stopped in front of Alpha Lee's house. He had dropped off Ben and Susan first so he could be alone with her to say good night. He walked up the steps to the front door with her and bent to kiss her lips very lightly. Then he bent lower and kissed her just at the point of the deep V of her neckline, where a shadow of cleavage showed, and his hands slipped around her to cup her breasts under her open coat. "Mmmm, baby ... Very nice," he whispered.

Alpha Lee could have slapped him ... but she didn't. She was mesmerized by an intense sensation that flooded through her, like a powerful chemical suffusing her blood; exciting ... wonderful ... just as she had read in many romantic novels. She smiled up at him uncertainly, and then, reaching up to cradle his face in her hands, she stood on tiptoe and kissed him very softly. Mark wrapped his arms around her and pressed her body tightly to his, so that she could feel the hardness of him against her. It was the most wonderful feeling she had ever experienced.

"Alpha, will you go out with me again?" he asked.

and she whispered, "Yes."

I'll call you, babe. Thanks for a great date."

"Thank *you*, Mark. It was fun."

Alpha Lee knocked softly on the door of her parents' bedroom. "I'm home," she said, and her mother answered, "Okay, Alpha Lee ... good night."

The next weekend Mark took her to a movie, "The Outlaw", which had been advertised as being quite risque. Alpha Lee was surprised, because the movie wasn't as "naughty" as many of the romantic novels she had read. Jane Russell and her lover, "Billy the Kid", embracing in the hay, fully dressed ... she didn't see what the fuss was about. Mark's arm was around her shoulder. He leaned close and whispered, "That actress is famous for her big boobs," he said, "but she's got nothin' on you, baby," and he stroked Alpha Lee's breast. She gently moved his hand away. But he simply moved lower to caress her thigh, from her knee to the crease of her groin. "Honey, let's go," he said softly.

Alpha Lee was overcome with the flood of sensation that swept through her. "Ohhh ... Mark ... please ...," she turned toward him breathlessly and he kissed her with much more passion than she had seen on screen. "Mmmm ...Mark, please, just let me see the ending ...just a little longer." He pulled away from her and stood up. "I've gotta have a cigarette. I'll wait for you in the lobby ... okay?" He made his way to the aisle and went downstairs. Alpha Lee felt abandoned, but she concentrated on the last moments of the movie. She had told Mark she had to go straight home from the theater, because she had homework that was due Monday. He was annoyed, but he asked if she would go out with him next Saturday.

She smiled with delight. "Oh, yes, Mark, I'd love to," and he kissed her passionately, while his hands were exploring the shape of her body until she was dizzy with that strange sensation

The next Saturday night, Mark had arrived at six to take her out to dinner. Alpha Lee was very excited; her first dinner date! She had dressed carefully, still with the "tempting innocence" ambience in mind. Mark kissed her just as soon as they were in the car together. His tongue pushed between her lips to explore her mouth, and again she felt the disturbing rush that took her breath away. After dinner, he drove slowly to a public picnic area, deserted on this cold winter night. Again he kissed her deeply, forcing her mouth open, and his hands caressed her until she was weak and breathless. He took her hand and placed it on his crotch; she felt a hot, hard lump. Alpha Lee was filled with conflicting emotions, guilt the one she recognized most strongly. "Do you want it, baby?" Mark was whispering in her ear.

"I ... I don't know ..." she managed to murmur, Alpha Lee was startled when he pulled away from her and started the engine. What did I do wrong, she wondered, as Mark pulled the car out of the shadowed park.

"I want to take you to meet my brother and his family," he told her, reaching over to squeeze her knee. She was a little relieved that he was not taking her home ... dumping her.

"Well ... that would be nice," she answered hesitantly. The high state of excitement was fading and she began to feel more control. "You live with them, don't you, Mark?"

"Yeah .. just a mile out of town on the old Mill road," he answered. "Well, whaddaya know, Allie ... there's nobody home," Mark said with pretended surprise. his sister-in-law had told him early last week that they would be spending the weekend out of town with her family. "Well, come in and see my digs, anyway." He unlocked the door and led her into the darkened house. "Would you like a beer, honey?" he asked her as he helped her out of her coat

"No, thank you," she answered.

"Well, how about a rum and Coke?"

"Hmmm ... that sounds nice," Alpha Lee answered. "Just a little bit, please, Mark." She sipped her drink tentatively. The rum added a burning, bitter flavor to the familiar taste of Coke. She took very small sips, and she felt a strange dizzying sensation flooding through her. The sensation was exciting, but the taste she found unpleasant, and did not finish the drink. There had never been liquor of any kind at the Evans home, and this was something totally new to her. Mark sat beside her on the sofa and took her in his arms. He pushed her back against the armrest and his hands caressed her body. Alpha Lee had a vague sense of guilt, or danger, but it was overwhelmed by the exciting thrill she felt

He stood up and led her into another room. "This is where I stay," he said. He turned down the covers on the double bed. With his hands on her waist, he said, "Take off your sweater, babe ... it sure is pretty, but ... I think there's something even prettier under it." She pulled the sweater over her head, exposing a bra of pale blue satin and lace. "Wow! You sure dressed up pretty for me, honey," he said, reaching around to unfasten it. He slipped the straps down over her arms as she stood entranced, unable or unwilling to resist him.

He bent to kiss her breasts. "What a gorgeous pair of knockers. Wow! Take off your skirt, honey. I'll be right back." He went into a nearby bathroom, leaving Alpha half exposed and weak in the knees. This can't be happening to me, she thought. I'm dreaming . Mark was back in a moment, barefoot and naked except for his shorts. He pushed Alpha Lee's light blue panties down below her knees; she was wearing a garter belt and stockings. "Just leave that," he said. "It looks real sexy. ... Oh, look at that pretty red curly hair," he said softly, tangling his fingers in her pubic hair. "Baby, you're the prettiest thing I've seen for a long time." He took her in his arms and lifted her onto the bed. "Allie, is this your first time?" he asked her as he fondled her.

"Yes," she whispered.

"You're a virgin! God, Allie, it's my first time, too, then ... I've never done it with a virgin before. This is gonna be really special for both of us, baby ..." As he continued to kiss her breasts and massage her between her legs, she began to moan softly and to writhe against him, and suddenly she gave a choking cry and pressed her hand urgently upon his. His fingers probed and he felt the pulsing of her orgasm.

"Oh, that's good, honey, ... Good." And he moved to lower himself on her. He pushed her legs apart and tried to enter her. She flinched and cried out. "It'll hurt just a little, honey, the first time, but then it'll feel so good ... just hang on, sweetheart." He withdrew and continued to caress her with experienced hands. A second time he tried to enter, this time with more pressure. He could feel the tension in her body.

Alpha Lee felt a hot, tearing pain, and she tried to stifle a scream as she twisted away from him. "Stop, Mark! Please ... it hurts! STOP!" she cried, as he persisted in pushing against something inside her that would not give way.

"Please, honey ... just once more and it'll be over," he murmured into her ear. "Allie, I love you, baby, I really do," and again he thrust hard. Still the hymen would not yield. "What the hell ... there's something wrong here ...," he said, withdrawing at last as Alpha Lee tried to hold back tears of pain. "Damn!" he said as he rolled over away from her. He stood up beside the bed. "Alpha, come here," and he took her hand and pulled her up to stand close to him. "Honey, I'm hurting for you," he whispered, pushing her hand hard against his erection. "Please ... go down on me, honey ... please.

"What?"

"Just go down on your knees and take it in your mouth. Give me some lovin' with your mouth, honey, please." He pushed her down. Alpha Lee had never heard of such a thing; in all her reading she had never encountered any-thing like this. She stared at his erection in disbelief. The condom was covered with blood. Alpha Lee felt a wave of nausea in addition to the sharp cramping pain. She looked down and saw blood running down her legs and pooling on the floor. She felt terrified and slightly faint.

"No, Mark, no, no, no ... please take me home now. I'm sick ... I can't ..." Holding her head firmly, he tried to thrust into her mouth, but she cried out and pushed him away. "*NO!* STOP IT! *STOP!*" she screamed, scrambling to her feet. He's going to rape me. she thought! She backed away from him, terrified.

"Shit!" he hissed, and hurried into the bathroom. She dressed quickly, and finding a box of facial tissues on the dresser, she pulled out a thick stack and stuffed them into her panties. I hope that will hold until I can get home, she thought, near panic. She wiped the blood from her legs and mopped at the puddle on the floor, and then she stepped into her shoes just as Mark emerged from the bathroom, fully dressed. "Let's go," he said shortly. Then he looked at the bed, and saw a large bloodstain where they had lain. "*DAMN IT, LOOK AT THAT !"* he raged. "What the hell am I gonna do with that mess! You didn't tell me you were having your period. Shit!" He ripped the sheets from the bed; the mattress was also stained. Mark was livid. "Let's get outta here," he said angrily.

"I'm not having my period, Mark ... the blood is from when you hurt me! Don't you see what you've done? I'm hemorrhaging! Oh, God, I hope I'm not ruptured or going to bleed to death!", and she began to cry.

Mark snatched a folded newspaper from the coffee table as he strode through the living room. "Here," he said, thrusting it at her. "Put this on the car seat. I've got enough shit to deal with, without having my car messed up too." He drove too fast down the dark streets without speaking a word, and stopped in front of the Evans home with a jolt. "Okay, you're home. That's what you wanted, here you are." He didn't move to open her door; he didn't touch her or look at her. As she got out of the car, she noticed that there was blood on the newspaper where she had sat. "Take that with you," he said coldly.

"Goodbye, Mark." He was staring straight ahead, motionless and silent as stone. She turned from him and walked up the porch steps without looking back. The tires squealed as he pulled away from the curb. Alpha Lee climbed the stairs slowly; she was exhausted, humiliated and frightened. Her mother heard her and came out of the bedroom, blinking at the light. "Did you have a good time, Alpha Lee?" she asked with a sleepy smile.

Alpha Lee immediately stood straight and controlled her voice tightly. "Mm-hmmm. Very nice," she lied. "We had dinner at the Classic Lounge, and then Mark took me to meet his brother and sister-in-law. They have two really cute kids." She had seen a photograph in Mark's room of a pretty woman with two small children. Alpha Lee was amazed at how easy it was to deceive ... to lie.

"Well, good. Better get to bed now. Will you go to church tomorrow?"

"Oh, yes, Mother ... we're going to sing a special Lenten litany," Alpha Lee said in a matter-of fact tone that belied her inner turmoil. She was careful not to turn so that her mother might see the stain on her skirt. "Good night, Mother." She smiled and backed into her bedroom.

Alpha Lee washed her panties, her stockings and skirt in the bathtub as quietly as possible, pressed them in absorbent towels, and then hung them in her closet to dry, so her mother wouldn't see them. She hoped the wool skirt wouldn't shrink ... it was her best skirt, light blue and gray with pleats all around ... the High School colors. The bloodstain came out, she knew, only because she had washed it immediately in cool water, before the stain had set. Why couldn't I do it? she asked herself. Why couldn't I have sex with Mark? There's some-thing wrong with me, she thought tearfully. There's always something wrong with me! I hope I'm not ... damaged, so I can't ever make love, or have a baby! I'll have to go to a doctor. How can I do that? she asked herself miserably. The only doctor Alpha Lee knew was old Dr. Bennett, who had delivered her and her brother James, and who had treated them both for chicken pox and sore throats throughout their childhood. She could *NEVER* go to him with a problem like this!

She put on a sanitary pad and her pajamas and turned down the covers. She was torn by conflicting emotions; she had really wanted to fall in love, to discover the thrill of sex with a handsome man who said sweet things to her, just like in the stories. But instead, here she was, utterly worn out and hurting, with that old familiar feeling of humiliation, of inadequacy, of being "different" ... and of being used. What of the bizarre thing he had demanded of her? "Go down on me, baby," he had said. It was unbelievable, she thought. ... He hurt me, and he never even said he was sorry, she realized, and suddenly her misery turned to anger. Mark! She thought. He is hateful and selfish. He didn't even care that he hurt me. It *WAS* like rape! I hope I never see him again, she thought. Before she turned off the light, she glanced at Jan's picture on the wall behind the door. Oh, Jan, she thought forlornly, you're the one I want to love! You wouldn't hurt me,

I know you wouldn't ... She touched the drawing with her finger; the smudge of charcoal on her fingertip made her feel as though he had somehow responded to her ... She kissed away the dark smudge. Oh, Jan, I love you. Alpha Lee climbed wearily into bed at last. She prayed passionately: Oh, God, please forgive me for what I did. Please help me to be normal! Please take away the pain and stop the bleeding. Oh, God, please let me fall asleep. I'm so tired ... Her prayers were answered before the clock struck one.

Chapter 3

"Ft. Lewis, March 1 "Dear Alpha Lee,

"I got your *BEAUTIFUL* charcoal just after we got back from our cold soak mission, and I forgot to mention it in my last letter, I was so weary that night. Anyway, I brought it along to TE, and a secretary saw it, and you'll never guess what she said, Alpha Lee! She said, 'That's my grand-father's fishing camp. Do you want to buy it?' And then the Personnel Manager said, 'My wife runs an art boutique, how much does this artist get for his work?' I let him take it home that night, and he said his wife would pay $20 each for TEN duplicates, and he gave me a 20 dollar advance. So here's the money order for twenty, and I made him bring MY copy back. I have it up on the wall where I can see it while I work. If you don't want to sell to her, it's all right, just send the money back and let me know. That could be a big job for you, and maybe boring. She also wanted to know if you have other works you wanted to sell. I guess she handles different kinds of original art from local artists. You wanna be a local artist?"

"I asked the secretary if she was serious about selling the fishing camp. She said she was ...it has been empty a couple years since her grandfather died, and it's only a couple miles from TE. I told her I'd need a place to rent in August, and I asked her what shape it's in, and if they would rent it. She said her grandfather had lived there year round, and she brought in the key so I could look at it. I drove out there today and met her husband. It's a really gorgeous place, Alpha Lee, but needs a lot of sweeping out, since it's been empty so long. It has electricity, a huge fire-place, a wood-burning kitchen range, two bedrooms and an inside toilet. Frank said the well had a new pump just a couple years back, and the roof was sound. They'll rent it to me for a year for $60 a month and leave all the furniture in it, even the ice-box. Boy, it's been years since I bought ice for an icebox! Have you ever seen one? But maybe I could find a used refrigerator somewhere. Anyway, I'm sure thinking about it. All the apartments in Tacoma are $65 and $75 a month unfurnished.

"Here comes the big question, Alpha Lee: If I can rent this place right away, and send you a plane ticket, would you consider coming out here and spending the summer painting on the porch, just like you said you dreamed of? The cabin has two bedrooms with double beds.. I intend to come back east for Labor Day, so I can bring you back in time for college, if you aren't a rich and famous artist by then. You could bring Susan along too, to protect you from me on Sundays. It might be good for Susan to be in a new environment for a while, sort of on her own.

"Susan's problem really scares me, hon. I don't know much about child abuse, and I sure as hell don't understand the abusers, but I just think the victims could have repressed feelings of remorse and pain, and even guilt, I suppose hon, if she IS willing to talk about any of it to you, it could be good therapy.

"Who should be the aggressor in a love relationship? Tough question. If a girl wants to meet a boy, I guess she needs to at least make eye contact. A nice smile helps, too. If she wants him to kiss her, she needs to use some kind of body language to make him feel he won't be slapped if he tries. Any guy worth his salt can tell if a girl is inviting a kiss. "If two people in love want to be really together, maybe they need to sort of meet each other half way. If one is aggressive, and the other too reticent, it might not be satisfying for both. I believe both partners have needs and rights, and they need to talk about it. I wouldn't think of being sexually aggressive with anyone I wouldn't want to marry, and I don't think you would either. Wow ... deep discussion there, Alpha Lee."

Please think over my offer. I hope your parents will let you do this, and I hope you want to. I would be so pleased to have you come here for the summer. When I look at the charcoal drawing you made, I see just one thing missing: *YOU* should be in that picture, sitting at your easel on the pier. That's *MY* dream, Alpha Lee. "Love, Jan"

"Brick City March 6 "Dear Jan,

"Wow, ten copies at twenty each is $200! That'll pay a lot of tuition. I spent the money for board stock, and I have three copies ready for the spray fix, as soon as I buy some more. Yes, yes, and yes, I'll make the ten copies, and send the art dealer some other stuff to look at, too. It's funny ... all my life I've really only made drawings for people I love, and I have just given them away, mostly. Now maybe I'll have a chance to earn a few bucks from something I've always done just as a pastime, and had lots of fun doing it. I sure do need to earn some money. Things are slow around here; I haven't found any kind of job since my cousin's store went south. Just baby sitting now and then.

"Jan, I have read your letter of March 1 over and over ... it's so exciting I can hardly grasp it! But I am uncertain about what you are expecting from me, and about what I am expecting of you, and about whether it would be 'proper' or not. I let Mother and Daddy read it too, and they aren't very enthusiastic about this. In fact, I think Daddy is sure you just want a girl to live with. . Are you making me a proposal or a proposition? Or are you (I hope) just offering me a chance to come out and paint in that beautiful setting, and sleep in the second bedroom? Jan, my heart tells me *YES, YES, YES*, go to him the day school is out, but my head (and my parents!) keeps saying *NO! NO! NO!* Maybe all he wants is a housekeeper, a cook, and someone to 'play house' with, now that his sweetheart has left him. Maybe when I get there I'll find Louise already staying in the master bedroom, and I'll only be the cook and the housekeeper. Please explain to me what sort of relationship you have in mind, sir, and I may be better able to make a decision. My parents are concerned that I would be returned to them penniless and damaged goods as well, with a broken heart. Oh Jan, tell me your intentions are completely honorable. (Well, honorable at least.)

"I feel that you and I never had a 'real' date, since you were going steady with that Salt Lick person at the time of the Jr - Sr banquet. That seemed like sort of just a friendly event, a school activity that we shared although, Jan, you must have known it meant a lot to me to have you as my escort that night. I was so proud to be with you! I wanted so badly to go to the prom with you, too, even though I knew that wasn't possible. We haven't really had any time 'together' ... alone ... in the sixteen months since we first met in math class. In a way, I guess, this exchange of letters is sort of like time alone together, isn't it? We have become much better acquainted, and much closer, I think. It means more to me than I can tell you to have a friend like you, even if you're so far away, to 'talk with' via letters.

"Reading your letters is like reading a good book; I can hardly wait for the next 'chapter', to hear of your adventures in a life that is fascinating to me. (The story of the Cascades crossing at Snoqualmie, which I *did* look up, was wonderful to read about, even though it must have been an ordeal in real life.) When I read your words, I can almost hear your voice, as if you were here talking to me.

"Yes, Jan, I *do* want to come to you, to live in your fishing camp with you. I want to be able to *REALLY* hear your voice. I want to fix your Sunday dinner ... to cook on that wood stove, which will be a real adventure for me! And, of course, I want to spend hours and hours finding out just what I can do with my art in such a beautiful and different setting ... that is a challenge I'm finding hard to resist.

"My father has never even met you. Here you are, propositioning his 'little girl' to live with you for a summer, and he doesn't know you at all. Maybe Mother met you just in passing, but neither of them knows anything about you, or your family or anything. Jan, would you write a letter to Daddy, to sort of introduce yourself, and to elaborate on what you have in mind? He is a reasonable person (*SOMETIMES!*), but he's also a very protective parent. If you are serious about this, a 'letter of introduction' would help, I think. Daddy is well-organized and logical, and I think you are too, and he would respond to that in you. Actually, he'd probably love to come out there himself! It's the kind of place he'd enjoy, because he loves wilderness and nature, but he's never been able to travel.

"If you're serious about inviting Susan too, that would be a good point. I would like to have her with me, if I can come. Maybe it would help my parents to go along with my coming, if Susan could come too. I think it would be sort of scary to be alone in the north woods while you're soldier-ing or working almost all the time! And I agree with you that it would probably be really good for her to have a change of scene. Please write to the McAllisters, too. So, my precious friend ... I can only give you this tentative answer to your exciting invitation. Oh, Jan, I hope I can do this! I thought I would never see you again, and now ... maybe ... I can see you under a whole different set of circumstances. Maybe ... who knows, Jan?

"I'm going to end this letter the way you've been ending yours: "With Love, Alpha Lee"

"Ft Lewis March 13 "Dearest Alpha Lee,

"Holy cow, I didn't think I would stir up such a duststorm with one little letter. Let me be as honest as I can be with you, sweet. I didn't make the offer in jest, *AT ALL.* "I'm very anxious that I don't do anything rash while I'm still on the rebound from Mona. It's only been two months. I don't know how long I have to wait before I can trust my emotions. I have the greatest respect for you, Alpha Lee, and I sure as hell don't want to hurt you in any way. Having said all that proper stuff ... Alpha Lee, I think I'm in love with you. Can you fall in love through letters? The letters have surely helped ... I love your mind, the way you look at life and the way you can express and share those observations. But it's not just that; I remember so clearly the way you look, and even the way you feel, Alpha Lee, from those short minutes we danced in your living room that one time. I remember the smell of your hair ... I find myself wanting to touch you again. So it's not just the letters; there's chemistry there, too. Maybe there always has been.

"If we hadn't known each other so long, and didn't have such respect for each other, I would think my emotions are all rebound. God knows I am lonely, but I don't think I'm grasping at straws. If I were desperate for a girl, I could call up Louise, I'm sure. But I haven't seen Louise, I don't want to see Louise ... she's *not* 'my cup of tea', to quote from a valentine I saw recently. But you, you sweet woman, I am asking you for a *three month date* in my very rustic log cabin. You can paint to your heart's content, or find a job any number of places, if you choose. You might be able to earn enough to pay your tuition for a semester, or maybe a full year. I'll pay for the food, and try my best to be home every Sunday, all day. Meanwhile, we'll get a chance to get to know each other, and find out how we really feel. You surely won't be living in the Ritz, and I'll be working and study ing so much that you may get so lonely and bored you'll just want to go home and forget about me. I know my schedule is enough to choke a mule. I got into this schedule when I needed to keep busy, and I didn't have to consider anybody but myself. I'll have to be on the base every morning at 7:30 or 6:30 if I eat chow there (sometimes on Saturday too.) With classes two nights a week and work three nights, I usually don't get to bed until 11 or 11:30. I usually work all day Saturday, too.

"You won't have to do more than your share of housekeeping or cooking, and you won't have to worry about bolting your bedroom door. If you come out here a virgin, and it is your choice, you may go home a virgin. What-ever you bring with you will be yours, and whatever you earn while you are here will be yours. I'll buy you a round trip ticket on the plane, so you can pick up and leave if you can't stand me or get bored to tears here. Alpha Lee, if we don't take this opportunity to really get to know each other, when will we ever be able to be together to find out just how far this relationship can go? Let me say this: If I let myself miss out on what promises to be the most perfect and beautiful relationship I'll ever know, how could I ever forgive myself? You're on my mind all the time. Unless something drastic happens, I may live out here for years, and who knows where your talent could take you ... Greenwich Village, Paris, Rome? So before you take off to search for your fortune somewhere out of reach, where I might never find you again ... please come and spend this summer with me. "*Please say YES*, dear one. *Please..* "Love, Jan "

P. S. I forgot: I'll write a letter to your father just as soon as I get this one ready to mail.

Jan sat staring at the typewriter, trying to get into the mind of Harry Evans, whom he had never met...a father whose daughter he had just invited to live with a man he had never met, over two thousand miles away from home. God, Jan thought, no wonder he says no. This letter had better be good, he told himself. I've gotta sell myself as the best guy Alpha Lee will ever know, and the offer I've made as the best opportunity she could hope for. Hey ... that's a cinch, he thought with a wry grin. Nothin' but the truth!

"Fort Lewis, Washington "March 13, 1949

"Dear Mr. And Mrs. Evans, "Let me begin by telling you that I greatly respect your lovely daughter, Alpha Lee. I can imagine that you are quite proud of her, and her many talents and accomplishments. Since we have never met, I want to sort of introduce myself to you. I am nineteen years old; I was born in Waters, and I lived there all my life until I left for a one-year hitch in the Army last August. My parents still live near Waters on a small farm. My father was injured in a train wreck several years ago (he was a fireman) and now he raises broiler chickens to sell, and my mother (an ex school teacher) gives piano lessons. They are good, hard working people. I love and respect them very much. I also have one older brother, at WVU..

"I met Alpha Lee for the first time when she was working at the jewelry store, but we got to know each other when I transferred to Brick City High School for my senior year in order to take some college preparatory courses that I couldn't get at Waters High. Alpha Lee and I shared a math class and also Glee Club. We had some good times singing together in school.

I am sure you are aware that she has been offered the possibility of earning a few dollars by making and selling copies of a landscape scene of a rather quaint-looking log fishing lodge beside an estuary of Puget Sound. This picture was copied from a postcard I sent her, and when she sent me her original charcoal drawing, people who saw it at my workplace (my part-time, after-hours job) were so impressed that the manager of a local Art Shop asked if it were possible to have duplicate 'original' drawings made for sale. I believe this shop is a sound business, with a reputable manager.

"During my Army enlistment I have worked weekends and some nights at a growing manufacturing concern near Tacoma, just a few miles off the base. The manager has offered me a position when I get out of the Army at the end of August, and the salary and benefits, including college tuition, are so attractive that I have decided to remain in the Tacoma area, working at this company (Takoma Elektroniks) and continuing my education - I plan to study engineering.

I do plan, however, to return to West Virginia for a two week vacation after my discharge. I understand that Alpha Lee also wants to attend college, which I must applaud, because of her intelligence; and her artistic talents should be fully encouraged. She has written to me that she would very much like to accept my invitation to spend the summer out here, where she can more readily pursue her artistry by being nearer the market for her work. I have offered her what is within my financial means: a plane ticket to fly out after her high school graduation, and a place to stay, rent free, during the summer. I understand that if she chooses to come, her friend Susan Remagen may also come along, and I assure you that both young ladies will be welcome, will be treated with respect, and will not be mistreated. I have a serviceable automobile, and it will be available to them on a shared basis.

"I have contracted to rent the exact fishing lodge that Alpha Lee copied in charcoal from the postcard, beginning April first. I plan to move in and make it my residence for some time. It is rustic, to be sure. A true log cabin with a stone chimney ... but it is comfortably furnished with the necessities. It has a combination kitchen/living room; two bedrooms, each with a double bed; and a bathroom with a tub and shower supplied with hot water from a coil in the wood range. The kitchen range is a wood - fired cook stove; at present there is only an icebox, but finding a used refrigerator is one of my top priorities.

"There is no central heating, just a large fireplace in the living room with plenty of wood available nearby; however, in time I hope to make some improvements as my earnings allow. The summers here are similar in temperature to those in West Virginia, so the lack of central heating during the summer should not be a problem. Mr. Evans, I hope very much that you and Mrs. Evans will agree to let Alpha Lee plan this adventure and pursue this opportunity to earn money for her college education, as well as to see a different part of the country. I can only ask you to trust me, and to believe that Alpha Lee is precious to me, as I know she is to you. I promise that I will protect her, respect her, and bring her home to you in late August. Please believe that I will do nothing to make you or Alpha Lee sorry she has come. "Sincerely, Pfc Jan Short"

Harry Evans read the letter three times before he handed it to his wife. "Well, he sounds like a decent young man. I sure wish I'd met him, though, before this thing came up. You say he's the one who took you to the banquet at Jackson's Mill last spring, Alpha Lee? But you've never had another date with him ?"

"Yes, Daddy. He was going steady with a girl from Salt Lick at the time, but since he was a senior in high school, he could go to the banquet, so he asked if he could be my escort. ... Daddy, and Mother, Jan is the best person I've ever known! He is so ... so *nice*, so respectful, and incredibly intelligent. I think you could ask any of the teachers at the high school, or any of the kids who knew him ... they'd say the same thing. Mrs. McAllister knew him from when she was a music director at 4-H Camp and he was a camper, and she really thinks a lot of him. He's really a good singer ... a tenor." Alpha Lee blushed at her own excited babble. Oh, I'm just so excited!" she giggled. "Please, Daddy, ... please let me do this! It's just the most incredible thing that's ever happened to me!"

"Alpha Lee, settle down. Your mother and I will make a decision."

"Brick City, March 19 "Dear Jan, "*YES, YES, YES, YES, YES!* I say *YES*, Mom says yes, and Dad says " ... W - e - l - l - l ..... I suppose so .... *IF* Susan will go along," which, for Daddy, passes for *YES!* "Jan, I am so excited. Can I possibly keep my mind on English Lit and Latin II and Journalism and even Graphic Art (no problem there!) when I'm so preoccupied with my wonderful plans for after graduation? There is *nobody*, Jan, *nobody* in the entire school, who has such great prospects for summer as Alpha Lee Evans, former mouse, soon-to-be world traveler and 'local artist' of Tacoma, Washington! Thank you, my most precious and dear friend, for this wonderful invitation. *We* -- you and I, sir ... are going to have a most memorable summer, I promise you that, Jan.

" Because ... Oh, Jan ... because you said some other words in your last letter that were maybe even more wonderful than your invitation. (I can't even dare to write those words down.) "Jan, maybe I don't really know what love is; I am so naive, so inexperienced in this sort of thing. For just a little while, I thought I was in love with Mark. It was romantic and thrilling, for a little while, just like the stories I have been reading. But that adventure ended in worse than disaster. ... But I don't want to let anything ruin my mood, so I won't think about that. I don't really know what love is, Jan. How does it start? The day you spoke to me in the jewelry store ... when I looked into your eyes ... there was ... *something.* I could almost hear it happen, and I didn't understand what it was. And after that first time I saw you, Jan, right up to this very minute, nothing has ever been the same for me. Is that love? How could it happen, between two complete strangers? I guess that's why it's so mysterious ... like it's something bigger than we are, we little people. "The respect and trust we share is so beautiful, so comfortable to me. Now that we know each other so much better, through exchanging letters, I am so happy that I know I can always trust you. We can 'be true' to each other by being true to ourselves. I know you understand what I'm saying. But now I'm ready and eager to go beyond these things, Jan. I want to touch you. Do you feel that way about me? If all of the minutes of our touching were added up, how much would it be? Just a few moments ... but I remember every second of it.

"Meet me at the airport, Jan, in two months. I can't wait. I can't write any more now. I'll mail this and write some more tomorrow. Maybe by that time I can be more calm. Love, my dearest friend ...Alpha Lee"

She sealed the envelope, put away her pen and crawled into bed feeling so full of joy that she could hardly sleep. It had only been three weeks since the terrible night with Mark; she had not heard anything from him in that time, which was a relief to her, because she didn't want to talk to him. The pain she had suffered, and the frightening bleeding, had stopped after one day, and she had abandoned the idea of seeing a doctor.

The next day was Saturday. She started another copy of the charcoal after doing her chores, and then she called Susan. "Susan, I have the most incredible thing to tell you! I don't even want to tell you on the phone ... can you come over here? Or could we go to a movie this afternoon?"

"Well, maybe we could ... I'll ask Nancy. Are you gonna make me wait in suspense? What's it about? Mark? Or Jan? Please ... give me a hint."

"Okay ... it IS about Jan! Oh, Susan, I can't wait! Go ahead, ask Mrs. McAllister if you can go with me this afternoon. I don't even know what's on, do you?"

Susan returned to the phone in a minute, her voice full of excitement. "Yes!" she said. "D'you want to stop by here on the way? We'll walk up town together. You're driving me crazy, Alpha Lee," she giggled. Susan heard the doorbell just as she finished lunch. "Alpha Lee ... I didn't expect you so soon. I've gotta comb my hair and put on some lipstick ..."

"I came early because I want you to read this," she said, handing Susan the first page of Jan's letter. Susan grabbed the letter with a squeal of excitement. When she came to the line, "You could bring Susan with you ...," she jumped up from her chair and hugged Alpha Lee, laughing and screaming.

"Oh, Alpha Lee ... can we go? *Can we*? I can't believe he's inviting *Me too!* ... Nancy!" she called, running to the kitchen. The girls shared Jan's letter with Mrs. McAllister, who was speechless at this bold proposal. "Alpha Lee, what do your parents think about this?"

"They've thought and thought about it, Mrs. McAllister, and Daddy is still kind of on the fence; but I'm pretty sure they will let me go, *if* Susan can come along, too. I really want her to ... I think I'd be sort of scared to do this by myself. Susan could get a job out there, Jan says ...there seems to be a lot of opportunities. Please think about it, Mrs. McAllister! It would be so wonderful to see those mountains and the Pacific Ocean."

"And Jan," Nancy finished for her. "Let's face it ... *HE'S* the really big attraction," she laughed. "Are you and Jan ... umm ... going together?"

Alpha Lee laughed happily. "Well, if you can call exchanging letters with three thousand miles between us 'going together', I guess maybe we are," she said. "We've never even had a real date ... although Jan did take me to the Junior-Senior banquet last spring."

"I thought Jan was going with Mona Dee Brooks," Nancy said."They were very close for a long time, I think."

"Yes, they were. But Mona broke up with him just after Christmas. She is engaged to a boy she met in college, Jan said. He was really hurt."

"I see," Nancy said slowly. "Alpha Lee, do you have any thoughts that maybe Jan is just lonely for a new girlfriend? I know that's a cruel thing to say, ... but it does happen. Is he perhaps, 'on the rebound' from his break-up with Mona?"

"He wrote about that, Mrs. McAllister. Maybe that's why he started writing to me. But we've been exchanging letters for several months, and we've gotten to know each other quite well that way. Even before that," Alpha Lee murmured, her eyes on the floor, "we had a sort of special relationship. I've always really liked Jan. He is not only the most intelligent person I've ever known ... he is so honorable and kind. I trust him absolutely, Mrs. M. He is *THE BEST*," she finished, and she looked up at Nancy, her eyes sparkling.

Nancy smiled. "Yes, Alpha Lee, I do know what you mean. Jan is an extraordinary young man. ... Well, Susan, Dr. John and I will talk about this. Are you girls going to the movie? You'd better hustle.

"Brick City, W. Va. March 20 - Late

"Dear Jan, "I am really trying hard to keep my head on straight, to be calm and serious so I can make sensible plans. But it's hard, Jan, because I am so excited about the prospect of making this huge long trip to ... well, to another world. A different life. *AND* to see *YOU*, my precious friend, for a long lovely summer. I keep asking myself, 'Am I dreaming?' I talked with Susan, and she, of course, went crazy ... you know how she is. Mrs. McAllister was sort of cautious and didn't promise anything. She wants to talk with her husband, of course. But

I'll bet they'll say *yes*. I think it would be great therapy for Susan to be on her own. I'll keep my fingers crossed!

Okay, Jan, so how do we proceed? My graduation is May 19, exactly two months from today. Two short months! The time will fly. I'm not an experienced traveler, Jan. Actually I've only been out of the state once, when we went to Pittsburgh in 1946 to see the sights. Of course Susan has been in several states, but she doesn't remember much about them. I want to get started just as soon as graduation is over; the sooner the better. My next goal in life after graduation is to 'Go West', like the Forty - Niners of a century ago. Well, Jan, I'm sort of a Forty - Niner, too -- that's what we members of the Class of '49 call ourselves! It will be so wonderful to see you, standing there waiting for us at the airport in Tacoma or Seattle or wherever the ticket says. I don't even think I'll be afraid of flying my first time, since the plane will be taking me to be with *you!* I get shivers just writing 'to be with you'. Jan, I feel *so adolescent!*

"Thank you for sending me the picture of you and Fred and your huge tank transports. You look so great, Jan. In spite of your dislike for Army life, I think it's been good for you! You must be a bit huskier than you were a year ago; when I saw you last summer at the bank, you were absolutely thin! And you have a promising job, and your superior officers think well of you ... and now you're going to have not one, but *two* girls living with you in that rustic home off base! I think, sir, as they say, 'You've got it made!' And so have I, dearest friend. I can't ask for anything more. 'To be with you' ... that's my theme song for tonight. Or maybe, 'I'll see you in my dreams'. It's true. "Much love, "Alpha Lee"

While the girls were at the movie, Nancy found in the mail a letter from Jan. She quickly opened it and read:

"Fort Lewis, Washington

"Dear Dr. and Mrs. McAllister, "You may have heard from Alpha Lee Evans that I have invited her to fly out to Tacoma to visit me, and to spend the summer painting and drawing for an Art dealer who has admired and sold some of her work here. I know that this is a big challenge for Alpha Lee, because she has never been so far from home before. I have suggested that maybe Susan might be interested in accompanying her and staying with her while she is here. There are plenty of jobs here if she would be interested in working. I will be moving soon into a rustic fishing lodge near Puget Sound, not far from Fort Lewis and the city. This would be where I'm proposing that the girls could stay, rent-free, for the summer. It's a beautiful setting, with Mt. Rainier providing a spectacular view out the kitchen window."

"This is a camp, whose principal embellishment is indoor plumbing and an attached fishing pier, furnished adequately but not quite like the usual home in town. There are two bedrooms, each with a double bed, an ice-box (for the moment) and a wood burning kitchen stove. But if Susan enjoys the outdoors and 'the simple life', I think she could have a great experience spending the summer here with Alpha Lee, *if her* parents agree.

"I am working at an electronics research and manufacturing firm on my evenings and week-ends, and I have only Sunday off, so the girls would have a lot of time to do as they choose during the weekdays. I think it would be a great vacation experience for both of them; a chance to be 'on their own'... a maturing experience. And I must confess, I would love to have them here. Sometimes this Army life is boring, frustrating and lonely, especially since I'm so far from home that I can't make trips back there. I will, however, finish my hitch at the end of August, and I'll come back to West Virginia for a couple weeks before I return to my job here, which is so promising and interesting that I plan to stay with it. My boss has promised college tuition for an engineering course and other benefits if I continue to work for them, and I've decided that it may be a better deal than if I would come back to enroll at WVU. This is the kind of work I'd like to have as a long term career.

"Alpha Lee tells me that the Glee Club has reverted to an all-girl group ... too bad. I think the harmony is better with a mix of voices. My experience last year singing with the group was great ... I'll never forget it. I came to Brick City HS for the Math and foreign language, but Glee Club was the 'icing on the cake'. I've always enjoyed singing, and I miss it nowadays. Maybe if the girls can come, we can 'jam' a little bit ... maybe we can harmonize out on the pier on Sunday evenings. 'A cappella', of course; my log cabin doesn't have a piano, worse luck!

"Please think seriously about my invitation to Susan. I really hope she and Alpha Lee can come to stay for the summer. I promise to respect and protect both these lovely young ladies so long as they are here. "Hoping to hear from you soon... with a *YES* answer! "Pfc Jan Short"

Chapter 4

Alpha Lee was finishing another copy of the fishing lodge charcoal when her mother called from downstairs that she had a telephone call. She put down her charcoal stick and hurried down the stairs. It was Ben. He asked abruptly, "Alpha Lee, have you been dating Mark Messersmith?"

"Well, we did have a couple of dates, Ben. He took me to a movie and dinner, ... but I'm not going out with him any more," she said. She could not tell Ben the reason why.

"Damn right you're not, honey. ... Oh, sorry, Alpha Lee, that wasn't very nice. I'm just so mad at the guy! Would you believe ... he was picked up by the sheriff yesterday and hauled before a magistrate because he abandoned his pregnant wife, Alpha Lee, *AND* his two children! I couldn't believe it! The creep is married to a woman he met when he was in England ... his wife lives in Delaware now, and he hasn't been supporting them!" Alpha Lee couldn't even speak. She felt humiliated beyond endurance. "Alpha Lee, I feel so bad about fixing him up with you for the Valentine Dance. I had no idea, I swear. He seemed like an okay guy, but he's a worthless son of a bitch! Did he ... do anything to you, honey? Did he try anything?"

"Well .." she hesitated. "I guess you could say he did, Ben. He hurt me."

"You mean he hit you, Alpha Lee?" Ben's voice was outraged. "You should bring charges against him! What a bastard!"

"No," she said, "he didn't hit me, Ben. He was just too ...aggressive," she told him, remembering Jan's words: sexually *aggressive* ... yes, he had certainly been that. Ben was silent for a long moment. He's guessing what happened, she thought. He knows. When he spoke, she could hear the pain in his voice.

"Alpha Lee, I'm so sorry I got you into this. I just feel awful," Ben said.

"I'm okay, Ben. I'm all right now ... I think. Thank you for letting me know this, even though it makes me sick! I sure don't hold it against you. The Valentine dance was fun. He seemed really nice. How could either of us known? I hope he's gone. I don't want to *ever* see him again."

After Ben hung up, Alpha Lee remembered the picture on the dresser in Mark's bedroom ... the woman with the baby and the little boy. The picture had been turned face down, and she had picked it up to look at it while Mark was in the bathroom. That was his wife, she thought angrily. I hate him! Alpha Lee snatched a jacket from the closet. "Mother, I'm gonna ride my bike for a while," she called, and Nell Evans answered something about taking a sweater because it was chilly out. Alpha Lee had read somewhere that when one was angry or upset, physical activity helped to dispel stress. She jerked her bicycle from the garage and went flying down the street, her mind seething with angry thoughts. When she heard a car horn too near her, she slowed and pulled closer to the curb. I've got to pay attention! she thought, ... or I'm going to be in even more trouble! She toiled up the grade at the end of Center Street slowly; she could already feel her anger cooling. She stopped at the top of the hill to catch her breath.

The sky was bright blue and the sun was bright, but the breeze still had the chill of winter. Even so, there were bright yellow and purple crocuses blooming in a nearby yard. Alpha Lee felt a sense of peace.

Thank you, God, for *NOT* letting me have sex with Mark ... at least not completely. I was terribly upset at the time, but I'm glad now that it couldn't happen ... now it's over, and I won't ever be with him again. With a last glance at the crocus, their colors brilliant in the sunshine, Alpha Lee started drifting down Center Street toward home.

The phone rang as Mrs. McAllister finished breakfast Saturday morning. She put down her coffee cup. "Hello."

"I have a night rate telegram for Mrs. Nancy McAllister."

"I'm Mrs. McAllister."

"Do you have a pencil? You may want to write down some numbers."

"Yes," she said, reaching for the note pad. "Go ahead."

"'Sending Alpha Lee ticket for NW Airlines flight 317 from Pittsburgh to Seattle Saturday May 21 departing Pittsburgh 10 AM. Susan more than welcome, and many jobs available. Many companies need receptionists, clerical help, and general assemblers. I will meet flight in Seattle. Please convey message of love to Susan and Alpha Lee and Nancy...(signed) Jan Short.' ... Shall I read the numbers again, Mrs. McAllister? May I mail the telegram to you at 500 Center Street?"

"Yes, please." Susan came down the stairs just as Nancy hung up the phone. "Oh, Susan, good morning, honey. Here's something you'll be interested in," and she handed her the scribbled note. "Oh ... can you read it?" Susan scanned the note quickly.

. "*YES!*" she almost screamed. "Oh, Nancy, this is so great!" She threw her arms around Nancy and they both laughed.

"Susan, are you sure you want to do this? Don't forget, Jan's letter described the lodge as being pretty primitive. No hot water heater ... an old kitchen stove that heats with wood ... and it's way out in the wilderness. You aren't used to that sort of thing. Don't be too hasty."

"Well, I have gone camping sometimes ... with the Remagens. We stayed at a state park once that was just like that. It was fun!" Then she became quite serious. "Nancy, I'll get a job, like Jan suggested. I'll get to be on my own, and make my own decisions. I'll meet new people, and be able to see a different part of the country. I think I *NEED* to do this."

"Susan, it's good to hear you talk this way ... I think you're saying that you want to challenge yourself, to grow up. I think you want to trust yourself, and you want us to trust you." Nancy hugged her close. "I'm glad you feel this way, Susan. It's time. ... So ... let's call right now and get a reservation on that same flight. We'll plan to drive to Pittsburgh the day before and spend the night in a hotel. Would you like to do that? Maybe if we leave early enough, we could do some shopping."

"That would be super, Nancy! I'll watch you make the reservation so I'll be sure I can take the same plane with Alpha Lee."

"Susan, I want you to make the call, and make the reservation yourself. Just ask the operator for Northwest Airlines in Pittsburgh. Then, tell them you want to be on that flight."

"Okay! And then I'll ride my bike up to Alpha Lee's and show her this note, and then we can start making plans. Oh, I just can't wait! Nancy, this is all so thrilling! Is it really happening?" After dinner Susan wrote a note to Jan to enclose in a card she had begged from Alpha Lee "You're always sending cards and things to people," she had said to Alpha Lee. "Do you happen to have one of those 'thank you' cards? I'd like to send one to Jan. He was just *so* kind to ask me to come along. He didn't have to do that, you know. But Alpha Lee, I'm glad he did. I'm just so excited I can't sit still! Are we dreaming?"

"Dear Jan, "Thank you so much for inviting me to come with Alpha Lee to visit you this summer. I am so excited about it! I made reservations today for me on that same flight, and we'll be going to Pittsburgh Friday, and stay in a hotel so we'll be there in plenty of time. Nancy says if we start early enough we can even do some shopping in Pittsburgh on Friday. "I'm looking forward to seeing you again, and also to seeing the Rocky Mountains and the Northwest. I hope I can find a good job. Thank you, thank you, Jan! "Your friend, "Susan Remagen "P. S. I think Alpha Lee loves you!"

"Brick City, March 26

"Dearest Jan, "Your telegram came to Mrs. McAllister just after breakfast this morning with the flight number and date, and Susan and I are on cloud nine. She copied the telegram for me, and Mrs. McAllister made Susan call the airline herself and make her reservation.

Mrs. McAllister is going to drive us up to Pittsburgh on the 20th, and take us to the flight. We even have a reservation at a hotel for that night. She is so sweet. Jan, I'm so excited I hardly know what to say. Mother and I have started making a list of the things I will want to bring, and I made a count-down calendar so I can X off the days before I leave. Susan will get a beautiful guitar for graduation, (but she doesn't know it yet ... she has practiced lots on an old one that belongs to Dr. John) and I'm sure she'll want to bring it along, so we'll have music when we have time to sit by the fire. (Do you need a fire in June? Maybe not. Oh well. It was such a pleasant thought.)

Or maybe when we sit on the pier, dangling our toes in the water. Now there's a pleasant thought, too! "Jan, it's only eight weeks from today! I won't make this a long letter, since I am going to bribe my brother to take it to the post office so it can go out on the Sunday morning truck. I sent three more copies of the charcoal by parcel post today. I'll try to make them all exactly alike so the dealer will be happy. Has she sold any yet? Your original copy is the ONLY one with just a tiny shadow of a sunken boat showing, just to the left of the lodge. I meant to put that in all of them, but I left it out of the first three copies by mistake.

"Mother's getting dinner, and I need to help. Wish you were here, to be our guest. Do you like meat loaf and baked potatoes? I guess I'll get to cook for you soon! I hope I can get the hang of cooking on that wood stove. Mother said her mother had a wood-fired cooking stove, and she tested the oven temperature just by sticking her hand in the oven! She baked biscuits every day. Grandfather Selby didn't care for light bread as much, she said. Oh, Jan this will be such an adventure! I can hardly wait to get started ... but first I have to graduate. "All my love, " Alpha Lee"

"March 27, 1949 "Dearest Alpha Lee,

"What a week! I rented the fishing camp this week, starting April first. Frank wanted two months' rent, and the electric company wanted a $25 deposit, and the phone company said they don't have any wires within a quarter mile, so we can't have a phone right now, maybe in three months. (That will be too late for you ... sorry!) The good news is that the camp is on two acres of land, and all the wood we want is free for the chopping. There is an axe in the wood-shed. I brought it back to the base and sharpened it on the grinder, and I'll chop up some wood when I have time.

"I made reservations for your flight out here on the 21st out of Pittsburgh. I'll send you money early next month for bus fare to catch the plane. I don't know how else you could get up there. I'll enclose the plane ticket with this letter; I paid cash for it last night at the airport after I got off at TE. Honey, I promised you I'd give you a return ticket too, but after all the expenses this week, including car insurance, a new front tire, the rent, the plane ticket, and tuition for the summer term, I'm all tapped out except for gas money so I can get to work. I want to get some sheets and pillows and blankets before you get here, and have a little food in the larder, so I'd like your permission to delay buying the return ticket until you get here.

"If your folks are adamant about it, I can wire the Farmer's Bank and take it out of savings there, but I hate to break into that account if we don't have to. That's my rainy-day college money if this doesn't last out here. (Honey, please bring out three blank savings signature cards from Farmers Bank.)

The money order is for the first three charcoals, love. She put my copy on display and has orders for fifteen (15) now, not 15 total, but 15 *MORE*. She said she had numbered each piece, and promised her customers there would not be more than 100 copies made. That sounds like way too many to me! Too much boring work for you. She is begging me for more of your work to display and sell. The original will go on LOAN to the museum in Seattle this week. She wants me to help write a little book to sell for 25 cents that tells 'about the artist'

. "Frank, (Naomi's husband), gave me the key so I could get a little cleaning done, and when I came out this morning Frank and Naomi were busy soaking the curtains in soapy water, and scrubbing the floors. I did a lot of cleaning in the kitchen and washed some windows. I'll bet my mom is doing this same kind of stuff ... she'll be into spring house cleaning just about now. She cleans *everything*, and we men always had to keep out of her way! ... except when she needed furniture moved.

"I checked what pots and pans and forks and spoons and such were there, and I think there's enough to get started with. I asked Frank about a used refrigerator, and he said he works for a place that sells them, and he thinks he can get one and put it in for an extra $4 or $5 per month, so I told him to please find us one. The electricity won't be on until April first, but there is a pitcher pump in the sink, so we could get water for cleaning. It is good, clean, cold water. To get hot water, we have to build a fire in the wood range in the kitchen.

"I'll have two GI paydays before you get here, and four checks from TE, so I don't think we'll go hungry. I need your help on what to buy beyond hand soap and towels, and dishwashing soap. I'll look for a used washing machine, but the ads I've seen in the paper are asking a terrible price. We may have to use some dishpans, or take your pretty girly clothes to the Chinese laundry. I'll string up a clothesline on the porch for rainy days, and there are LOTS of those. I just added clothes pins and line to my shopping list. (Hmmm -- I wonder if I can find clothes pins that were made in Richwood, West Virginia? Could be! They make a bunch of them there.) I couldn't have guessed that setting up housekeeping could cost this much. Honey, I want so much for you to be happy here, but everything is so rustic and primitive. The furniture is all 'old mother -in- law', and the silverware and dishes are old dime-store brand, and the lights aren't nice lamps, but just bare bulbs in the middle of the ceiling with strings hanging down that you pull for ON or OFF.

"Our one really big luxury is the view ... Mount Rainier and Puget Sound. There are lots of gulls and pelicans, and wild ducks and geese, beautiful birds, Alpha Lee. And the surrounding forest is huge old-growth pines. The driveway down from the highway goes down and down to the water, through huge pine trees of some kind. The view of the mountain *is* just like the picture, and I know it will be even prettier when you get here. Lots prettier, sweetheart. I'm so excited! Enclosed please find a ticket to your summer home, which, I hope, will be a happy place for both of us.

"All my love, Jan"

"Brick City April 3rd "My dearest Jan,

"My ticket to adventure arrived yesterday, and I'm so excited! Jan, my parents did not see your letter that said 'round trip ticket', so please, *please* don't worry about it for now. I *will* stay for the full three months and beg for more. I just hope you will truly *want* me to stay. Having a pair of giggly girls in your life every day might make you decide you want to be a bachelor forever! (God forbid!) Dear Jan, don't worry about doing a lot of shopping, and having the shelves full of food and everything spiffy clean. We'll arrive with our suitcases full of clean clothes, enough to last a week, at least, and we can go with you to the grocery after we have planned some meals. Girls like to do that, you know. We'll even bring our own towels and wash cloths, and our own special bath soap and shampoo. We *can* use brands boys use, but we prefer our own with nice soft perfumes that make the boys notice. (Have *you* noticed?) My mother gave me a couple of candles to have in case the lights go out sometime (or if we want to eat our canned beans by candle light).

I've done some thinking, and I came up with sort of a basic list of things we'll need to have on hand for the first few days. ... 4 bed sheets; 2 blankets; 3 pillows (any kind, even toss pillows) 2 extra rolls toilet tissue dishwashing soap & a big dishpan 1 can beef stew; 1 can pork & beans 1 loaf of bread (till I can learn to bake biscuits in that stove!) 1/2 dozen eggs; 1 pkg bacon 1 box All-Bran or Corn Flakes &1 qt milk 1 can of applesauce (or some fresh fruit would be nice) Susan and I love to shop, so we can get more stuff when we find out what we need. She knows we'll be roughing it. In fact she took out a library book on camping. And I'm looking at James's Boy Scout manual. What a really great book that is!

"Don't forget, Mrs. McAllister is sending $20 a week for Susan's 'room and board'... she insists on that. We all know you're working two jobs because you'll never get rich in the Army ... but we also have great confidence that you will get a good education and some day have a very responsible job for which you'll be highly paid.

"I'll cash that money order tomorrow and buy some more stuff so I can make more copies of that charcoal to sell, so we can buy more bacon and eggs, and maybe even some fresh fish and hamburger. I want to make you an apple pie when I get the hang of that cookstove! You know they say 'The way to a man's heart is through his stomach' (which is kind of a revolting thought!), and I *do* want to reach your heart!

"Oh Jan, I'm as happy as a child on Christmas Eve. I'm going to get on my bike right now and take this to the post office. "Lots of *LOVE* to my favorite soldier ... "Alpha Lee"

Bicycle, birthday, sheets, blankets, Jan repeated as he walked into the main PX. He had drawn two nice checks from TE since he paid the rent and with a half hour before class time, he wanted to do some shopping. "Hey, what's that?" He saw a set of oil paints in a large wooden case on sale for $24.95. The sign read: CLOSEOUT -- INCLUDES EASEL and 12 CANVASES. He asked the clerk. "Is that really a good price?"

"It's a fantastic price. The set was $29.95, without the easel, but this is the last one and the manager said he wanted to get rid of it. It's the best easel we sell. We always carry the same brand of oils, too."

"I'll take it then, thanks." This'll be a surprise for Alpha Lee's birthday, he said to himself. Sheets, blankets, bicycle. Oh, there's the white goods. The sign said FREE PILLOWS; in smaller print, 'Buy package of two sheets with matching pillowcases on sale and get two free pillows, only $7.49 for all.' He grabbed a yellow set and a rose set and headed for the cashier. He priced the blankets and shook his head. Fourteen ninety-five each. Have to wait until payday for those. He remembered seeing a roadside stand with hand-woven Indian blankets. How much were they? He tried to recall. I think they were only ten bucks each, and they were pretty. If I stop there tomorrow on my way to TE, three days before GI payday, I might get a bargain, he thought. As he guessed, he was able to buy two blankets the next afternoon for sixteen dollars for the pair. One had an eagle pattern, the other had a smiling gray wolf.

Chapter 5

As the big plane lifted from the runway, Alpha Lee pressed against the window, watching the ground fall away beneath them. Beside her, Susan sat tensely, her eyes tightly closed and her hands clutching the armrests in a white-knuckle grip. "Oh Susan! You're missing this ... it's so exciting!" Alpha Lee said. "Did you feel the lift when the wheels left the ground?" Susan didn't reply. The DC-4 climbed into the smoggy sky and Alpha Lee watched the buildings and landscape of Pittsburgh grow smaller and smaller, the cars, trucks and buses crawling along the highways like so many toys. Beyond the city, the hills were brilliant green with new spring growth; the rivers wound like silvery blue ribbons, crossed by toy bridges here and there. The higher they climbed, the more the ground was obscured by Pittsburgh's smoky pall. Alpha Lee turned away. "We're on our way to Detroit, Susan," she said. "Can't you relax and just enjoy it?"

"Tell me when we get to Seattle," Susan said.

It would be a very long day. Northwest Airlines Flight 317 carried fifty-two passengers and also a load of mail. There would be many stops along the way in northern cities Alpha Lee knew only as names on a map: Detroit, Milwaukee, Minneapolis, Billings, Spokane. It would be dark when they reached Seattle at 10:15. Alpha Lee would reset her new watch (a graduation gift from her parents) to Pacific Time, three hours earlier than the familiar Eastern Standard. She fumbled in her purse to find a notepad and pen. The sights she was seeing from her window, now that the thick city overcast had been left behind, were so interesting she wanted to keep notes to discuss with Jan. The textures of the landscape below ... cities, forests, hills and valleys, golf courses and crop lands, the shadows of clouds moving across the land, the blue of the lakes and ponds reflecting the sky .. were exciting to her, and she vowed she would paint it from memory. This is abstract art I can enjoy, she thought. She was thrilled, but a little frightened when they flew over Lake Erie ... out of sight of any land.

The landing in Detroit came after lunch, and was only a short stop to pick up mail and a few more passengers; through passengers were advised to remain in their seats. Smog lay over this city too, but their take-off lifted them above the low cloud layer and back into sunshine. They pulled out their books to read for a little while after the plane leveled off. "What are you reading, Susan?" Alpha Lee asked. Susan showed her the book, a romance novel with a lurid cover. "Oh, yeah, I read that," Alpha Lee said. "I'm reading 'The Postman Always Rings Twice.' Did you see the movie? It was really tragic, but good anyway. Lana Turner and John Garfield. Mmmmm," she said with a smile.

"No, I didn't see it," Susan said. "I think it was on while I was ... with the Remagens, and you know they wouldn't let me go to movies."

"Well, the movie was not as ... umm ... explicit as the book is, of course." After a long pause, Alpha Lee asked in a whisper, "Susan ... did you ever have sex?"

Susan looked up quickly. "*NO NO*, of course not!" she answered indignantly. "Why would you ask me such a thing!"

"Well, I'm sorry. I just thought,maybe since you and Ben have been going together for such a long time, and I know he loves you."

"Of course not! Ben knows better than to try anything with me. I would never speak to him again!" She squirmed in her seat and turned back to her book. After a few moments, she turned to Alpha Lee. "Have *you?*"

"Well-ll ... almost. Sort of. Don't you ever tell, Susan!" Susan was immediately interested.

"With who? Mark? Are you gonna tell Jan? Are you going to sleep with Jan, Alpha Lee?"

"Oh, stop it, Susan! He probably wouldn't even want to," she said, hoping that wasn't true. "Mark hurt me, Susan. He was awful. Did Ben tell you about him? ... That he is married, and even has children? The sheriff actually picked him up for abandoning his family. I felt so terrible about it. We had three dates. Ben didn't know when he introduced us."

"No, he didn't tell me that! Oh, Alpha Lee, that's awful." Long pause. "How did he hurt you?"

"He just tried to ... you know. He pushed hard inside me, and ... there was blood, lots of it. I was scared to death. Oh Susan, I wanted to do it!" she cried. "Some of it was exciting and wonderful, and I just couldn't stop. At first he was nice to me; he said sweet things, and he kissed me as though he meant it, just like those lovers in the books. He even told me he loved me, Susan! But he didn't mean it ... he was just trying to get me to . . . you know."

"Yeah," Susan said. "Oh, Alpha Lee ..." and Susan squeezed her hand ... "that's just awful. Did you tell your mother?"

"No, I just couldn't. I had to wash my skirt, Susan, because there was so much blood. I've been praying that I'm not ... damaged, or something, so that I can't ever have children. Or even have sex normally with somebody I really love and want to marry."

"Like Jan?" Susan asked.

"Maybe like Jan," Alpha Lee answered with a shy smile. "He is the *BEST*, Susan. I love him." Then she added, "Even though we've hardly even touched each other. We've never really kissed ... he just kissed my cheek the night of the banquet, and again when we had a chance meeting by the bank when he was leaving for the army. I love him mentally, Susan. I fell in love just through letters." She turned to Susan with a radiant smile. "But there's more to it than that, Susan. There's some kind of magic that I can't even explain. I hope he feels it, too."

"Alpha Lee, that's just beautiful. Do you suppose I'll ever be able to feel that way about any-body? Ben is nice to me, and he kisses me sometimes, but I haven't felt anything magical yet." She hesitated before continuing, her eyes downcast. "Actually, I have felt something that I won't call magic, exactly. It's sort of embarrassing. Especially when I can tell he's... umm ... excited, or whatever you call it. But that's when I break away and stop everything. Because I'm afraid."

"Gee, Susan, I guess we've both got problems, haven't we? Because I'm afraid, too. I must find a doctor out there and find out if I'm all right, after what Mark did to me."

"Alpha Lee ... honestly, now ... don't you think sex is really disgusting?" Susan asked. "It's like your privacy, and your rights, are just destroyed. I feel like hiding in a dark closet sometimes ... dressed in sixteen layers of clothes, with a ski suit on top of everything else, zipped up to my chin!" Alpha Lee laughed at that. "Susan, you are weird." And then she sang softly, "'Someday he'll come along, the man I love ...' and the man *you* love, too, Susan. You'll see. Maybe he's waiting for you in Washington State" and she gave Susan a rapturous smile. "But his name *ISN'T* Jan."

Jan's week seemed interminably long. He and Fred taught a class four days, and worked four nights at TE, since the professor had a speaking engagement in Seattle on Friday, and had canceled his class, leaving them free to work. Still, each hour passed very slowly. He had spent the previous Sunday in the lodge, scrubbing all the dishes and pots and pans, washing the windows, and hanging the curtains that Naomi had washed.

Finally the day came when the girls would arrive. The bulletin board held no surprises that Friday ... his Saturday *and* Sunday would be free. On Saturday morning he had breakfast at the base and then drove to TE to work a full day. By mid-afternoon, anticipation was making him jittery, and concentration was difficult. It helped when Professor Heiden came by to chat, taking his mind off his evening rendezvous at the air-port. Jan had been assembling a new prototype in the lab; when he finally had everything wired according to the drawing and placed in the new metal chassis, he re-checked the power cables and felt he was ready to run the "smoke test". The Professor had asked to see the first fully assembled test, so Jan called him on the lab phone. The new modification tested out perfectly, and the Professor was all smiles, he was so pleased. "Friend, this calls for a drink!"

They walked to the soft-drink dispenser in the break room and Professor Heiden provided the coins. Checking the bottoms of the bottles for their source, Jan found his to have been produced in Kansas City; this entitled him not only to a free drink, but to an extra dime for getting the bottle from the longest distance. "Hey, Jan, this is your lucky day!" the Professor said with a smile as he handed him his winnings. "Naomi tells me you've rented her fishing lodge to live in. Jan, I think that's a good move. The location is handy to everything, and it's a beautiful setting. Do you like to fish?"

"Oh, yes, sir. I think this is a pretty good deal, even if I don't look forward to having just a wood stove for cooking and heating water. But they gave me a good price, and I'll need a place to live in a couple of months anyway when my enlistment is up. With my Class A pass, I can live off base now ... I just need a phone close so the Army can get me if they need to call me. The phone company says it will take some time to string wires that last half-mile or so, but the Captain said as long as they can call Naomi, it'll be okay." He took a long drink from his Kansas City bottle.

"Jan, from what Naomi told me, you're going to have company living with you for the summer. Isn't your artist friend flying in tonight? Jan, if there's anything we can do to help make you comfortable, just ask."

"Thanks, Prof. Yes, their plane's due in at ten. Alpha Lee's best friend is coming out, too ... I'm not sure what she'll find to do ... maybe she'll want to work here as an assembler or some-thing. I think we have everything we need at the lodge for now ... except a decent refrigerator. I sure hope it won't be too rustic for those girls. They're both city girls, but I think they're pretty good sports. Money may get a little tight, but with the hours I'm getting here, I think we'll make it okay."

Milwaukee, Minneapolis, Billings. The landings, the airports, the takeoffs seemed to follow each other at long intervals, all much the same. The girls read, dozed, talked, through an endless afternoon. In one of the forward seats a baby cried; the pressure change before landing caused pain in his ears. Somewhere east of the Rockies the stewardess served dinner, or what passed for it, to the passengers. The girls hadn't known meals were included as part of the flight service, and they were delighted with the chicken sandwiches, chips and fruit and cookies. They had enjoyed the peanuts and soft drinks that had been offered periodically through the long day. Once Susan chose wine, which she had never tasted before. "I think I like Coke better," she decided. Now the sun was lower in the sky; Alpha Lee's watch said 9:30, Eastern time. The prairie far below was changing to a broken landscape of lone buttes and small mountains; a residue of snow still on the summits revealed the higher peaks. The Rocky Mountains! Alpha Lee felt a thrill of excitement. I never dreamed I'd see them ... especially from above.

Alpha Lee hummed the melody of one of the All-State Chorus songs. "I can't wait to tell Jan about All-State," she said. "Wasn't it wonderful, Susan? How did that many people manage to keep together? ... when the music was so complex, especially. I'm so thankful that Mrs. McAllister chose me to go."

"Yeah, it was really nice. You know, Alpha Lee, I'm going to miss singing with the Glee Club more than anything else about school. Maybe we can join a chorus or something at Wesleyan, since we're not going to commute."

"I'd love that," Alpha Lee agreed. She resumed her humming, and Susan joined in. The girls sang the words softly in harmony, and then went on to sing other songs they had sung together. The nearby passengers quieted to listen, or sometimes joined in, if the song was a familiar one. Susan said, "You see, Alpha Lee ... those popular songs always make love sound like it's all just holding hands and dancing and hugging and kissing. There's nothing at all about getting hurt, or exposing yourself to a man ... an almost total stranger." After a pause she added, almost to herself, "Or even someone ... someone close to you ..." She stopped, embarrassed, and then added, "The romance part is wonderful, but the *other* part is .. scary. Don't you think? Scary and disgusting."

"Well, Susan, there must be something about sex that isn't disgusting ... everybody does it, I guess. Actually, I *want* to do it ... with the right person, and under the right circumstances. Although I'm not sure what that would be. I suppose things work out ..."

"Alpha Lee," Susan said suddenly, "you've seen animals do it, haven't you? Like dogs, or chickens? It looks *DISGUSTING!* When Ben told me about artificial insemination that they do with the cattle, it seemed to me that would be much better. Neater. Less dangerous." She turned to Alpha Lee and whispered, "Can you imagine a huge bull doing that to a cow? Wouldn't they hurt each other?

"I'd think so, but I guess they don't hurt each other seriously," Alpha Lee agreed. She paused a moment. "Susan, just imagine *elephants!*"

"Oh my gosh!" Susan exclaimed. "How could *they* do it? How about whales, deep down in the ocean?" Dinosaurs!...snakes....alligators, Susan offered, incredulous. "I've even seen bugs doing it ... they were attached at the ends of their bodies. They could even fly while they were connected! Weird and disgusting. *SPIDERS!*"

Alpha Lee nearly screamed. "*Eeeeew*! And then the female *eats* the male!"

"It serves him right," Susan said, laughing. "Imagine monkeys doing it," she said. "They'd be almost like people, wouldn't they? Except hairier. Disgusting!" She tried to stifle laughter. "Gorillas!" Alpha Lee giggled.

"Dragons! Schmoos!" She doubled up with laughter. In the seat in front of the girls, a small boy turned around to peer curiously at them, only his eyes and nose visible over the back of the seat. By now the girls were laughing uncontrollably, and the child watched them, his eyes round. Alpha Lee looked at him, still giggling, and asked, "Is your name Kilroy?"

He grinned and shook his head vigorously. "Donnie," he said. That sent Susan into another fit of laughter.

Alpha Lee quickly drew on her notepad the "Kilroy" character often seen by GI's: a round face, just eyes and a long drooping nose, peering over a fence. Beneath the face were the inevitable words, "KILROY WAS HERE." She tore off the sheet and handed it to the child. "This is Kilroy," she explained, "and you looked just like that." The little boy stared at the cartoon for just a moment, and then he, too, began giggling. That set the girls off again, and all three of them couldn't stop laughing.

Leaving work at five, Jan stopped for supper at the nearby diner, and then drove to the lodge to make up the beds with the new sheets. His hands were so jittery he wondered if someone had "laced" his coffee. He checked the basket of mixed fruit Sgt. Herndon's wife had given him. She had said, "You'll find out one thing about women, Jan. There's never enough fruit or flowers to suit 'em. You just set this in the middle of the kitchen table, and you'll make a hit." He checked his watch ... eight o'clock, an hour yet before time to go to the airport. He built a fire in the range to make coffee, then unloaded a small suitcase of clothes he had brought from the barracks, and placed everything neatly in the chest of drawers in his bedroom. Still finding himself with forty-five minutes to spare, he sat down in the rocker by the empty fireplace and read the lesson in his electronics textbook again. The rain was pelting down, drumming against the window. Then he saw headlights flashing through the front window. Someone was driving down his lane. When the pickup got closer, he saw it was Naomi's husband Frank, with a refrigerator strapped on in the truck bed! Even in the rain, they made short work of getting it into the lodge and plugged in. When they had loaded the old icebox into the pickup and covered it with the tarp, Jan thanked Frank heartily, and watched him go up the road.

And then it was time for Jan to head for the airport ... he wanted to allow himself more than a full hour for the drive. Driving through town he was glad he had the extra time: the wet streets were crowded with cars full of high school students celebrating their graduation. Jan felt a moment of nostalgia, recalling his own experience only a year ago at Brick City. It seemed so long ago.

North of town he finally had time to think, and his thoughts tumbled over each other in a nervous confusion: What have I gotten myself in for, he thought. She's used to living in a nice home, with her own bedroom, and all the modern conveniences ... will she be happy to stay in that no-frills place? ... She's been on that plane all day ... will she be so tired she'll want to go right back home and crawl into her own pretty bed? Is she used to cooking for herself? Will she be frustrated with the wood range? .. Will she take one look and think everything's so ugly she just can't stay there? I didn't even stretch out on that bed ... I wonder how lumpy that mattress is? ... Lord, I hope she isn't a real citified girl that can't adapt to what I can offer her. ... No, she's not like that! ... Oh God, I surely hope all this will work out, somehow. I want her to love this place, and to want to stay here with me ... I know she'll be homesick; if she gets mad at me for anything she'll be a hell of a long way from home, and not even a telephone so she can call her mom. Oh, God ... I really have a lot to learn about her, and about women in general. Wish my sister had lived.

And what about Susan? Will she be okay here? I wonder if she's ever been away from home before? ... Should I kiss Alpha Lee at the gate? How will I know what she expects of me? ... Oh, come on! Surely I'll be able to tell ... won't I? Jan, he said to himself, you're either in tall clover or burnt-out broomsedge, and you may not know which for a couple of days.

It was twilight when they landed at Billings, and fully dark when they left Spokane. Susan was asleep, her head tilted back against the head rest, her mouth open slightly. The stewardess spoke: "We'll be landing in Seattle in approximately twenty minutes. The temperature is sixty-eight degrees, and there's a light rain falling. The captain will begin the descent sequence in about fifteen minutes."

Seattle! Alpha Lee began to feel butterflies in her stomach. Can this be real? The next stop ... only half an hour, she thought. Jan will be waiting. Or maybe he won't be there! Maybe he will forget to meet us! What will we do, at night in an airport a million miles from home? ... *NO!* He won't forget us ... not my sweet Jan. ... Is he really 'my sweet Jan'? Maybe he won't feel that way at all ... maybe he does have another girl friend by now, somebody tall and beautiful and sexy. Oh, God, please don't let that happen! ... The plane is turning ... Why are we making a turn like this? Maybe the pilot just barely missed crashing into a mountain! Those mountains are so huge, and we aren't flying very high ... My ears are popping again ... we're descending! How do I look, after this long day in a tight little seat? My dress is mussed, I'm sure. I should have worn some-thing else. ... And my hair ... I've got to comb my hair and check my lip-stick. Maybe another little touch of cologne ... I want to be pretty for him. Will he kiss me ... or just shake my hand? ... I'll be really cool. I'll wait for him to show how he feels. I'll just be friendly, that's all. We *are* good friends. ...At least we have been ... just through our letters. I don't really know him very well ... maybe the Army has changed him. Maybe he'll be rude and crude, after living with all those other guys all this time. Maybe he'll think I'm too ... babyish, or immature, or something. Maybe we'll find out we can't stand each other, living so close together in that cabin ... *NO! NO! NO!* she agonized. She prayed the universal young girl's prayer: Oh, God, please let him love me!

Alpha Lee clutched Susan's hand, unable to endure her feeling of alone-ness and uncertainty any longer. "Wake up, Susan! We're almost ready to land! We're near Seattle!" Susan yawned hugely.

"Already?" she asked. "After only a thousand hours of flying? Wow."

"It's past one A.M. our time, Susan. Did you re-set your watch? It's 10:05 Pacific Standard Time."

The stewardess said, "Fasten your seat belts, please. We'll be landing in fifteen minutes. Thank you for flying Northwest." And again Alpha Lee felt her stomach turn over; her heart was pounding. Oh, Jan! ... God, let him love me, please!

The plane came to a standstill at last, and Alpha Lee and Susan scrambled for their carry-on bags, Susan picked up the guitar case, and they worked their way forward with the other passengers. "You go first, Susan," Alpha Lee said nervously.

Oh no, he doesn't want to see *me*," she said. "It's *YOU* he'll be looking for. Go on," and she gave her friend a firm push.

"Thank you so much for a nice flight," Alpha Lee said to the two stewardesses. The girls could now feel the cool moist air from the open door. The air had a strange scent they couldn't recognize ... the ocean scent!

Jan watched as they rolled the steel stairs to the plane sitting just a few yards outside the gate. Finally, the door was opened, and he watched the people deplane ... a frazzled-looking young mother with a fussy baby; a priest; a couple of middle-aged men in expensive suits ... business executives, he supposed. Two Air Force officers and a Naval officer in uniform with lots of decorations, Jan noted, as he saluted sharply. Six ... seven ... eight soldiers he didn't need to salute, they weren't officers. He recognized one of them, a private who was one of the Mess Hall crew. Next came a tall blonde wearing a coat with a fur collar ... she must have boarded in Minneapolis, he thought ... it could be still wintry there. And then ... *NOBODY!* My God, did they miss the plane? But then another face appeared in the doorway: an elderly lady, being helped to the stairs by the stewardess, who turned her over to the airline ramp attendant who ran up the steps to assist her. Next came a woman with a little boy, groggy with sleep, who held his mother's hand and carried a piece of paper in the other hand. Jan saw a master sergeant hurry to meet them; he swung the child up and embraced the woman. The boy, wide awake now, showed his paper to his father, who immediately laughed, and the child gestured back toward the plane where more passengers were beginning to emerge. Two more soldiers, three sailors ... probably coming back from leave. Lucky guys. ... Will I know her, after not seeing her for nine months? Will she have changed? Girls do change a lot between their junior and senior years. He tried to recall Alpha Lee's junior class picture in his yearbook back home ... just a bit plump in the face, big glasses with cheap pearlized plastic frames; but, 'five foot two, eyes of blue', he thought, and a really nice figure ... I'll know her.

Alpha Lee swiftly looked over the few waiting welcomers on the tarmac, and she saw Jan. Oh, God, he looks so beautiful in his uniform, she thought with an overwhelming surge of emotion. I can't wait one more minute to touch him! ... No, no, be cool, don't rush him, she tried to tell herself. Susan screamed with joy when she saw him, and they began to descend the stairs. Jan saw two girls finally emerge from the open doorway of the big DC-4 and walk carefully down the rain-slick steel stairway onto the pavement. He couldn't believe his eyes. It *HAD* to be them ... he *KNEW* that was Susan ... tall, blonde, her head bowed and her back characteristically bent, wearing a slim navy-blue skirt and a checked shirt. He saw her broad smile ,heard her excited scream. She was carrying a guitar case and an over-large pocketbook. That was Susan, no doubt. But Alpha Lee *HAD* changed ... she had lost seventeen pounds over a year's time, and couldn't be described as "plump" anymore. She had saved her money from working at the jewelry store and from occasional baby- sitting jobs, and she had bought herself a new pair of glasses with dainty gold frames that looked like jewelry. She was wearing a soft white summer dress with cap sleeves that fit her snugly, and her dark red hair hung over her shoulders, a mass of coppery curls. Her full skirt billowed as she descended the stairs, revealing her slim legs. Then she waved and smiled at him. Wow! Jan thought.

What a picture! God, she is truly beautiful! He walked quickly to meet them through the light Seattle mist. And there were those crystal-blue eyes, the self-conscious, tentative smile, the faint smell of lilacs, recalling his mother's lilac bushes in the front yard at home ... Jan managed to greet Susan and grasp her hand in a welcoming shake, and then Alpha Lee lifted her arms to him, and he pulled her close against him. When he kissed her, her lips were parted, and he was aware of a faint taste of peppermint. She melted into his embrace, and he could feel the pressure of her generous breasts, her stomach, the hard mound of pubic bone, the length of her thighs, and a fragmented thought swept through his consciousness: this is no hello-at-the-airport kiss ... this is bedroom kiss, a behind-closed-doors kiss ... He felt the familiar rush of desire; it's been such a damned long time, he thought, and he felt a moment of foolish panic that everybody at the SeaTac Airport would notice his erection. Alpha Lee was whispering something in his ear: "Jan, I love you! It's wonderful ... just as I dreamed it would be ... *Better!*" And then they both remembered Susan, who was making a determined study of the surrounding scene, deliberately not watching this private- public moment between her friends.

"Hey Susan!" Jan cried heartily. "Sorry, hon, ... we just sort of got carried away, didn't we?" and he wrapped one arm around her waist. "God, it's good to see you girls! How was your flight? Other than just plain long?" Without even waiting for an answer, he led them swiftly through the drizzle into the terminal building. "I shoulda brought an umbrella! We'll get your bags, and then we'll be off to our summer camp! Are you ready for this, ladies?" He laughed, overcome with excitement and pleasure. "Oh, Susan ... do you need to call home? There are telephones over there."

"I won't call tonight, Jan; it's way after midnight back home; I just reset my watch to Pacific Time a little while ago. But Nancy said I should send a night wire. Can you tell me where to find the telegraph office?"

"Sure ... the Western Union desk is just over there on the right. Why don't you go ahead and do that, and Alpha Lee and I will get the luggage. You can meet us at the baggage claim. Just follow the signs. Okay?" When they were alone again, Jan turned to Alpha Lee. "Congratulations on your graduation, sweetheart." He kissed her again, this time with deliberate restraint.

"Thank you, Jan. I felt so ... exalted, I guess, when I got my diploma, and a moment later I felt sort of alone and small and uncertain." She turned to him with a brilliant smile. "And then I thought of coming out here to you, and I felt wonderful again ... strong and brave and ready for anything;"

"You can put things so beautifully ... God, Alpha Lee, you smell so sweet," he whispered. "I just want to inhale you ... And you look so pretty. I didn't remember how beautiful you are." Then, more matter-of-factly, "Did you have anything to eat on the plane? Are you hungry?"

At last they were settled in Jan's car. As he pulled away from the parking lot, Susan yawned and said, "Wow, Jan! It sure feels good to be on the ground again! I guess I'm an Earthling. I'm not crazy about outer space."

Jan laughed. "How was the flight, really? You didn't get airsick?"

"No, no," Alpha Lee answered. "It was really pretty smooth, except when we came down through the clouds to land. We landed and took off *so many times*, Jan."

"Could you see the big mountains?"

"No, it's been dark ever since somewhere in Montana. But Jan, I saw so many beautiful scenes down below. I want to paint a dozen pictures. It was so exciting."

"I sort of envy you, Alpha Lee. I've never flown on an airliner. Just a short flight in a little Piper Cub a long time ago. Since then, every time I see one of those little planes, I remember the promise I made to myself: Someday I'm gonna have my own plane. Someday I'm gonna fly, Alpha Lee. I swear, I'll do it."

Chapter 6

Jan turned into the dark lane, heading steeply downhill, just beyond Frank and Naomi's house, and Susan gasped. "Are you lost, Jan? This looks like the forest primeval!"

"Not at all, Sweet Sue, we're only a half mile from the lodge. You can see our porch light ahead now."

"It's eerie dark, with all these giant trees," Alpha Lee said. "Are they redwoods, Jan? I've never seen anything so tall!"

"No, I think they're Douglas fir, but they are tall, and they sing when the wind blows." He stopped the car just off the porch, and turned to her with a smile. "Well, girls, here we are ... home." The rain had stopped at last. Jan opened the car doors and the girls stepped out onto the hard damp sand..

"Oh, Jan ... this is so exciting. The air smells wonderful!" The dark pines whispered softly in a slight breeze, releasing drops of rain. There was a feeling of limitless space, as though every-thing stretched far in all directions ...the sky, the sea, the great dark forest. Alpha Lee touched Jan's arm as if to reestablish his closeness and her connection to him.

She spoke to break the overwhelming silence: "As remote as this place seems to be, we still have neighbors close by. That's nice. Do you know the people up by the road, Jan?"

"Oh yes, ... they're Frank and Naomi Massey, our landlords. Naomi's a secretary at Takoma Elektroniks. This lodge belonged to her grandfather." When they reached the door, Jan unlocked it and then turned to Alpha Lee. "I've been looking forward to this little ceremony. I'm gonna carry you across the threshold, sweet woman." He picked her up and kissed her, and, with Susan following behind laughing, he carried her through the door into the big room that served as living room-dining room-kitchen. He kissed her again, and set her down facing the easel, and turned on the light.

"Oh Jan, what's this?" she asked in surprise. "That's partly for your graduation, and partly for your birthday, which, I happen to know, is just a few days away. I'm sorry that Uncle Sam wouldn't let me attend your graduation, but maybe we can make up for that with a big birthday celebration. You know, if we work this thing right, we can find something to celebrate every weekend!"

Alpha Lee laughed. "That sounds like fun! I love to celebrate! Jan, thank you for this nice easel ... and oil paints, too! Wow ! I've never had a chance to try oils. Can I ever live up to your expectations? I feel like I'm a real artist! I'll work every day."

"Well, fine ... but leave a little bit of time for other things, sweet. We're gonna have a great summer, you betcha." He turned to Susan. "No, Susan, I didn't forget you. There's something for you on the dresser in the bedroom on the right." Susan rushed into the bedroom he indicated, giggling with delight. She came back in carrying a song book with the music written for a guitar.

"Thank you, Jan!" she said, riffling through the pages. "How did you know I was going to get a guitar for graduation? This is just great!"

He smiled. "Maybe a little birdie told me."

"Look, Alpha Lee ... here's 'Faraway Places,' and 'My Happiness' ...'Lazy River' .... This will be just great, Jan. We can harmonize, and I'll play accompaniment.

"Jan, I can hear the waves splashing out there," Alpha Lee said.

"Are we near the water, Jan?" Susan asked.

"Just out the back door. Don't you remember the picture?"

"Oh, yeah. There was a fishing pier for a back porch, wasn't there?"

"Shall we go outside and take a look? I think the moon is shining just a little by now ...," and he led the girls out the back door. Pale moonlight filtered through the thin overcast, illuminating the water and deepening the darkness of the vast forest that surrounded the lodge as far as they could see. The calls of loons and night birds made a strange music.

"Jan, this is just incredible," Alpha Lee said softly, slipping her arm around his waist. "This is the quietest place I've ever been. The sounds of the birds seem to just heighten the silence." She looked up at him, her eyes shining. "How can I ever thank you for bringing us here?"

"Just be happy, sweetheart. That'll be all the thanks I need." He held her in his arms and she snuggled against him, overwhelmed by emotion. As they went inside, Jan asked, "Are you girls hungry? Would you like some coffee, or some fruit? We have peanut butter, and some crackers."

"Do you have milk, Jan?" Susan asked. "I *am* kind of hungry. Coffee sometimes keeps me awake. And tonight I *don't* want to be kept awake!"

"Oh Jan, you did get a refrigerator!" Alpha Lee exclaimed as he opened the door to take out the milk.

"Frank brought it tonight, and only raised the rent five bucks. a month."

"It's nice looking ... and it freezes ice cubes, too. Oh, I'm glad, Jan. That wlll make grocery shopping and cooking a lot easier."

"Well, yeah ... but please don't plan on spending a lot of time cooking, Alpha Lee. Let's keep it simple. I didn't ask you to come out here to be my cook!" Jan sat on the couch while the girls sat at the kitchen table eating apples and drinking milk.

"Girls, we're going to be sharing a pretty small house here, and I think we should have a couple rules. When a door is closed, knock, and don't go in unless you are invited. When the door is open, everything is fair game. I'll try to remember to put the toilet seat down, and when we leave the toilet be sure the door is left open so the next person who needs it knows it is vacant. Everybody agree?"

"Easy," Susan said with her mouth full of apple.

Now, to continue ... The bedroom to the right of the bath is yours, girls, and to the left is mine. We have to burn a fire in the kitchen range to heat water, but it only takes about twenty minutes to get enough for a bath. There are extra towels and wash cloths in the bottom drawer of the chest in your bedroom. I haven't gotten any extra sheets because I didn't have the money, but I did get two extra keys for the lock on the front door, one for each of you. ... Now, let's see ...Oh, I almost forgot. I found a couple of second-hand bicycles ... they're out on the pier. We can go for rides if the tires will stay up. I have fishing poles in the woodshed, too. Do you like to fish? There's plenty of fish out there in the sound."

"It's so peaceful here, Jan. Have you spent many nights here?"

No, the sheets on both beds are brand new, but I think we're gonna break them in pretty soon. You girls have had a long day, and I know you've gotta be worn out. There might be enough warm water left to wash your face, I did have a fire going before I left for the airport. We could start it again if you want to soak in the tub."

Alpha Lee took the empty tumblers to the sink and rinsed them, then she came over and sat down on the couch beside him. She kicked off her shoes and pulled her feet up on the couch and leaned back, her head on his shoulder. Jan put his arm around her and pulled her close to him. "This is going to be a wonderful summer," she said dreamily.

Susan got her guitar and walked over. "Move over, I want a hug too." She sat on the other side of Jan, and he put his arm around her, too. She strummed some chords on her guitar, and sang softly, "Lullaby, and good night," and Jan and Alpha Lee joined in, remembering when they sang that song at Brick City High School, long ago and far away. When the song was over, Susan said, "Jan, thanks for letting me come out here. I promise to never get in the way of whatever the two of you want to do."

"I'm glad you could come along, Susan. I'm afraid my schedule would make Alpha Lee very lonely without you here. And she might not have been able to come at all without you."

"Well, I'm really happy I'm here, and I'm glad you'll have tomorrow off, but right now I'm going to wash my face and go to bed. Which side of the bed do you want, Alpha Lee?"

"The side by the window, please, unless you want it. It doesn't really matter, Susan. Tonight I could probably sleep on the floor."

"Jan, can I hang my guitar on these pegs?" Susan gestured toward the wall by the fireplace.

"Sure, they're for hanging guns, and if they're strong enough to hold guns, they'll hold your guitar okay. That'll be a good place for it."

She hung up the guitar and said, "Good night, my dear friends," and kissed both of them on the cheek. "I love you both," and she went toward the bedroom.

Alpha Lee stood. "I guess I'd better go, too," she said reluctantly. She took off her glasses and rubbed her eyes.

"Not yet." He pulled her down on to his lap. "Alpha Lee, you look so pretty. You've lost a lot of weight, haven't you? I was surprised when I saw you get off the plane ."

"Thank you for noticing," she said with a smile. "It's been fun making new clothes."

"And you have beautiful new glasses. I like those much better than the old ones. You know, I've never seen you without your glasses, Alpha Lee. You have devil eyes, honey. You're so beautiful I could kiss you."

She put her arms around his neck and closed her eyes. "*Do it,*" she whispered. They barely noticed Susan walking through to the bathroom.

Alpha Lee was awakened the next morning by small careful sounds from the kitchen: water running, the metallic sound of the fire door on the stove being closed. Her "body clock" told her it was mid-morning, but her watch on the bedside table displayed a quarter past seven. The sun was shining brightly on the blue water she could see out the window. She put on her short summer robe, and ran a brush through her hair. Susan was still fast asleep. Alpha Lee walked barefoot to the door, opened it quietly, and entered the kitchen area, closing the door behind her. Jan was putting plates, cups and silverware on the table

. "Good morning, pretty lady," he greeted her with a smile. "How was that bed? I hope you had a good rest."

"I feel great, Jan. I think I fell asleep the minute I closed my eyes. It'll take a while, I guess, to get used to Pacific Time. Susan and I may get drowsy as soon as we finish supper until we adjust. . . . Oh, that coffee smells so good! I'll go brush my teeth and wash my face, and I'll be right back for a cup.

"First things first, sweet." He pulled her close and kissed her. Then said, "Alpha Lee, when you kissed me at the airport, it just blew me away. I want a lot more kisses just like that."

"I'm glad, Jan ... because I want that, too."

Jan started bacon frying and took eggs and butter from the refrigerator. Uh, oh, he thought. I can think of one thing we need: a toaster. Hmmm I wonder how I can toast bread? Maybe on a rack over the burner opening? I'll have to watch it carefully. I'll try this old popcorn popper. It oughta work, upside down. When Alpha Lee reappeared, he assigned her to the toast detail while he fried the eggs. She poured two cups of coffee while the bread was toasting. "Jan, this is going to be such fun! It'll take a while, I think, to get the hang of using the oven. I'll try biscuits soon ... they're easy." Susan came into the kitchen, rubbing her eyes and yawning. "G'morning, folks," she said. "That bacon smells so good. Can I have some, too?"

"Mornin', Susan. Did you get some rest?

"Well, for a while, anyway," she answered sleepily. "Jan, will the water be hot yet, so I could take a bath?"

"Hmm ... I'd say give it another ten minutes, Suz. Why don't you eat breakfast first while you're waiting?"

"Okay. No eggs for me, please ... if I could just have a couple slices of bacon and some toast. Is toast possible?" Then Susan noticed Alpha Lee taking two slices from the popper. "Oh, yeah, that works, doesn't it? But you have to really watch it, don't you?"

"Here you go, Susan," Alpha Lee handed her a plate with two slices of toast, and Jan added the bacon. Susan sat down at the table, and Alpha Lee brought her a cup of coffee.

"Hey, I think I have some jam for your toast," Jan said, opening the cup board. "My sergeant's wife, Sally Herndon,, donated a jar of homemade huckleberry jam. They grow up here like crazy, I guess. Did you ever pick huckleberries, Alpha Lee?" He opened the small jar and handed it to Susan.

"Once ... Mother made jelly or something. I was just a little girl, and I thought I'd *never* get my bucket full of those tiny little berries. They have the best flavor, don't they? ... Mmmm." She sniffed the open jar of jam.

"We're ready, Alpha Lee. Two eggs for me, one for you ... sunny side up, as they say in the diner. A breakfast fit for a king. Hey, I feel like a king this morning! ... with two beautiful princesses in my castle."

Susan finished her breakfast and went into the bathroom with her clothes. As they lingered over a second cup of coffee, Alpha Lee asked, "Jan, would it be possible to go to church today? Do you ever go? I just feel like I want to, after the long trip and everything that's happened this week "

"Sure, honey, that'd be nice. I've only gone to church a half-dozen times since I've been here. My mom would be upset to know that. Would you like to go to the base chapel? That's the only place I've gone to church, except for the Catholic service at Christmas."

Alpha Lee brightened at the suggestion. "Oh, yes, Jan, that would be interesting! I'd love to see your chapel. I suppose it's a sort of all-faith kind of church?" she asked.

"Yeah, I guess you'd say that ... sort of basic. Non-denominational, I guess that's the description. What about Susan ... will she want to go, or has she rejected religion completely, because of her so-called father?"

"No, she hasn't ... I asked her last night, and she said yes, she'd like to go. I'll take a bath, too, and we'll dress for church, then." She rose, picking up the dishes. "That was a wonderful breakfast, Jan. I didn't know you could cook!"

"Well, frying eggs and making coffee isn't exactly cooking. but I guess I could survive on my own. I fixed my own meals occasionally at home, when Mom wasn't there. Only the simplest stuff. I'm not hard to please." There was water heating on the stove for dishwashing. Alpha Lee filled the dishpan and put the dishes in the hot sudsy water. "Just leave them soaking for a minute, Alpha Lee. I want to show you something." Jan guided her out the back door to the pier. "Take a look at that, honey." Toward the east Mt. Rainier rose majestically against a sky of deepest blue, the sun lighting up its snowy summit. The effect was highly dramatic; the snow sparkled brilliantly. Dark pines far away made black shadows against the mountain.

After a long moment, Alpha Lee spoke,"Jan, that is so beautiful ... it takes my breath away. The mountain is just too glorious! I must try to paint it, if I can. It's like a study in turquoise and silver, all those far distant ranges by the big mountain. At first I thought it was clouds, but I can see that it's the mountains. Is this the Cascade Range?" she asked. "When you wrote about your adventure crossing the Snoqualmie Pass, I looked at the atlas and found that, and Seattle ... even Fort Lewis was on the map. I didn't realize how far west you were ... all the way to the Pacific Ocean."

"Yessir, we're on the edge. Would you like to see the base after church today, Alpha Lee?"

"Yes, I would, Jan. I want you to show me everything you've described in your letters. I want to visit Tak-Elek, too, sometime. Maybe even a drive up to Snoqualmie some Sunday afternoon, if it's not too far. It'll be different in the summer ... I'll have to try to imagine those high snow-banks along the side of the highway."

"Maybe not, Alpha Lee. There may still be the remains of last winter's accumulation, even this late. I'll tell you, honey, that was *real winter.* I don't need any more of that, *EVER*." Standing close behind her, Jan encircled her with his arms.

He was silent for so long that she turned to face him and asked, "A penny for your thoughts, O Master of the lodge."

"Alpha Lee, I was just thinking how wonderful it is to have you here with me, sleeping in my house, ... to wake up with you here in the morning and to have breakfast together. There's a peaceful feeling in my heart, knowing that you'll be here tonight, and tomorrow, and tomorrow. It just seems natural and right." She turned to face him and raised her arms.

"Yes, Jan, I know. I feel like I belong here with you. Aren't we lucky, with all that's happened to us in our separate lives, to be able to come together like this? I am so thankful!"

It was Communion Sunday, and the sermon was short. The Chaplain bade all who would to come to the altar to accept the Sacrament, and in their turn Jan and the girls went up the aisle together. They knelt at the altar rail, Jan between Alpha Lee and Susan, both of them dressed like fine ladies, even wearing gloves and hats. Jan humbly thanked God for his many blessings, especially the privilege of having these beautiful friends with him. Jan introduced the girls to the Chaplain as they exited the service. "We hope you will enjoy your visit to the state of Washington," Captain Durbin said as he shook Susan's hand, and then Alpha Lee's. "Will you be here long?"

"We hope to spend the summer here," Alpha Lee said, "and then return to West Virginia for college in September. This is a wonderful place. This morning I saw Mt. Rainier for the first time ... it's breathtaking!"

"Yes, and you're lucky to see it ... often there are clouds that obscure the view. But as summer comes along, the foggy conditions will change, and you'll be able to enjoy it many days. During winter months ... *and* fall, *and* early spring! .. we don't always have very good visibility. Do come back again, girls, and Private Short. It was nice to hear you singing."

Jan asked the girls if they would like to have lunch at the mess hall. At first Susan made a grimace, and said something about "beans, beans, beans", but Jan explained that the food really was good, especially on Sunday. "You've been listening to too many Army jokes, Susan. They do feed us pretty well, considering how many mouths there are to feed. Being in the Army really teaches some of these guys to appreciate what's offered. Some of them came here and turned up their noses at things they wouldn't eat at home, but when you have to work hard every day, you get hungry enough to try just about whatever's served."

They stood in line at the mess hall with a hundred other soldiers and some visitors. Jan saw Fred already seated, and Fred motioned to him to come and sit at his table. Jan paid for the girls' lunches and they carried their trays to Fred's table. He rose as they approached and offered his hand when Jan introduced him. "Alpha Lee, Susan, meet my pal Corporal Fred Harris from the flatlands of Kansas. Fred, Alpha Lee Evans and Susan Remagen."

"Nice to meet you, ladies. ... Hey, Private, it looks to me like you've got it made! All these guys here just have to live with each other, while you have two gorgeous gals to brighten up your place! Alpha Lee, you're the artist, right? You do nice work, ma'am, very nice!"

"Thank you very much, Corporal Harris. Jan has told me about your work at TE and also about the big tank haulers. I hope I can see those."

"We'll see 'em today, Alpha Lee," Jan said. "Fred, Susan's from Brick City too, where I graduated from high school. We met in Glee Club. Susan's the number one soprano ... sings like an angel."

Fred grinned at Susan. "Art *and* music! Hey, I get it! You girls are gonna bring some culture to this hayseed country boy! Well, he could use it. Matter of fact, so could I! I hope we'll see a lot of each other this summer. My girlfriend's gonna come up here from Kansas the first of June, after her college term is over. Maybe we can get together for some fun."

"Would that be Veronica?" Alpha Lee asked. "Jan told me about your getting a valentine from her after you came back from Yakima."

"Yes, ma'am, that's my Ronnie. We went steady through two years of high school. She's majoring in Education, to be an elementary school teacher."

"Jan, you're right," Susan said as she pushed her tray aside. "This food is really good ... best baked chicken I've ever had. Lots better than hot lunch at school. ... Jan, could Corporal Harris go with us when we tour the base?"

"Are you available for an hour or so, Fred?" Jan asked.

"Sure, I don't have a schedule for this afternoon. I was just gonna write a letter or two, but I can do that later. Sure, I'd like to go with you to show off this fascinating place."

Jan drove to the motor pool. The gate was locked, but through the chain link fence they looked at the huge lineup of various trucks, jeeps and other vehicles. "See the tank riding on that big trailer? That's one of the beasts we've been working with," Jan said, pointing to his right, near the fence.

"You're lookin' at some tonnage there, ladies," Fred added. "Those big monsters just barely crawl on a grade of any degree at all. We have to coax them along ... talk sweet to 'em, and feed 'em nice warm fuel when the weather's cold."

"Oh, yeah ... you should just hear Fred 'talkin' sweet' to 'em," Jan said with a laugh. "He has some choice words he throws at 'em now and then. Over there are what we call 'six-by-sixes' ... it means six hubs and all six get power to turn 'em. They're the work horses we use to haul all kinds of stuff." They drove by the barracks where Jan and Fred had bunks, but could not go in.

Then they drove to the main Ft. Lewis ... the main base, and stopped near the Division Headquarters to gaze at Mt. Rainier visible across the huge lawn Jan called the Parade Ground. "Are those administrative buildings, Jan?" Alpha Lee asked, pointing to a cluster of large brick structures lining the parade ground.

"No, those are the permanent barracks, for the GI's stationed in these Regiments. Fred used to live there," Jan explained. "But when they needed drivers to man the motor pool where we work, he had to move to the wooden barracks of Easy Company. They ran out of space in the permanent units and had to build those ugly pine buildings during the war to accommodate the increased number of troops."

"Where's the PX, Jan?" Susan asked. "Can we go shopping there?"

"Not today, Susan. It's closed on Sunday. The main PX is just around the corner by the Enlisted Men's Club and the bowling alley. We'll go there another time. Let's go to see Takoma Elektroniks, where Fred and I spend most of our non-soldiering hours."

There were two cars in the parking lot when Jan pulled into the Takoma Elektroniks facility. Two men and a woman were just leaving the building, locking the door. They looked up and waved at Jan; the taller man got into his car and left, and the other man approached their car. He had the blocky build of a one-time football player, with thinning sandy hair. He was dressed in a neat summer suit, with a white shirt and narrow tie; Alpha Lee wondered if he had been to church, too. "Jan, you're just the man I need to see. Where's your artist? One of these pretty girls, I presume?

"Yes, you're looking at my beautiful artist friend, Mr. W. Please meet Alpha Lee Evans and, in the back seat, Susan Remagen, both from West Virginia. Girls, this is Charles Williamson, our VP of Accounting and Personnel."

"Pleased to meet you, ladies. Hi Fred. Let me get Jane over here," Mr.Williamson said, and he turned and called to the tall, stylishly dressed woman, who was putting some things into the car. "Jane! Your artist is here." He turned to Alpha Lee. "Miss Evans, did you bring your tools with you?" Alpha Lee smiled winningly at him.

"Oh, yes. I have plans to do a lot of painting and sketching while I'm here."

"Well, good. I wonder if you could do a sketch for us for the cover of a brochure we're developing? We just need a likeness of this little box, a little larger than life charcoal would be fine. Of course we could make a photograph, but a drawing would be so much more aesthetically pleasing ... a touch of class, if you will. Here's the catch, Miss Evans: We really need it by Thursday ... we're in a bit of a time crunch. Is that possible?"

"Yes, that won't take long. I'd love to do that for you ... you've been so good to my friend Jan."

"Oh, we'll gladly pay you. And as for Jan ... well, he's been pretty good to us, too! ... Jane, meet Alpha Lee Evans and Susan Remagen, Jan's friends from West Virginia. Girls, this is my wife Jane. She operates the Arte Schacke."

"Hello, girls ... Welcome to the Northwest!" Jane Williamson's voice was deep and husky for a woman. She extended a bony hand, with expensive looking rings on several fingers, the stones sparkling in the bright sunshine. "Alpha Lee, I'm so excited to meet you, dear! My goodness ... you are quite young, aren't you? I expected someone fortyish. You must have been working at your art for most of your life, Alpha Lee, to have achieved such a mature mastery at your age."

"Thank you, Mrs. Williamson! Yes, I've probably spent more time drawing than I should have, really. Before I tried charcoal, I just used crayons, and colored pencils. I'm just beginning to try oils."

"Well, dear, your work is the hottest thing going this year. My local customers seem to consider the sketch of the fishing lodge as a charming representation of this area, as well as a very nice piece in its own right. So when can we expect you in the shop?"

"Well, we haven't made any plans yet ... we just flew in late last night. But surely soon ... within the week, certainly. I'm looking forward to seeing your shop."

"Will you have a car to drive?" Alpha Lee looked at Jan questioningly. "Yes, she can use my car sometimes, Mrs. Williamson. We'll work something out."

"I hope so... if not, call and I can come for you. Say, Alpha Lee, could you and Susan both have lunch with me tomorrow about one o'clock? The curator of the Seattle Museum, Mr. Arthur, will be here, and he asked specifically to meet you."

"Susan, is that okay with you?" Alpha Lee asked.

"I guess so," Susan answered.

"Here's my card, Alpha Lee. The shop is just a block that way," she said, pointing down the street, her rings flashing brilliantly. "You can't miss it ... The Arte Schacke. I usually just park here and walk; they seem to always have plenty of extra space. Were you able to bring more copies of the fishing lodge with you? ... I hope?"

"Yes, I have five more copies ... I'll bring them tomorrow."

"Wonderful. Has Jan told you we have ten more unfilled orders? This thing is phenomenal! Especially for charcoal, which usually isn't that much in demand.

"Really?" Alpha Lee said, a little surprised. "I wouldn't have guessed."

"Well, do bring them along. I'll see you tomorrow, at one, girls. Nice to meet you both." She flashed them a brilliant smile, and turned to her husband, signaling that she was ready to go. Mr.Williamson ended his conversation with Jan and Fred and the two of them left.

"Jan, does she always talk so fast? I could hardly keep up with her," Susan said.

"I've never met her before, Susan. All of my dealings with her have been through Charles. The Williamsons are from Minnesota, so they have kind of a different accent." He turned to Alpha Lee. "Charles told me on Friday that there were more orders, but I don't think he told me how many. Are you getting tired of making copies of the same old thing, Alpha Lee? Don't let her schedule your life, honey. I'd like to share a little of it. Make that a *lot* of it."

After they returned Fred to the base, Jan asked Alpha Lee, "Do we need to find a grocery store on the way home?"

"I think we should, Jan," Alpha Lee said. "I don't know what you have on hand, but I guess we should plan some meals and get what we need so we won't be missing things when we start to cook. Maybe some fresh veges and some more milk. And some baking supplies." She took her note pad from her purse and began writing a list. " And potatoes. I promise we won't spend a lot, or take a long time, Jan."

"I'll buy the groceries this time," Susan said. "No argument, Jan," she added, as he started to protest. "I have money from Nancy to pay my way. You've already spent a lot to make us feel welcome and comfortable. Besides, I want some cookies and some more chewing gum."

As they left the market, Jan asked, "Alpha Lee, can you drive a car with a clutch?"

"Sure, Jan. Our old Chevy has a standard transmission. The Driver Education car was an automatic, but that's the only car I've driven that wasn't standard."

"Okay ... how about if I drive back past the Arte Shacke to T.E., and you drive home from there. That'll give you a feel for this car and help you familiarize yourself with the route. You can haul me up to catch a ride with Sarge Herndon tomorrow morning at seven, so you can have the car to go to lunch with Mrs. Williamson. How about you, Susan? Do you have your license?"

"Yes. I took Driver Ed. in the same class as Alpha Lee. I haven't done much driving, though, Jan ... but I could. I'd like to try driving this car sometime."

"We'll plan on that sometime soon," Jan told her. He pointed out the Arte Schacke as they approached. "There it is. I've never been inside ... but *look*, Alpha Lee ... there's your charcoal in the showcase window. You *are* a local artist! And sort of a famous one, too! Let's stop and look in the window."

Alpha Lee was surprised and pleased. "I don't know what the fuss is all about, really," she said. "Why do so many people like that picture so much? When I made that for you, Jan, I never dreamed anyone would pay any attention to it. And frankly, I'm getting bored with making copies. I want to move on to something else."

"Well, just tell her that. A 'limited edition' will just make the originals more valuable. I'd like to see something in color, honey! I want to see what you can do with that big mountain," he said with a grin as he pulled into the T. E. parking lot. "Okay, you take the wheel and drive around the lot once or twice to get the feel. Then I'll direct you home, and Susan, you can write down the directions." He found a note pad and pencil in the glove compartment and handed them to Susan. As they approached the turn-off to the lane leading to the lodge, Jan told Alpha Lee to pull into the driveway of a small log house almost hidden by trees. "This is our turn-off, Alpha Lee, and this is where Frank and Naomi Massey live. They're our landlords, and they have a phone. Naomi works for Charles at T. E. ... she was the one who recognized your charcoal because the lodge was built by her grand father. Let's stop and visit them a minute."

Frank was working on his pick-up, and they could see Naomi in the garden nearby. Frank looked up, wiped his hands on a dirty cloth, and said "Hi, Jan. I see your beautiful girlfriends made it in last night. How'd you sleep with all that pulchritude in the house?" He grinned at the girls.

"Fitfully, Frank, to be sure. Meet Alpha Lee Evans under the wheel, and Susan Remagen in the back seat."

"Nice to meet you, ladies. How's the refrigerator doing?"

"It's perfect, Mr. Massey," Alpha Lee responded. "Works like new, so far. Thank you for bringing it."

"I thought if I waited long enough we'd get a good one. Lucky it turned up just in time ... I just bought it last night."

Naomi walked over to the car, smiling as she took off her sunbonnet. The girls saw a tall, big- boned woman with a stately posture and a wide smile that exposed perfect, even teeth. Her long black hair was pulled back in a single thick braid, and she was wearing shell earrings in her pierced ears, even while she worked in the garden.

"Hello, Jan! Welcome to Washington, girls ... I'm pleased to meet you both. I'd shake your hands if I didn't have so much dirt on mine. I'm planting my beans and onions and tomatoes today."

"You can grow a garden here, so far north?" Alpha Lee asked. "The season must be pretty short, isn't it?"

"But the days are long, Alpha Lee, and the northern light is wonderful for growing things. My grandfather used to have the best garden, just down there by the woodshed," she said, gesturing toward the lodge. "He just grew everything. This sandy soil is easy to work, and things grow very fast. I have extra tomato plants, a variety developed especially for this area ... and lots of seeds, if you'd like to try planting a few things."

Susan was enthusiastic. "Let's do it, Alpha Lee! I love fresh garden tomatoes! ... But how do we dig it up?"

"You could use my little push plow ... this sandy loam is easy to work. It just needs to be broken up and the weeds dug out. Jan, let's load it into your trunk. Maybe there's still an old hoe in the woodshed."

"Yeah, I believe I did see one down there, Naomi. Are you girls serious about this?" he asked. Both of the girls reassured him that they were. "

Jan, Millie had her baby last night, so we're out of a receptionist for a while," Naomi told him. "I won't be able to get a thing done except answer the phone tomorrow ... she'll probably want two weeks off."

"Millie finally had her baby? Did she have a boy, like she expected?"

"Oh yeah ... we half breeds are never wrong about that, you know. ... Hey, if you girls are looking for work, I've got a lot of openings. Our new building is ready, and we lost five high school girls this week. They graduated, and went up to Boeing, they did. Said they heard rich bachelors were a dime a dozen up there, and they were going hunting with a full quiver. If either or both of you are interested, just be up here at seven, and I'll haul you back and forth ... no bother. You can wear anything you like up there, too. It's no fashion show. We need gals for assembly, and inspectors, and now a receptionist, till Millie can come back."

What does the receptionist do?" Susan asked. "Maybe I could do that for two weeks, I worked in the school office sometimes."

"Just answer the phone, and welcome a few visitors. I'd have to spend a little time training you on that switchboard. My office is close to the reception area, and our phone system is only ten lines. If Millie could do it, anybody could!"

"I'd like to try it," Susan said. "I can type a little, too, if that helps."

"That's really good! We can use another typist. Come up in the morning, if you're interested, and you can ride back and forth with me. Now, let me get you some tomato plants, and the seeds. You'll want beans, and squash and lettuce and carrots and onion sets ..."

As they drove slowly down the pebbled lane to the lodge, Susan said, "Maybe I'd better not plan to have lunch tomorrow with you and Mrs. Williamson, Alpha Lee. It's you she wants to see, anyway. D'you think you can drive to the art place by yourself?"

"I guess so, Susan. Will you just fix a sandwich to take along for your lunch?"

"Sure, I can do that. Jan, what did Naomi mean when she called herself a half-breed? Is she part Indian? She sorta looks like she is."

"Yes, you're right, Suz. Her great-great-grandfather was the famous Chief Leschi of the Nisqually tribe. He was murdered by white men."

"Hmm ... I never heard of that tribe, *or* that Indian chief," Alpha Lee said.

"Well, he was famous out here. There were lots of small Indian tribes here in the northwest in the old days. They had a different lifestyle from the Plains Indians. They lived mostly off the sea ... caught and dried lots of salmon, I guess, and they even hunted whales. You'll see some old totem poles when we drive around next Sunday. Naomi's mother was a full- blooded Nisqually -- one of the few left, she told me."

"She walks like a queen," Susan said. "So straight and tall. She's not exactly pretty, but she is certainly striking. I think she's proud of her Indian heritage."

Chapter 7

The girls were glad to be "home" at the lodge. While they changed from their church dresses, Jan changed into his fatigues, unloaded Naomi's small plow and went to find the hoe in the wood shed. Susan emerged from the bedroom wearing a white T-shirt and red shorts. "I'm going out on the pier to practice on my guitar," she told Alpha Lee.

"Okay. I've gotta think up something for supper," Alpha Lee said as she put the groceries away. "Maybe we can just have sandwiches for supper tonight, and a can of those beans." As Alpha Lee explored the kitchen to discover what food and utensils were available, she heard Susan singing. ...Her voice was rising to full volume in response to the vast space surrounding her. She sang: "When I'm calling you...ooo... oooo ...." "The Indian Love Call" that she had heard many times at the Remagens'. Jeannette MacDonald was one of her stepmother's favorites, and she had grown up listening to recordings of operettas.

Jan finished pushing the five-pronged cultivator plow through the soil in the small garden patch and came back into the lodge. "Wow ... just listen to her! I've never heard her sing more beautifully "

"Ah, Sweet mystery of life, at last I've found you ... Ah, at last I know the secret of it all.." As Susan ended her song, there was applause and shouts of "Bravo!", and Jan and Alpha Lee, exchanging a puzzled glance, went out on the pier to see who was with Susan.

"Look what I caught with my guitar!" she said with a bright smile. Two young fishermen had pulled up to the pier and were tying their boat to a piling. They had several fish on their stringer, and they were taking some off and putting them on the pier.

"It wasn't the guitar," one of the boys said. "It was that million-dollar voice. It lured us right onto the rocks! ... or would have, if there were rocks." He extended his hand to Jan. "I'm Roddy Williamson, and this is my brother Jon. We live just a short distance over that way ... two coves over ... and we've been cleaning our fish here on the pier, since nobody seemed to be using it." The younger boy, Jon, waved and attended to cleaning the fish.

"Roddy, this is the couple I'm staying with Jan Short and Alpha Lee Evans. Jan, Roddy just graduated from the College of the Pacific, he says he's going to teach science and music at the high school next fall. *And* he has a dance band."

"Really? ... Nice to meet you, Roddy, ... Jon. Where do you play?"

"We've been doing the service clubs at North Fort and out at McChord Field. We're only a five-piece band," Roddy said. "You haven't seen us?"

"No ... I've been working nights and Saturdays at Takoma Elektroniks. Your dad wouldn't happen to be the chief accountant there, would he?"

"Sure is! And you're the Jan Short who has saved them a bunch of money and time. You're going to work full-time out there in a couple of months, I understand. Well, Jan, I'm glad to meet you."

"Thanks, Rod. Yeah, your dad is a good personnel man and a good friend. We just saw him earlier this afternoon at T. E. I was showing the girls where I work, and he and your mother were just leaving," Jan said. "I'm renting the lodge for the time being, and the girls are spending the summer here. They're going back to West Virginia for college in the fall.

"Hey, could you folks use some nice fresh fish for supper?. Good fishing here in the estuary. Jon, you have some fillets ready?"

"Yeah. Is this enough, Miss? I can clean another in just a minute."

"Oh, I think that will do nicely!" Alpha Lee told him. "They look like they're nearly a pound each. Are they good fried?"

Jon grinned at her. "That's the best way, fried in butter, and drizzled with just a bit of lemon juice."

"Jon, I never saw anybody clean fish so fast," Jan told him. "You're *GOOD!*"

"Well, it's not like I haven't had plenty of practice," Jon answered with a grin. "We live just about a mile from here, and we fish a lot."

"What kind of fish are these, Jon?" Jan asked. "I've never seen any like that, with both eyes on one side."

"They're flounder, Jan. They lie on the bottom, and they're a salt water fish."

Jan laughed. "I guess that's why I never caught 'em in West Virginia! How much is a license to fish here?"

"You don't need a license to fish in salt water, Jan, for flounder," Roddy told him. "Trout or salmon, though, you need a stamp."

"Really? Hey, Alpha Lee ... we can have free fish any time, I guess! What kind of bait do you use, Rod?"

"We usually use minnows, but they'll hit little pieces of shrimp, right on the bottom."

"Well, thanks for the fish, guys," Jan said. "And, Susan, thanks for luring these unsuspecting fishermen onto the rocks, just like the Lorelei, on the Rhine!"

"Hey ... speaking of Susan ... Jan, could she sing and play her guitar during intermissions for us? I could pay her something, and she'd be a huge hit with the GI's. Susan? Would you consider singing for us two nights a week?"

"Gee, Roddy ... I don't know I've never done anything like that ... And I'm not very good on the guitar yet ..."

"You're plenty good enough," he insisted, "and I can help you with the guitar. I could pay you fifteen dollars a night to do two intermission slots of about ten minutes on Friday and Saturday."

"How would she get there and back?" Jan asked.

"Mom goes with us almost every gig," Roddy replied. "Dad works so much he's never available. Mom could pick her up and be a proper chaperone."

Jan turned to Susan questioningly, and the girls exchanged a long look. "We'll talk about it," Alpha Lee told Roddy.

"Well, guys ... thanks for the flounder," Jan said. "Hope we'll see you around. Ladies, we need to get these babies into the skillet. Can we fry some of those taters to go with 'em, Alpha Lee?"

The Williamson boys waved as they pushed off. The low sun gilded the waters of the sound, changing the deep blue of the morning into bronze, and Mount Rainier, filling the southeastern sky, reflected the golden afternoon light. Sea gulls wheeled and cried above the water in the distance. Alpha Lee lingered a moment, overwhelmed by the color and shape of the landscape.

"Jan," she murmured, "thank you for bringing us here. I love this place."

On Monday morning dawn came slowly, through a veil of slanting silvery rain. The great mountain was lost to view; the water of the sound was gray and choppy. Alpha Lee marveled at the different colors she had observed in the sea waters in such a short time.

Jan told the girls that he would eat his free breakfast at the base, but he made a pot of coffee and drank a cup with them after he awakened the girls. They each ate a piece of Sally Herndon's fruit, Susan had fixed her sand-wich the night before, and she tucked a couple of cookies and an apple into her bag. "I hope there's a Coke machine at T. E.," she said, and Jan assured her that there was.

Jan and the girls hurried out to the car at 6:35. Jan drove toward the base after dropping Susan off at Naomi's, while Alpha Lee took careful notes of the route so that she could drive back to the lodge alone. Jan stopped at a small white house with lots of roses blooming after driving about a mile. "This is Sergeant Herndon's place," he told Alpha Lee. "I'll ride to the base with him. He sort of supervises the driving classes we teach. Are you sure you can find your way back, honey?" Jan asked.

"I think so, Jan. Everything looks different in the rain, though. I'm gonna look at these directions carefully before I start out; maybe I'll rewrite them, that'll help fix them in my mind. *IF* I get totally lost, I'll stop somewhere and call Naomi to get myself back on the right track. She gave us the T. E. phone number."

"Okay, sweet. Fred'll bring me back late this evening, after class. Enjoy your lunch with Jane Williamson. I sure hope the rain stops before noon." He kissed her gently and got out of the car, and ran up the steps through the rain to the porch. Sergeant Herndon met him at the door, ready to leave for the Fort. With a final wave, Jan jumped into the sergeant's car and they pulled out and headed away.

Alpha Lee found her way back to the lodge without difficulty. She found the sense of solitude a little daunting at first, with the drumming of the rain the only sound to be heard. It would be nice, she thought, to have a radio. I feel as though I am *in* that charcoal picture, she thought, with all of the shades of gray surrounding me . She shook off her morose thoughts and, checking the coffee pot, she was grateful to find there was a cup remaining, still hot enough to be comforting. Her first priority, she decided, was to write a letter to her parents; she could mail it in town. When I finish this, she thought, I'll start on the sketch for Mr. Williamson. I have plenty to do!

After writing a brief letter home, she found the the light was not adequate for drawing with charcoal. She decided she would explore the cabin and familiarize herself with every part of it. She unpacked all of the things she had brought with her, but was stymied by a lack of closet space. She would ask Jan to put up a clothes-line, or a rod of some sort, to hang clothes on. Everything was wrinkled from being tightly packed in the suitcase. I'm just going to have to buy an iron, she thought. There's no way I can get along without one for three months!

She looked in the kitchen cupboards and drawers to discover what kinds of implements were there, and to her surprise and delight, she found an oven thermometer. NOW I feel better about trying to bake, she thought. Jan had showed her how to start a fire and to control it to some extent with the draft door and the damper, but she did not want to do that for the first time when she was alone.

She walked into Jan's room. "Well, there *is* a radio!" she said aloud. It was a clock radio with a battered case and one knob that didn't match the others. I'll bet he rescued that from somebody's wastebasket, she thought with a smile. She turned it on and found some pleasant music. She smoothed Jan's bed, straightening the covers and fluffing the pillows. She lay down on the bed, overwhelmed by a strange sense of longing. The pillow still held the faint odor of his hair... I love him, she said with a sense of wonder. I am here, in this strange place, far from everything familiar, and my love is here with me ... She turned to lay her cheek on Jan's pillow, and stroked it lovingly with her hand. She closed her eyes, and as the rain drummed softly on the roof, she fell asleep.

She was awakened in only a little while by the radio announcer's voice, a harsh contrast to the soft music, as he related the news of strife in Korea. I'm not sure where Korea is, she thought drowsily. ... Hmmm ... I fell asleep on my host's bed, just like Goldilocks! "Someday my prince will come," she sang softly, and then ran out of familiar words. The clock on the radio showed ten forty - five. Still plenty of time, she thought.

She looked through all of the clothes she had brought to find something with the least wrinkles. She settled on a silky knit skirt and top ensemble that she had made to wear to church at home, hoping it wouldn't be too dressy for the occasion. The five copies of the charcoal picture were in her portfolio; she checked her hair in the bathroom mirror one last time and went out to the car, thankful that the rain had stopped.

She had no trouble finding the Arte Schacke. She was amazed at the size of the gallery; it seemed much more spacious than it looked from outside. There were the works of more than fifty artists displayed ... some prints from the masters, but most appeared to be originals from local artists she didn't know. She saw some pieces that appeared to be Indian folk art.

Jane Williamson saw her come in and emerged from her office with a well-dressed man with longish gray hair and a moustache. I'm not over-dressed, Alpha Lee thought, observing Mrs. Williamson's smartly tailored suit and perfectly chosen accessories. "Alpha Lee, good morning!" she exclaimed with a charming smile. "I want you to meet Mr. Darius Arthur of the Seattle Art Museum. Darius, this is our visiting artist from West Virginia, Miss Alpha Lee Evans. Did you bring the charcoal copies, dear?"

Alpha Lee murmured, "Yes," and extended her hand to Mr. Arthur's grasp. "Hello," she said. "It's nice to meet you. I hope I can see your big museum while we're here."

"Hello, Miss Evans. By all means, you *must* visit us; we have a wonderful collection. Your charcoal has had a phenomenal reception. Do you work in other media ... oils, perhaps? Pastels?"

"I'm just beginning in oils, Mr. Arthur. It's very exciting. In the past I worked only with colored pencils, and a little watercolor, so this is quite different for me."

"Yes, it would be. Do you have anything finished for us to see?"

"No, not yet," she said. "Maybe in a couple of weeks. ... Here are the charcoals, Mrs. Williamson," Alpha Lee said, handing the portfolio to Jane, who took the parcel into her office. "Actually I think it would be very helpful to me to study the work of other artists. Back home I don't have access to very much original art."

Jane returned, carrying an umbrella. "Shall we go to lunch now?"

Jane chose to sit with Alpha Lee in the back seat of Mr. Arthur's big car. "Roddy told me about meeting Susan ... he was quite excited! Has she thought about singing with his band?"

"Yes ... we talked about it last night, and I think she's inclined to say yes ... *If* we can work out transportation and some kind of ..umm ...chaperoning ... Is that the right word?" Alpha Lee asked hesitantly. "She really needs an adult she can trust to sort of support her. She's had a difficult life." Alpha Lee paused, wondering if she had said too much; then she added, "Also, she's never performed solo for that type of audience, so she's a bit nervous about that; but, Mrs. Williamson, when she begins to sing, she just loses herself in the music. I don't think the audience will bother her at all, once she gets into it."

"Wonderful! Roddy will be so pleased. Don't worry about those other details, Alpha Lee. I promise we'll take good care of her. Thank you for telling me. ... Do you think she could start this Friday?"

"Maybe ... you could call her at T. E. She'll be working there temporarily, until the receptionist comes back. She ... Millie, I think ... just had a baby."

"Yes, I heard. Well, I'll do that, Alpha Lee. Darius, Alpha Lee's friend has a lovely singing voice. She was singing on the pier and my boys were out fishing. I think they thought they were hearing an angel! ... or perhaps a mermaid," Jane said, laughing. "She's a lovely girl."

"Mrs. Williamson, that was a wonderful lunch! Thank you so much. Mr. Arthur, I'll look forward to seeing you at the Art Museum. I hope Jan and Susan will want to come, too."

"It's a pleasure to know you, Miss Evans. I have to confess ... we here on the west coast seldom meet folks from West Virginia. I'm afraid your state has a rather humble image in the popular press and culture. It's good to discover how wrong that is. You're a charming ambassador for West Virginia. I'd be happy to meet your friends ... please persuade them to come with you when you visit us." He shook her hand warmly and gave her his business card.

"Alpha Lee, thank you for bringing the copies," Jane said. "If, as you told me, you want to limit the total number of originals to fifty copies, I'll raise the price of those remaining, and I'll see if I can make some prints, which could be sold at a lower price, to fill the continuing demand. I have print-making equipment in the shop here ... do you have time to look around the shop? We also make frames. ... And I will call Susan in a little while. ... And, dear, you must call me Jane ... please."

Alpha Lee was back at the lodge by mid-afternoon. The light had improved so that she was able to work on the charcoal Mr. Williamson had asked for, and she had the small piece finished in a hour. She opened the oil paint box and examined the small tubes. Zinc white, she read. Rose madder ... Prussian blue ... cadmium yellow. Such interesting names. I wonder if Monet and Raphael used pigments like these. I suppose they would have had to mix their own ... Now, what can I paint? Something easy and simple, just for practice ... She chose a red apple from the bowl on the table, rubbed it against her skirt to heighten the shine, and began making the outline on one of the pieces of canvas board. Let's see, she said to herself, which shade of red? Vermilion? No ... too bright. Crimson lake, maybe ...

Susan arrived a few minutes after five, bouncing into the house with a smile. "Hi! That's the easiest ten bucks I could imagine, Alpha Lee ... all I did was sit behind a desk and answer the phone and smile at whoever came in. I think I'll enjoy this job! Naomi says they'll only need me for two weeks ... Millie will be back, she said, because she needs the money. She isn't married ... she lives with her parents, Naomi told me. ... Oh, Alpha Lee, that's pretty! You're catching on to the oil paints quickly!"

"Thanks, Susan. The blending is easy ... it's just sort of messy. I think I'm gonna need some rags to clean things up with. ... Susan, would you like a cup of tea? I'm thirsty, and I want something warm! That means building a fire. Shall we try it?"

"Tea sounds great, Alpha Lee. Did you have a good time with Mrs. Williamson today? How was lunch?"

"Oh, Susan, it was wonderful! We had smoked salmon .. I had never even heard of that. It was so delicious! And crab legs, I hate to mention it looked sort of like spider legs, except huge! .. and red and white. I wonder what the actual animal looks like. You have to crack the shells with little pliers, Susan! ... to get the meat! It's sort of weird and drippy. Anyway, the meat inside the shells was *so* good. White as snow, and sweet. You dip each bite in melted unsalted butter. I'll bet nobody in Brick City eats that!"

Alpha Lee was placing small sticks of kindling wood on top of a small log in the firebox, and she struck a match and dropped it in. "Mr. Arthur invited all of us to go to the Art Museum in Seattle. I'd love to do that, if we can find a time when Jan could go, too. There ... I think the fire's taking. It'll be ready in a few minutes. Fill the teakettle, Susan."

Alpha Lee found two teacups in the cupboard. "Did Jane call you today, Susan? She wanted to know what you decided about singing for Roddy's band."

"Yes, she did, and I told her I would try it. I'm supposed to do the first 'gig' ... that's what they call a performance...on Friday night. So soon! I have to talk to Roddy, to find out what he wants, and how I should dress, and stuff like that. She said maybe he'd drop by T. E. tomorrow and we could talk." Susan got up and went to the cupboard. "Tea always tastes better with cookies," she said, bringing a handful of ginger snaps to the table for them to share.

That evening the girls worked in the garden. The sandy soil dried quickly and was easy to work, as Naomi had told them. Jan's plow had dislodged the weeds, and they pulled them out easily and raked it level. They set in the tomato plants Naomi had donated, and planted rows of vegetables. "Alpha Lee, the mosquitoes are getting bad!" Susan said. "I'm going inside"

Alpha Lee had kept the fire going so that they both could take showers before Jan came home. The evening was long, the sun setting finally just before nine o'clock. By that time the girls had eaten a light supper of sandwiches and fruit. Susan wrote a letter to the McAllisters, and then one to Ben, giving them an address so they could write in return. Naomi had suggested that they just have their mail sent to the T. E. address for the duration of the summer.

Jan would not be home for more than an hour. The girls walked out on the pier to watch the fading colors reflected in the water and to listen to the cries of the sea birds. Clouds were thickening again far away over the water. Susan brought her guitar and strummed easy chords, and the girls sang softly in harmony the lovely hymn, "Now The Day Is Over", another song they had sung in the chorus at Brick City High School. Alpha Lee felt a twinge of nostalgia; the Glee Club experience she had enjoyed so much was over forever. Would she ever again have the pleasure of singing as part of a group?

Soon the mosquitoes drove the girls back inside. "I'm getting sleepy, Alpha Lee," Susan said with a yawn. "What time is it back home?"

"Hmmm well three hours later than here. After midnight, Susan. I wonder how long it'll take our bodies to adjust to Pacific Standard Time?.... Do you want to take a shower while the water's still hot?"

"I guess I should." Susan stood, and she suddenly straightened to her full height. "Alpha Lee, I wish I could walk like Naomi. Like an Indian queen," and Susan extended her arms slightly and walked across the room.

"Oh, Susan, *YES!* That's beautiful. I guess the Indian women used to carry things on their heads ... maybe that's how they learn the habit of walking that way. ... Susan, we could practice doing that, couldn't we!" She was excited at the prospect. "I'm so short, I need to learn towalk tall. And if you're going to be a performer, you really should practice walking like that ... like a queen! Let's see ... what can we balance on our heads ..." She looked around the room. "We could start with books or our purses!" She carefully placed her purse on top of her head, and walked slowly, arms extended. Susan quickly followed suit. They could take only a few steps before the purses fell off, but they kept at it until they began laughing, and could no longer sustain the dignity that such walking seemed to require.

"We'll practice *every day*, Alpha Lee!" Susan said with animation. "Won't Jan be amazed when we can do it really well ... just like Naomi?" She hugged Alpha Lee in her excitement. "And Nancy! Just wait till she sees the new *ME!*" Susan laughed with delight, and then strode majestically into the bedroom, holding her purse in place with one hand.

"A great idea, Susan!" Alpha Lee said. Privately she felt jubilant that Susan was interested, at last, in overcoming the posture problem that everyone seemed to notice but Susan herself. We'll do this, Alpha Lee resolved. We'll practice together every day, and I hope it will make a permanent difference.

Susan was in the shower when Alpha Lee heard a car in the lane. She hurried to the door, and Jan was just emerging from Fred's car in the drizzling rain. She waved to Fred even though she couldn't see him in the rain and darkness, and Jan ran up the steps to the door. "Welcome home, soldier," she said as his arms enfolded her, and their kiss was a reprise of the very first one they had shared, at the airport, in the Seattle drizzle.

Chapter 8

After midnight on Thursday night, two young bear cubs splashed in the shallow water of the estuary at low tide. One of them snagged a small rainbow trout with his claws and flipped it out onto the bank. The other cub grabbed it and trotted toward the lodge, with the first cub close behind. They fought over the fish on the porch, growling and bumping against the log wall, right under the window beside the bed where Alpha Lee and Susan slept. As they scuffled and growled, they knocked over the bicycles with a crash, and one of them fell off the pier into the water, which startled the cubs, and they yelped and ran, leaving the mangled fish behind. The mother bear approached, grunting loudly to call them. Alpha Lee and Susan were jolted awake by the tumult that seemed to be almost in the room with them, and they ran from the bedroom. Alpha Lee slammed the door behind her ... just in case.

Jan was awakened by panicked voices. The first thing he saw when he opened his eyes was Alpha Lee, barely covered by her sheer white nylon pajamas as she bent over him, her hand gripping his shoulder, shaking him awake. He reached up to pull her down beside him, welcoming her into his bed. But she resisted, pulling back from him. "*JAN*, JAN, there's something *BIG* and heavy outside ... I think something is trying to get in!" she cried urgently. "Get up, Jan! Do you have a gun or something?"

Then he saw Susan, too, whimpering and trembling in the moonlight that filtered through the curtains. They could hear, not far away, grunting and squealing. Jan wasn't sure what was out there, but he knew they were safe behind the cabin's thick log walls. "Nothing can get in here, Alpha Lee. You're safe. Come on, get in bed with me, both of you. Don't worry. Come on, Susan ... there's room for all of us." He reached out to clasp her hand; it was ice cold. Both of the girls hesitated for a moment, exchanging a doubtful look, but then they both crawled into the bed, one on each side of Jan, and he pulled them close. "Now ... do you feel better? Just go to sleep. I promise nothing will hurt you. Not even me."

Jan's body, and the bed, were warm and comforting, and the noisy threat apparently was over; the girls' fear quickly diminished, and they relaxed. But Jan was not relaxed; he found himself sandwiched between two beautiful female bodies, confined to a narrow space and unable to move without touching them. He was acutely aware that he was dressed only in his GI undershorts; but nature called. "Alpha Lee, I have to go to the bathroom," he whispered. "Just stay right where you are, please." He crawled over her carefully, stroking her face, and she caught his hand and kissed the palm. "Stay right there, please, sweet." As he passed the window, he looked out; nothing in sight. The light from a hazy half-moon illuminated the calm waters of the sound.

When he returned to the bed, he had to crawl over Alpha Lee again, and he was aware of the soft scent of her perfume. As he lay down in his narrow middle space, Alpha Lee turned toward him, her head against his shoulder, her arm across his bare chest. He circled her shoulders with his arm and pulled her close. Susan's breathing was deep and regular; she had fallen asleep already. "Are you comfortable, honey?" he whispered.

"Almost," she answered softly, and then she raised herself on one elbow and found his mouth with hers. "Mmmm ... " She ran her fingers through his hair and stroked his neck and shoulder. Jan could not resist any longer; his hands moved over her body, drinking in the smoothness and curves that had tempted him for days.

"Alpha Lee, I want to make love to you," he whispered urgently. "I want you so bad. But not here, not in this situation ... *dammit*." He pulled away from her. "I've gotta get out of here. I've got to cool off ..."

"Yes, me too ... dammit." She giggled softly at her own uncharacteristic language. "Let's go in the kitchen," she suggested. "Susan's asleep." .

Jan found a pair of fatigue pants and pulled them on while she covered Susan with the wolf blanket. She stopped by her bedroom and put on her short robe. When she came out of the bathroom, Jan was making a fire in the range. Alpha Lee came to stand close beside him, and they watched the flames spread from the kindling to the larger pieces of wood.

"Jan, I'm sorry we disturbed you. What could that have been out there? It was a really frightening way to wake up. We were sure it was coming through the window ..."

"I don't know, Alpha Lee. We'll look around when it gets light."

Jan banked the fire so it would stay hot for coffee and showers later, and he took Alpha Lee's hand and led her to the table. "Now, love, you sit here, and I'll sit across the table from you so we can talk for a little while without getting into trouble," he said to her with a smile.

"Okay," she agreed. "Yes, we do need to talk ... privately. I want to tell you some things that are hard for me to talk about, but I want you to know." She was silent for a long time, trying to compose her thoughts. "Jan, you said you wanted to ... to make love to me. I want that, too ...although I am not experienced in this sort of thing ... and I have to confess that I'm afraid."

"Afraid, Alpha Lee? You mean you're afraid of getting pregnant?"

"Well, that, too," she answered. "I just *CAN'T* let that happen, of course. But there's more, Jan." Another pause, she twisted her hands nervously. Jan took her hand and raised it to his lips. "I need to tell you about what happened when I was with Mark."

"Alpha Lee, you don't need to tell me anything. That's *your* business ... and besides it's history. You don't owe me any explanation."

"Yes, I *do*, Jan, because it affects *us*." She took a deep breath. "Mark is older than we are and, I think, pretty experienced with women. He was very ... umm ... aggressive, Jan. He made all of the right moves to make me want to ... Well, you know ... to arouse me, to make me want to have sex with him." Alpha Lee's eyes were downcast; she couldn't look at Jan while she spoke. "He .. I mean, we ... did actually try to do that; but there was a problem. He couldn't do it, not all the way. I think there must be something wrong with me, Jan. He tried, and he pushed hard, and he wouldn't stop, even when I tried to push him away ... and there was blood all over, and it hurt, it hurt so bad." She began to cry. "Jan, I'm afraid! Maybe he hurt me so that I can't do it ... or maybe there's just something wrong with me that I can't do it anyway, ever!" She dabbed at her eyes with the olive drab handkerchief Jan handed to her.

"Oh, Alpha Lee ... I'm sorry he hurt you, honey! That's a *hell* of a way for a guy to act. Have you seen a doctor since then?" She shook her head. "You *must* do that. We'll find somebody who can examine you, honey. I won't bother you at all, Alpha Lee, until you feel like you're ready."

"Jan, even at the time, it was *you* I really wanted, even then. I wanted to find out about love ... but it was *you* I wanted to be with, for that ... not Mark. He was good-looking, and he said sweet things to me, for a while, and I couldn't resist him, and didn't want to resist. But, Jan, he was *so mad* at me because he couldn't do it all the way! He was furious, and he took me home and just dumped me. But that's not the worst of it." She wiped her eyes again. "Ben called me later ... he had found out that Mark is married! He has two children, and his wife ... she lives in Delaware and ... is pregnant. That was the last straw, Jan. I hoped I'd never see him again, and I won't. He had to go back to her ... the sheriff served him with some kind of papers to force him to support his family. I hate him!"

"You don't need to hate him, Alpha Lee ... that'll just make you bitter, and make it harder for you to love anybody. What you need to do, sweetheart, is forget about it. It's over, and you won't be hurt any more. I'm sure a good doctor can help you, if there's some kind of problem. Sexual intercourse is the most beautiful and thrilling thing a couple in love can experience, and I want you to have that with me ... when you're ready. When you're not afraid any more."

At Jan's words Alpha Lee broke down and cried in earnest, both for the bitter memory of her humiliation, and because she was so moved by Jan's tenderness. She rushed to him, and, kneel-ing in front of him, she hugged his knees and lay her head on his lap.

Jan groaned deeply. "Ohhh..... God, Alpha Lee, don't do that!" He stood, with effort, pulling her up with him. He grasped her buttocks with both hands and pressed her hard against himself. "I'm gonna have to go out and jump in the water and swim a couple laps across the sound!"

"I'm sorry ... Jan, does it hurt when it gets so hard like that? Mark said, 'I'm hurting' ..."

"Well," Jan said, "the guy may be a *bastard*, but I sure can understand his pain." He moved away from her. "It doesn't hurt like a charley horse, or like a toothache, or a punch in the jaw ... It's just more like a desperate need, an urgent desire that blocks out everything else. Maybe more like a man who's starving to death, facing a table full of his favorite food. No, it's worse than that! Although I've sure never been *that* hungry. Right now I'm hungrier for you than I've ever been for anything in my life."

"What will happen? Does it just go away?'

"Yeah, it'll go away ... but not very fast, with you standing just inches away from me."

"I guess that means we'd better go to our separate rooms," she said. "I wish I could sleep with you till morning. What time is it, Jan?"

He looked at his watch. "Five till three," he answered. "Yeah, we've gotta get a little more sleep. Dammit." They walked together to Jan's bedroom; Susan was not there. "I didn't see her walk past us," he said, surprised. "Must have been when we were making the fire. ... Alpha Lee, will you sleep in my bed till morning? I promise, I won't touch you. I just want you lying there beside me."

She was silent for just a moment. "I don't think so, Jan. I don't think we can do that. I couldn't keep from touching you, love. And you *do* need to get some more rest. We've ruined your night's sleep."

He sighed. "Yeah, you're right. But that's every man's dream, to have his sleep 'ruined' by a beautiful woman in his bed who can't keep from touching him. Good night, sweet love," and he kissed her very lightly, only their lips touching.

"Oh, gosh ... it's Friday!" Susan woke up suddenly. She could hear Jan's radio alarm faintly from the other room. "Alpha Lee, wake up!" Susan said, shaking her vigorously. I hope this day goes ver-r-ry slo-o-owly, she said to herself, so I'll have time to work up my courage for tonight.

Alpha Lee stretched luxuriously, and began to smile even before she opened her eyes. Then Susan remembered the adventures of the previous night. "Hey! I'll bet I can guess what's on *your* mind!" Susan said. "Alpha Lee, tell me I didn't do what I think I did last night ... get into bed with a *man!* I hope it was just a dream!"

"Well, it sure was dreamy, Susan," Alpha Lee agreed, still smiling that secret smile. "You do remember the monsters outside the window, don't you? Would you rather have just stayed in here and fought them off when they came in the window?"

"What was that, Alpha Lee? D'you suppose there'll be footprints, or teeth marks or something out there? Or maybe even blood?" Susan was scrambling into her working clothes. She put on the navy blue skirt and the shirt she had worn on the plane; the outfit had been hanging on the rod Jan had installed, and in five days, most of the wrinkles had smoothed out.

"I guess we'll find out," Alpha Lee replied.

When the girls walked into the kitchen, the back door was open, and they saw Jan outside on the pier. He found muddy footprints and tufts of coarse hair and a half-eaten fish. Bears! he thought. "Good morning, ladies! I think we've solved the mystery of the night monster. I think you were visited by some bear cubs. See those footprints? ... like a chubby little boy's prints. They're still damp. And this is the remains of the prize they were fighting over, I'll bet." Jan picked up the remains of the fish gingerly by the tip of the tail and flung it into the water. "Frank told me there were a pair of cubs roaming the woods around here. I don't think they'd hurt you ... they'd probably high-tail it for the deep woods if they saw a human ... but Mama Bear is something else. If she thought her babies were threatened, she could do a bunch of damage. *DON'T* go walking in the woods alone, either of you. Hear?"

"Hey, Jan, " Susan said. "Look ... where's the other bicycle? That's the crash we heard, Alpha Lee. They knocked the bikes down. Oh, look ... I see it ... it's in the water!"

"Well, so it is. Damn. I'll have to fish that out and wash it off ... the salt water will corrode the metal in no time at all."

..."I can do that, Jan. I'll be here with nothing to do but art, art, art. I'll wade in the water when the tide's low and fish out the bicycle, and I'll douse it with pump water. Maybe it'll need to be oiled or something ... do you think, Jan?"

"Yeah, it will. I'll take care of that. ... Oh, another thing, girls ... *don't* put garbage outside of the lodge. That'll attract the bears for sure, and they'll pester us to death. I'll have to take the garbage to the base to dispose of it, or maybe leave it off at T. E." Then he laughed. "I don't know what I'm complaining about ... first time in my life I've ever slept between two beautiful women!" He winked at Alpha Lee. "Think I'll write to Ben and tell him what he's missin' out here at summer camp," he told Susan with a wicked grin.

Susan was appalled. "*DON'T YOU DARE*, Jan Short! Don't you tell a soul! Anyway, all we did was sleep. ... We were *scared*, Jan ... we really, really were! Isn't that true, Alpha Lee? ... It was *her* idea, Jan ..." He was laughing, enjoying her fluster, as he followed her out the door.

After work, Susan had borrowed an iron from Naomi and was pressing her beautiful new party dress that Nancy had bought for her in Pittsburgh. The fabric was a lustrous ivory faille, with narrow stripes of maroon edged with tiny gold threads. The skirt was full and flaring, the bodice closely fitted with a deep neckline. "This dress was so expensive ... we got it at Kaufman's, remember? I'd never been there before, of course. I love it, but I didn't know where I'd ever wear it. Nancy said Jan would be wanting to go to dances ... do you think that's true?"

"Maybe she doesn't remember Jan very well," Alpha Lee said with a rueful smile. "Or else she didn't believe what I told her about his schedule. When would he go to a dance? He works *all* the time. Don't I wish ..." she said. "Maybe when Fred's girlfriend comes to town, they'll both take an evening off and take us out."

"Not *us*, Alpha Lee. I'm a working girl." Then Susan smiled brilliantly. "Isn't that exciting, Alpha Lee? *Me*, Shy Susan, singing for a room full of handsome soldiers! Am I dreaming?"

"It's incredible! You'll be GREAT, Susan. Just remember: *NISQUALLY*." That was the code Alpha Lee had devised. Whenever she or Susan noticed each other slumping, or forgetting the queenly walk they'd been practicing, that was the whispered word they'd use to remind each other to stand tall, to walk regally.

"Oh, yeah ... *nisqually*." Susan immediately straightened to her full height, even at the ironing board. "Alpha Lee, thank you *so much* for helping me do this! I just feel so confident, and so pretty, when I'm walking that way. You've really helped me a lot."

"Well, it works for me, too, Susan! Alpha Lee, former mouse! I feel that way, too. It's so wonderful to feel pretty, isn't it?"

"It really is! And not to feel guilty because feeling pretty is sinful. You know, Alpha Lee, vanity is one of the seven deadly sins. That's what my father taught me. God loves you if you're humble."

"Well, I'm sure he does, Susan ... but I think he loves us anyway. That's the way I learned it."

"That's a lot nicer," Susan said with a bright smile. She was silent for a moment, and then she said, "Alpha Lee, when I went back through the living room last night, I saw you and Jan in there by the table ... you were hugging each other so tightly ... Alpha Lee, I had strange feelings, just watching you for a minute." Susan kept her eyes fixed on the ironing board. "The way you hold each other ... the way you kissed when you met at the airport ... Alpha Lee, it's better than the movies." She looked up and met Alpha Lee's eyes. "I can almost feel the love you have for each other. I never saw, or felt, anything like this before. It's the most beautiful thing I've ever seen."

"Yes ... it is beautiful. I feel like I've won the jackpot, Susan. I'm rich, I'm pretty, I'm blessed. I hope you'll feel just exactly like I do someday." Alpha Lee smiled blissfully.

Then she looked at her watch. "Susan, you must hurry and get dressed. Jane will be here in a minute! Aren't you finished ironing that?"

Susan was brushing her hair when Jane arrived. "Hello, Alpha Lee! This is a nice little place, isn't it?" she said, looking around the lodge. "Is Susan ready to go?"

"Yes, here I am, Mrs. Williamson. I'm ready." She lifted her guitar down from the peg and picked up her purse.

"Susan, what a lovely dress! You look beautiful. The men will be delighted with you." She noticed Susan's low-heeled white slippers. "Hmmm. Susan, what size shoe do you wear?"

"Oh, Mrs. Williamson, I have huge feet. I wear eight and a half," she replied.

"Well, thank you very much, Susan," Jane said wryly. "I wear nines myself! ... but narrow. I wonder ... I have a pretty pair of high heeled gold sandals ... I wonder if you could wear them. Would you like to try them on? We can stop back by the house for a minute and see if they would fit you. They'd look so pretty with that dress, with the gold accents. The spotlight will pick up those little gold threads, you know ... they'll really sparkle."

"I'd just *LOVE* to wear high heeled gold shoes!" Susan said enthusiastically. "Please, let's try them! ... Bye, Alpha Lee. I wish you were going, too."

"Maybe next time, Susan. Jane, thank you for picking her up. I'll be in soon with some more charcoals. ... Good luck, Susan," and she whispered into Susan's ear, "Nisqually! Don't forget!" Susan straightened her back, and followed Jane out the door with a graceful stride.

Jane stopped at a handsome stone ranch-style house only a couple miles from the lodge turn off, situated on high ground above a shallow cove. Susan got out of the big car and followed Mrs. Williamson into the house. "Wait here a minute, Susan, and I'll bring the shoes," Jane said, and Susan sat down on a broad leather sofa and looked around in fascination at the beautifully furnished room. There were many paintings and sculptures displayed, furniture of an exotic design Susan had never seen before, and a wide expanse of mirror tiles above the stone fireplace. Jane returned a moment later carrying the shoes. "Here we are ... try these on. If they're not too narrow, you're welcome to wear them."

Susan slipped her feet into the glamorous sandals. The heels were gracefully slender and the narrow gold leather straps criss-crossed over her foot. "Hmmm ... maybe just a bit snug across the instep, but of course you won't be doing much walking. What do you think, Susan?" Jane asked.

"I love them," Susan said softly, standing to attempt a few steps. "I love them! Yes! I can wear them, Mrs. Williamson. The straps give just enough so that I can wiggle my toes ..." She walked across the room, her back straight, her carriage "queenly." Nisqually, Susan told herself.

"Oh, Susan, that's lovely," Jane said. "Would you like to wear earrings, dear?" She offered Susan a pair of golden hoops, and when Susan's eyes lighted up, Jane clipped them in place. Susan looked at her reflection in the mirror, enthralled. Jane followed her eyes. "Now, Susan, all we need to complete the picture is a lovely smile."

Susan was so filled with joy that this was an easy request. She did indeed smile, as she breathed, "Thank you so much, Mrs. Williamson!"

Jane was deeply gratified. Susan did look like a performer. Now, if only ... When Roddy's band had finished its final upbeat number before intermission, he led Susan onstage where a tall stool had been set up for her. As Jane had directed her, she bowed slightly when Roddy introduced her and smiled brilliantly at her audience, turning to acknowledge the applause from several directions. She seated herself, turned her attention inward, closed her eyes briefly and stroked her guitar. She sang a short verse and then began the chorus: "Dream ... when you're feelin' blue ..."

In the audience Jane listened and was very pleased. And her mind was filled with ideas. How far can we go with this child, she wondered. I wish ... I wish ...

It was almost time for Jan to return from work at T. E. Alpha Lee hurried to put away her oils. She had been painting an arrangement of a pitcher filled with wild flowers and a drape of cloth beside it for practice on textures and the play of light. She dipped her brushes in a small jar of turpentine and cleaned her smudged fingers. What a nasty smell, she thought, and she went to wash her hands after setting the brushes in their container outside on the porch. I hope that won't attract the bears ... surely they wouldn't like that smell. She took off the faded shirt she wore to protect her clothing and left it on the porch rail also.

She had just washed her hands and was rubbing scented lotion on them when Jan opened the door. He looks tired, she thought. His days are too long. She hurried to welcome him. Maybe he's too tired to want me to ... But Jan was not too tired to take her in his arms and kiss her long and soundly. As she felt his desire for her, her own response awakened; and then he gently withdrew from her. "Alpha Lee ...," he breathed, "you're gonna drive me crazy. If we have to be 'just friends' for the time being, we're gonna have to find some way to cool it. Not an easy thing, sweet heart." He smiled to soften the words, and kissed her lips gently with distance between them.

"Jan, would you like some coffee?" Alpha Lee asked, backing away from him as well as his subject. "The fire is still warm ... or maybe a shower? I know you must be tired. What do you need?"

"Don't even ask," he told her with a wink. "But, yes, a cup of coffee sounds great as a second choice."

Alpha Lee poured the coffee and found a couple of Susan's ginger snaps to accompany it. She sat in the rocker while he lounged on the couch. "Thanks, honey. ... Alpha Lee, I've been for-getting to mention something we need to talk about. Susan said something about you girls not commuting to college next fall. Are you going to be able to stay at the dorm? Or have your plans changed somehow?"

"Oh, Jan, how have I managed to forget to tell you! Yes, my plans have changed a lot, and every time I think about it, you're at work or at the base, and here we are, after a whole week, and I haven't told you!" She pulled her chair closer. "I think I told you that I took a class in Graphic Arts last year ...Yes?. It was taught by Mrs. Petrovsky, the wife of the basketball coach at Brick City. She is a very talented lady and an excellent teacher, and we got along really well. That's partly the reason I enjoyed that class so much.

"Well, Jan ... Mrs. Petrovsky has taken a job at Wesleyan. They haven't had much of an art department there ... if at all. The new dean felt that this was a serious deficiency in their curriculum as a liberal arts college. I guess they did have an art professor years ago, but he served in the air corps and was killed in action. The school is really still recovering from the lean years of the war when enrollment was down. Now that all those GI's have enrolled, they're making an effort to build up their class offerings. ... This is what Mrs. Petrovsky told me." She stood to pick up Jan's empty cup. "There's a bit more, Jan ... could you drink another cup?" When he nodded yes, she refilled it and carried it to him.

Alpha Lee resumed her story. "So Mrs. Petrovsky will be teaching several classes ... water-color, oil painting, maybe even sculpture ... and hiring graduate students, maybe, to take over some classes. But here's the exciting part: You know I told you that I did win a very small scholarship when we took the tests at Brick City last winter. Well ... she asked me if I'd be willing to relinquish my scholarship ... it would be awarded to somebody else if I did ... in ex-change for a grant that would amount to much more ... full tuition for the year, room and board, textbooks ... if I would act as her assistant."

"Wow, honey! That sounds like a great deal. What would you be doing? Is there a time commitment involved ... so many hours a week?"

"I think the actual responsibilities and duties ... hmmm ... I think that's called the job description ... hasn't been written in final form yet. But I'd be helping her in whatever way she needs me ... nitty-gritty things like ordering supplies and doing secretarial work, and also helping the students if she isn't able to handle all of the demands. Jan, I'm dazzled by all of this. I can't believe there isn't someone more experienced than me for this work. I told her that ... and she just said that she thought we could work together more harmoniously and effectively ... those were her exact words ... than anybody else they could find for her. Isn't that exciting? Am I really good enough to do this?"

"Honey, you are good enough to do whatever is asked of you, and more. Don't ever forget that. But will you be able to take the classes you want to take, and the core classes that are required?"

"Josie says yes. ... That is, Mrs. Petrovsky. I'll have only one actual art class this year; I had planned to take oil painting, but hey, Jan, I'm already doing that!" She laughed. "I just had myself a class this very evening. Did you see my picture?" She took the painting she had been working on from its place against the wall where it was drying. "This is just an exercise, Jan ... just to build my familiarity and skill with the oil so I can try something more serious."

Jan sat up and studied the painting. "Well, I'm no critic, Alpha Lee, but it looks to me like you're doing it! This is nice. Has your work with the colored pencils helped you with blending the colors and putting what you see on paper? Or canvas, as the case may be?"

"Yes, absolutely. It's totally different from the pencils, of course, but ... well, maybe not *totally*. Yes, it has helped. The medium is very different, but some of the skills are familiar. I have to tell you, Jan ... it sure *smells* different! I don't like the turpentine one bit, but I have to get used to it." She returned the picture to its corner. "Anyway, I will have to take some core classes. English Composition is required, and some kind of social studies course, maybe history ... and would you believe, philosophy and religion? Wesleyan is, after all, a church-sponsored college."

"Alpha Lee ... I'm almost afraid to ask ... are there strings attached? Is there a time commitment? Would you have to agree to stay for several years? That would be ... " He trailed off, unwilling to verbalize his thoughts.

"No, no, no. There was nothing said about tenure ... I think that's what they call it. If the art department develops the way Josie plans for it, there will be other professors hired the next year, and the whole structure may change. She would surely have a *real* secretary and other paid staff by that time. The only condition for this grant is that the assistant must live on campus, in the dorm. *Unmarried*." She looked at the floor, twisting her hands in her lap.

"Unmarried," he repeated. There was a long silence. There's no commit-ment between us, he thought. No promises ... He could not know that her own thoughts were exactly the same, and her emotions as confused as his own.

Roddy brought Susan home a little past midnight. Alpha Lee had tried to wait up for her, but had finally fallen asleep on the couch, her book falling to the floor beside her. Susan could not resist waking her; she herself was wide awake and bubbling with excitement. "*Alpha Lee!* Please wake up ... I just have to tell you about my *gig*!"

She had sung six popular songs during two intermissions; the troops had whistled and clapped for her, and brought her back for two encores. The gold shoes were beautiful and fit her just fine, she said. Jane had even dabbed her with a bit of expensive Schiaparelli perfume! Yes, she had remembered "*Nisqually*", and she had remembered to smile, smile, smile, as Jane had insisted. Roddy seemed pleased with her performance. She would perform again *TOMORROW* she said -- this time at the air force base a few miles away ... McSomething, she couldn't remember the name ... something about music, she thought. McChord! That was it. She even danced once with Roddy ... he was a super dancer, she said, and *so* nice. Tomorrow she would write to Nancy and tell her all about it. ... After fifteen minutes of exuberant rapid-fire reporting, Susan finally realized that she, too, was exhausted, and the two girls tiptoed to their room, and were asleep in minutes.

Chapter 9

Saturday morning began, typically, with rain that dropped the temperature several degrees. The fire in the cookstove felt good as the biscuits baked; Alpha Lee had finally decided to try baking in the unfamiliar wood-fired oven. She had to check often; but the baking time was short and they were golden brown and nicely risen when she took them out. She had found some honey in the farm market, and breakfast became a real treat with fresh coffee and warm apple-sauce to accompany the biscuits. Jan was pleased.

"Hey, Alpha Lee ... I thought nobody could make biscuits as good as my mom's, but I think you've done it. I won't tell *her* that, though," he told her with a wink.

"Good for you, Jan. I'm glad they turned out okay. I was afraid I'd burn them, or they'd just dry out, if the heat wasn't high enough. They *do* taste pretty good, don't they? And this honey is delicious."

Susan emerged from the bedroom, stretching and yawning. "Hmmm ... Good morning, folks. I guess I overslept. But I deserved it, didn't I? ... After such a great night last night." And she began regaling Jan with a description of her first performance at the service club.

"Is Roddy's band pretty good, Suz?" he asked.

"I think they sound great, for such a small group," she answered. "Roddy plays the piano, and he is good on guitar, too. Jon is the drummer. He just graduated from high school this spring ... he's the same age as we are, Alpha Lee ... he's a Forty-Niner, too. There's a trumpet player ... sometimes he plays trombone. I think his name is Ricky something. And then there's a sax player who also plays clarinet, and an amplified string bass. They all play other instruments sometimes. I think they're a pretty talented group. Sometimes they play polkas ... the guy on the bass guitar can even play an accordion." Susan was enthusiastic. "I love it! I've gotta plan what I'm going to sing tonight, and practice a while." She buttered a biscuit and helped herself to the applesauce. "Gee, Alpha Lee ... you're getting good at this cooking thing. If the art career falls through, maybe you can be a big time chef!" She grinned mischievously.

"Well, doesn't that sound glamorous!" Alpha Lee replied sarcastically. "Susan, what are you going to wear tonight ... the same dress you wore last night? Will it need to be washed ... or does it have to be cleaned?"

"No, I think I'll have to find something else for tonight. I have my navy blue suit ... I could wear the skirt with a fancy blouse or maybe that white angora sweater ... but I'll have to talk to Jane about what to wear, if I'm going to perform twice a week. This could be a problem. I just can't go out and buy a bunch of special clothes ... I'll end up losing money on this job."

"Hey, Susan ... the guys would love you in a sweater," Jan said with a leer. "Wouldn't matter much what you wore with it."

"Oh, *JAN!* Cut it out!"

Jan chuckled at her embarrassment. "Matter of fact, I'm gonna cut out right now. I'll work till five o'clock this evening, and then when I get home, we'll get all gussied up and go to McChord to see the beautiful Miss Susan Remagen do her stuff for the flyboys. Alpha Lee, I'll take the garbage along to T. E. Do you need anything from the market?"

"Oh, yes, Jan, just a few things. I have a list. Just a minute, I'll find it."

"Jan, will you take me to McChord, or should I just leave things as they are, and plan to go with Jane?" Susan asked.

"We can probably take you, Suz. What time did Roddy say to be there?"

"About eight, I think. My performance won't be for at least a half hour later, but he wants me to be there in plenty of time so we can check out the room and the crowd and stuff. D'you think we can get there by that time?"

"I don't see why not ... unless it takes you girls a lot of hours to get your-selves ready. I'll call Jane from work and tell her she won't need to pick you up. ... Okay, then, I'll see you sometime after five. I hope the rain stops."

"Okay, Jan. See you," Susan replied.

"Thanks for the great breakfast, sweet," he said to Alpha Lee. "Maybe I'll give you a raise, you're such a good cook." He kissed her cheek, took the grocery list, and headed out into the rain.

Charcoal weather, Alpha Lee thought, as she looked out from the doorway at the landscape, all but devoid of color. Jan's black car climbed slowly up the white-sand driveway bordered with dark dripping pines under a gray sky. No wonder the folks out here found my charcoal so appealing, she thought. It's real.

Susan looked through the clothes she had brought with her that hung on the rod in the bed-room, hoping to find something she had overlooked that would be suitable to wear to her performance that night. "I wish we could wear each other's clothes," she said. "But you're so much shorter"

"Yeah, there's not a whole lot we can share," Alpha Lee agreed. "Most of mine are homemade, because most of the time I can't find quite the right size. A size 14 is too tight across the bust, and a sixteen is way too long in the waist. And sometimes they're too tight, too."

"You have big knockers," Susan said with a smirk.

"What!"

Susan giggled. "Knockers ... that's what the boys call them. Last night, when I forgot 'Nisqually' for a minute, Roddy said, 'Knockers up, Suzie'", and she raised both hands chest-high in fists with the thumbs extended up. "He calls me Suzie," she explained. "Anyway, when he said that, Jane hollered at him '*RODDY!*' That's no way to talk to a lady!'" Susan mimicked Jane's deep voice.

Alpha Lee shook her head. "Boys are so weird. They have all these dumb names for our breasts. 'Boobs'. Where did that come from?"

"Tits ... like we were cows or something," Susan agreed. "Jugs. It's stupid."

"D'you suppose there are silly names for *their* body parts?" Alpha Lee wondered.

"Oh, sure. You've heard of 'cock', haven't you? And 'dick', and 'balls' ..."

"*End of conversation*, Susan," Alpha Lee said firmly, and strode back into the kitchen to clear the breakfast table.

Susan tried on Alpha Lee's full, swirling white skirt with the short-sleeved angora pullover sweater and decided that, while it was an awful lot of white, it didn't look bad. The skirt was shorter than she would have wished, but Alpha Lee pointed out that the mid-knee length might just possibly be acceptable to a room full of soldiers. Susan burst into a fit of giggles at that, and decided she was right. The gold locket Ben had given her glittered between her "knockers" against the furry white sweater, and they both pronounced the look rather cute. She did wear her low-heeled white slippers this time, and wished she still had Jane's golden earrings to complete the picture.

When Jan arrived, he immediately whistled at Susan in her fetching white attire, and assured her that she would be "a big hit with the guys."

"Well, okay. But this is going to be a constant problem until I can figure out how to get some more 'career clothes' without going bankrupt. Alpha Lee ... I think I'll write to Nancy first thing tomorrow ... Oh, gee, make that Monday ... and ask her to send me some of my stuff from home. That'd be cheaper than having to buy things. My white graduation dress ... remember it? It has a double row of gold buttons down the front. And the flowered sheer print I wore to the Sermon; the Baccalaureate, do you think that would be appropriate? Nancy would know what would work, wouldn't she?"

"'Scuse me for changing the subject," Jan said, "but what smells so good, Alpha Lee? I sure hope it's supper," he said, following his nose to where she had opened the oven door to take out baked pork chops and scalloped potatoes. In a skillet on the stove sliced apples were sizzling in butter and cinnamon. "Boy, what did I do to deserve this?" he asked. "I'm gonna do it often!" Alpha Lee smiled winningly at his praise.

"'The way to a man's heart ...'", she quoted.

"Baby, you've found it," he said, hugging her vigorously.

Susan covered her pretty white costume with her bathrobe while she ate dinner. "I can't afford to dribble pork chop grease down my front."

"Good thinking, Susan," Alpha Lee said with elaborate sarcasm. "Slop-piness is a sin at this point ... we don't have any alternatives. I hope Jane can help us make some decisions about clothes. *If* I had my sewing machine ..."

"You're going from a cook to a seamstress, is that the plan?" Jan asked. "Seems to me you're sort of stuck in Home Ec, honey. You're an artist, remember?"

"Well, I *do* like to sew ... there's art involved in that, too, you know. We could come up with something nice for not much money. I wonder if Naomi has a sewing machine ... "

"I'll ask her," Susan said.

After dinner, Susan went to the bedroom to apply her make-up and brush her hair. Jan helped pick up the supper dishes as Alpha Lee filled the dish-pan. "Honey, I'm gonna gain weight if this continues," he said. "The U. S. Army can't *NO WAY* compete with great food like this, fixed by the prettiest girl in town. I feel like a fat cat. Come here and let me eat you up!" He came up behind her, turned her around and kissed her hard, as her hands dripped soap bubbles on the floor.

Alpha Lee laughed when he released her. "Jan, we've got to hurry up and get ready! Let me finish here while you shower ... if you want to ... and then I'll get dressed as fast as I can."

They arrived at McChord Air Force Base a few minutes before eight. The guard looked at the sticker on Jan's windshield and nodded. "Where do you want to go, sir?"

"To the Special Services dance. Can you point me that way?"

The airman indicated a wide avenue through the base. "Three blocks down and turn left ... you can't miss it." He had spotted Susan in the back seat with her guitar. "Excuse me ... is this the blonde singer everybody's talking about? ... The special performer that's on tonight's bill?" He smiled broadly, exposing a mouth full of very big teeth.

"You're right, private," Jan said. "Meet Miss Suzie Remagen. You gonna be able to come in for the show?"

"I guess not ... not this time," he said regretfully. "Will you be back next Saturday, ma'am?"

Susan smiled at him brilliantly. "Gee, I hope so," she said in her most soft and sexy voice. Alpha Lee had to hide a smile. "Can you come to the show next week, Private ... umm ... Cochrane?" she asked, reading the name from his ID patch.

"I sure hope so, ma'am ... I'll look forward to it!"

"Well, I'll look for you ... okay?" Another engaging smile.

"Yes, Ma'am!" The private grinned and waved them on their way, giving a snappy salute for the benefit of the girls.

"Susan, you're performing already, and you aren't even there yet!" Alpha Lee said, laughing.

"Well, Jane told me to 'connect' with my audience ... she said I should perform as if I'm singing to each one of those soldiers personally. She said to smile and make them feel special ... one at a time. So ... that's what I'm doing!" she said. "... Besides ... he was kind of sweet, don't you think? ... Even if he wasn't very good looking."

"Suzie, you're gonna be a big success at this ... I can see that right now," Jan said. "You've found your calling, kiddo."

Jan drove ahead down the street until he saw the big brightly lighted building on the left. A poster near the door announced "Music by Roddy Williamson's Band of Outlaws, with a Special Guest Performer." "That's our Suzie!" Jan said with a grin.

Jan took the guitar case, and with a girl on each arm entered the room. Uniformed men and civilians turned to look as they made their way across the room. They immediately saw Jane Williamson as she rose from her seat and came to meet them. "Come over to my table. The show has just started. Susan, Roddy will want you backstage soon; your first perfor-mance will be in about twenty to thirty minutes. Do you folks want anything to drink?"

They ordered Cokes and settled themselves at Jane's table. Roddy's next piece was a slow romantic ballad, and Jan asked Jane and Susan to excuse them as he and Alpha Lee moved to the dance floor. "It's been a long time between dances, sweet," he told her. "Over a year ago, in your living room. Our lives sure have changed since then. I wouldn't have it any other way."

"Do you really mean that, Jan?" she asked in a whisper.

"You know I do. I love you, Alpha Lee." She lay her head against his chest, eyes closed in sweet contentment.

The next number was a fast boogie woogie that was beyond both Jan's and Alpha Lee's dancing experience. They were content to rejoin Jane at the table; Susan had left. "Mrs. Williamson, I'd ask you to dance this one with me, but I think we'd both regret it," he said with a wry grin.

"Thanks anyway, Jan ... that's not my cup of tea, either. May I have a rain check for some other number? With Alpha Lee's permission, of course."

"Of course," Alpha Lee agreed. "I'd love to watch the two of you dance!"

Finally, Roddy introduced "Our special guest performer, Miss Suzie Remagen, the pride of Brick City, West Virginia!", and with a dazzling smile and bows of acknowledgment to all corners, Susan took her place on the tall stool, sitting straight, and lost herself in her guitar and her song:

"They asked me how I knew
My true love was true ...."

Her voice filled the utter silence of the room. Alpha Lee felt tears of pride fill her eyes. She's wonderful, she thought. She's perfectly at ease. Oh Nancy ... if you could only see her ... Jan squeezed her hand, and she knew he could read her thoughts.

Chapter 10

On Monday Jan and Fred ate lunch with their five tank-transport students at the mess hall. They had almost finished their meal when Sgt. Ed Kraskovic walked over to their table with a cup of coffee and a cigarette. The sergeant was a huge man, over six feet tall and massively built; his kitchen whites made him look even bigger. He sat down at a vacant space, nodded to Jan and grinned at Fred. "I was just tellin' Corporal Spivak in the kitchen about our li'l adventure at Yakima. You just about got enough cold soakin' to do you, didn't you, Harris?"

Fred waved his four-fingered hand at him. "Ed, I think Jan and I both got enough cold soakin'. But Jan here, he's warmin' up every night with a girlfriend in his cozy shack, and I can't do nothin' but sleep in the barracks with a bunch of stinkin' gi's and wait for my apartment ... middle of the month, they tell me."

"Well, you just let me know when the house-warmin's gonna be, and I'll bake you a li'l ol' cake for the party. I hear you're gettin' married when that gal comes out from Kansas."

"Yeah, Ed ... Ronnie and I have already set a date with the Chaplain in the north base chapel. Jan's gonna be my best man," Fred said. "You can bake me a little cake for that day, for sure. I'd say, somethin' white, about three feet tall ..." and he measured the distance between outstretched hands, " ... with lots of icing roses and ruffles, and one of those plastic bride and groom things on top." He added, "The groom should be in dress khaki's, of course."

"Hey, Corporal ... hold on there! That there's a whole 'nother project! You plannin' on servin' cake to the whole dam division? Hell with that! Get yerself a caterer. And start savin' lotsa bucks."

Jan said, "Ed, is that offer good for me, too? How about making me a small birthday cake? My gal's gonna celebrate her eighteenth on Thursday."

"No kiddin'? Well, what's her name? Write it down on this napkin here, Jan, an' I'll just make her a nice li'l cake with her name on it. You can pick it up Thursday when you get off. ... Ya know, you two guys are my favorite truck drivers ... 'specially after you spooked that dumb fat-ass lootenant the way you did!" He chuckled, his cigarette dangling precariously from the corner of his mouth. "Did these guys tell you'ns about the cold-soak mission to Yakima in Feb'rary?" he asked the driving students. "Tell 'em, Fred. These guys need to know how lucky they were not to be along on that fiasco. ... Jan, I'll see ya Thursday evening ... okay? Harris ... we'll talk about that weddin' cake." And the Messmaster sauntered back to his kitchen.

Alpha Lee shook the rainwater from her umbrella and opened the door at the Arte Shacke. It was early; no customers were on the streets yet, and maybe traffic would be slow all day, unless the rain stopped soon.

"Hello, Alpha Lee," Jane said with a bright smile. "You're early today, ... I just opened a minute ago. Did you bring some more copies, dear?"

"Yes ... but I am frustrated, Jane. I'm having a difficult time working with the charcoal on these dark days. The light at the lodge isn't very good when there's no sunshine. We just have bare bulbs hanging from the ceiling in the middle of the room. Do you suppose I could work here? It's so nice and bright in here ..."

"I think that's a great idea, Alpha Lee. Of course you could work here! Let's see ... would you want to work in the studio shop in the back? ..... Oh, no, wait a minute! I have a better idea. Let's move some of the pieces from the window, and set you up right there, where the passersby can see you working! Don't you think that would be great?" She was enthusiastic, swiftly making room in the display window. "You wouldn't mind working ... publicly, so to speak? ... would you? I think it would attract attention, don't you?" She paused in her busy-ness to determine Alpha Lee's reaction to her suggestion.

"Well ... why not, Jane? I could do that. This window is one bright spot on the wet gray street. Yes ... I can do that. I did bring along my paper and charcoals in the hope that I could find someplace here with good light." She opened a packet that was well wrapped against the rain, producing two finished copies as well as her supplies.

..."This is all I could do since I was here last. It's been a busy weekend, *and* a rainy one."

"What will you need, Alpha Lee? An easel?"

"Yes, a small one. At the lodge I just work on a tabletop, but it would make more of a show if I work on the easel so the drawing is visible. And something to sit on ... preferably a stool, if you have one here. ...... And an old cloth to wipe my hands."

Jane set up one of the copies of the fishing lodge, framed in a broad white mat and a silvery frame, beside Alpha Lee's stool, and quickly made a placard with her name on it in calligraphy. "There we are ... now we're ready for a crowd to assemble to watch you work. Are you comfortable?"

"Yes, this will do fine, thank you," and Alpha Lee began the too-familiar outline that would begin her drawing.

"Alpha Lee, I was *SO* pleased with Susan Saturday night. She has such a talent. She seems to be really warming to her little job, don't you think? I think she enjoys performing for these men."

"Yes," Alpha Lee agreed. "It's a little strange ... she seems like every man's sister, or girl-friend, when she's performing, and yet she is pretty uncomfortable in personal relationships. I've read about that; I guess some of the most famous movie stars and singers are more at ease behind their facade as a performer than they are in real-life situations."

"I'm sorry that she has this problem," Jane said. "Can you tell me what caused her to be so sensitive, Alpha Lee? Or is it too confidential?"

Alpha Lee hesitated. Jane had been very kind to Susan and seemed truly interested in her success and well-being. After a moment's consideration, she said, "Susan was mistreated, Jane. She was ... umm ... molested ... and even beaten sometimes, for several years. She is very uncomfortable around boys ... in a close relationship. She's okay with Jan; he's so kind to her; and besides, she knows he is *my* boyfriend and she isn't worried about him getting too close. She treats him like a brother, although she doesn't have a brother."

Jane was shocked. "I can't believe it! How could anyone do such horrible things to that sweet girl? Who was it ... some demented neighbor?"

Again Alpha Lee considered for a moment, and then spoke. "It was her father, Jane. He was a minister." Alpha Lee finally found the courage to say the terrible word. "They say her father raped her."

Jane was silent, horrified beyond words. She turned away in distress.

Alpha Lee continued: "Susan is with foster parents now. Her foster mother is the music teacher who was director of the Glee Club at high school. Mr. McAllister is a retired doctor. They both love her very much. Sending her out here must have been a risky decision for them; I think they thought it would be good for her to get away to a new location and be on her own, with Jan and I to sort of watch over her. And so far, it has been. It's been great. She has just blossomed."

Jane was so upset that she left the room for a moment to regain her composure. The problem was far more serious than she could have guessed. This child needs all the love and help she can get, she said to herself. And Roddy must know what to expect, and not try to ....

The door bell jingled; Jane dabbed her tears away and returned to the showroom. "Oh, hi, Fran! Do we have a foursome for tomorrow night?"

A short woman in hospital scrubs was turned toward Alpha Lee as she entered the room. "Hi, Jane. Yes, Rosemary and Marsha are okay, and Joyce will take my place for the duration. I'll be back in a couple of weeks ... think you can play without me?" Without waiting for an answer, she asked in a soft voice, "Jane, who *IS* that in the window? Don't tell me that's the charcoal artist!"

Jane smiled brilliantly. "As a matter of fact, it is! Come and meet her. ... Alpha Lee, this is Dr. Frances Sparks, my bridge partner when she's not gallivanting around somewhere .... Dr. Sparks bought one of your first copies. Fran, meet Alpha Lee Evans from West Virginia. She'll be spending the summer out here with us. We hope she'll do a lot more artwork for us."

"Well, Miss Evans! I am surprised. Are you still in school? I love that charcoal ... mine's lucky number seven. I've had so many nice comments on it. I have it on the wall in my office."

Alpha Lee wiped away the dark dust before she reached to clasp Dr. Sparks' hand. "Thank you so much," she said. "I graduated from High School just two weeks ago .. although it seems like much longer. so much has happened."

"Do you have time for other projects, since you've had so many requests for copies of this drawing?"

"I'm working in oils when I have a chance. I had such a difficult time doing the charcoals on days like this ... our lodge has poor light on rainy days. We ... my two friends and I ... live in this actual fishing lodge, Dr. Sparks," she said with a smile. "It's quite rustic ... it wasn't built for an artist's studio."

The door bell jingled again, and Jane excused herself to attend to the customer. "You are a medical doctor, is that right, Dr. Sparks?" Alpha Lee asked. "Do you work in a hospital?"

"Yes, and I also have a clinic." She looked at her watch. "And I must go. I'm leaving on vacation tomorrow, and I have things I need to clear up before I go. I'm so glad I met you, Alpha Lee. Maybe you and Jane and I can have lunch sometime when I get back."

"Doctor ... do you have just a minute, please?" Alpha Lee managed to say in spite of acute self-consciousness. "Could you please recommend someone I could see for ... umm ... a sort of personal matter?"

"Are you ill, Alpha Lee? Is there something I could do for you ... an examination, ... or something like that?"

"Yes ... something like that," Alpha Lee said, her eyes downcast. "I'm not sick ... I just need some advice, maybe ... or something."

She seemed so ill at ease that the doctor made the obvious guess. "Alpha Lee, are you pregnant?" she asked softly.

"Oh no, no," Alpha Lee answered, blushing deeply. "But I do need an examination."

"I am a gynecolocist, Alpha Lee ... a 'female doctor', as some folks say. Would you like to see me in my office when I get back from my trip? I could schedule you for sometime in June. Every girl your age should have a physical exam anyway. Let me give you my address and phone number, and you can call my office for an appointment ... if it's not urgent."

"That would be just great, Dr. Sparks," Alpha Lee said, smiling with relief. "I'm so glad I met you. I will call ... I'll do it today."

Alpha Lee returned to her work feeling confident and optimistic. A woman doctor! she thought. That's just perfect. I won't feel so ... strange with her. Yes! What a lucky break that I came here today!

Jane finished taking an order from her customer, who had brought in a piece of needlepoint to be framed. When the door bell jingled as the customer left, she returned to Alpha Lee. "I'm so glad you could meet Fran ... she's a dear friend. We've been playing bridge every Wednesday evening for years. Do you play, dear?"

"No, I never learned bridge," Alpha Lee said. "Mother and Daddy used to play long ago when I was little ... I can just barely remember. But they haven't played either, for a long time. Dr. Sparks seems very nice."

"Yes ... she's going to California for a while," Jane said. After a long pause, she said, "Alpha Lee ... do you think that Susan would consider working here with me a few days a week? She'll be finished at Tak Elek at the end of this week, I believe ... is that right? ... Yes. I could use

someone just to be here to greet customers so I could work back in the shop when I need to. I could train her, and pay her a small stipend. What do you think?"

"Do you really mean that, Jane? Susan really does need something to do, rather than just sit around the lodge all day. It doesn't bother me; I can keep busy with my art, and fixing dinner for Jan, and the time just flies. But I think she would be bored. Why don't you call her at T. E. and ask her to stop in to talk about it?"

"The more I think about this, the more excited I get, Alpha Lee! She could play her guitar when I have receptions and showings for local artists. They do that in the big-city galleries. ... There's so much I want to teach her. ... I must say, I am so pleased that she is learning not to crouch and slump the way she did the first time I saw her ... she looked almost ashamed, or depressed, or something. ... Well, since you told me about her history, I guess I can understand, perhaps, why that became a habit with her "

"Exactly, Jane. Whenever she performs, she becomes a different person ... she stands straight; you'd never guess she had such a heavy burden on her shoulders. But other times, she forgets, and so we've been practicing at home ... we remind each other to be aware of our posture. This new career she has with Roddy's band has done wonders for her. Nancy ... her foster mother, will be amazed, *if* Susan can just keep it up when she goes home."

"She's such a beautiful girl *and so* promising. The posture problem is the first challenge; then maybe we can go beyond that. I really do care about her, Alpha Lee. I love my boys dearly, but ... it's such a joy to be with a sweet young girl. And both of you are just a delight to me."

Alpha Lee thanked her with a warm smile. Yes, she thought, what a lucky break I came here today! Alpha Lee stayed through Jane's lunch break, assuring her that she could greet any customers (there had been very few on that rainy morning), and just take their messages and promise them that Jane would contact them soon. One woman did come in during Jane's absence, curious to speak to the girl who was drawing in the show window.

"That's a nice picture," the woman said. "I can't afford a real drawing, but I've heard that prints will be offered ... I'll come back when they're ready. Are you from around here?"

"No," Alpha Lee said. "I'm just spending the summer here; I'm from West Virginia."

"Oh, really? I have a cousin who lives in Richmond," the woman said brightly. "Do you live anywhere near there?"

Alpha Lee smiled. "No ... that would be Richmond, VIRGINIA. It's a long way from my little town, in a neighboring state. I live in WEST Virginia... just next door to Virginia."

The woman looked puzzled. "I don't know anything much about West Virginia. What's it like?"

"Well, we have mountains ... not as big as the Cascades, not as high. Our mountains are covered with forests ... hardwoods, mostly. Maples and oaks and poplars. There are beautiful colors in the fall when the leaves turn. And there are lots of coal mines. And the roads have lots of curves and ups and downs."

"Hmm ... sounds very scenic. How did you happen to make this picture? Surely this scene is local, isn't it?"

And Alpha Lee explained how she had originally made the first drawing from a postcard from a friend who was stationed at Fort Lewis. ... The woman thanked her, and asked Alpha Lee if she would put her name on the waiting list for one of the prints.

When her customer left, Alpha Lee called the number Dr. Sparks had given her. The receptionist looked over the doctor's schedule.

"Dr. Sparks will not be in her office until after June 20," she said. "The first opening I have for a new patient examination would be on June 22nd. This would have to be done when you are not having your menstrual period. If that date is okay with you, we could schedule you for 9:00 AM."

Alpha Lee had hoped for an earlier date; but she accepted the appointment and made a note of time and date. She would have to find out how to get to the office. I'm afraid to drive through this big city alone, she thought. Maybe Jane can give me directions ... or maybe I can ride a bus.

She would also have to find a way to pay for the examination. I hope it's not terribly expensive, she worried. Maybe I'll have to use all of my earnings from the charcoals to pay for it ....

When Jane returned, Alpha Lee gave her the two copies she had finished, packed up her supplies and left the Arte Schacke. It had been an entirely rewarding day. Now she needed to get back to the lodge to fix dinner; meat loaf with tomato sauce, mashed potatoes, salad ... she had one of Naomi's early tomatoes to mix with the greens ... and I'll bake those muffins Jan likes so much, she thought. We'll just have ice cream for dessert; I don't think there will be time to bake anything else today. Susan would ride home with Naomi, and Fred would bring Jan home; then after supper he would go to work at T. E., as usual.

Alpha Lee was setting the table when she heard Naomi's car coming down the driveway. In a minute Susan came in, full of news about her day's work. "Naomi said we could use her iron again, Alpha Lee. I told her everything we own is so wrinkled it looks awful. Maybe we could use hers just one more time, and then we'd better try to buy one, don't you think?"

"Absolutely. I'm tired of looking so shabby," Alpha Lee replied. "Oh, there's Jan," she said. "I wish I had thought to ask Fred to stay and eat with us. I like him. Jan says his girlfriend from Kansas is coming to Tacoma soon. Maybe we can get together ..."

The door opened, and Alpha Lee greeted Jan with her arms lifted wide, and he walked into her embrace. With his lips close to her ear, he whispered, "Honey, if there was nothing for supper but this, I'd still be a happy man. You always feel so good. And smell so sweet," and he kissed her hard.

"Are you guys *ever* gonna get finished with that smoochy stuff? I want to tell Alpha Lee my great news!" Susan washed and dried her hands and reached into the cupboard for cups and a glass for herself. "Alpha Lee, Jane called me today and asked me if I would want to work at the Art Schacke when Millie comes back! Isn't that great?"

"Wow! It *is*, Susan. ... Jan, we'll be ready to eat in minutes. Everything's done. Susan, what would you be doing?"

"Just basically the receptionist thing at first. She wants me to come in next week, or earlier if I can get some time off, and she said she'd train me ... tell me about the stock and how to greet the customers ... that sort of thing."

"Well, I think that would be an interesting place to work. Probably more so than T. E."

After dinner, Jan thanked Alpha Lee for another delicious meal. "Those bran muffins are not only super, they bring back memories of that day at your house, when we went up to your bed-room to look at your artwork. I sure missed my chance that time, I could have kissed you right then and there, and saved a bunch of time."

"No ... it wouldn't have worked. We just have to let things happen in their own good time. But it is a nice moment to remember. And I *am* glad you enjoyed the All-Bran muffins, both then and now. ... Will you be home before ten, Jan?" she asked.

"Yeah, for sure. Hey, I happen to know that your birthday is coming up soon. Thursday, right? We *are* going to celebrate, honey. But not a lot on Thursday night ... that's a work day and I won't have much time to spend with you. But I have some special plans for this weekend ... so don't schedule a bunch of ironing, or garden work or anything, will you?"

Alpha Lee smiled brightly. "Oooh, that's exciting! I promise, I won't do a thing! I'll just get dressed up and sit and wait for something great to happen." She reached up to kiss him. "It's sweet of you to remember. Bye ... see you later."

The next day there was another reminder of her birthday: Susan brought the mail from Naomi that had been delivered for them, and there was a pretty card from her mother and father, with a twenty-dollar bill enclosed. Her mother's note was very short, but Alpha Lee could sense the love and concern behind the few words. I'll have to buy something special with this, she thought, and write to them to tell them how much I appreciate it. There was a card from her brother James, too mischievous and teasing, it made Alpha Lee laugh, and realize how much she missed him. He had enclosed his picture, posed with his best friend in front of the High School. Alpha Lee felt a twinge of nostalgia. I'll never be there again, she thought, at least not as a student.

She placed the cards on the mantle, feeling a bit misty. My first touch of homesickness ... she thought.

Chapter 11

Thursday morning was the first day of the week that dawned with a real sunrise, the fog and drizzle of the previous days gone at last. Jan surprised Alpha Lee by staying for breakfast with her and Susan on this, her real birthday. "The guys at the Mess Hall will miss me, I'm sure, but hey ... it's my sweetheart's birthday, and I want to spend all the time I can with her. Just watch out for a Jeep full of MP's, they may come out to get me and drag me back there, kicking and screaming."

"Soldiers *don't* kick and scream, Private Short," Susan said sternly.

"Oh, Jan ... this is a treat! A real gift, honey, having you here with us to start the day."

Jan had suggested having breakfast out on the porch, in the cool of the morning, and they spread a blanket and sat cross-legged, "Indian fashion", to eat their French toast and applesauce. "Our happy birthday celebration starts early, sweet," he told her. "Susan ... ready?" And the two of them sang "Happy Birthday to You."

Alpha Lee laughed and clapped her hands like a child. "Beautiful, beautiful! Such great harmony! Thank you, nice people! ... Hey, would you believe I'm finally eighteen. I thought it'd never happen, it's taken so long."

"That's true," Susan agreed. "I've been eighteen since April, and Jan for ages and ages."

"Well, actually I stopped being eighteen last October," he said.

Alpha Lee scanned the nearby forest nervously. "I just hope the bears don't decide to join us," she said, her eyes wide in mock terror. "Do bears like French toast?"

"You betcha ... they like everything," Jan teased her.

The sun cleared the faraway mountaintops and sparkled brilliantly on the waves of the sound, and the birds sang their territorial claims in a sweet clamor. "You sure picked a pretty day for your birthday, Alpha Lee," Jan told her. "I hope it stays nice for you all day, so you can do your art-work right here at home. We'll get back as soon as we can for dinner tonight. Susan, tomorrow is your last day at TE, right?"

"Yes. Millie came by yesterday with her little baby boy, he is just so cute! Her mother will watch him while she works. She seemed like she was anxious to come back to work."

They finished their breakfast and brought the dishes inside. As Jan kissed Alpha Lee goodbye, he said, "*DON'T* fix dessert tonight, hear?"

She looked at him inquiringly. "We can just have ice cream again, I guess," she said. "Bye, love."

Susan changed from her pajamas and robe into her work clothes, and made herself a sandwich to take along for lunch. "I'll bring the iron when I come home tonight," she promised. "See you later, Alpha Lee."

Alpha Lee could not resist trying her hand at painting in the morning sunlight. The rhododendron was beginning to bloom in the understory of the nearby pine woods; the beautiful color and the sparkling golden light that filtered down in the less densely forested areas tempted her to try her hand with the oil paints. She set up her easel some distance from the lodge and eagerly began. Viridian, she decided, with some Prussian blue mixed in for the shadows. And rose madder for the rhododendron blooms ... She spent most of the morning working, until the light began to change so profoundly that she could no longer capture the effect she had wanted; it would have to wait for another perfect morning, she decided reluctantly. How long would that be? As she began to assemble her materials to return to the lodge, a movement caught her eye. She looked up quickly and her eyes locked with those of a small bear. She froze in terror, recalling Jan's warning about the danger of the mother bear, who probably was nearby.

While she stood motionless, her mind was in a tumult, assessing what her next move should be. 'Non-threatening' was the command that thrust itself most forcefully into her mind. She very slowly gathered her canvas and her paintbox, and, deciding to abandon the easel and brushes, she backed away from the cub toward the lodge. When she took the first step, the bear turned and bounded in the opposite direction. She almost fainted with relief. Still she moved slowly, walking backward in case the mother bear, like a dog or cat, might be provoked to pursue if she just turned and ran. But she saw nothing moving in the woods. Still, she decided she would not try to bring in her easel until Jan came home.

Well, she thought, that's enough excitement for me today. And my painting isn't too bad, at that. I guess I'll live to paint another day. Thank you, God! I'm not going to spend a lot of time cooking today, she decided; it's *my* birthday, after all! We'll just have hot meat loaf sandwiches, and some fried potatoes with onions ... how he does love potatoes! And I don't have to fix dessert ... Hmmm. I wonder why he said that.

So Alpha Lee spent the afternoon making two more copies of the charcoal, of which she had become thoroughly tired, and then, just to amuse herself, she drew some sketches of costumes she had dreamed up for Susan. Who knows, she thought, *maybe* I can borrow a sewing machine. And *maybe* Jane or Naomi knows where I could find some material that isn't too expensive.

At last, when the water had warmed enough, she enjoyed a long bath and shampooed her hair under the shower. By the time Jan came home, she was refreshed, perfumed and fetchingly dressed. Her efforts were not lost on Jan; as always, he made it clear how much he enjoyed coming home to her. Maybe just because it's my birthday, she thought for an instant, his kiss is especially sweet tonight ... "I'm the luckiest guy in the entire U. S. Army," he murmured in her ear, "*And* the state of Washington ... you can throw West Virginia into the mix, too," he added extravagantly. *Mmmm*! Good! Happy birthday again, sweet lady!"

"Wow!" Susan exclaimed. "I sure hope my birthday gets this kind of a celebration! Breakfast outside in the sunrise ... A good-looking guy kissing me till I faint ... And *who knows* what's still to come!" she added mischievously. She was carrying a box wrapped in colored paper and tied with a bright ribbon, which she brought to the table and set down like a center- piece.

"Here's Naomi's contribution to your birthday," Jan said, handing Alpha Lee a bottle of wine, also adorned with a bow. "She made it herself from grapes from her family's vines."

"Oh, my goodness! This is just *too much*!" Alpha Lee cried. "I thought you said we weren't going to celebrate!"

"I still have some plans for the weekend, honey," Jan said. "This is just some small stuff to let you know we love you on your special day. ... Now, there's one more item. I'll be right back," and he went out to the car.

"Susan, thank you for the present," she said. "I can't wait to open it."

"Oh, yes you can," Susan said. "Just wait till Jan brings in his gift."

He came in carrying a large cardboard carton. "Now, sit down in the rocking chair, Alpha Lee," he told her, and he brought the box to place on the floor in front of her. "Open it," he said.

Alpha Lee was mystified. She opened the box, and there was a tiny black kitten, stretching up its full length to try to escape. Alpha Lee screamed with delight. "Oh, Jan! It's darling! It's *so* cute! Mmmm " She held the little creature close to her cheek. "It's just precious ... Jan, you are too good to me! To us ... it'll be Susan's pet, too."

"You like it, do you? Well, then, that's fine. You're not allergic, or a cat-hater ... Good. It's a female ... maybe we'll have to have her spayed someday. But for now, all we need is a little bowl of milk *And* a box of sand."

Alpha Lee handed the kitten to Susan and threw her arms around Jan. "Thank you so much, my precious friend! This is the most perfect gift you could have given me." And she kissed him again eagerly.

"Now, let's do have supper," Alpha Lee said. "I know you have to go back. Do we want wine with our meat loaf sandwiches? ... Maybe not. We'll try it later tonight, or maybe Saturday. You mustn't drive to T. E. and work with alcohol on your breath ... do you think?"

"Good thinking, sweet," Jan answered as he washed up for supper. "Meat loaf sandwiches? Sounds good to me."

But the surprises were not over yet. Susan's gift was a small travel iron, which delighted Alpha Lee. "Thank you so much, Susan! Now we won't have to borrow Naomi's any more. I guess all my complaining paid off ... you knew exactly what I wanted! Where did you get it?"

"Jan and I made a secret trip to the PX," she said. "We're having an affair, you know."

Alpha Lee laughed. "This is one busy guy!" she exclaimed.

Jan excused himself and went to the car again. "What's going on?" Alpha Lee asked Susan. "Surely he hasn't got something more, after all of this."

"Don't bet on it," Susan said.

Jan entered the lodge carrying a small square cake with a candle burning in the center, amid a wealth of colored-icing decorations. "Happy Birthday again, sweet!" Jan said as he placed it in front of her. "Compliments of my friend in the mess hall, Sergeant Kraskovic! ... Sarge is a hero of the Battle of Snoqualmie Pass, by the way. Now, make a wish and blow out the fire!"

Alpha Lee was delighted all over again. "Oh, Jan ... this is just great! Look at all the fancy flowers and squiggles! AND 'Happy Birthday to ...to Alpah Lee'!" She laughed . "Sergeant What's-his-name is an artist with icing ... even if he did slightly misspell my name. ... Okay," and she closed her eyes for a moment, and then blew hard on the candle, and the flame gave way to smoky fumes.

"I'll bet I can guess what your wish was," Susan said.

"Just never mind, Susan," Alpha Lee said firmly. She went to find a knife and some small plates. They ate their cake with coffee instead of wine, while the kitten lapped up the milk Susan had put down for it, and then set about exploring every part of the lodge.

"Time to go, sweet. That cake was pretty good, wasn't it? Chocolate ... my favorite. I'll give Sarge a big kiss and tell him it's his thanks from you."

"Better just wait and let me do it myself," Alpha Lee suggested. "He might punch you right on your puckered lips." And when he puckered up at the suggestion, she kissed him herself. "Bye for now, sweet Jan. Thank you so much. You sure do know how to DO birthdays."

Chapter 12

Friday: Was it possible to have two clear days in a row? The brilliant blue sky was arrayed with mackerel-scale clouds, an almost certain sign of impending rain. But then, impending rain was the rule in the Pacific Northwest. Alpha Lee decided she could not waste the golden morning light; she determined to return to the place where she had begun her painting and put on the finishing touches. Surely the bears would not be there two days in a row. Jan had been concerned when she told him of her encounter with the bear cub, and warned her to be extra careful ... not to go far from the lodge alone. "My goodness," she said, "you sound just like

Grumpy, warning Snow White to watch out for the wicked witch!"

She set up her easel and mixed her paint, green and gold. This'll only take a little while, she thought. Just a few more touches will finish it.... And the bears spent the morning elsewhere, so the work went well. The rhododen-dron bloomed beautifully on Alpha Lee's canvas, and reminded her of home, where it would be blooming now in the West Virginia woods.

In the afternoon she busied herself with the new iron Susan had given her. I never thought I'd enjoy ironing, she said to herself; but it was a pleasure to see her clothes looking the way she wanted them to. The Chinese laundry they had found in town did a good enough job at washing the girls' clothes, but the ironing was an extra expense, and Alpha Lee preferred to do her own anyway. She and Susan washed their undergarments by hand and hung them on the clothesline Jan had put up for them; they dried quickly and needed no ironing.

There was still time left in the long afternoon to do some garden work. Their little vegetable patch was thriving, as Naomi had promised, with the frequent rain and long hours of clear sun-light; the beans and carrots were up, and the tomato plants were blooming already. Twenty minutes of easy hoeing took care of the weeds. Will the bears eat our tomatoes before they're even ripe, she worried? I sure hope not.

At half-past five she heard Naomi's car at the top of the driveway, and a few minutes later Susan burst into the lodge. "Alpha Lee, *what* am I going to wear? I forgot to figure that out!" Susan wailed. "Jane will be here to pick me up in an hour and a half! Help me find something! The week just went by so fast!"

"Oh, Susan, don't panic! That sweater worked so well last week ... would you want to wear my light blue one tonight? It'd look great with your hair. And just wear your slim navy skirt. Don't you have a silk scarf ... that floral print one? That'll work, until we can find some new outfits."

"Yeah ... that would do," Susan agreed, calming down a bit. "Is there hot water? ... Oh, yeah, of course there is. I'm gonna take a shower," and she rushed into the bedroom to find her clothes.

I hope she knows what she's going to sing, Alpha Lee thought, shaking her head. She's right, the week has flown.

When Jane arrived at seven, Susan was dressed in shades of blue, and Alpha Lee was combing the long blonde hair back, where it was secured with a rubber band which was hidden by the flowered silk scarf tied in a big fluffy bow. "Susan, whatever you wear, you always look so lovely," Jane exclaimed.

"Thank you!" Susan said with honest delight. "And thanks to my fashion advisor here! Alpha Lee's a genius. You know, I didn't pack clothes with the idea of performing twice a week I just mostly brought casual things that are comfortable and not too hard to take care of. I'm just gonna have to find some way to get more outfits to wear, Jane. I hope I don't have to spend all of my money ..."

"Susan ... Alpha Lee ... I've been meaning to tell you: There's a consignment shop in town that sells second-hand clothing. Several of the well-to-do ladies in Seattle and Tacoma take their clothing there ... some-times after only one wearing. I've taken a few things there myself. Would you like to shop there someday?"

The girls both spoke at once. "Oh, that would be perfect!" Susan said.

"We'd love to! What a great idea!" Alpha Lee added. "You know, Jane, I've been wishing I could have brought my sewing machine out here. Of course that would have been impossible, I know, but ... I could have made Susan some pretty things for very little money. And I really love to sew, especially my own designs."

"Really, Alpha Lee?" Jane laughed. "Your talents are amazing, dear! I can make that wish come true without a bit of trouble: I have a portable electric machine that I never use! I never did much sewing ... just repairing split seams now and then, and I made some pillows from my needlepoint long ago, and curtains for the boys' bedrooms when I was in my 'domestic' phase. Please ... do take the machine. I'll get it out and you can pick it up right away soon. Or one of the boys can bring it out to you."

"Do you mean that, Jane? That would be just wonderful! You are a fairy godmother, Jane, really! You just keep making nice things happen. ... Now ... the next question is obvious: Can you direct me to a fabric shop? Is there someplace that sells remnants or mill-ends? We want to buy as cheaply as possible."

"I'm sure there's such a place, Alpha Lee," Jane said. "Let me check around; one of our bridge club members sews a lot, even makes quilts. She would know every fabric outlet in the area. I'll call Marsha tomorrow. ... Susan, are you ready to go? ... Alpha Lee, I'll be in touch."

"See you late, Alpha Lee," Susan said as they left the lodge. "After midnight, for sure. You don't need to wait up. Thanks for doing my hair, I like it this way." She smiled warmly and waved, and they drove away.

Alpha Lee was left with the supper dishes to clean up while the kitten played around her feet. She was finished in only a few minutes; supper had been very simple, just a salad and crackers with peanut butter, and a scoop of ice cream. We'll save the rest of the cake for when Jan's here, she had decided. That sergeant at the mess hall ...I wonder if I'll ever meet him, so I can really say thanks, and tell him I heard about the "Battle of Snoqualmie Pass" ... I sure hope Jan will take me there someday, she thought. I want to see that place ... but in the summertime! I'll just have to imagine the deep snow and awful cold.

It was only seven-thirty; Jan wouldn't be home for at least two hours, and Susan not until midnight. The sun was still high. I must take advantage of whatever time I have to get those tiresome charcoals done. I'll be SO glad when I finish number fifty! Well ... it won't be long. She took her sketch pad and charcoals out on the porch and began.

By the time the sun had set, she had finished two more copies. Forty bucks, she told herself. This is just too easy. But the mosquitoes were beginning to be annoying. Pity they spoil the evening; it's so beautiful out here with the sunset colors reflecting in the sound Another scene to be painted, she decided. I'll have to wear long sleeves and burn a citronella candle, but maybe I could do it someday.

Alpha Lee soaked in a bathtub frosted with bubbles; the bubble bath was a graduation gift from her cousin Edith. The kitten was sleeping on the bath mat beside her. She decided to call it Sunshine, and she sang the country song, "You are my sunshine, my only sunshine, You make me happy, when skies are gray ..." It was true -- the kitten would be an amusing companion on the days when it was too wet and gloomy outside to do anything much. ... Just wait till I get that sewing machine, she told herself. I'll spend some of my money at the PX for a bright lamp so I can sew even when it's too dismal to draw or paint! It was an exciting prospect.

It was half past nine when Alpha Lee dusted herself with lilac-scented talcum powder and put on her short summer pajamas ... pretty satin "tap pants" with flared legs and a matching top with pastel blue embroidery and tiny buttons down the front ... another graduation gift. She put on her short robe and combed her hair, and she thought about Jan. He'll be here soon ... and we'll be alone. Something stirred inside her. I love him, she thought for the hundredth time. I want him to ... What do I want?

She polished her nails and touched her throat with cologne, and checked the stove to make sure there was enough fire left to make coffee, in case he wanted a cup. And then she heard the car, and she ran to the door.

When Jan opened the door, he saw Alpha Lee in her scanty white robe, barefoot and bare- legged, her glasses abandoned somewhere. There was something in her eyes that held him, that answered questions he didn't need to ask. When he held her close against him, her body felt soft and unconfined, and her kiss was hungry. "Jan, my darling ... I love you so much," she whispered.

"Let me take a quick shower, honey. I'll be out in ten ... no, make that seven minutes."

Alpha Lee took off her robe and walked barefoot outside onto the pier. The moon was waxing toward full; the increasing mackerel scales were silvery, revealing a few stars ... a beautiful, romantic night, she observed. The loons called occasionally, and the spring peepers sang some-where nearby. In only a few minutes ... less than seven ... Jan came close behind her and encircled her with his arms.

She turned to face him. He was wearing only his olive drab shorts. "Mmmm ... you're so warm and damp ... like you were newborn, Jan. It feels so nice." She reached up to cradle his face in her hands, and kissed him softly, her lips parted, inviting him. His tongue tasted her mouth, and desire increased in both of them.

But there were distractions: "Let's go inside, honey," he said. "The skeeters are gonna eat us up, with all this bare skin exposed."

"Do you want a cup of coffee, Jan?" "I can fix it in a minute .."

"No, not now. All I want right now is *you*." He opened his arms n an invitation. Alpha Lee. Come here, please."

She went to the sofa and stood before him. When he embraced her, his hands touched the bare skin under her pajama top, and moved down to stroke her bare legs. "Mmmm ... Jan ... I want to lie down beside you, for just a little while ... "

"What are you telling me, sweet? Are you not afraid any more? Are you okay ... ?"

She shook her head. "Nothing's changed ... not yet, but soon. I still can't go all the way ... you know. But, Jan, I'm not afraid ... I just want to be close to you, to touch you, to love you ..."

"Come on, honey." He stood and took her hand. "Come into my room. I want those same things, too." He lifted her onto his bed, then turned his back to her and put on a condom. She turned down the eagle blanket and the sheet, and they slipped under the covers together. Moonlight fell slanting across the bed, and an owl hooted far away across the estuary, its call muted by the soft splashing of the tide.

Jan pulled her close and kissed her tenderly. "Honey ... I don't want to hurt you. I'm not sure ... how far can we go?"

"Hmmm ... about ninety-eight percent, my darling engineer," she told him.

Jan laughed out loud. "Oh, Alpha Lee ... it's fun to love you!" He tickled her ribs and she giggled and twisted away from him. He sat up beside her and unbuttoned her pajama top. "Beautiful," he breathed, stroking the soft skin, touching the hard nipples, and she moaned softly. Her breast filled his hand. "Honey ... I've wanted to do this since that day when I faced you across the counter in the jewelry store ... your cousin asked you to try on the locket I wanted to buy. You were wearing a blue sweater ..."

She covered his hand with her own. "Yes ... I remember. I knew. I knew when I looked into your eyes. That moment was the beginning for us, Jan ... and we didn't even know it."

They clung to each other, their hands exploring every secret place. He touched the silky skin between her thighs, and his fingers reached the curly pubic hair. "Alpha Lee," he whispered, "can I take your pajamas off?"

"Mmm-hmm," she answered. "Your shorts, too ... they're scratchy." And then there was just skin against skin, and pleasure beyond enduring.

"You're wearing one of those rubber things," she said. "I want to feel your real skin, love ..."

"Not this time, sweet ... that's the final two per cent. I can't make you pregnant."

"No ... but someday, I hope ..." She stroked his hard penis tenderly. "Please, Jan ... I want to feel your weight on top of me now ... Come, love, please come to me!" and she pulled at his hips until he moved to lie full length on her. Her knees were flexed and wide apart as she opened herself to him.

"Alpha Lee, every word you say cranks me up another notch. I can't last another minute, sweetheart," and he thrust against her as close as he could go without penetrating. He fondled her breasts, kissing her nipples until she moaned with pleasure, until suddenly her orgasm came and her hands pressed urgently on his buttocks. And at last Jan was overwhelmed with the intensity of his need, and his climax came like an explosion. "*Oh my God, Oh my God,* Alpha Lee ..." His voice was a ragged whisper. "I love you!"

They lay together, spent and drowsy, overcome with pleasure, kissing and touching gently. "Jan ..." she said at last, "thank you, love, thank you for that. I could die happy right now. Actually I thought maybe I *was* dying ... I felt out of this world, when it happened. Jan, do people ever die from love ... from sexual ecstasy?"

"I dunno, honey," he mumbled sleepily. "But what a way to go." After a moment he added, "Don't die on me now, Alpha Lee. That was so good it hurt ... but we've still got that hundred percent to go for, honey. ... Oh, Lord, Alpha Lee ... you're the best thing that ever happened to me. That's not very original, but I'm not up to creative speaking right now. I'm used up, sweet-heart. God, it feels good."

"How long has it been for you, Jan, since ... the last time?"

"Since I left for the Army," he said. "Seems like a hundred years ago. God, I needed it *so much,* Alpha Lee." He turned to her and kissed her again.

"Didn't you ever make love to that girl, Louise?"

"Oh, hell, no. I don't do it that way. Maybe some of the guys do, I don't know ... there's plenty of girls around to serve them ... believe me, plenty. But I can't do that; actually I'm afraid to do that. I'd *never* want to go down that road, just screwing around with anybody who acts like an easy mark. I think it'd be like an addiction, like alcoholism or something. I'd hate myself." He rolled over to face her and cupped her breast in his hand and kissed her nipple again, tasting, nibbling, and she responded urgently. "Oh, Alpha Lee, I only wanted you. There needs to be something besides just the physical act. There needs to be love ... at least for me there does. ... Honey, I need to go to the bathroom for a minute. Don't move ... stay right there, please."

He walked naked through the dark house and returned in a minute. To his surprise, he already had another erection. He found another condom and lay down beside her. She turned toward him and laughed softly. "You said you were 'used up' ... it feels like you're not used up at all, love ...not yet," and she stroked him rhythmically until he groaned deeply with the painful pleasure of desire. "Do it," she said, "do it again, love ... Yes!" He mounted her once more, pressing against her, their curly hair tangling together as he thrust again and again, penetrating only slightly ... and then with a shudder, he came again, with the sensation that all of the blood in his body was draining away in a flood of pleasure.

It was some minutes before he could catch his breath and roll away from her. "Oh sweetheart ... that was so good ... so good. ... Did I mash you ... can you breathe at all?"

"I'm breathing, love. And I'm praying my thanks to God for you, and for letting us be so close. I'm *so glad* you could do it again. It makes me feel so rich, like a queen, that I can give you pleasure like that."

But now it was after eleven; the moon was high, and their time alone was running short. "Jan, I need to go to my own room. I don't want Susan to find us like this," Alpha Lee said. "I don't know how she'd react. She says sex is 'disgusting', and I guess, for her, it must have been. I may tell her when the time is right, if I can, that we've made love. But she might be shocked or something, if she found us in bed together."

"Yeah, I guess you're right. But I hate for you to go. The normal thing, the best thing, is for us to fall asleep together, all relaxed and happy, and wake up tomorrow and do it again. Someday, sweet ... we'll do it right. One hundred percent. With interest." He kissed her again, long and deeply, and the sweet tingling began again; but they reluctantly pulled away from each other. Alpha Lee put her pretty pajamas back on, and Jan found his olive drab shorts. He walked with her to her own room, and when she turned down the eagle blanket and the pink sheet, he lifted her onto the bed and kissed her goodnight.

Chapter 13

When Alpha Lee walked into the kitchen on Saturday morning, she was surprised to find a beautifully wrapped gift on the table. Susan was still asleep; she heard water running in the bathroom and knew that Jan was up; a new fire was burning briskly in the stove. She filled the coffee pot and set the table for breakfast. Only cereal and fruit this morning, she thought. They were all going to have to cut back on the calories, she decided. I can't bear to gain back the weight I worked so hard to lose. It wouldn't have hurt Jan to gain some more, but he had asserted that he didn't want to have to buy new uniforms in a larger size at this point in his Army career.

He emerged from the bathroom in his Saturday work clothes for his shift at T. E. He caught Alpha Lee in his arms as she stretched to reach cups from a high shelf. "Morning, my favorite bedfellow!" he murmured into her ear. "Are you rested from your exertions of last night?"

"I feel absolutely wonderful, love! I think I could leap tall buildings in a single bound!"

"Great. It's the best exercise there is, isn't it? I feel pretty damn chipper myself. Maybe we could leap together ... whaddaya think?"

"Well ... let's think about it over breakfast. Maybe you should just go out and earn some 'dough' so I can make some 'bread' instead ... dammit," she said with a mischievous grin.

"Adam's curse ... Alpha Lee's curse, too, I guess," he agreed, pouring two cups of coffee. "Hey ... what's this?" Jan said, pointing at the fancy gift. "Did Santa Clause come while we were sleeping? Is it Christmas already?"

"I don't know, Jan ... Susan must have brought it in." There was a card with the gift, and Alpha Lee looked at it. "It has my name on it ...," and she opened the card. It was beautiful, adorned with flowers and sparkles. "Oh, Jan, it's from Jane! ... for my birthday! ... Look what a lovely verse! She is so nice to us!" She showed him the card.

"Well, that really is nice," he said. "You know I forgot to get you a birthday card, with all the stuff that was going on. Susan and I were right there at the PX, and both of us forgot to get a card for you. Now we'll have to wait a whole year for the next chance. ... Go ahead and open the package, Alpha Lee."

"Let me fix our breakfast first, Jan. Just a minute," and she filled two bowls with cereal and sliced a banana, half in each bowl, and poured in milk. "You can go ahead and eat while I open my present," she said.

She removed the fluffy silver bow carefully. "I'll save this to put on your birthday present," she said, and she removed the pink flowered paper. She opened the box, and there was a small bottle of perfume. "Oh, Jan ... this is so beautiful ... It's called 'Platine'. I've seen advertisements in Vogue magazine. See the little flakes of platinum floating in the bottle? This is *so* expensive, Jan. I can't believe it." She opened the ornate glass bottle and touched a drop of the perfume to her wrist, offering him a whiff.

"Nice," he agreed. "But I think I like the lilac you wear better. It's one of my favorite smells ... even before I met you, I loved the smell of lilacs. Mom has huge bushes all around the house, and it smells wonderful in the spring. ... But, yeah, this kind is nice, too. Jane likes you a lot, honey. She's a classy lady, for sure. ... Flakes of platinum, you say? What do you want to bet it's tinfoil? That'd cut way down on production costs, and the company's profits would be fantastic."

"Oh, Jan! You think like a capitalist! This job at T. E. is doing strange things to your point of view. I'm gonna believe it's platinum," she declared. She set the box and wrappings aside and attended to her cereal. "Jan, the lilac scent that you mentioned belonged to Grandmother Evans. Remember her?"

"I never met her, Alpha Lee, not even for a minute ... I only remember you saying she would fuss if she saw you riding in my car if I brought you home. You haven't mentioned her for a long time ..."

"She died last summer, when you were working down south. She'd been bedfast for a long time, and not very coherent. It was so sad. The doctor said she had cancer."

Jan was lingering over a second cup of coffee, so Alpha Lee continued: "Grandmother was very short ... shorter than I am, maybe only five feet tall, and quite round, until she wasted away from the cancer. She was born in England, but her family came to America when she was a baby. She had silvery hair that curled around her face and was pulled back in a round bun in the back, fastened with big hairpins ...

"Grandmother's Avon lady used to come to see her every two or three weeks, a big lady, Mrs. O'Haver. She always smelled so good! Mrs. O'Haver gave Grandmother samples of the perfumes, little tiny glass bottles, and she gave me a tiny little lipstick sample, a rosy pink shade, with the name 'Passion Pink' printed on the bottom in tiny letters. I was thrilled! Mother never bought cosmetics, not even face powder or hand lotion. I loved that kind of stuff. I still love things that smell nice."

"Me, too," Jan said as he rose to go. "Especially *you*. You're the best smelling thing I've ever come across." He nuzzled her neck to smell the lilac talcum powder, and kissed her just as Susan came into the kitchen, stretching and yawning, in her robe.

"Oh, for Pete's sake, are you guys at it already? You start kissing before I'm even awake. Hi, Alpha Lee. Bye, Jan, you're off to work. 'Hi ho, hi ho, it's off to work you go,'" she sang as she found a bowl and a spoon.

"Bye, Susan," Jan said, and gave her a smacking kiss on the cheek. ."You get one too." And he waved as he left them.

"Oh, Alpha Lee, you found the present from Jane! Let me see," she said. "Oh, my gosh, look at that! It's gorgeous! She asked me to deliver it to you. She said she was sorry it was late. I just told her about Jan giving you the kitten and the birthday cake from the mess hall on our way to the club, and she stopped and bought something ... I didn't see what it was ... and had it wrapped right there in the store! We were just a little bit late, but Roddy didn't mind. Isn't she sweet?"

"She really is, Susan. I wish she and Nancy could meet ... wouldn't they like each other?" Susan nodded, her mouth full of cereal.

When Jan returned home for supper, he had important news for the girls. "I forgot to tell you last night. Wonder what made me forget ...?" he asked, pretending to be puzzled. "And I forgot it again this morning. Anyway, Fred's girlfriend from Kansas, Veronica, is arriving next Saturday on the train with her mother. He wants us to meet them. Fred and Ronnie are going to be married the next weekend at the north fort chapel. How about that?"

"Oh, good! I've been looking forward to meeting her. They're going to be married so soon, Jan? Isn't that sort of sudden?"

"No, Alpha Lee, it isn't. They've been dating since maybe they were sophomores in high school, and they just got back together after a year of separation. They are ready, believe me, honey. Fred has an apartment lined up in town that'll be available Saturday, he'll be moving out of the barracks right after the wedding. ... And he asked me to be his best man, and both of you are invited to the ceremony!"

The girls were excited at that. "Wonderful! We should do something special with them, or for them, shouldn't we? Could we invite them and Ronnie's mother out for dinner or something? Maybe next Sunday evening?"

"Hey, that would be a good idea. I'll ask Fred when I see him tonight.... Now, I have a request to make. I haven't even mentioned it to Fred, but, Miss Remagen, would you please sing an appropriate song for the wedding service? I just got that idea on the way home. It'd be really nice to have special music, don't you think?"

"Sure I could, Jan. I'd love to. Hmmm ... what would be a good wedding song ... Help me decide, guys, so I can practice. They have a piano at the chapel, don't they, Jan? I wonder if Roddy would play for me ..." She wandered into the bedroom to dress for her performance at McChord. Tonight she had resigned herself to wearing the striped party dress from Kaufman's again. It would be a different audience.

Jan had promised "something special" for the weekend. He andAlpha Lee went to church at the chapel, and then had lunch at the Mess Hall again with Fred. "Is Sergeant Krakovitz on duty? Oh, that's not right! What's his name, Jan? Kraskovic! Yes ... thank you, Fred. Is he working today? I'd like to meet him and say thank you for the birthday cake."

"I'll go see," Jan offered. "I want you to meet him. He's quite a guy."

As Jan walked toward the kitchen, Alpha Lee said, "Fred, I'm anxious to meet Veronica. Jan told me a little bit about your reconciliation ... or whatever it was. I'm happy for you."

"Yeah, it's great. I think I was headed down the wrong road. When I broke up with Shirley, she gave me the damnedest cussing out I've ever had in my life! That woman could put a drill sergeant to shame. She even told me she was pregnant, which I was sure wasn't true. And a week later I saw her at the service club hanging on to another guy, just like she used to do with me. She didn't stay home and cry over our bust-up, for sure. She wouldn't even speak to me. ...

"Ronnie and I go 'way back. We started going together in high school, when she was sixteen and I was seventeen. She's a sweet kid, and pretty as a picture. You'll like her. ... Where's your friend today, Alpha Lee?"

"She stayed home today. Roddy Williamson was coming over to give her a lesson in classical guitar. She's very talented, Fred ... she'll pick it up in no time. She has a real musical gift. ... Oh, here comes Jan with ... Is that Sergeant Kras --?"

"Kraskovic," Fred muttered behind his hand. "Hi, Sarge! What's for supper?"

"Pot luck, Harris ... take a chance. ... "Well, hell-O! Is this pretty li'l thing Alpah Lee, Jan? Pleased to meetcha, Miss. How was that birthday cake?" He grabbed her hand in his huge paw and shook it vigorously.

"Hello, Sergeant Kraskovic! Thank you so much for that nice cake. It was *so* good, and *so* pretty! I was totally surprised. Jan put a candle on it, and I made a wish and blew it out, and ... who knows? ... Jan says you're making a wedding cake for Fred and Ronnie. Is it gonna be huge and tall, with lots of fancy decorations, and wedding bells on top?" she asked.

The big man laughed. "Not in my kitchen, Miss! I tole Fred he'll hafta scale down his specs, and maybe we can do business. ... Nice to have you eat lunch with us, Miss ... hope to see y'ns again!" And the sergeant smiled around his cigarette and returned to the kitchen.

"Where are we going, Jan?" she asked as they headed out of town.

"I'm gonna take you to the top of the world, honey," he said. "We're heading for Snoqualmie Pass ... the site of my only combat experience, with the infamous Lootenant Sumovich ... although that's not what the troops called him."

Alpha Lee laughed. "Yes, I remember from your letter. How far is it to Yakima, Jan? Will we drive all the way ?"

"No, not today. It's just about an all-day trip, even in a car. And there's nothin' much to see when you get there. It's just an artillery range where they can practice firing big guns ... howitzers, bazookas, stuff like that. They even have old tanks and trucks out on the range for targets"

Jan drove for several miles until they encountered a sign: SNOQUALMIE PASS CLOSED DUE TO SLIDES. DETOUR VIA RT. 169 TO YAKIMA. "Well ... damn. There goes my plan. We'll have to try it later in the summer, Alpha Lee. Let's just drive on 169 toward Mt. Rainier, and see some pretty scenery."

The land became increasingly more rugged and steep as they approached the great mountain. There was snow on several of the high peaks, and deep blue lakes that mirrored the sky. Every-where the enormously tall Douglas firs and other evergreens grew in endless forests. "I'll betcha there's plenty of bears in those woods, Alpha Lee ... big ones, grizzlies. Don't think I'd want to be lost in there. It's like we're in a different world from West Virginia, isn't it?"

"Yes, it is. I could never have imagined it. I'll have lots to write home about. It really is beautiful out here, Jan ... but I do feel like an alien. Tell me, honey, are you really ready to live and work out here indefinitely, so far from home?"

"I really am, Alpha Lee. It's a great challenge. I'll be doing what I like to do, and what I think I can do pretty well, and working with people I respect. I'll miss the West Virginia hills and my family, of course, but I can come back to visit. I think I'll be making enough money eventually that travel won't be impossible." He was silent for a long moment, and then he reached for her hand. He slowed the car and pulled off on a wide shoulder beside a sparkling blue river, switched off the ignition and turned to her. "The only thing that really worries me is that you won't be here with me. How am I gonna manage being here alone again, with you so far away? That scares me."

Alpha Lee turned away, her face somber. "I can't imagine how we will do it, Jan. In fact, I'm not *going* to imagine it. I'm not going to worry about it, or be depressed or afraid about it. I'm just going to *forget* about it, and when the time comes, we'll face it, like so many other people have had to do ... like during wartime, when husbands and wives have to be separated, some-times for years. I guess you just do what you have to do. ... Didn't John Wayne say some-thing like that in one of his movies?" she said with a wry smile. "'A man's gotta do what a man's gotta do.' And a woman, too."

Jan smiled, too. "You know, honey, I had a conversation just like this with Mona when I left for the army ... only she was the one who was afraid, and I was the one who was being realistic and brave. ... God, I hope our being apart won't end the way it did that time, sweetheart ...," and he reached to pull her close to him.

Her hands framed his face and she kissed him tenderly. "Jan, I swear to you: You are my only love, forever. There will be no letter of goodbye from me. I can't know how it will be for you ... but for me, you are my love, and that is not going to change, I swear it, no matter what."

They left the car parked safely off the road and lingered beside the river for a while, sitting on a huge gray rock in the warmth of the high mountain sunshine. The sparkling snow-covered bulk of Mt. Rainier pushed high into the deep blue sky like a living presence, listening as they talked. "Jan, this is so nice, just being alone together. You told me we would do 'something special' this weekend, and this really has been special to me! And I still have Snoqualmie to look forward to! Thank you, my precious friend. If this is part of my birthday celebration, it's been wonderful. I think birthday number eighteen takes the prize ... it's been the best ever!"

"Well, it's not over yet, Alpha Lee," he said. "We'd better head back toward Tacoma. We still have a dinner date."

"You're not serious! Jan, can we afford that? And what about Susan?"

"We're gonna afford it ... I put that in my budget a long time ago. And what about Susan? Well, I'm much obliged to her ... that twenty-buck room-and-board contribution she gave me from Nancy and the doc helped make it possible. Let's go, honey."

When they arrived back at the lodge, it was quiet and empty. There was a note from Susan: "Roddy's taking me to his house. I'm invited to the Williamsons' for dinner. See what you missed? .... Suzie R."

"Oh, Jan ... look! Roddy brought Jane's sewing machine!" She took off the cover and was delighted to find an almost-new machine with a box of accessories included. "This is a deluxe model, Jan. I can do all kinds of stuff with it ... *IF* I can figure it out. Look, a buttonhole maker, and hemmer! Now I've got to find some place to buy material cheap. We need to make some clothes for Susan for her performances."

"Does Roddy give her a clothing allowance? Seems to me she could lose money on this job."

"I hope she can break even. She loves it, and it's been so good for her. Haven't you noticed how much she enjoys it and how energized she is?"

"The thing I've noticed, Alpha Lee, is her posture," Jan said. "She walks so straight now, it makes such a difference. It really shows off her good looks and her nice figure. I guess you can't put a price on that."

Alpha Lee's smile was brilliant. "We've worked on that, Jan. I'm so proud of her. I can't wait till Nancy sees her."

"I just wonder what her relationship with Roddy is. I'd think that sooner or later, he'd make a move. She's a gorgeous and talented girl, and she's gotta be giving his band a boost. How could the guy *not* be attracted to her? Can she handle that?"

"I don't know, Jan. She hasn't mentioned a thing about him making a pass at her, or anything like that. Jane may have warned him to go easy with that kind of stuff. I did tell her just a bit about Susan's problems. She seemed so interested in Susan ... I thought she should know."

"Well ... I'm glad about that. Suz seems to be having a good time. Wonder how the guitar lesson went today. ... Well ... anyway, here we are all alone in this love nest again. What'll it be, sweetheart? Should we go to dinner, or go to bed?" he asked her with a wicked grin.

"I guess we should go to dinner, since you put it in the budget," she said. "We can go to bed when we're dead broke!"

"And still feel rich," and he kissed her, his hands caressing her breasts.

He took her to a restaurant with a small dance floor; they ate veal cutlets and the trimmings, and they danced slowly, holding each other close. On the way home, they stopped for ice cream cones, and sat in the car on a high bluff overlooking the sound, where the full moon shone on the ripples, and the pattern was repeated in the silvery mackerel scales scattered across the sky. It would rain tomorrow, surely.

Chapter 14

"Alpha Lee, Jane has big plans for us today, if you don't have something going on," Susan announced as soon as she walked into the kitchen on Monday morning. "We had the *best* time yesterday! Gee ... I don't know where to start."

"Well, start with Jane's big plans for today," Alpha Lee told her, "so I can get ready for whatever it is."

"We haven't even seen each other since breakfast yesterday!" Susan said. "That's amazing, isn't it? Roddy took me to a movie after dinner last night. We saw 'Twelve O'Clock High', with Gregory Peck and Robert Stack. It was a great movie, but sad , a war story, with Flying Fortresses. Jan would have loved it ... Anyway, we didn't get back here till you were fast asleep. I'll bet you have lots to tell me, too."

"I sure do," she said. "I was so pleased to see the sewing machine when we came back from our drive. We thought you'd be here to go to dinner with us. Jan took me to a nice place for dinner, but I guess you had a nice evening, too, with the Williamsons. ... Well, so what about Jane's plans?"

"The sewing machine is a good place to start. Since the Arte Schacke isn't open on Mondays, Jane suggested that we go shopping at some of the fabric outlets her friend Marsha told her about. In fact, Marsha is even going with us!"

"Great! I love to shop for sewing material and stuff. I even made some sketches the other day, Susan. I forgot to show them to you. We've both been so busy." Alpha Lee said. "When will we go? Is she picking us up?"

"Yes ... she said she'd come out about half past nine, unless she heard from us, and we'll go to the Seattle Art Museum first, and then to lunch. Then we'll meet Mrs. Burks ... that's Marsha ... and we'll go to the fabric shops. And then, if we have time, we'll go to that second-hand place she mentioned, where rich ladies sell their designer clothes. It's called the Encore Shoppe. Won't that be fun? Is that okay with you? Or do you have some other plans?"

"No, that'll be just fine. Sounds like lots of fun. It's not a good day for art, anyway ... too dark and wet out. If it's like this tomorrow, I'll go to the Art Schacke with you and do my charcoals in the window again. That worked fine last week."

Alpha Lee was setting out cereal bowls and coffee cups; Jan had left early for breakfast at the base. "She'll be here by nine thirty, you say? Well, let's eat a quick breakfast and get dressed for shopping. It's only eight fifteen, we have plenty of time. ... How did your guitar lesson with Roddy go?"

Susan was enthusiastic, as usual. Roddy had brought some music books and his own guitar, and had given her the first steps in classical guitar instruction. Much more complicated, of course, than the easy chording she had been doing to accompany herself when she sang popular songs. "But I'm getting it, Alpha Lee. Playing the piano makes it easier to learn other instruments. ... By the way, Roddy said he'd accompany me when I sing at Fred and Ronnie's wedding. He suggested 'Always' ... that's pretty and romantic, easy, and not too long. Do you think they'd like that?"

"Of course they will. Wouldn't anyone? ... Will you sing at *MY* wedding, Susan?" Alpha Lee asked with a twinkle in her eye.

"What? Are you and Jan gonna get married? I thought ..."

"No, no, Susan ... I'm just kidding. Wishful thinking. Someday, maybe. We had a *WONDERFUL* romantic day yesterday. I met Sergeant Krav ... Oh, gee, I can't ever remember his name! Well, THAT wasn't the romantic part! But it was fun. The cook at the mess hall who made the birthday cake. Kraskovic, that's it. He's huge, Susan ... the biggest man I've ever seen. He's going to make a wedding cake for Fred and Ronnie. ... And then we drove partway to Snoqualmie Pass, but the road was closed due to mud slides."

"What's a snow qualmy pass? Sounds scary. I never heard of that."

"It's a long story.... Anyway, we drove up into the mountains, toward Mt. Rainier, and then we went out to dinner, and we danced ... and we had a wonderful time talking about ... the future, and the past, and all kinds of stuff. Oh, Susan ... Jan is so wonderful. I love him so much. He is the best person I've ever known."

"Alpha Lee, I've heard that so many times I'm tired of it. '*The best*' -- you *always* say that. It makes it sound like the rest of us have to settle for seconds."

Alpha Lee giggled. "Sorry, Susan. I just got lucky. ... So, are you finished? We should clean up this stuff and get dressed. And I'll show you those sketches."

Alpha Lee chose a neat pale blue tailored dress from the rod in the corner, and took a pair of stockings from the dresser drawer. "Monday is washday, Susan. THAT's what I had planned. Exciting, hmmm? I'll do it tomorrow ... or the next day. I can't hang the undies outside to dry anyway. ... I think we should dress up a little to go to the museum. We shouldn't look too casual or we'll give West Virginia a bad name." They laughed. "As if it doesn't have one already. Well, anyway ... we should look as nice as we can.

Your pretty white striped dress should probably be cleaned, shouldn't it, Susan? Wear your navy suit and that scarf. Did you write to Nancy to ask her to send your graduation dress?"

"Yes, and yes. I think the Chinese laundry does dry cleaning, don't they? I couldn't possibly expect to get a package from Nancy for several more days. I hope I get it before this Friday, though. ... Oh, Alpha

Lee, I forgot to tell you something really *important* and exciting: Roddy asked if I would consider actually singing *WITH* the band!"

"Really, Susan? That's exciting! It would definitely mean some rehearsal time, though. Would you get paid more?"

"Oh, yes, he offered me an extra ten dollars for each performance. Isn't that great, Alpha Lee? *Maybe* I can afford my clothes!" They both laughed.

They heard Jane's car in the driveway at twenty past nine, and were ready. Susan grabbed the umbrella and they hurried out to the car. "This rain will dampen our day, I'm afraid, girls," Jane said. "It's much nicer to go shopping when it's dry, but we west coast folks just have to take what we get, and this is what we get most of the time! You both look sweet. Are you ready for a big day?"

"Jane, I think they're *all* big days! Thank you so much for the lovely perfume. I just absolutely love it! You are so nice to us. And the sewing machine, too! I was so happy to find that when Jan and I got home last night. Your machine is much better than what I've been using at home. I just used Grandmother's old Singer, which is a treadle machine. It's practically an antique, but I've made lots of clothes on it."

"Well, dear, I'm glad to make it available to you. Marsha will meet us after lunch, and then we'll go shopping for material. Do you have anything specific in mind?"

"No, not really, Jane ... for me it seems to work better to just see what's available and get my inspiration that way. We're going to be limited by what we can afford."

As they drove north toward the city of Seattle, Alpha Lee noticed highway signs pointing the way to SeaTac Airport. "Oh, look, Susan ... there's the road to the airport where we landed! See the planes coming in?"

"Oh, yeah!" She turned to Jane. "We landed after dark ... ten fifteen, I think it was, and it was raining ... Jan drove us to the lodge. Of course we couldn't see much along the way. We were so tired we probably wouldn't have seen much even if it had been in the daytime. It took us all day long to get here from Pittsburgh."

"Was it your first flight?" Jane asked.

"Yes. I was scared to death! But Alpha Lee just stared out the window and described everything she saw down there," Susan said. "And in less than two months we'll have to do it again!"

Jane laughed. "Why not just stay out here? Both of you have good careers started."

"But we both have scholarships to West Virginia Wesleyan College. We have to go back. Besides, I would miss my foster parents and my friends in Brick City ... wouldn't you, Alpha Lee?"

"Yes," she said. "Jan and I were talking about that yesterday. He is not looking back; he said he likes it here, and he's so involved in his job at T. E. that he wants to stay. I'm afraid I'll miss him terribly when he leaves us to come back here."

It took almost an hour to reach the museum, a sprawling gray granite building with brass Roman letters across the front, flanked by broad green lawns. There were weathered totem poles spaced in the grass, at least a dozen in all, with fantastic animal faces carved and painted on their full length. "Look at that!" Alpha Lee exclaimed. "I've seen pictures of totem poles, but I never dreamed I'd really see them!"

"They are one of Seattle's truly unique attractions, girls," Jane said. "Each one is different, made by artists from different Indian tribes in the area. The representations are symbolic of tribal totems, or animal spirits that are sacred to each tribe. This ancient art is practiced today as it was centuries ago ... handed down through the generations to whatever tribe member ... always a man, is chosen for his skill. These Indians," Jane continued, "did marvelous things with wood. The forests are all around, and they used forest products in many ways, whereas the Plains Indians that we're more familiar with, had a different environment that determined their lifestyle. People adapt. ... And that's your history lesson for today," she said with a smile. She parked the car and as they walked toward the entrance she said "Well, Alpha Lee, I think you're going to be surprised."

The rain had diminished to a fine misty drizzle. Under their umbrella the girls took a few minutes to scrutinize the totem poles that were near at hand. "Is there a totem pole for the Nisqually tribe?" Susan asked.

"I don't know. I think there's a list of them inside," Jane said. She led the girls up the granite steps into the cool, dim building. The reception area was decorated with many examples of Indian art; many of the pieces were quite ancient, most of them made of wood or shell. Jane stopped at the desk and registered, and spoke to the receptionist. In a moment Mr. Arthur appeared, smiling broadly.

"Welcome, Jane. Hello, Miss Evans! So nice to see you again," he said, grasping her hand in both of his. "We have a surprise for you."

"Hello, Mr. Arthur," Alpha Lee responded. "This is my friend Susan Remagen, she's from Brick City, too, my home town in West Virginia." Susan smiled and offered her hand, and Mr. Arthur shook it briefly and nodded with a smile.

"Jane, have you told the girls about our special exhibition?" Mr. Arthur asked as he led them into a hallway lined with paintings and sculptures.

"No, I haven't, Darius. This is your show," she said.

"Well ... during the summer months, we are showing a special exhibit of local art; that is, pieces by local artists as well as artwork that showcases the Pacific Northwest, its scenery, its people, its culture, its history. Please come this way."

He stopped in a lighted alcove beside a wide entrance. "Before we see the special exhibit, ladies, I want you to see this ..." He gestured to a painting, larger than life size, of a stern-faced Indian in full regalia, erect and imperious looking "This is Chief Seattle, for whom our city is named. He was one of the great chiefs, wise, intelligent and visionary. Please take a moment to read the plaque that describes him." While the girls studied the information beside the painting, Mr. Arthur and Jane talked quietly nearby.

"Wow," Susan said. "He must have been a real hero. Don't you wish we could have known that, Alpha Lee? I've never even heard of him."

"Well, we don't know much about any of the Indians, do we? Just what we see in the movies, when they come riding over the crest of the hill in their war paint, yelling and shooting arrows. They were individual people, and I'm sure there were heroes and bad guys, just as there are in any group of people. Maybe they'll make a real movie about Chief Seattle someday. Why not? I'd be first in line for a ticket."

As they walked into the huge gallery, they saw a wealth of art in many different mediums, much of it obviously Indian, but more modern than what they had seen in the entry way. Abalone inlaid pieces, exquisite woven baskets, carved wooden masks, bowls and other artifacts polished to a high gloss, worked leather and pieced fur, shellwork, woven garments with intricate patterns. And then, to Alpha Lee's amazement, she saw her own charcoal drawing, framed in gray weathered wood with a silvery sheen, spotlighted in the center of a collection of scenic paintings, small sculptures and drawings. She turned to Jane in astonishment; Jane just smiled encouragingly and put her arm around Alpha Lee's shoulder.

Mr. Arthur beckoned to a small group of men and women with cameras and clipboards, and they converged around the display. "This is Miss Alpha Lee Evans of West Virginia," he told them. "She has loaned us for our special exhibit this example of her work. Miss Evans is a high school graduate, who will be attending a college in her home state on a grant she earned through her art. ... Miss Evans, these people represent several publications across the state and also from other states. Would you consent to an interview?"

Alpha Lee could not speak for a moment. Then she remembered something she had heard recently: "... You are good enough to do anything that's asked of you, and more ..." She smiled her most convincingly poised smile, and answered, "Of course," and she nodded to the reporters as she had seen Susan acknowledge her audience at the Service Clubs.

There were flashbulbs in her face as they photographed her beside Mr. Arthur, who held her charcoal; there were questions that she answered as coolly and forthrightly as she could. There were pictures, too, with Jane, who was identified as "the owner and proprietor of the Arte Schacke in Tacoma, where Miss Evans' work was first discovered, and where she sometimes actually works on her pictures." And privately Alpha Lee was amused and amazed at "all this fuss over a little old gray charcoal picture copied from a postcard."

Finally the press people shook her hand and went their way with photos and notes, and Alpha Lee turned to Susan and laughed, and turned to Jane and hugged her. "Mr. Arthur wants to take us to lunch, girls, in a little while. ... Darius, give us another half-hour to look at some of the other pieces. I want the girls to see some of the Oriental art."

He nodded and smiled. "Take your time. I'll see you all at about one," and he walked off n the direction of his office.

The girls were dazzled at the collections of exquisite porcelains, carved jade in fantastic designs, painted silks, folding screens decorated with delicate pastoral scenes. There were fans with intricate stylized flowers and lustrous kimonos printed in exotic patterns, and an informational display describing the ancient production of silk. Jane, who had visited the museum before many times, was enjoying the beautiful objects again, and was delighted with the girls' awed reaction.

"Well ... what do you think? Have you seen enough to satisfy you for one day? I really hope you can come back here again when Jan can be with you. I think he'd enjoy this, too, especially seeing your work as part of the collection, Alpha Lee."

"It's almost too much to comprehend, Jane. Just incredible. Absolutely, I will do my darnedest to get Jan here. Maybe even next Sunday." She turned to Susan. "Oh, no, not next weekend ... that's when Veronica and her mother are coming, isn't it? We'll be very busy next weekend, *and* next."

"Corporal Harris's fiance from Kansas? Yes, I think you're right, Alpha Lee. Well, as soon as possible, please schedule a return trip when you can spend more time. There's much more to see on the second floor."

They ate lunch at a tea room decorated with a floral and garden motif near the museum. Marsha Burks was waiting when they arrived. She was a short stocky woman with straight dark hair pulled severely back into a bun, well-dressed and quick with a smile. "Hello, Darius , Hi, Jane! Who are these pretty girls?" And Jane introduced them, and they were escorted to a small round table with a view of the Sound. Jane suggested that the girls try the crabmeat salad, which was served with a cup of deliciously flavored clear broth and small crusty rolls with sweet butter. For dessert there were thin wedges of cheesecake garnished with fresh raspberries -- another treat the girls had never tasted.

Darius Arthur signed the check and thanked Jane for bringing the girls to the museum. "Please do come back and see us again, Miss Evans, and Miss Remagen. And whenever you have something to show us in oil, Miss Evans, I'll be delighted to see it. I'll be in to see Jane now and then, so we'll be in touch. Marsha, Jane ... have a pleasant afternoon. I'll look forward to seeing you again." He made his way to the door, and the girls followed, with Jane and Marsha.

The fabric shops were fascinating to Alpha Lee. She conferred with Susan about certain pieces, and picked out a heavy maroon taffeta that she thought would go nicely with the striped party dress. "I'll make the bolero out of this, Susan, and we'll get enough to make a sheath dress, too ... that'll make two outfits ... maybe three. Let's see ..." and she looked around at the piles of bolts. There was a folded length of lacy nylon material in almost the same color. "This is exactly what I need," she said. "Perfect! I didn't even dream I'd find it in a matching color ..."

They drove to two more shops, and Susan and Alpha Lee chose two more pieces of discounted fabric, after examining them carefully to find possible defects. Marsha wanted them to see a display of Chinese silks. "This is called 'raw silk', Alpha Lee. Did you ever see this before? Notice the slubs - the thick irregular threads in the fabric. That's a Shantung weave, named for a province in China. It's usually sold undyed like this, in the natural color of the fiber. You do know that silk is made by ugly little worms, don't you?" she asked with a grin.

Susan grimaced. "Just like spiders make webs," she said with a shudder.

"Oh, I don't care ... it's so beautiful! I've never sewed real silk before. They just don't carry it back home; it's too expensive. The people I know just buy nylon if they want something dressy. But this is much richer than nylon ... it just feels so luxurious, and the texture, the colors, the lustre, are wonderful! ... Oh ... look at this ..." Alpha Lee lost herself in an assortment of silk velvets in rich jewel colors. "Oh ... I love this ..." She picked up a piece of deep blue velvet and draped it across her arm. "It feels heavenly ... it must cost a fortune." She looked at the tag. "*Flawed*", it said. "Reduced to $4.25/yd." Alpha Lee scrutinized the piece carefully. There was a pulled thread near the selvedge that ran the length of the piece, marring the perfection of the luster. I could cut it to avoid that, she thought. This piece is so beautiful I just have to have it ... Three yards, she thought. I could make a wonderful dress with a swirling skirt ... Jan would love it. She picked up the piece and carried it to the counter, feeling just a trace of guilt at her self-indulgence. "Three and a half yards, please," she said, and pulled out the twenty- dollar bill her mother had sent for her birthday, which she had tucked away in the "secret compartment" of her billfold to save for "something special". This was definitely special, she knew.

The Encore Shoppe was another adventure. There were extravagantly glamorous gowns that were fun to look at, even though they were far too expensive and too formal for Susan's needs. But there were some pretty sweaters." Those guys just love sweaters," Susan said.

"You're not surprised at that, are you?" Jane asked, laughing. "Go ahead ... get a couple. They're only three dollars apiece. Just be sure they're not damaged." Susan chose a soft pink one and a grey angora, both with short sleeves that would be wearable in summertime. "Watch out, Susan ... the men will be wanting to *FEEL* that grey one, it looks so cuddly soft!"

There were barely-worn shoes, which Susan tried on in her size. "Black peau de soie, with high heels, Susan. Perfect," Jane said. "Now, let's find something in black to match them. Blondes look wonderful in black." There was a dress with a glittery sleeveless bodice and a sweeping skirt of layered sheer material, sprinkled with sequins. "Perfect!" Jane said again when Susan tried it on, twirling to show off the fullness of the skirt. "That would be perfect for your performance. I'll buy that one for you. My treat! Roddy will be *so* pleased!"

Susan felt a guilty thrill; despite her vow never to think about her parents again, she couldn't help but imagine what their reaction would be if they could see her in this frankly provocative costume, dancing around in high heels. "I love it, Jane! Thank you to pieces!" and Susan hugged Jane, both of them laughing with delight.

It was after six when they reached Tacoma, and nearly seven by the time Jane delivered the girls to the lodge. This was Jan's night to eat at the base and go to class; Jane offered to buy the girls a hamburger or whatever they wanted for supper, but they declined. "We have plenty of sandwich stuff here, Jane," Alpha Lee said. "You've really spoiled us today. But it was wonderful! How can we ever thank you?"

"You just have, dear," Jane said. "It was great fun for me, too. I pretended I had two beautiful teen-age daughters. What a treat!" She kissed each of the girls on the cheek.

"Jane ... I just don't know what to say," Susan said. "Thank you so much, for everything. I love the dress ... and I loved the museum, and the shopping. You are so sweet to us ..." Susan was getting misty. She swallowed hard and said, "I'll see you tomorrow.."

Alpha Lee said "I'll come, too, if it's too rainy and dark to draw inside the lodge. Bye ... and thanks again, so much!"

Jane waved and pulled away, up the driveway, leaving the girls tired but elated. The sandwiches could wait. With a shared look of total accord, they tore open their packages to re-discover their treasures.

Chapter 15

I have my work cut out for me, Alpha Lee said to herself; or rather I should say I am cutting it out for myself. She had a lustrous swath of deep wine-colored fabric spread on the kitchen table and spilling onto the floor, which she had covered with newspapers begged from the T. E. office. The pattern for Susan's bolero was pinned to the material, and she was cutting the fabric, modifying it as she went along. I can have this finished for her to wear on Friday, if she wants to ... maybe the matching dress, too; it shouldn't be difficult ... it's a simple pattern and I won't have to change it.

She had practiced sewing on Jane's electric machine, and after a few tries felt confident she could use it for all the normal stitches.. It was another rainy day out; she had gone with Susan to the Arte Schacke in the morning and again worked in the well-lighted window while Jane gave Susan a crash course in how the business operated.

"The most important thing, dear -- even more important than finding what the customer is asking for ... which you'll learn more completely by practice is to make him or her glad they came in. You are a lovely girl, and I want you to give them your very best: stand tall, smile warmly, be sincerely interested, speak courteously, and listen when they speak."

"That's what you told me about my performances," Susan said with a smile. "I guess those are good rules to apply to people ...anybody ... where-ever you meet them."

"Exactly! That's just what I wanted you to grasp, dear. Your attractive-ness gives you an advantage; it draws people to you. The rule is: Don't blow it!" She laughed at herself. "You can be a great help to me... that's why I want you to be here. You can make my customers comfortable, so they'll want to come back again. Good public relations ... I think that's what they call it. ... Alpha Lee, are you doing okay? Do you need a drink of water, or a cup of coffee?"

"Oh, thank you, Jane. Yes, I would love a cup of coffee, if you have some made. I'm just finished with my first copy, this is a good time for a break." She sprayed the drawing with fixatif and left it on the easel in the window, and she stepped into the showroom, stretching. "I get a little tired when I sit and work with my hands too long, It makes my back muscles cramp. Thank you," she said as Jane handed her the coffee.

Jane called for Chinese food to be delivered at noon, and they took turns "watching the front" so everyone had some time in the back room to eat. The girls had never tasted the exotically seasoned vegetable combinations, but they both agreed they were delicious. "And low-calorie, too, for sure! I wonder if I could cook up something like this," Alpha Lee wondered. "I don't know ... the spices aren't familiar at all. I don't think I'd know what ingredients to buy. Maybe we'll just have to get food like this at a Chinese restaurant. Thank you, Jane, for lunch. I really like this stuff!"

Alpha Lee finished her second picture before two o'clock, and drove home. Susan would walk up to T. E. and ride home with Naomi at five. Sunshine the kitten greeted Alpha Lee at the door, and she was delighted to pick up the little creature and cuddle for a while. But when she unfolded the taffeta yardage and it overflowed the table onto the floor, she put the kitten in her bedroom, since it seemed to enjoy clawing playfully at the fabric. "Sorry, little Sunshine ... we can't have snags in our pretty material."

The electric sewing machine hummed along until Alpha Lee realized she had to stop and get supper. Scrubbed potatoes went into the oven with breaded chicken pieces. There was still some peach cobbler left from last night; she would warm it in the oven when the other things came out.

Susan came in at half-past five. "Mmmm ... something smells so good! I'm glad you're the cook, Alpha Lee, I don't think I'd do such a good job. I wonder if Jan has ever eaten that stuff like we had for lunch, what was it? Chow something?"

"I think it sounded like 'chowmane'," Alpha Lee answered. "I'll ask him. It *was* good. Haven't we had some wonderful new things to eat, Susan? I never expected that when we came out here. We couldn't possibly find that kind of thing at the A & P back home, or at any restaurant I know."

Susan went to the bedroom to change from the "nice" outfit that Jane had asked her to wear into her red shorts and pullover shirt. Alpha Lee heard Fred's car come down the driveway and she hurried out the door to speak to him. Jan grabbed her for a quick hug, and she greeted them both. "Hi, Fred ... would you want to eat with us tonight? I don't pretend to be as good a cook as Sergeant Kras ... whatever ... but you're invited."

"Hey, Alpha Lee ... that's the best offer I've had for a long time! But...I have an appointment to meet my landlord in ... about 30 minutes, it looks like," he said, checking his watch. "I've gotta grab a hot dog and hustle downtown. Can I have a rain check?"

"Of course. Did Jan tell you we want you and Ronnie and her mother to come for dinner next Sunday? I hope that'll be possible ...?"

"Yeah, I do too! Thanks a lot. Jan's been tellin' me you're the best cook he's ever seen ... except his mom, of course," he added with a wink. "Sure, I'll tell Ronnie and Loretta we're invited. I want you to meet them. ... See you in a while, Jan. Bye, Alpha Lee."

"Another great down-home meal!" Jan said, after enjoying his supper. "I should walk to work, to lose some of those calories. Next week, Alpha Lee ... nothin' but bread and water!"

"Sure, sure," she agreed, dismissing the suggestion. "We'll see you after while, Jan. I'm going to get back to the sewing machine." A quick kiss and he was gone.

By Friday morning the bolero was finished, and the matching maroon taffeta dress needed only to be hemmed. It had been fitted closely to Susan's figure and was very glamorous, with only narrow straps instead of sleeves, so that her well-tanned arms and back were bare. The bolero had short sleeves and fastened at the center front with a small flat bow; the sides were cut away at a sharp angle from the center, exposing an enticing area of bare skin above the low neckline of the dress. Susan was delighted, if a bit self-conscious in such a daring costume. "Alpha Lee," she said as she observed herself in the mirror, "is that me? I look like a movie star."

"Yes, you do," Alpha Lee said with satisfaction. "I wish I could do your hair in a glamorous upsweep, but that's beyond me. Maybe we can have it done at the beauty parlor sometime. ... Now, take off the dress and I'll hem it. It'll only take a half-hour, that skirt is so slim. I don't think you could walk very comfortably if it weren't for the slit."

Susan hurried to dress in her more modest outfit for her workday at the Schacke, and waved goodbye as she walked out the door.

When Jan arrived home that night after class, he found Alpha Lee cutting another piece of fabric ... this time it was the sheer nylon in the same shade as Susan's sheath dress and bolero. "You're really into this business, aren't you, honey? Funny .. Mona was good at sewing, too. She made a lot of clothes. And her friend, Gail, planned to make a career of designing clothes. Did you get Susan's dress finished so she could wear it tonight?"

"Yes . Oh, Jan, I wish you could have seen her! She looked wonderful in that ... like a real professional performer. A star. And she just glowed ... I know she felt beautiful. ... Would you like a cup of coffee, sweet? ... Or anything?"

"Yeah, I'd like 'anything'," he said, taking her in his arms. "How about a communal shower?" he whispered in her ear.

"Ooooh, Jan," she murmured. "You could probably talk me into it ... but I don't want to get so involved ... just yet. Please, let's not go too fast. It almost scares me, what we did last Friday." She pulled away gently, and he sighed.

"I guess it was just too good to last," he said with exaggerated pessimism. "Well, then, just give me a cuppa coffee," and he slouched on the sofa.

"Tell me what you did today, love," she asked as she poured his coffee.

"Not much, Alpha Lee. Life in the U. S. Army is dull, dull, dull. I drove a six-by-six -- that's one of those big trucks I showed you ... remember? I drove one of 'em to the central commissary for mess supplies for Sergeant Kras; and then after lunch I helped Herndon fix the lights on one of the older buses. I think the battery cable must've come loose while it was running at night, and the driver didn't get it stopped in time, and both headlight bulbs burned out, along with a bunch of other stuff. The driver said the heater fan sounded like a siren, so I think the generator must have run away without the battery to keep the voltage down."

Alpha Lee was listening with a bewildered look on her face. "I never heard of such a thing. Those big trucks sure are different from regular cars like I can drive. How do you know about all of this stuff?"

"Well ... I did work with heavy trucks back home, you know ... when I hauled coal. Not just driving 'em, but learning about how they worked. You're right, there are some big differences in these military vehicles, but it's pretty elementary ... you catch on pretty fast to the special features, because they have to follow basic engineering principles. Fred and Sarge know all about six-by's ... they've been driving them and fixing them a hell of a lot longer than I have, so I've learned from them. This problem today ... thank goodness it doesn't happen very often, 'cause it's pretty complicated and expensive. It can mess up a lot of electrical stuff. We got it pretty well ironed out by three o'clock, and then I fixed some flat tires ... Are you still listening, hon? Or am I putting you to sleep? I *told* you it was boring. Aren'tcha glad you're not in the army?"

She laughed. "Yes! My days are much more interesting than that! ... if today was typical. But, love ... I am impressed with your mechanical genius, even if I don't know much what you're talking about."

Alpha Lee had put away her sewing tools and the material by the time Jan finished his coffee. He took his shoes off and was stretching out on the sofa when she suddenly came to him and lay down on top of him, surprising him with kisses. "Hey, what was that crap about let's not go too fast?" he asked as his hands stroked the length of her body.

"Pay no attention to that girl at the sewing machine," she whispered. "She's weird."

Chapter 16

The Sunday pot roast was cooking slowly in the oven with potatoes and carrots, a bay leaf and an onion, when they heard Fred's car in the driveway. The extra extension had been put in the table, which was set for six; Alpha Lee was thankful that there had been enough plates and silverware for "company". Naomi's grandfather must have had large fishing parties here long ago. Or Frank and Naomi had just stocked the place for their renters.

Jan went to the door with Alpha Lee. "Hi, buddy," he said to Fred. "Where'd you find these pretty women?" Alpha Lee saw a tall suntanned blonde with long hair like Susan's, and a warm smile. The older woman was shorter and a bit heavy, attractive behind heavy glasses, her hair colored an unlikely shade of strawberry blonde, and the longest red-polished nails Alpha Lee had ever seen.

"Jan, Alpha Lee," Fred said when they were inside, "meet my best girl, Veronica Benton, and my next best, her mother, Mrs. Loretta Benton, from Hays, Kansas. They grow 'em pretty back in the Sunflower State." There were handshakes all around.

"We're so glad to meet you," Alpha Lee said. "Did you get rested from your long train trip?"

"Yes, thanks," Loretta Benton replied. "Alpha Lee, is it? I think Fred said you're from West Virginia, way back east. I've never been there. Do you live anywhere near Winchester? A friend of mine moved there."

Alpha Lee exchanged a glance with Jan and laughed. "Not really," she said. "Actually, I've never even traveled in Virginia. Brick City, where I live, is in central WEST Virginia."

"Mom, it's a different state!" Veronica said with an embarrassed laugh. "Alpha Lee, something smells wonderful! Fred says you're a famous cook. How'd you get so good at it at such a young age?"

"'Famous'?" Alpha Lee laughed. "That's a bit much! I just help Mother a lot back home, and we just fix ordinary stuff. Learning to use this strange old stove was interesting, though. I'm still not totally confident about that. Fred says you're going to college to be a teacher, is that right?"

"Yes ... elementary. I've wanted to do that since I was in second grade, and fell in love with Miss Walker. I wanted to be just like her. I still do. I've just finished my second year, so I guess I'll transfer my credits and finish my degree at College of the Pacific." Then she discovered Sunshine, the kitten, who had stretched her paw out from under the sofa to grab at Veronica's foot. "Oh! Look at this! Is this yours, Alpha Lee?" She picked up the kitten, petting and tickling its underneath. "Oh, you precious thing! What's her name, Alpha Lee?"

"She is my Sunshine, when skies are gray," Alpha Lee said, singing the words. "The skies are gray a lot out here, Ronnie. This little critter is good company when I'm here alone. Sunshine is my birthday present from Jan."

"I love her! Fred, this is what I want for *my* birthday," she said, turning to him with a smile.

"Well, I just *might* be able to afford somethin' like that, Ronnie," and then aside to Jan, "D'you suppose Millie has any more kittens to give away?"

Susan came in from the pier, where she had been practicing with her guitar, and was introduced to the guests. "You girls could be sisters!"

Fred exclaimed. "Jan, do you have a camera? How about takin' a picture of these pretty women?"

Jan asked them to go back out on the pier, with the sound and the forests as a backdrop, and he took pictures of everybody; then he asked Fred to take a couple of him with Alpha Lee and Susan. "You can send a print back home in your next letter, Alpha Lee," he said.

After Alpha Lee had served pineapple upside-down cake and coffee, she suggested that Jan and Susan show the guests around the place while she cleaned up the dinner dishes. Then they all piled into the station wagon and drove along the scenic highway overlooking Puget Sound, with a view to the east of majestic Cascade Mountains.

On the following Saturday afternoon, Jan and Fred stood together in their dress uniforms in the sanctuary of the north base chapel with Captain Durbin, waiting for the bride. There were two dozen or so guests: Charles and Jane Williamson, the Professor, Sergeant Herndon and Sally, and even Sergeant Kraskovic and his petite girlfriend Lou Anne. Alpha Lee and Susan, in their best freshly pressed summer dresses, sat beside Naomi. Roddy was at the piano, playing romantic popular music.

And then Roddy began to play the traditional wedding march. Six-year- old Cheryl Herndon, dressed in the lacy pink dress she had worn for Easter, walked slowly up the center aisle, scattering pink petals from her mother's roses, and behind her came Veronica on her mother's arm. She was wearing a short white cotton embroidered dress and a shoulder-length veil fastened to a ribbon headband, and she carried some of Sally Herndon's pink roses wrapped in netting. She looks like a princess, Alpha Lee thought; and Jan's thoughts were a jumble: ... Someday, I hope ... Will my bride look some-thing like that? ...'Five foot two, eyes of blue' ...? When? And where ...? He felt a lump in his throat.

Mrs. Benton gave away her daughter into Fred's keeping and came to sit with Alpha Lee, dabbing away her tears. The traditional words were spoken; the traditional prayers were said; Fred took the gold band from Jan and slipped it onto Ronnie's finger. And then Susan took her place, facing the bride and groom, and with Roddy playing accompaniment, she sang,

"I'll be loving you, always
With a love that's true ... Always ... "

As she sang, she took Veronica's hand and Fred's hand in hers, and sang directly to them, looking into their eyes. This isn't a performance, Jan thought; it's a blessing from Susan's own heart, given in the style that's her very own.

After the service, there was Sergeant Kraskovic's beautiful cake, which was somewhere between the lofty architectural creation Fred had teasingly requested and the Sergeant's "li'l ol' cake" he had declared was all he could produce. He had cadged two of his K.P. crew into helping serve the cake and punch, and the little reception was entirely satisfactory to all present ... a gift to the honored couple from the Williamsons and Professor Heiden.

Jan took the evening off from work at T. E., since Fred would not be there either. The newlyweds had been waved on their way toward a short honey-moon somewhere near the sea, and Jan had asked Mrs. Benton if she would like to go with him and Alpha Lee to see Susan perform at McChord Field Service Club.

Fred had told Jan earlier that his prospective mother-in-law was a real estate agent, long since divorced from Veronica's father, who had carried on an affair with his secretary for a time. After the divorce, he and the girl had married and moved to California, and Veronica had not heard from him since, except for one birthday card when she was twelve. She had sent a graduation announcement to that address, but it was returned; so her father appeared to be lost to her. Veronica had told Fred that her mother had been seeing a man regularly for the past two years, and she thought Loretta would probably marry him now that she, Ronnie, had left home.

Tonight would be Susan's last performance playing her guitar and singing during intermissions only; she had rehearsed with the band several times, and would be their regular vocalist beginning with next Friday's performance. But tonight she was perched on her high stool as usual, singing sweet love songs and the occasional upbeat number. She had just finished singing "Mona Lisa," which had been a recent hit for Nat King Cole, and when the applause ended, she stepped down from her stool, and looking over her audience, she took the micro-phone and said, "Roddy has told you that I'm from a little town in West Virginia. Do you guys know where that is?" There was some laughter, some scattered clapping, a few loud "No"s. "Well -...," she said, "it's *WEST* of Virginia, for Pete's sake!" That brought more laughter and applause. "Are there any troops here from West Virginia?" she asked, searching for response. One serviceman held up his hand and called out, "*ME!*"

Susan clapped her hands and asked, "Would you please come up here with me, soldier?... and a big sunburned fellow with a sandy crew cut pushed away from his table, grinned at his companions and sauntered to the stage to stand self-consciously beside Susan. "What's your name, soldier?" she asked, holding the mike up to him.

"Corporal Calvin Moneypenny, Ma'am," he said. There was some quiet laughter at his unusual name.

"Great!" she said. "There's lots of Moneypennys in my home county. Where are you from, Corporal?"

"Braxton County, Ma'am," he answered.

"Okay," she nodded, "... Been there. Corporal, do you know what day next Monday is?"

He thought for a moment, and then his face lit up. "That's West Virginia Day, Ma'am, June twentieth!"

"*RIGHT!*" Susan cried. "The banks'll be closed in Charleston, and Brick City, where I come from, and Flatwoods!"

"Well, ma'am ... I don't think there is a bank in Flatwoods," he said. There was a bit of laughter.

"You're probably right," she agreed. "Well, Corporal, can you sing?"

"Ummm ... well ... maybe just a little, ma'am ... hillbilly music mostly."

"Great!" Susan said enthusiastically. "D'you know the words to the West Virginia state song, Corporal Moneypenny?"

He grinned. "Oh, sure. Everybody back there does. We learned that in junior high."

"Okay, Corporal, let's sing it for these nice folks who couldn't find West Virginia on a map of the United States to save their souls... Ready?" and she struck a few chords

"Oh, the West Virginia hills, How majestic and how grand With their summits bathed in glory, Like the Prince Immanuel's land ... "

Jan and Alpha Lee were watching, fascinated, as Susan effortlessly held her audience. He squeezed Alpha Lee's hand and grinned at her. Even Loretta Benton seemed to be enjoying herself. When Susan and the corporal finished the chorus, she kept strumming as she said, "Come on up here, Jan ... Alpha Lee," and she beckoned insistently. "Private First Class Jan Short and his girlfriend, Alpha Lee Evans, are my friends from back home. Jan's from Fort Lewis ..." There were scattered '*boo!'s*, which Susan dismissed with a scolding frown. "Come on, Jan ... Alpha Lee. Sing a chorus with Corporal Moneypenny and me!" And they made their way to stand beside Susan, and they sang in four-part harmony the final lines, with Jan trying to sing bass:

"Oh, the hills .... Beautiful hills How I love those West Virginia hills --

If o'er land or sea I roam, still I think of happy home,

And my friends among those West Virginia hills!"

Loud applause filled the room as the quartet finished. Susan stood on tip-toes to kiss the corporal on the cheek, which made him blush and fidget a bit, and brought more cheers, then he shook hands with Jan and Alpha Lee, and made his way back to his table, grinning broadly and acknowledging the applause of his mates. Roddy had returned and was thoroughly delighted with Susan's impromptu performance, giving her a quick hug as she turned to leave the bandstand amid loud applause and whistles. "Honey, you are the *BEST!*" he whispered in her ear.

Chapter 17

Another rainy Monday; I won't do the washing today, Alpha Lee said to herself. After breakfast she settled herself at the kitchen table with writing paper and pen to write to her parents. It had been nearly two weeks since her last letter to them, and there was much to tell. Susan was ironing and listening to music from Jan's clock radio, which she had borrowed from his room. She sang along with the popular songs. "When I finish this, I'm going to write, too, Alpha Lee. I need to write to Ben. He'll think I've forgotten him."

"Well, have you? Maybe you're falling for Roddy," Alpha Lee suggested.

"That's silly, Alpha Lee. Roddy is just a very special nice friend."

"Hmmm ... 'very special nice friend'. That doesn't sound very far from a crush to me," she replied. "Do you have a rehearsal today, Susan?"

"Yes ... this afternoon. He said he'd come out and pick me up." Pause. "Now, Alpha Lee, don't get any ideas. This is strictly business.

Actually, it's really exciting! Singing with the band will be entirely different. I wonder if it will be hard to do ..."

"*NO*, Susan, it won't. Anything that has to do with music, you just pick it up right away. You have a gift."

"Gee, Alpha Lee, thank you. You say such nice things. ... You have some gifts, too, you know ... you're a wonderful artist, and a great cook, and the best friend anybody could hope for." Susan picked up her finished ironing and came over to hug her. "This has been the *BEST* summer I've ever had in my life."

Alpha Lee smiled winningly. "You betcha!" she said, using one of Jan's favorite expressions.

"Tacoma, Washington June 20, 1949

Dear Mother and Daddy,

Tomorrow we will have been here just one month. It has been a great adventure! How can I ever thank you enough for letting me come? We've had such an exciting week! Last Monday we went to Seattle with Mrs. Williamson, the lady who runs the art gallery. She took us to the Art Museum." Alpha Lee tried to describe their experience -- the totem poles, the interesting art, the thrill of seeing her own work on display, being interviewed by the reporters; she would send the clipping. "Yesterday (Sunday) was Jan's free day, and so we borrowed a boat and went fishing in the estuary. We caught some flounder. They are very flat, and have both eyes on one side because they lie on the bottom, partially covered with sand. I fried them in butter and sprinkled them with lemon juice, and they were so good! Much better than the frozen fish we get at the A & P. Jan likes to fish; he and his brother used to fish in the West Fork, but fishing in the salt water in the sound is very different.

. "We went to church at the base chapel yesterday ... that made two days in a row we were there, because we went to the wedding of Jan's friend Fred on Saturday. His girlfriend from Kansas came up here to get married, and they will live off-base in an apartment. She is very nice; she was going to college to be a teacher, and her credits will transfer to the college here."

I have only eight more copies of the charcoal drawing left to do now, thank goodness. I'm so tired of it! (even though it's made me a LOT of money!) But I've been doing some oil painting with the oils Jan gave me for graduation. I have one picture that I will send you, or maybe just bring it with me when I come back, of the pine woods and rhododendron near our cabin. Last week I started a portrait of a half-Indian lady who lives near us; this lodge was built by her grandfather a long time ago. She has very interesting features and I asked her to pose for me. The portrait is almost finished; I can do the rest without her having to pose again, I think. Mrs. Williamson asked me to let them exhibit it at the Seattle Art Museum in their special collection of 'local art', and I guess I'll do that. Jan and I plan to go up there next Sunday so he can see the museum, and I'll take it along. I'm looking forward to going there again ... we didn't have time to see everything last week when we were there.

"Susan is having a wonderful time. Just a minute ago she said, 'This has been the best summer of my life.' (Mine too!) She has been a big hit at the service clubs where she sings with a band. I thought maybe she would just want to stay here and make a career of doing this ... she is a wonderful performer and the troops love her. But she says no, she still wants to come back with me and go to college.

I have made two outfits for her to wear when she performs. The lady who runs the art gallery, Mrs. Williamson let me use her electric portable sewing machine! It's great. Someday I want one of my own. It's lots of fun to sew for Susan; she is so beautiful, she looks good in anything.

"I must tell you: Jan has been so good to us. He is a true gentleman. He is so kind and generous! He is doing so well in his electronic work that he is planning to return here after a couple of weeks' visit at home in August and September, and just continue to work for this company. They have offered to pay his tuition at the college here for night classes. I will miss him a lot.

"I wonder how your big garden is doing. We planted a little one here ... tomatoes, lettuce, onions, carrots and beans, and some kind of squash I've never heard of. Everything grows really fast here because there's so much rain, and when the sun comes out, it is very clear and bright, and the days are very long.

"I miss you! I hope someday you can come out here and see this wonderful country. The mountains, the ocean, the pine forests ... it's beautiful. I look forward to hearing from you soon. James, too.

Love, Alpha Lee"

Susan had to borrow a page of Alpha Lee's stationery for her letter; she marked out "ALE" at the top and printed her own initials, "SER", for Susan Elaine Remagen, above the markout. I wish my name were McAllister, she thought wistfully.

"On the shore of Puget Sound, June 20, 1949

"Dear Ben,

I wonder how your summer is going. Is your summer school class hard? I would think so. College Chemistry sounds awfully hard to me; I'm glad I won't have to take that for my major. I'm having the best summer I ever had in my life, Ben! I have been playing my guitar and singing during intermissions for a small band at the service clubs near here, at Fort Lewis on Fridays and McChord Field on Saturdays. It is *so* great when those servicemen clap and cheer for me!

"The scenery is so beautiful, Ben. There is a huge mountain with lots of snow on its crest that is just in front of you no matter where you are... that's Mt. Rainier. (I think it's named for all the *rain* that we have! Most days it rains.) Our lodge is right on the edge of Puget Sound. Do you know where it is? Look at a map of Washington state, the north-western corner. Our back door opens onto a pier, and there are all kinds of sea birds around.

We were almost invaded by bears one night! Two little cubs came right up onto the porch beside our bedroom window! Alpha Lee and I were scared to death ... but Jan takes good care of us. "Jan and Alpha Lee are really in love, Ben. The way they look at each other ... it's like they're just drinking in the sight of each other. It's better than a movie to see them together. I *LOVE* them both so much.

"Alpha Lee has been making beautiful clothes for me to wear when I sing. She dresses me like I was her favorite doll! The costumes she makes make me feel beautiful, Ben. Alpha Lee thinks she is dumpy and fat, which is silly ... she really looks pretty since she has lost a lot of weight and has fallen in love. *THAT* just lights her up.

"I have a new job, five days per week ... I'm sort of a receptionist at the art gallery in town. A lady named Jane Williamson (mother of the band leader, Roddy) runs the place, and she is *SO NICE* to us. She treats us like a really loving aunt, or something. She takes us out to lunch sometimes and we have the *best* meals ... wonderful sea food and strange new things like Chinese food. She took us to Seattle last week to the big art museum there. Alpha Lee's charcoal drawing of our lodge was on display there, and there was a crowd of reporters with flash cameras who interviewed her, and her picture was in the newspaper! She's busy all the time making copies of the charcoal and painting with the oil paints that Jan gave her for graduation. She's getting really good at it. She's painting a portrait of our neighbor, a part Indian lady, and it is beautiful ... it's going to be displayed at the Seattle art museum too.

"Ben, I really do miss you a lot. Please write to me. I love it here, but I'll be glad to get back home to be with you, and with Nancy and Doctor John. You have been so sweet to me, to put up with my craziness. I think I have a lot to make up for when we get together again.

"I hope to hear from you *soon*, Ben. IF you can find time between your Chem. homework and helping your dad with the animals, please write and tell me all about your summer.

XOXOXO Susan"

Susan enclosed a clipping in Ben's letter, a photograph taken by a reporter at the McChord Field performance last week. She had been surprised when the flash bulbs popped, and amazed to see her own picture in the Sunday entertainment section of the newspaper. Roddy brought the paper out when he came to give her her weekly guitar lesson. She planned to ask Naomi to save their Sunday paper for her, so she could send a clipping to Nancy, too.

She wrote a letter to Nancy, telling her much the same news as she had reported in the letter to Ben, and thanking her fervently for sending the clothes she had asked for ... her white graduation dress, a billowy flowered summer skirt she could wear with the new pink sweater, and her gray suede dress shoes. Nancy had surprised her by sending a new dress: sheer white cotton sprinkled with navy blue polka dots, sleeveless to expose her suntanned shoulders, a full skirt to float as she danced. There was a narrow red patent belt to buckle around her waist.

"Oh, Alpha Lee ... isn't this just darling? I love it!" she gushed as she whirled in the rippling skirt. "Everybody picks out the cutest clothes for me. I really do feel like a star, with my own wardrobe staff!"

By noon the rain had stopped, and the sun was beginning to burn through the lingering mist. Alpha Lee had renewed hopes of getting her hand washing done, after all. Lunch was peanut butter and jelly sandwiches and a glass of milk, with an apple for dessert. Roddy arrived shortly after, and came in for a moment's visit before taking Susan to rehearse with the band in the Williamson garage. "D'you want to go fishing after rehearsal, Susan? We could start at the cove behind our house, and I could deliver you back home over the water."

"Well .. that sounds like fun," she said. "I don't know how to fish, Roddy, You'd have to teach me that. Will Jon be along, too?"

"No. Jon has a part time job with the newspaper, so he'll be leaving right after rehearsal. And Mom's off to the beauty parlor this afternoon. Suzie, do you know that Ames Brothers song 'Till Then'? I'd like try that soon."

"I've heard it ... I don't know all the lyrics, but it's a pretty song, and sounds really easy."

"Okay, we'll work on that. We need to do some more upbeat stuff, too. ... Alpha Lee, what're you up to? Is that a portrait you're working on? *HEY!*, it's Naomi! ... only prettier. That's beautiful. Is that a native costume you're putting on her?"

"Yes, Roddy. She let me borrow it so I could finish this at home and she wouldn't have to pose again. She said this robe belonged to her grand-mother ... she wove it herself ... she even dyed the wool with plant pigments. It has faded some over the years, but I can brighten the colors to make it look like new ... maybe."

"That's really special, Alpha Lee. Will you sell the painting, or is it for Naomi to keep?"

"I don't know, Roddy. I'll offer it to her, or if she'd rather have the money, I'll just split the price with her ... *IF* there's a buyer."

"'*IF* there's a buyer'? Are you kidding? Mom would probably like to buy it herself. It'll be beautiful, Alpha Lee. You really do great work."

The painting was a seated portrait, with Naomi's face partly turned to the left. Her distinctive Indian features were accented with slightly enhanced coloring, and her erect posture was characteristic. She wore a heavy necklace, a woven lacework of abalone, jasper and obsidian beads that Naomi had allowed Alpha Lee to borrow for the painting; it also had belonged to her grandmother. Her arms and fingers were adorned with highly polished incised copper bands, and in her right hand she held a carved wooden staff ornamented with eagle feathers. Alpha Lee had decided to call this work "Nisqually Princess".

"Thank you, Roddy! What a nice thing to say. The next thing I have to do ... and I want to get it done pronto ... is a wedding portrait of Fred and Veronica. Jan took pictures of them after the wedding, and I can paint from those, as soon as he gets them developed. That will be our wedding present to them." She laughed. "Maybe they'd rather have a can opener."

"Are you kidding? ... Of course you are. A real portrait painted by a real artist? Now *THAT'S* something special. I'll bet couples with hand-painted wedding portraits have fewer divorces! ... Well, Suzie, are you ready to go? Maybe you'd better bring along some baby oil, or wear long sleeves if you're gonna go fishing with me ... you could get a sunburn. You'll need sunglasses, too ... it'll clear off soon, and there's a hell of a glare out there on the water when the sun shines." Susan hurried to find the oil and a long-sleeved blouse, just in case, and then waved goodbye to Alpha Lee, and the two of them left, taking along the letters to be mailed from the Masseys' mailbox.

By late afternoon Alpha Lee had the figure finished, with the wool robe restored on canvas to its original colors, as she imagined them to be. Interesting, she thought, that these people who were so close to the earth had clothing that required colors made from earthy pigments: the ochres, the umbers, the siennas. And black formulated from charcoal made from wood from the forests that sustained them. ... All that remained to be finished was the background of the picture. She thought maybe a mountain range backdrop would be appropriate, with the black- green points of faraway pines below the snowy slopes ...

Jan would not be home for supper tonight; his evening class started early, so he ate at the Mess Hall on class days. By the time summer was over, he would have accumulated nine credits from his night classes at the College of the Pacific. His year in the army had not completely delayed his college education, as he had expected it would.

Roddy delivered Susan to the pier shortly after six o'clock, with a catch of flounder and two rainbow trout. Susan's face was a bit pinker than it had been when she left, and she was excited about her success with fishing. Roddy was invited in for a Coke, but he said he'd better get back home with his share of the fish for his mother. "If you don't want to fix them for tonight's supper, you can just keep them on ice, they'll be fine for tomorrow, and the next day, too. ... Suzie, could we have one more rehearsal maybe on Thursday evening? Just to kind of polish the performance and finalize our song sequence? I think we're gonna have a great gig on Friday."

"Sure, Roddy. I'll be working at the Schacke that day ... D'you want me to ride back to your house with Jan after supper, or ..."

"No, no ... just plan to have dinner with us, and ride home with Mom when she closes .. okay? I think Mom'd like to keep you all the time," he told her with a grin. "I'll see you then, honey." He kissed her cheek and waved. "Bye, Alpha Lee," he said, and returned to the boat.

"Just a nice special friend, you say?" Alpha Lee said skeptically. "You're gonna break his heart, Susan. Suzie."

"Oh, Alpha Lee, cut it out! I couldn't break anybody's heart if I tried. You've been reading too many of those books."

"Just you wait and see, sweet sister."

The painting would wait till tomorrow to be finished, she decided. She went out to the pier to clean her brushes and her hands with the offensive turpentine. The bears hadn't been seen again; maybe the turpentine fumes repelled them.

"We'll save the fish for tomorrow night," Alpha Lee said. "I think Jan loves trout; I'll fix that for him, and we'll eat flounder. I like it a lot, myself don't you, Susan? Maybe with baked potatoes, and a nice salad. And for tonight, Susan, just for the two of us, how about an omelet with some bacon bits? I have a nice early tomato that Naomi gave me, and some green onions."

"Ooooh, you're making me hungry. Sounds wonderful! Is there any more of the wedding cake left for dessert?"

"Maybe just a little. We can split it. Wasn't it beautiful? That great big sergeant sure is a wonderful baker."

"He is so cute! I love to hear him talk. He sounds so funny. He says, 'Nice to see you'ns,'" Susan said, mimicking the sergeant's Pittsburgh Slav accent in a deep voice. "'You'ns! ... Or 'Yu'ns' ... Where does that come from?" she asked, giggling. "He and Lou Anne make an odd looking couple, don't they? She's so tiny ... he could pick her up with one hand." Susan was setting the table while Alpha Lee assembled eggs, vegetables, bread to be toasted.

Alpha Lee said, "Wasn't that a great reception? Better than a lot of rich folks' big productions, I'll bet. I hope Fred and Ronnie had a wonderful honeymoon, overlooking the sea, even if it was only one night. ... And I hope they'll really live happily ever after." Alpha Lee smiled dreamily. "And I hope we can be good friends with Ronnie. She's so pretty and so nice."

Jan came home a little after ten, tired after his long day. Susan had showered and gone to bed. Alpha Lee opened the door for him and kissed him gently on the cheek. "Hi, honey," he said wearily. "Is there coffee?"

"Yes, I just made a fresh pot for us. You look tired, Jan. Hard day?"

"Oh, yeah. We had a minor accident at the driver training today... although maybe it wasn't so minor to the guy who broke his leg. He'll be out of commission for a while, I'm afraid. Some of these jokers are so careless ... they don't pay attention. You *HAVE* to give those big trucks and tanks your full attention, or they'll bite you."

Sunshine the kitten jumped up on the sofa beside him and batted at his hand. "Hi, li'l critter," he said, scratching its belly. "You know, honey, we'll have to leave Sunshine with Naomi, or somebody, when we leave for West Virginia. I'm sorry, but I don't think we should try to take her with us on the plane."

"I know, Jan. Maybe Ronnie would keep her."

"When I come back, I'll bring her back here," he said. "She'll be a reminder of my sweetheart who's so far away from me."

Alpha Lee put aside her hand sewing and came to sit close to him on the sofa. "There --," she said, "Now I'm not far away. Oh, Jan ... we have two beautiful months together ahead of us. The happiness I feel now, the memories that we'll always have, no matter what ... I think we'll be all the stronger for it, and better able to do whatever we have to do when we can't be together." She reached up to caress his face, touching his lips with her fingertips.

Jan wrapped his arms around her and pulled her close. He kissed her deeply and stroked her body, shoulder and breast, hips and thighs, until they both felt the awakening of that sweet familiar need. "I want to take you to my bed, Alpha Lee. I want you right now ...," he told her urgently. "But I know we can't. Dammit."

"Soon, Jan, love. I promise: just a few days ... one hundred percent."

Chapter 18

When Jan arrived at the Tak Elek plant on Thursday evening, he found a note on the engineering bulletin board, as was usual; the Professor was meticulous about keeping in touch with Jan and Fred, since he didn't see them often due to their late work schedule. He opened the envelope and read the Professor's note:

"Jan ... If there is any possible way for you to get three or four days' leave, we need you to fly to California and consult with the engineers and buyer at Lockheed in Burbank. They are very interested in the V-3 box, but really want to talk with someone from here who can discuss the temperature ranges and new features, and you know them better than anyone else who could possibly go. They have also discussed a new type of connector they would like to use, and you could assure them that we can make that change.

"We anticipate the trip would take three days ... one to fly down (airline schedules attached) ... one day with them, and fly back the next day. Of course we would pay all of your expenses, and pay you well for your time. We'll even throw in enough of a bonus so you can buy a sport coat and tie, and you can borrow a small briefcase from me that I hardly ever use. Jan, this is important to us. We would like for you to do this as quickly as possible, next week if at all possible. Please let me know."

Jan scratched his head. They want *ME* to go to California? Burbank... I think that's near Los Angeles . Wow ... several hours by plane, probably with a stop in San Francisco or somewhere. Let's see ... we're finishing a class tomorrow, and it'll be a week before the next one starts ... *MAYBE* the Captain would give me a three-day leave ... but what would the girls do? Would they be all right if I left for three days?

He thought about it: I really *WOULD* like to make that trip for the Prof ... and for *ME*. I could talk to the engineers down there ... I have met several engineers from Boeing, and didn't have any problem communicating with them; they were all nice guys. ... But would Alpha Lee and Susan be okay, if I left them alone here for that long? Even if they had the car? ... Jan decided he would talk to Alpha Lee tonight, after he got home from work.

He buried himself in his assigned job: 'bread-boarding' a newer version of the V-3 box that the Professor had sketched for him to make. He had found the new parts on the Professor's desk with a note asking him to try to get this done tonight. Why can't the Professor go? he wondered. Maybe he's going to see the wheels in the Pentagon about the contract T. E. is bidding. ... This was for a two-place night interceptor fighter that needed the new communications box.

The Professor had told him that the fighter contract would probably be won by Lockheed, but the commercial plane engineers were a different group from those in the fighter plant. He and Fred clocked out at ten, and he left a note for the Professor that he would check tomorrow about the leave and let him know immediately. The evening was chilly, and he smelled the pleasant aroma of wood smoke as they neared the lodge ... he knew that Alpha Lee was probably keeping a fire in the range to heat water so he could take a shower. She greeted him with a kiss that made him tingle, and offered him a cup of coffee, which he accepted gratefully. He waved at Susan, who was sitting by the fireplace strumming her guitar.

They sat down on opposite sides of the table; there was a plate of peanut butter cookies to tempt him, fresh from the oven. They each took one and smiled at the familiar old flavor that everybody's mom used to make. "What's new with my famous artist, sweetheart? Did you go in to see Jane today?"

"I sure did, Jan," she said. "I finished three more copies of the charcoal. I'm actually seeing light at the end of the tunnel! And speaking of light ... the light is so much better there in that window at the Schacke. There's only four more to do to finish the contract on the drawings. We looked at the print she made today ... it really is nice, Jan. She's talking about making a hundred copies! Is there any possible way that a hundred more people are gonna want a copy of that little old gray picture? She's going to advertise it in some art magazine for other dealers, and I'll get some money for each copy ... *if* anybody else buys them!" she said with a wry smile. "Jan, I could never have dreamed things would turn out this way!"

Jan smiled warmly. "That's great, honey. It doesn't surprise me any; I always knew you were a very talented lady. Boy, I sure am glad you came out here ... this never would have happened with you back in Brick City. ... What *WOULD* have happened to you if you'd stayed back home, Alpha Lee? And what would have happened to me, here all by myself?"

"I think we'd have been two lonely people, Jan. Unless you persuaded Louise to come and keep you warm!" She flinched as he pretended to punch her. "My summer would have been a waste of time, I'm afraid, some baby-sitting, --. maybe working as a waitress at the Coffee Shoppe. It's just beautiful, Jan, how our lives seem to be guided in this way. ... Are you finished with your coffee? Let's go sit on the sofa."

"Right!" he said. "Lots of good things have happened on that old sofa," he whispered in her ear, and he put his arm around her shoulder and they settled themselves close together.

He was silent for a long moment, considering the right time to tell her about the trip the professor had proposed. The time was now, he decided. "Alpha Lee, the Prof at T.E. wants me to try to get a leave and make a trip to Lockheed, in Burbank, California ... that's near Los

Angeles," he told her. "I would be gone three days ... flying down and back would take two days, with one day for the consultation. D'you think you and Susan would be okay if I did that the first three days of next week?"

"Oh, Jan, that sounds so exciting! Of course we'll be fine here." She snuggled close to him. "I'll miss you like the dickens, love, but I'm glad the professor values you so much that he trusts you to do this on your own. ...But Jan, does it take a whole day to fly to California? We flew out here from Pittsburgh in one day. I didn't think it was so far."

"Honey, I checked the schedules, and the best flight takes about four hours to San Francisco, and then I would have to change planes and fly another four to Los Angeles. It's about twelve hundred miles down there."

"Wow! Well, you have to do it. Don't you *want* to?" She looked at Jan. He was nodding yes. "We can get along. Susan has a ride to work, and I'll have the car to run errands. They will pay for the trip, won't they?"

"Oh sure ... they'll buy the ticket and give me advance money for the hotel and meals. The Prof's note even suggested there would be a bonus to cover a new sport jacket. I really don't have much in the way of civvies to wear, and I can't go on a business trip in uniform. I'd have to get a couple white shirts and a tie, too. I guess I could wear my G.I. brown shoes."

"And Jan ... you'll get a chance to see San Francisco ... maybe even see the Golden Gate bridge from the air. Mmmm ... I wish I could see that sometime. Can I go along, honey?" she added wistfully.

He smiled. "I really wish you could, Alpha Lee. Maybe someday. You know, I never dreamed I'd be asked to take a business trip for them, Alpha Lee. I just thought I'd be working on the drawing board or in the lab. But traveling for them, too --yeah, it *IS* exciting. You girls will be okay?"

Susan had been practicing some complex rhythms on her guitar and hearing only half of the conversation across the room. But at Jan's question she rose, hung her guitar on its peg and fastened him with a stern look. "Jan," she said indignantly, "you're not living with a couple of thirteen -year-olds here! We're *both* grown women, and women have been able to fend for themselves for a very long time ... usually better than men! Like during the war ... *lots* of wars! When they had to take care of their families all alone. Some of them even working in the factories, too. We'll be just *fine* here by ourselves. We're not even afraid of bears any more! Are we?"

"Well ...," Alpha Lee hesitated, only half joking. Then she brightened. "I guess the rule is, if bears come around, go jump into Jan's bed!"

Captain Ross's initial reaction to Jan's request for leave appeared to be a forbidding scowl; but then he said, "So what are you going to do with three days' leave, Short?"

"Sir, the company I'm working for part-time wants me to make a business trip for them ... to Los Angeles."

The Captain whistled. "LOS ANGELES ? That's a hell of a long trip! Short, you *DO* plan to come back after your leave, don't you?" He grinned. "I'm not gonna have to send the MP's after you, am I?"

Jan didn't hesitate. "Oh, no, sir. I'll be out of town for those three days, but my girlfriend won't be along, so I'll definitely be back."

The captain was stern. "Are you telling me that if she *were* along, you'd go over the hill, Private?" he barked; he was enjoying grilling Jan. But then he became serious. "Short, I don't normally involve myself in the off-duty life of my men, but I've heard about your girl friend ... the young artist. My wife tried to buy one of her charcoals, and the shop owner told her the full set was sold out ... so we'll have to take one of the printed copies. My wife said it is really a beautiful picture ... several of her friends did get the hand-made copies. ... Well, you have a nice trip... and a safe one ... and if the return flight is delayed, be sure to call in so we can cover your butt. Please ask the First Sergeant to step in, Short, so we can get your leave papers ready tonight."

The Nisqually Princess portrait was finished and ready to be delivered to the Art Museum as promised. Alpha Lee had changed her mind about the background; the scenic concept, she decided, would distract from the figure, which was itself rich with detail. So she set her princess against a simple monotone of burnt ochre, shading it just enough to give a dimensional feeling. The shining dark braided hair was shown off to advantage by the warm background.

"Honey, this is your best ever," Jan said, admiring the picture. "Have you shown it to Naomi?"

"Yes ... I took it up to show her, and I returned the stuff she lent me ... the staff, the neckpiece and the robe. I was sort of surprised at her reaction, Jan. She just didn't say much at all. She studied it a long time, but she just didn't say much. I asked her if she wanted to keep it, and she couldn't even decide on that. I told her I'd promised it to the museum, at least for a while. I made that promise before it was even finished; and she didn't seem to mind that. I guess I'll have to ask her again if she'd prefer to keep the picture, or to get half of what it brings. She seems to need some time."

"I hope the museum buys it," he said. "I think it'd be a shame for it to be hidden away at Frank and Naomi's house where nobody would ever see it."

"Well, I wouldn't begrudge it, Jan. She's been so good to us ... to you, and to all of us. And this represents her heritage, which, I think is more important to her than she lets anyone know. If she wants it, I'll be glad for her to have it. ... Now the next project for me is the wedding portrait of Fred and Ronnie. Did you pick up the photos?"

"No, I haven't ... I forgot about them. I'll do that tomorrow, honey."

"Jan, would it be possible for us to take the painting up to Mr. Arthur on Sunday, before you have to leave for California? I'd like to get it where it belongs as soon as possible." She was putting away the dishes while Jan drank the last cup of coffee at the table. She sat down across the table from him. "And besides, I want you to go to the Art Museum so I can show you all the beautiful things we saw! Do you think we could do that on Sunday, Jan? We could leave early. We could skip church this time."

"Hmmm - yeah, I guess we could do that. I must go somewhere and see if I can find a jacket. I'll try to do that tomorrow; I'll take a long lunch. And I'll stop by the PX and pick up those pictures."

"Do they sell clothes at the PX, Jan? Maybe the price would be better there than in town."

"Only military stuff, Alpha Lee, except special order, and I don't have time for that. I guess I'll have to venture downtown to one of the men's stores. I'll bet the prices will blow me away. Wonder where Roddy buys his stuff?"

"Well, you can be sure that *he* wouldn't be blown away by any prices," she said. "If you can't find anything, maybe we could look around in Seattle. ... Would there be any stores open on Sunday, do you think?"

"I dunno ... it's a big city; there might be some place open. Damn... this is the hardest part of the whole business, just getting gussied up for the Lockheed people. ... Well, honey ... I hate to tell you this, but I'm bushed. Give me one of those earth-shaking kisses, and I'll drag myself off to bed. ... Unless you have a better idea ... I hope?"

"I have ideas, my sweet love ... Oh, Jan, I wish I could stop thinking about what we did last Friday. You're right .. I think it's addictive. I never dreamed it would go so far." She spoke in a rush, her eyes closed, her cheeks flushed pink. She stood and walked to the window, deliberately putting space between them. "We'd better just say good night, and wait till another time for .. other things. I'll try to wait up for Susan; it'll only be another half hour or so till she'll be bouncing in here, full of excitement about her gig. She sure does love it." Jan followed her to where she stood and his arms encircled her from behind. She quickly turned to face him, and his embrace lifted her off her feet. He held her high and buried his face in her bosom. "Ohhh -- Jan, Jan." she breathed, "I love you so much!" When he set her on her feet, their kiss was almost too intense to deny.

Susan just turned over and fell asleep again when Alpha Lee got up to dress on Sunday. Roddy wasn't due till eleven for her guitar lesson. She had told Alpha Lee she'd offer him a light lunch ... a sandwich or salad. "If I'm lucky, maybe he'll take me out for lunch!" she had said coyly.

"I'll just bet he would. You two are getting as thick as thieves," Alpha Lee said, yawning, as they had climbed into bed the night before.

"'Thick as thieves'? Now what kind of a crack is that?" Susan said, pretending to be insulted.

"Thick as thieves," Alpha Lee repeated. "Night, Susan."

Jan and Alpha Lee were in high spirits as they traveled north toward the city of Seattle. "I love my sweet sister Susan," Alpha Lee said, "but I love spending time alone with you even more! ... Ooohh, isn't that a wicked thing to say?"

"Well, if you hadn't said it, I would have," Jan answered. "We sure had a great day last Sunday and I'm figgerin' to repeat it!"

As they approached the exit to SeaTac airport, Jan remarked, "We'll be back here early tomorrow morning, honey. You won't have any trouble finding your way back home, will you? I might be able to get the Professor to take me to the airport."

"No, I want to do it, Jan. ... Tell you what: Why don't you just drive into the airport from here, and show me where to turn to park, and to get to the terminal, so I can know my way around?"

"Good idea. We'll just do a dry run, that's what we'll do," and he signaled for a turn and took the SeaTac exit.

"Okay ... now I do feel more confident, Jan. Maybe Susan will come along tomorrow. But if she doesn't want to, I'm sure I can do it alone. ... Oh, Jan ... I never dreamed I'd say such a thing! Here in a huge strange city. Driving around Brick City and even to Harrison didn't do much to prepare me for this. I'm getting so brave and so self-sufficient. I know I won't have ANY trouble getting started in college next fall. I had been sort of worrying about that."

"I'm proud of you, honey, you aren't a shy little girl any more; you're becoming a strong woman. Like I told you: Coming out here has been great for you ... and for Susan too. For this soldier, it's been better'n Christmas!"

When they arrived at the Seattle Art Museum, Jan was as impressed at the totem pole display as Alpha Lee and Susan had been. "Wow! Those things are really something, aren't they? Amazing! Where's the one from the Nisqually tribe?"

"I think it's on the other side, Jan. There's a chart inside that tells about them. I must tell Naomi about this. I wonder if she's ever been here."

When they entered the museum, Alpha Lee asked for Mr. Arthur, and he appeared in a few minutes. He smiled with pleasure at seeing her. "Miss Evans! I'm so glad you came back. This must be Jan? Good to meet you, Private Short," he said as he shook Jan's hand when Alpha Lee introduced them. "Did you bring us something today?" he asked, indicating the wrapped package Jan was carrying.

"Yes," Alpha Lee told him. "This is 'Nisqually Princess', painted from life. Our neighbor is a descendant of Chief Leschi."

"*REALLY?* Come," he said, "Let's take it into my office and unwrap it. We'll have to frame it appropriately," and he led them down a dim hallway. He closed the door behind them and quickly removed the wrapping. "Ohhh, Miss Evans ... this is very beautiful! ... Yes ... an actual squaw robe , the colors are so warm you want to touch it. Are these authentic artifacts ... the neckpiece and the staff? ... Yes, I was sure they were. Oh my, this piece is just lovely! ... I don't think I have ever seen anyting so authentic. Now, what are the terms? Can I make you an offer?"

"Well ... I guess you can, yes," Alpha Lee spoke slowly, taking Jan's cue. "I'm not sure it's really for sale, though ... I offered it to Naomi, who posed for me. If she decides she would prefer to have money instead of the picture, ... yes, I'll sell it to you. ... Although I would really like for Jane to have a chance to display it at the Arte Schacke sometime," she added. "She hasn't even seen the finished picture. I owe her that."

"All right," he said. "Why don't you two go ahead and tour our collection while I confer with some of my directors? And then in a couple of hours, we'll get together and I'll take you to lunch, and maybe we can come to an agreement." He smiled brightly and opened the door.

Alpha Lee was delighted to show Jan through the museum, beginning once more with the imposing portrait of Chief Seattle, and proceeding to the 'local art' exhibit where her encounter with the reporters had taken place beside the display of her charcoal drawing. They spent a short time in the Far East Room, where she had enjoyed the Oriental masterpieces, and then they ventured upstairs to see what they could find.

There were many maritime paintings of sailing ships tossed on dark waves, whalers attacking huge whales in the open sea, and raging sea battles with cannons blazing as tall masts came crashing down. There was a documentary collection on the explorations in search of the fabled but non-existent "Northwest Passage", with looming icebergs menacing the fragile wooden ships and another section devoted to antique artifacts used in the salmon harvest both by native fisher-men and the later

European- American entrepreneurs who made salmon fishing and shipping a major industry in the northwest. There were historical photographs from the time when Seattle became the jumping-off place for gold-seekers bound for the Klondike in 1897, provisioning for their quest in the shops of the city ...

The time passed all too quickly. It was half-past twelve when they returned to the lobby, where Mr. Arthur was waiting. "There you are!" he said. "Did you find something interesting on the second floor? That section is my favorite, I think. I'm a native of Seattle, and the city's history always fascinates me."

Mr. Arthur took them to lunch at a teahouse where they ate teriyaki at a small table in an exotic garden setting, and drank fragrant tea from little cups that had no handles. He offered Alpha Lee $500 for her new painting, "Nisqually Princess", which astounded her so that she could hardly answer. "Well! ... Umm ... Mr. Arthur, how would it be if we left the painting with you for a while, and I'll ask Naomi again if she wants to keep it, or if she'd prefer a share of the price. Would it be possible for you to photograph the picture, so I could have something to show my parents, and maybe for Naomi to keep if she decides to sell it?"

"Certainly, Miss Evans. I'll do that. Actually we have extensive photo files with photos of all of our pieces for insurance purposes. I'll frame the painting first, and then I'll take a picture and send you copies. You can call me collect, or just come up again, and we'll finalize the deal. I do hope your friend will agree to sell it ... it's a truly beautiful piece, quite unique ... we have no other single portrait paintings of Indian women."

He drove them back to the Museum in his luxurious black Lincoln, and, after they had searched for and found the Nisqually totem pole, which Jan and Alpha Lee Alpha Lee quickly sketched on a notepad, they left the Museum to attempt shopping in downtown Seattle. Jan found a service station that was open, and he pulled in and asked directions to the business district. He bought a city map. "This may come in handy in the future, Alpha Lee. If I'm gonna live up here for a while, I could use a map of Seattle." He studied the map for a moment and then drove slowly down the street looking for street signs. Suddenly he realized he was in a left turn only lane. "Damn! I didn't want to go that way ... well, I guess I'll have to go around the block," and he made the turn.

In only a moment, Alpha Lee exclaimed, "Oh, Jan, look, what is that? There are racks on the sidewalk. Can you stop? This place is open!"

"What the hell?" The sign said, "ELI'S EMPORIUM -- Something for Everybody!", and it looked like the shop was most of a block long. Jan saw the familiar triple-ball symbol that identified the place as a pawnshop... but this one was monstrous. There were people everywhere including sailors in their brilliant whites and many GI's. It reminded Jan of a carnival. There was even a parking lot next to it, and Jan drove in and found a space.

"This may turn out to be a lucky accident, Alpha Lee," he said. "See? There are clothes for sale here! Who'd have guessed it? Wouldn't it be something if I found a coat here in a pawn-shop? That'd be something to tell the Prof!"

Alpha Lee was busily shopping, looking over the jumble of wares that seemed to include everything imaginable. There were the usual cases of jewelry, including diamond rings that made her wonder if they represented broken hearts, weddings that never happened, marriages that went wrong. ... "Oh, look at this, Jan! This is exactly what I need!" She picked up a small brass lamp with a shade that was not very clean. "I could clean this up, and use it on the table when I'm sewing ... maybe even painting, and it would be a big help. Let's see, Jan, it's only four dollars! There's a little dent in it here, but that doesn't matter. I'm going to get it!"

Jan was looking through a rack of men's suits and jackets, not very hopefully. Alpha Lee put the lamp on the counter, telling "Eli" (or one of his clerks) she'd be back to pay for it shortly. She joined Jan and quickly dismissed several suits, many of which were out of style, faded, not too clean. "What size, Jan? About a 38, maybe?"

"How'd you guess? That's what I wore when I graduated. It might still be the right size."

She continued to sort quickly through the racks, checking sizes on the ones that seemed good enough for a second look. "Hmmm, this one is nice-looking, Jan," she said, pulling out a light blue jacket with a tweedy slubbed finish, flecked with tiny silvery gray threads. "Single-breasted... that's good. Yes ... this one is a size 38, Jan. Try it on."

"You have a thing about blue, don't you, Alpha Lee?" he teased, but he did try on the jacket, and looked in the mirror. A dark fifty-ish man with a bushy moustache appeared. "That's a very nice coat, don't you think, sir?" he asked, smoothing the shoulders. "Silk tweed, made in Hong Kong, hardly worn ... only $29.95. Very stylish."

"It's a good fit through the shoulders, Jan," Alpha Lee said. "Do you think the sleeves are a bit too long?"

"No, I think the price is a bit too long, Alpha Lee!" Jan said indignantly. "Thirty bucks for somebody else's jacket! That's way too much." He hastily started to take it off.

"I can give you a good deal on this fine coat, sir," the salesman said in an ingratiating tone. "It fits you so well ... it appears to be tailor-made for you. You'd have a hard time finding anything else anywhere at a comparable price, sir. But I'll tell you what I'll do: I'll give you your choice of a necktie, absolutely free, if you decide to take it. You won't regret it, sir!"

"I regret it already," Jan grumbled. "It's just too much."

"How about *two* neckties?" Alpha Lee said sweetly. "Jan looks so good in a bow tie," she said to the salesman. "It would be a good idea to have a choice ... don't you think, Jan?"

He hesitated, looking into Alpha Lee's deep blue eyes that, at this point, he thought, looked distinctly conspiratorial. "Well ... what do you really think, Alpha Lee? You don't think it looks too flashy, or something? Or too shabby?"

The salesman looked downright injured. "I beg your pardon, sir, this is one of our finest jackets; it looks like new. It probably cost three times this amount when it was purchased. This is a tremendous bargain ... especially if I give you *two* ties at no additional price. Maybe the lady would like to choose?" He flashed a brilliant smile at Alpha Lee, who caught the ball and returned it in kind.

"Oh, yes! Please, Jan ... let me find you some nice ties to go with it," and she went busily about her task, looking through the display of hundreds of ties. Jan had a feeling that she had won this round. His clothing allowance from the professor was fifty dollars, and he had bought two white shirts and two pairs of socks in Tacoma; he still needed a pair of slacks. "Eli's Emporium"seemed to be his best bet at this late date, but he hated to be conned into buying by the likes of this sleazy salesman.

Alpha Lee brought her choices for Jan's opinion: the long tie was a silvery gray silk with regimental stripes of navy bordered with narrow lines of maroon and white. The bow tie was an intricate paisley, gray, red, sky blue and black. He had to admit they were good-looking, and went well with the jacket. "We'll take it, then," he told the salesman, eager to get out of Eli's. But he still needed a pair of slacks.

"Jan, " Alpha Lee said hesitantly, reading his mind, "do you have pants to wear with the jacket?" She knew he was thoroughly tired of dealing with the salesman. "Let me measure you" She found a tape measure and wrapped it around his waist. "Thirty-one," she said. "Do you know the length? What are your uniform pants?"

"Damned if I know," he answered testily. Nothing would do but he must try on a pair of dark gray wool slacks. They were too long.

"Seven fifty," the salesman said. "That includes free alteration, sir."

"Give us credit for the alteration," Alpha Lee said. "I'll do that at home; we don't have time to wait."

The salesman was a bit flustered, but rose to the occasion. "Five dollars?"

Jan looked at Alpha Lee, and she nodded slightly. Jan knew she was satisfied, and he was desperate to finish this transaction and get out of Eli's Emporium. "Done," he told the salesman. The jacket, the slacks and the two ties were bundled into a paper bag and the cash was exchanged. Alpha Lee paid for her lamp with her own money; Jan hadn't the energy to argue with her.

"Ohhh, honey --," Jan sighed as he closed the car door, "Am I ever glad to have that over with! Thanks for helping me find something decent. I sure am glad you were with me. That guy .. that place ... gives me the creeps. I hope I never have to darken their door again. ... Can you really shorten those pants tonight?" he asked doubtfully.

"Of course. I've shortened pants at home for James. It won't take long with that neat hemmer on Jane's machine. ... Oh, Jan, I knew you were dying to get out of there. But we really had a pretty successful shopping trip. You will look *so* nice! I haven't seen you dressed up nice since the Junior-Senior Banquet! Except in your uniform, you look wonderful in that." She smiled happily at him, and he felt much better.

"How about a Coke ... or maybe some ice cream? ... before we start home?"

"That sounds great, Jan. ... Do you need to look at this map?"

They found their way out of downtown Seattle and followed a broad highway that seemed to lead straight toward a wide expanse of water. "Where are we going, Jan?" Alpha Lee asked. "Are we going to cross that huge lake? Or is it a river mouth, or ...?"

"No, this is Lake Washington, Alpha Lee. The bridge ahead there is the world's longest floating concrete bridge. It's built on pontoons ... I guess it must have been cheaper than sinking piers down into the lake. I've heard of it, and you can find it there on the map ... but I've never driven across it."

"How can you have a floating concrete bridge, Jan? That doesn't sound possible! Even if it's full of air holes like Swiss cheese, how could concrete possibly float?"

"Well, it displaces the water ...," Jan started to explain.

"Never mind," she said. "Don't even try to convince me. Rocks displace water, too, but they don't float."

But they did drive across, and the bridge stayed firmly in place. Jan said, "*if* we continue on this road, we'll end up on top of Snoqualmie, Alpha Lee. I really want to take you there some-time, but I'm afraid we don't have time to go that far today. It's past three o'clock now, and we still have a long drive home. What do you think?"

"I agree, Jan. I have a pair of pants to shorten," she said. "Let's just go on home ... it's been a busy day. But I do want to see the famous Snoqualmie Pass. Let's make plans to do that ... the very next pretty Sunday. Just the two of us. Maybe we could take a picnic ..."

Chapter 19

Jan's Monday morning flight from SeaTac was scheduled for a 7:30 a.m. departure, which required an early trip to the airport. Susan chose to sleep in on this day off from her work at the Schacke.

At the airport, Jan and Alpha Lee shared a tender goodbye kiss, then he headed for the check- in counter carrying a small suitcase he had borrowed from Susan, and Professor Heiden's brief-case. The plane taxied from the gate on schedule, but had to wait near the runway for a short time while another plane landed. When the pilot received clearance, Jan was amazed at how quickly the big DC-4 accelerated on the runway with the power of four roaring engines. He heard the whine of the pumps as the landing gear and flaps were retracted, and soon they were flying above the clouds. He immediately recognized Mount Rainier and its sister mountains off to the south. The pilot made an announcement on the intercom: their flying time to Portland with a nice tailwind would get them there on time ... and the weather was beautiful along the way. As the flight progressed, the pilot spoke again, naming Mount Rainier, Mount St. Helens, and finally Mount Hood, as they passed in sight of each peak. He said they would be on the ground in Portland only twenty minutes to add more fuel and a few more passengers. The weather from there to "San Fran" promised to be clear.

South of Portland, they flew very near Crater Lake; the beautiful deep blue lake, nearly circular and six miles wide, which had been formed a millennium ago in the caldera of an extinct volcano. The pilot continued with his commentary: Crater Lake was more than 6,000 feet above sea level, and was located in a large national park bearing its name; they might enjoy visiting there some day, and Jan vowed to do just that. He had brought a camera with him, and was busy taking pictures as they passed. He was happy that he had splurged and bought color film.

"We'll be landing in San Francisco in about thirty minutes, sir," the pretty stewardess told him as she tapped him gently to wake him from a nap. "You have time for a cup of coffee if you would like." When he nodded, she poured a cup for him from her cart.

Jan sat with his face close to the window as they flew south past the Golden Gate Bridge, the Oakland Bay Bridge, and the skyline of San Francisco, with countless ships of various sizes tied up at what seemed to be a thousand docks -- passenger liners, ferryboats, Navy ships ... he was sure he saw a battleship, an aircraft carrier and several destroyers steaming through the waters of the huge bay. Jan was fascinated at the sight.

The San Francisco air terminal was enormous. Jan had to hurry along, carefully noting the signs to the various gates, to catch his flight to Burbank on a different airline. His connecting flight was ready to board, and, looking out the window, he saw a giant Lockheed Constellation sitting at the gate ... the first time he'd ever seen one so close. He thought this was one of the most beautiful airliners, with three vertical fins adorning the back of the fuselage.

The pilot's first announcement after takeoff was terse: "We may have some bumpy weather near Los Angeles, folks. There's a weather front moving in now. I expect we'll be flying in clouds the last hour or two, and landing in a gentle rain with low clouds. We'll try to pick the smoothest way through, and we should be landing pretty much on time.

You might want to keep your seatbelts fastened loosely. Our flight crew will be serving you lunch as soon as we reach our cruising altitude."

Jan enjoyed his lunch in bright sunshine and smooth air as they droned south. He gazed at the mountains off to the east, wishing he had a telephoto lens for his camera. As they approached Bakersfield, the pilot's weather predictions proved true ... they flew into a large cloud mass, and Jan felt for the first time the plane's uneven flight as it flew through alternating updrafts and downdrafts. All he could see through the window was fog, with streams of water moving by as they flew through showers. The pilot talked to them frequently, assuring them that they were nearing the airport, and would be on time when they landed, in a light rain.

Alpha Lee was tense as she very deliberately navigated the route Jan had indicated for her. Once out of airport and on the highway, she felt more sure of herself, heading for home. It was still early; the sun was streaming down brilliantly. This is a good day for growing things, Alpha Lee thought. Maybe we can pull some little onions from the garden today.

Susan was up when she returned home, enjoying a day-old doughnut from the dozen they had bought yesterday. "Can I have one, too?" Alpha Lee said as she picked up the coffeepot to see if there was any left. She poured the remaining coffee into her cup.

"So our soldier boy is flying somewhere up there in the wild blue yonder on his way to sunny California, is he? I'll tell you, Alpha Lee ... he's really doing well in that company, isn't he? They must think a lot of him. He's only been working there for a little while, hasn't he?"

"Yes, but he's solved problems for them, and come up with ideas for improving their products. They can see he is really talented in electronics. I'm so proud of him, Susan ... he is ..."

"... '*the best!*' Yes, Alpha Lee, I know, I know. 'It seems to me I've heard that song before ...,'" she sang. "Hey ... I could sing that at the club, couldn't I? It's a great song!"

"You sure could. I love it. ... Susan, you know what I'd like to do while Jan's gone?" Alpha Lee asked.

"Go out with somebody else?" Susan guessed. "Naaah ...NOT THAT."

"Right!" Alpha Lee declared. "No ... seriously, Susan. I have a favor to ask you. Would you pose for me? I want to paint your portrait."

"You're kidding," Susan said. "Why do you want to paint *my* picture?" she asked, honestly puzzled.

"Because you are beautiful. Because I'd love to do it for Nancy and Dr. John. Because I love to paint with oil. Because ..."

"Okay, okay. Well ...," Susan said, "I guess so. Why not? Sure. When I get famous, I'll use the portrait you painted on my concert posters." She smiled brilliantly. "What do you want me to wear?" Suddenly she was apprehensive. "You don't mean ... in the nude, do you?"

"No, of course not," Alpha Lee said with a chuckle. "No ... I want you to wear your white striped dress that Nancy bought you at Kaufman's, and I want you to hold your guitar. I have it all figured out in my mind. And I'd really like to get started on it today, while the light's good."

Naomi had reserved a room for Jan near the Burbank airport, and the Professor had told him just to take a cab: "It's only a buck, and you'll be tired enough when you get there. The offices of Lockheed are nearby, so you can grab a cab over there in the morning. You have an appointment at 9:30 with Tom Stilesman, the buyer. He'll come out to the lobby to meet you and take you around."

As Jan checked in at the hotel, he asked for directions to a restaurant. The room clerk told him of three or four not far away, and suggested one nearly across the street. "They really have good seafood there, if that's your pleasure," she said. "The little place down a block is open for breakfast about six. They make their own fresh doughnuts, too."

He thanked her and carried his bag to his room. Looking around, he discovered the window overlooked one end of the airport runway, and he spent a few minutes watching planes landing, nearly all of them airliners. The telephone rang, and he answered. "Jan, this is Tom Stilesman at Lockheed. How was your flight down?"

"Just great, Mr. Stilesman. The weather was perfect most of the way, and we got in right on time."

"Good. Jan, I've had a meeting added to my morning schedule, so I won't be able to see you tomorrow at all. Could we meet tonight for an early dinner? I can't stay out late, but I do want to meet you. I could pick you up in about twenty minutes. By the way, dinner down here doesn't require a jacket and tie ... this is California, you know. Bill Sykes is the engineer who wants to see you tomorrow ... so when you come in just ask for Bill."

Their dinner meeting was a pleasant one; Jan judged that Tom was several years older than himself; he had gone to college in Michigan, and was a former Navy pilot who had done his primary flight training at Jackson's Mill, near Jan's home, and they had many things in common. Tom drove them to his favorite seafood restaurant in Pasadena, near the Rose Bowl stadium, and Jan was back in the hotel by nine, his stomach content after a dinner of broiled flounder stuffed with crab meat. He turned on the television and watched part of a play, and then the news. He marveled at a television in a hotel; back home in Waters and in Brick City he didn't know *ANYONE* who had a TV. and here they had them in hotel rooms.

On Tuesday morning Jan had an early breakfast at the little restaurant with fresh doughnuts ... and for the first time experienced the miracle taste of orange juice that had been squeezed from tree-ripened oranges. He was amazed at the difference from the canned juice he was familiar with at home and at the mess hall. Back in his room, he turned on the television; he had a half hour before time to get in a cab ... and he listened to the news. The violence in Korea was worsening. He had to think for a minute to remember where Korea was; but there on the TV was a map right before his eyes. Someplace you don't ever hear of, he thought.

Jan reflected for a moment about what he might expect at this meeting. He had not been at all intimidated by the prospect of meeting the buyer; he felt that the buyer's main goal in business was to choose suppliers they could trust to deliver good quality on schedule, and who offered a fair and competitive price. Engineers, on the other hand, tended to know much more about the product they specified, and could ask a lot of questions dealing with all the technical details. Jan felt some butterflies, but he also felt confident that he knew as much about the V-3 box as anyone. That's why I'm here, he thought.

Alpha Lee had not told Jan about her appointment with Dr. Sparks; she decided it would be better to tell him after the fact, hoping that all would go well, and she would be healed and whole in a few days. So on Tuesday she drove to the nearest bus stop, parked the car and caught the bus that Dr. Sparks had suggested; it would bring her within half a block of the clinic. Susan had ridden to town with Naomi as usual, because Alpha Lee had preferred to keep this appointment a private matter. She worried about the fee; I have to go through with this, she told herself, even if it meant spending the income from her artwork. There it was: The Sierra Street Clinic, just ahead. She walked quickly in the entrance, found the waiting room and spoke to the receptionist. Her appointment was in five minutes.

"Hello, Alpha Lee! How are you? I'm glad to see you again. Just sit down and let's talk a minute," Dr. Sparks said, indicating a chair covered in green plastic. "Did you notice the charcoal in the lobby when you came in?" she asked with a bright smile.

"Yes," Alpha Lee said in a very small voice. The doctor perceived immediately how uncomfortable her patient was. "Are you not well, Alpha Lee?" she asked.

"No ... I feel just fine, thank you," Alpha Lee replied, and she swallowed hard and continued. "I told you I think I need an examination. I've never had that kind of an examination, Doctor ... you know. I am really healthy, but ..."

"Please go on, dear," the doctor said. "Is there something wrong?"

"Well, Doctor ... I had a sort of ... umm ... injury, some months ago. In March. I had a lot of bleeding and pain. I don't know whether there is any damage to my ...uh ... organs. That's what I need to know."

"Can you please describe the nature of your injury, Alpha Lee? Were you in an accident?"

Alpha Lee realized she had to be direct, clear, "frank and earnest"; this is a *doctor*, she told herself. Just tell her! ... "I was involved in an attempt to have ... sexual intercourse, Doctor. But he ... couldn't do it ... there was a blockage that must have ruptured or something. It hurt me a lot, and this person would not stop when I cried out. There was so much pressure, and sharp pain, too. And then there was a lot of blood ... the bleeding lasted for several hours, and I felt sort of like I had cramps for almost two days after-ward. .... I just have to know if I am going to be barren, or something." She was close to tears, both from fear and from embarrassment.

Dr. Sparks sighed as she made a notation on the form in front of her. "It sounds to me as if you were raped, Alpha Lee. This was someone you knew, that you were with by your own consent?"

"Yes. We had a couple of dates before this happened. I shouldn't have gone out with him again ... I should have known ..." Her eyes were down-cast, her hands twisting nervously in her lap. I thought I wanted to do that, but I couldn't; why couldn't I?

"Don't blame yourself. When a woman says, '*STOP!*', a decent man stops. It's not your fault. Some girls do have problems the first time. Have you continued to see this man?" Alpha Lee shook her head. "Good. Now, let's get back to the facts. Do you have cramps with your period?"

"Yes, usually. I just take aspirin and lie down sometimes."

"Okay. My nurse will help you prepare yourself for the exam. I want to see if there is any serious damage ... which I doubt."

"Doctor," Alpha Lee said, "Can you tell me how much this is going to cost ... just the examination?"

Dr. Sparks smiled and patted Alpha Lee's hand. "I have an idea about that, Alpha Lee. Just don't worry ... we'll talk about that in a little while. You can afford this." She opened the door and left the room, soon a motherly looking older woman entered. She was so short and plump she almost reminded Alpha Lee of Grandmother Evans, as she remembered her long ago when she was well.

As the examination progressed, Alpha Lee was profoundly thankful that it was Dr. Sparks, and not some male doctor, who was doing it. She couldn't imagine having a man perform such a procedure; she would *die*, she told herself.

Dr. Sparks said that she had found some scar tissue, which she was removing; this would diminish the cramping, she said. The damage was minimal, and the hymen was almost entirely breached; only a minor surgical procedure was required to open it fully. She smiled benignly at Alpha Lee, aware of how her patient was suffering, much more from embarrassment than from pain; a local anesthetic had taken care of any physical discomfort she might have felt. In twenty minutes the work was over, and the doctor reassured her that she would be just fine in a few days. She gave Alpha Lee a tiny sample bottle of pills that she said would reduce any residual pain.

After Alpha Lee had dressed, the doctor came back into the room. "I would like to see you again in a week or so, Alpha Lee. I strongly recommend that, since you're my patient for this procedure, you should be fitted as soon as possible with a diaphragm. This will enable you to take responsibility for yourself in the matter of sexual activity. You are eighteen; this is an important aspect of your health as an adult woman." The doctor was so matter-of-fact about it that Alpha Lee's intense embarrassment began to fade. She speaks as though it's perfectly normal and ... okay, Alpha Lee thought. She isn't scolding me, or judging me; she's only concerned about my health!

"So, this procedure should be healed in just a few days, and you shouldn't have any more pain during intercourse, or during your period, either. I can't fit you with the diaphragm today, we'll wait until the healing's complete, and al the swelling has gone down. Now, you asked about the fee for my work. I'd like to make you a proposition, Alpha Lee. If you would be willing to make me a companion piece for the charcoal drawing you made of the fishing lodge, I will consider myself amply paid. What do you say to that?"

Alpha Lee was stunned. "You mean ... you just want me to do another charcoal that will go with that one ... to make a sort of pair ... to balance or harmonize with that one ...? D'you mean that would be in payment for what you did for me today?" Then she broke into laughter. It was inconceivable. Dr. Sparks was laughing, too.

"Oh, Alpha Lee, I do think we can do business ... don't you? Yes, that's exactly what I have in mind. I won't even tell you what to draw; *YOU* are the artist, and I trust your judgment. In fact, I don't have an idea of what it would be; you can come up with something, I'm sure. Do we have a bargain, then?"

"Yes! I want to do this!" Alpha Lee said with animation. "This one will be an individual one- of-a-kind drawing, not to be reproduced at all... not even as a print! ... Dr. Sparks, how can I thank you?" Alpha Lee's eyes filled with tears in an excess of relief and delight.

"By doing just what you have suggested," the doctor answered, smiling warmly. " ... Now, Alpha Lee, you have about 45 minutes before the next bus. I want you to lie down on the cot here and rest for at least a half hour; by that time the anesthetic will have completely dissipated and you'll feel quite normal, I think; if you do feel any discomfort, just take one of these pills. Check with the receptionist on your way out to set up another time in a week, or after the holiday and we'll finish the job." She shook Alpha Lee's hand, smiled again and left the room.

Alpha Lee lay down on the cot as instructed and closed her eyes. Thank God, she prayed. Thank God! How did I ever get so lucky?

Chapter 20

The Lockheed engineer Bill Sykes was a rotund, jolly man in his mid-forties, Jan observed. His first question was one that Professor Heiden had provided the answer for: Could they change the connector? Jan assured Bill that they could, and asked for the Lockheed parts drawing, which he could use back in Tacoma to order parts. Bill asked if the higher temperature ratings had been thoroughly tested, and again Jan was prepared, showing him the results of many tests he had done in a test oven. They discussed the physical size, and of course Bill was asking for smaller and lighter ... weight and space being critical on all airplanes. Eventually, Bill asked if Jan had done any experimentation on incorporating voice-activated on-off and automatic gain control, which Jan was only vaguely familiar with; he asked Bill if this was available now in someone's product, or only someone's dream. Bill's reply was a long wish list of things he would like to have with the next model. Jan was busy making notes to share with Professor Heiden when he got back.. Some of these items were soon to be possible based on work he was doing, but some were just "blue sky,"

After an hour of technical discussions, Bill offered to take Jan to see the airplane assembly area. Jan was delighted, and was amazed at the vastness of the building, with room for many airplanes in various stages of construct-ion along the progressive assembly line. They walked to a mock-up of the newest model of the Constellation, and Bill pointed out where the V-3 boxes would be mounted, each of the four to be used taking only a third of the space behind a quick- mount panel. Jan immediately had a thought to offer Bill a modified box, mounted two per panel, but reserved this idea until he could discuss it with the Professor.

Alpha Lee had spent most of Wednesday recuperating from her surgery; when the time came to go to SeaTac Air Terminal to pick up Jan, she was feeling well enough, and almost brave enough, to go alone. Susan hadn't even come home from work at the Arte Schacke; she had a rehearsal with the band at seven thirty, and Roddy had invited her out for Chinese food. It had been a long, quiet, rainy day for Alpha Lee; she was grateful for the company of little Sunshine, who was a bundle of energy. Alpha Lee did find time to do a little of the detail work on Susan's portrait; the striped dress was tedious to paint, but this was what she had wanted for the portrait --Susan looked so beautiful in it.

The portrait was, like the "Nisqually Princess", a seated pose, with Susan's face in full profile, her hair swept high on her head in a "do" she had never worn; this was entirely Alpha Lee's invention. "One of these days, we'll go to the hairdresser and have it done this way, Susan," she had told her. "You'll look like a movie star. If I can go along and watch how they do it, maybe I could do it myself, and you wouldn't have to pay to have it done the next time." The guitar was held across Susan's lap, her fingers resting gracefully on the strings. Again, Alpha Lee had taken a bit of license, painting Susan's nails long and tapered, polished with a soft rosy shade. Ben's locket gleamed on her breast. Susan was enthralled. "Oh, Alpha Lee ... that is so lovely. Do you really think I'm that pretty?" she asked wonderingly.

"Everybody thinks you're that pretty, Susan, and you *are*, really."

"I'm gonna buy some nail polish exactly that color, and shape my nails just like you painted them. I *want* to look like that, Alpha Lee! Thank you so much."

It was almost time to leave for SeaTac, so Alpha Lee put away her paints and put her painting on the mantel to dry; she was afraid to leave it where Sunshine could reach it. Who knew what the rambunctious little kitten might do while the paint was still soft?

She turned on the porch light, picked up her umbrella and purse, and went out to the car. It'll be so good to have him back again, she thought. It's only been three days, but ... I have missed him so much. After a good supper with Bill Sykes, Jan returned to the motel to study his mechanical drawing workbook ... he had missed a class, and he wanted to read the material in case there was a quick test at the next session. He got a good night's sleep, and looked forward to a nice flight back, with lots of sight-seeing from the window. He was to be disappointed; the weather front had brought a layer of clouds all the way to Portland, and with only two hours in San Francisco between flights, he couldn't leave the airport.

Happily, his flight arrived at SeaTac nearly on time, and he and Alpha Lee met at the gate again, in the fine Seattle mist; but this time it was Jan who was getting off the plane, while she searched for him among the disembarking passengers. Nevertheless, the passion of their greeting definitely recalled to him that other one, at another gate, only a little over a month ago.

"Welcome home, Jan," she murmured, and she took his arm, and they walked together toward the baggage claim. In only a few minutes, they were settled in the car, and Jan headed for home.

"Did you have supper on the plane, Jan?" she asked him as they drove along, the windshield wipers going at slow speed to erase the mist as it accumulated.

"Yeah, I did. I had a good meal. Did you eat, honey, all alone at the lodge? Are you hungry?"

"A little ... but we can have coffee and cake when we get home. I made a 'li'l ol' cake' today. I was hungry for something sweet. ... Probably because *you* weren't there," she said coyly. "... Now, Jan ... tell me about your trip. Did everything go well for you?"

"Honey, this was a wonderful trip! ... For me, and also, I think, for TE. I had time on the flight back to write a long report for Professor Heiden. The engineer down there, Bill Sykes, is one of the nicest people

I have ever met. After we had a long technical discussion, he took me out in the hangar where they assemble the big Constellation airliners ... it is *so* huge, Alpha Lee! Then he took me into the mock-up for the *next* model they are working on ... a brand-new concept, this one will have turbo-compound engines, and will fly much higher. It'll be a great treat to fly on that one. And he showed me where the V-3 box will be installed, four of them on each plane! And they plan to build hundreds of the planes; they already have orders for over a hundred, and the prototype hasn't been finished yet. Can you imagine how much a contract like that is worth to T. E.?"

"No ... I can only imagine how exciting it must be to think you'll be with T. E. when they have such a great future in the works! Oh, Jan, it sounds so great!"

"I'll tell you, Alpha Lee, it really does. If I hadn't already been convinced that I want to stay with them, this trip would've clinched it. ... When I told Bill what the V-3 box can do, he gave me a list of what he *wishes* it could do ... and he has some really Buck Rogers ideas! Things that are going to be possible someday. What we are doing right now with the V-3 box couldn't have been done just a year ago, the parts hadn't been invented yet. The transistor was developed just three years ago. Professor Heiden was one of the first to use them in electronic gear for planes. He is so smart, Alpha Lee. He talked to me a couple weeks ago about a dream he has of building some kind of radio thing that works like radar, but under water ... he says it should be possible for ships to know how deep the water is, and for fishing boats to locate schools of fish ... even find ships that are on the bottom. He said it would be able to find ancient shipwrecks and buried treasure! He keeps searching for some kind of special crystal so he can build one that lasts, he says the best he has found only work for a few hours before they burn out, for some reason.

"One of the research projects he has money for this year is to build a radar simulator for bombers; that will let the bombardier "see" just as if he were flying over an enemy target, and will show exactly what the radar will see. I think I'll be working on that when I go full time. Alpha Lee." He turned to face her for a moment. "I'm just so damned excited about this little company! I'd like to buy some stock in it, but I just don't have any extra money. Not that any of the stock is for sale. I think the Williamsons and the Prof own most of it. But I plan to look into it, when the time's right. Maybe someday ...

"Anyway, I did have a wonderful trip ... but the flight down there is so long! Will someone ever make jet airliners that can fly passengers at 500 miles an hour? Wow, that plane would have a big market."

"What do you mean ... a 'jet airliner', Jan?" she asked.

"Alpha Lee, Bill and I talked about that ... he said he is sure several companies are working on designs right now ... and it will take about five or ten years for the engineering, and to build the proto-type ... based on the jet engines and wings we're using now for fighters and bombers ... huge jet planes that will carry 200 people at 500 miles per hour ... and fly coast to coast or to Europe in just six hours, maybe less. He says there are even people planning rocket ships that could go to the moon and back ... that's what *he* wants to work on, some day."

At last they arrived at the lodge; there were no lights inside. Susan was not home yet, apparently. Jan pulled Alpha Lee close and held her tightly. "Oh, honey, I had a great time in Los Angeles, but it's good to be back home again. I missed you."

"Yes, I missed you, too, Jan. The lodge seemed awfully empty without you. Just don't make a habit of this traveling thing, will you please?" She kissed his lips very lightly, but that wasn't enough; he prolonged the kiss and held her close for a while.

When they entered the lodge, the first thing Jan saw was the portrait of Susan, propped on the mantel. "WOW, Alpha Lee ...Is that what you've been doing while I was away? Honey, that is just beautiful. Does Susan."

"She didn't let him finish -- Oh Susan just loves it. she really thinks it flatters her a lot. Jan. It's almost finished ... I just have the background to fill in, and some more of those stripes to paint. That's a bit difficult, especially to get the gold highlights just right. But challenge is what I need, to develop my skills. I want Jane to see it when I get it done. Maybe she'll put it in the window."

"Jane will want that painting, Alpha Lee. She'll want to buy it. You'll break her heart if you send it back to Nancy and Dr. John."

"Well, that's where it's going to go. Maybe she can make a print from it to keep. What will *really* break her heart is when Susan herself goes back to West Virginia. She has a lot of emotion invested in my sweet sister." She made a fresh pot of coffee over the newly revived fire, and cut squares of warm applesauce cake, fragrant with spices and moist with raisins, for each of them. While they were eating, they heard Roddy's car, and Alpha Lee ran to the door. "I want to ask Roddy in for coffee and cake, too, Jan," she explained.

She reached the door just in time. Roddy was holding an umbrella for Susan, walking her to the door, when Alpha Lee opened it. "Hi! Roddy, can you come in for coffee and cake, please?" And he thanked her and accepted the invitation with a wide grin.

Jan asked how the rehearsals were going, and Roddy replied, "I think we're doin' good, Jan. This pretty girl," he indicated Susan ..."the one in Alpha Lee's beautiful portrait, has given us a new sound, and a new look. Don't you think it's about time for you and Alpha Lee to come to the club and see for yourselves?" He kept his eyes on the portrait, except to glance at Jan when he spoke.

"Yeah, we'd love to do that, and we'll plan on it soon, Rod. Right now both Alpha Lee and I have a bunch of irons in the fire ."

"We really do," Alpha Lee added. "Right now I've got to get started on that wedding portrait of Fred and Ronnie. That's my urgent project, and I can get a lot done on these lonesome weekend evenings." She paused and added, "But, oh! How I'd love to go dancing sometime before long in my blue velvet dress, which isn't even made yet."

"Well, get busy on it, honey," Jan said. "We'll set a date."

Roddy rose to leave. "Alpha Lee, thanks for the coffee and cake. That cake is really delicious. I've heard about your cooking ... you're getting famous around here."

"Thanks, Roddy. This is Daddy's favorite cake. We make one for his birthday every year. Mother ices it with a kind of icing made with Karo syrup, from a recipe that was on the Karo label during the war, when sugar was rationed. It's sticky as can be, but oh! so good."

Susan walked with Roddy to the door, and he bent to kiss her cheek as he left. "Thick as thieves, that's what they are," Alpha Lee whispered to Jan.

Chapter 21

Jan drove into the motor pool compound, pointing the big six-by-six at the grease rack. He saw Fred look up from his work and throw down his brake spring pliers, waving as he approached. "Hey, Jan ... didja see the duty roster for the Fourth? You and I both get to drive a band bus to Tacoma for the parade."

"Yeah, I saw it this morning, Fred. At least we didn't have to take that jaunt to Yakima some of the guys went on. I guess we're supposed to be at the band compound on the main fort at 0930. Do you know where it is?"

"Oh, that's easy enough, straight across the parade ground from Regimental HQ, near the big motor pool, in those temporary barracks next to the tennis courts. By the way, Sarge asked me to assign the buses, and I put you in your favorite bus, old 46-10,007. I figure we oughta fire up at 0845. Do you want to have breakfast out here? I can pick you up at seven."

"Yeah ... we can have breakfast here and let the girls sleep in. Old 07 is fine. I've never had the trouble with her that some guys seem to have. She's balky enough when she's cold, but I like that five-speed tranny."

"Okay Jan ... I'll pick you up at your lodge Monday at seven. We'll have five buses goin'. I assume you're gonna work tonight ... right?"

"Yeah, Fred ... much as I'd like to take Alpha Lee to the dance or a movie, I need that extra money ... I paid the rent again, and things are a bit tight. I'll be working all day tomorrow, too. What time do you think we'll be done on Monday?"

"Yeah, I understand 'tight'. I'll sure be glad when Ronnie's paychecks start rollin' in from the hospital. They only pay twice a month down there, starvation wage at that. ... Jan, best I can figure, the parade kicks off at noon, and we should be headin' back outa town by two or so, I'll tell Ronnie I'll be home by four-thirty or five. That oughta be safe enough. Are you guys goin' downtown for the fireworks?"

"I haven't heard of any plans for the Fourth, Fred. Whatever Alpha Lee and Susan want to do'll be fine with me. I like fireworks, and I suppose they do, too. Seems like the way to celebrate the Fourth of July. ... When we were kids, and you could buy fireworks at a stand along the road at home, we always had firecrackers to set off, all day long. But they're illegal to sell in West Virginia nowadays. The fire department in Brick City has a big doin's at the football field on the Fourth ... that's the only show in town."

When Jan told Alpha Lee that he and Fred would be driving a bus to the parade, she appeared downcast. "Oh, Jan, I was hoping you'd have the day off and we could celebrate the holiday somehow. Will there be fireworks anywhere near here? ... Jane said they used to go up to Seattle. But that's so far away, and the traffic would be awful, I'd think." Alpha Lee was sitting beside Jan on the sofa as he drank his coffee, putting the final touches on a new skirt for Susan to wear with her gray angora sweater.

"You're right about that, honey," Jan agreed. "Fred said something about fireworks. Let's find out where and what time. Actually, Alpha Lee, I can't complain about this special duty. They've been more than decent to me since this driving school started. Six of our drivers left yesterday for Yakima, and half of the others have to drive to a parade in Olympia tomorrow, so I guess I'd rather drive on Monday when TE is closed, and I can work tomorrow. We can use the money."

"Jan, I feel bad about that. You work *so* hard, so much. I wish you would let me help out on the rent and electricity. Jane has been paying me every time I take her the charcoals."

"Alpha Lee, please don't start that debate again," he said wearily. "You'll need that money for college ... we made a bargain, and for me, sweetheart, it was a great bargain. I'm so glad you could come out here," and he pulled her close to kiss her.

"Oh, Jan. I'm so glad you wanted me to. It's been better than I could have dreamed. I'm getting so much experience in my art, and being with you is ..." She ran out of words, but her eyes spoke to him. They held each other quietly, enjoying their time alone before Susan returned.

Then Jan said, "I need to start putting a few dollars back for your plane ticket, too, honey. When I get discharged, I'll get travel money back to West Virginia, so my ticket will be covered, probably both ways, on the mail flight."

Alpha Lee pulled away from him. "Jan, my ticket home is one thing I *do* want to pay for. Give me that much independence. I've made more money than I ever expected, and there's still time to make more. There are other things I want to paint that maybe I can sell."

"Well, you know what the budget looks like, Alpha Lee. Nancy's money pays for at least half of the groceries for all three of us. And if I can work four Saturdays, the rent is covered. Over-all, I've put a dollar a day in savings since you came out. And we've been to a couple dances, and a couple movies ... we're getting by pretty well, I'd say."

She held his head between her hands, and kissed him softly. "I'm not complaining, my darling Jan." She looked deeply into the eyes. "It's kind of fun, don't you think? Making do, cutting corners, watching the pennies, it's good practice for the future. It's a challenge. I don't really mind it at all." Then she pretended to pout. "But I *did* want to celebrate the Fourth of July, darn it. ... Actually, we're invited to the Arte Shacke to watch the parade, Susan said, and Ronnie sent a note saying she hoped we could do something together on the Fourth. So, maybe we can dream up something special

And so on the Fourth of July Alpha Lee and Susan drove Jan's car into town, picking up Veronica at their apartment at eleven, and they drove to the TE lot, which was still nearly empty. They walked from there to the Arte Schacke, where Roddy and Jane had set up chairs on the sidewalk so they could watch the parade. Jon was on hand with his camera, preparing to take pictures for the newspaper, and Jane had set out pitchers of iced tea and fresh lemonade as well, with crackers and smoked salmon bits, and cookies and watermelon balls mixed with straw- berries. In a few minutes Jan, Fred, and Sergeant Herndon joined them, having parked their buses at a school parking lot some ten blocks away; they would be free for about an hour, until time to return the band members to the Fort.

The Arte Schacke was near the beginning of the parade route. Leading the parade, the Second Division Band from Fort Lewis appeared, one hundred twenty men strong, led by their bagpipers in authentic tartan kilts, rather than the usual regulation trousers, worn with Eisenhower jackets. The girls applauded enthusiastically at their dashing appearance. Roddy was the first to ask the old worn-out question: "What do bagpipers wear under their kilts?"

Sergeant Herndon spoke up with an answer: "*Our* pipers wear regulation brown GI shorts, Rod -- they damn well better, or they're out of uniform. I don't know what the hell the Scots wear under theirs."

The watchers enjoyed an impressive array of bands and floats, as well as a unit of veterans of past wars, several of them dressed proudly in their old uniforms. As the final units rolled by, the bus drivers thanked Jane for her hospitality, and started the long walk back to their buses. "See you back at the lodge, honey," Jan said as he waved to Alpha Lee and turned away with Fred and the sergeant.

Fred dropped Jan off at the lodge at a quarter to five. Alpha Lee and Ronnie came out on the porch to greet them, and Alpha Lee said, "Fred, you and Ronnie are invited to stay for supper, we'll have a wiener roast on the pier."

But Ronnie was quick to answer: "Thanks, but we can't do that, Alpha Lee, Fred promised me we'd go to the movie on the main base this evening. And we'll still be able to see the fire-works over the water in Tacoma – that doesn't start till ten. Aren't you folks going to watch? Maybe we'll see you somewhere. ... Thanks, Alpha Lee, for picking me up. I really enjoyed the parade. Weren't those bagpipers beautiful?" Alpha Lee nodded in agreement. "Thanks for showing me all your sketches. You are so talented! Will you teach me to sew? I had Home Ec in school, but I was terrible at sewing. I'm better with animals than cooking and sewing."

Jan put his arm around Alpha Lee as they watched Fred's car go up the hill. "Did you and Ronnie have a good time talking girl talk, honey?" he asked with a grin. "And where's Susan?"

"I just love Ronnie, Jan!" she replied enthusiastically. "She is so funny. We had a wonderful time watching the parade. ... Susan is staying at Williamsons' ... couldn't you guess? She'll watch the fireworks with them. Maybe she and Roddy will watch from his boat. ... Anyway, Ronnie said she's been offered a chance to be a substitute elementary teacher in Tillicum, wherever that is, and the hospital will let her take that time off; actually she's just part time at the hospital, but she's been working there five evenings a week, helping to feed and cheer up and care for the young kids in the hospital. She really enjoys it, but it doesn't pay very much."

He took her hand as they turned back toward the house. "Well, Fred has a couple things going for him, since he's married. He gets some kind of a housing allowance, and he and Ronnie can shop in a big grocery store on the base called the Commissary, where things are cheaper than in town where we buy. And the Captain gave him another stripe after he lost his finger, because of his work on the school, not because of his finger, and that raises his pay. Fred's a good teacher. We work really well together. ... I'm glad you and Ronnie like each other, honey."

As they walked into the lodge, Alpha Lee asked, "Jan, are you hungry? We could have hot dogs and potato chips, just like millions of people are having on this holiday, if you want to. ... Actually I'm not too hungry right now, myself, I ate a lot of that wonderful smoked salmon Jane had , wasn't it good? Do you like it, Jan?"

"Oh, yeah, I sure do ... that was a real treat to me the very first time I tasted it. We don't get that kind of stuff back home, do we, honey?" Then he pulled her close to him. "Alpha Lee, I just realized that we're gonna be alone in this cabin for the first time in days, with Suz with

Roddy. I'll tell you what I'm really hungry for, sweetheart, *if* you can't guess." He kissed her deeply, his hands moving down to pull her against him. She raised her arms high and held him, pressing her body close, unmistakably offering herself to him.

"Jan ... Jan," she breathed into his ear, "I'm hungry, too. I want you entirely, completely."

"One hundred per cent, Alpha Lee? Is that what you're telling me?" he asked her between kisses.

"Yes, my darling engineer. Yes. All the way!"

Jan insisted he must "grab a shower," promising he'd be out in less than seven minutes. Alpha Lee spent the minutes in busy work, emptying and washing the coffee pot, putting away her sewing, leading Sunshine into her own bedroom to stay for the night. And looking into the mirror to see if she looked as radiant as she felt. She would shower, too; she had declined Jan's invitation to share the shower with him. "I'm not quite ready for that, love," she said; she still felt a bit shy about exposing herself in this way.

Jan appeared, barely dry from his hasty toweling off, and Alpha Lee in her short robe went into the steamy bathroom for her own allotment of minutes. When she finished, she was fragrant with the lilac scent Jan loved, and her hair was damp around her face in coppery curls that clung to her neck and shoulders. She was wearing the short sheer nylon pajamas Jan remembered from the night the bears came.

"Honey," he said, holding her at arms' length to stare at her full-length, "tell me why you brought these pretty little lacy things with you when you came out here to live with a raunchy soldier? Why didn't you pack your suitcase with long flannel granny gowns?" He grinned wickedly as he waited for her answer.

"Well-l-l- ," she said hesitantly, evading his eyes, " ... Umm, I had to consider what would, you know, pack better; those heavy gowns would be so bulky, you know, they would've taken up too much room in the suitcase?" She looked at him with a smile she hoped was "temptingly innocent".

"I'm not buying that,. I think you came out here to seduce me!"

For an answer, she threw her arms around him and pressed against him all the way down to her knees. "Is it working?" she whispered.

Jan laughed. "You betcha, sweetheart!" And they walked arm in arm into his bedroom. He closed the door behind them. Then Jan looked at her seriously. "Honey, did you see a doctor? Are you sure you're okay?"

"Yes and yes ... when you were in California. I had an appointment with a woman doctor, one of Jane's bridge partners. She came into the Arte Schacke one day and I met her; she bought one of the first copies of the charcoal. ... She examined me and fixed whatever was wrong, and told me I would have no more pain." She sat down on the edge of Jan's bed and smiled at him serenely.

Jan lay down beside her and took her in his arms, kissing and fondling her body. His touch was slow and very gentle, and she responded eagerly. He lifted her to lie on top of him, and when he entered her, he knew that her sudden muffled cry was not of pain, but of passion and pleasure. And when he kissed her, he tasted the salt of her tears that were not tears of pain, but of a surfeit of emotion. "Oh Jan, I love you so," she murmured as she caressed his face.

They lay together for a long while, drifting in and out of a shallow sleep, awakening to touch and to explore each other. The sun was still high, glittering on the waters of the sound and pouring in through the window above Jan's bed. He reached to turn on the radio, and tuned in a program of popular music. "Hey, honey," he said, turning to her, "I have a great idea! Let's dance."

"Well Okay," she agreed, reaching for her pajamas.

"No, no. Let's dance just the way we are. Just the way God made us." He stood and reached for her hand to pull her to his side.

"You mean ... you want to dance ... with our clothes off?" she asked incredulously. "Jan, are you crazy?"

He pulled her close and they moved together to the slow music. "Crazy like a fox," he murmured in her ear. "Mmmm ... Honey, every time we dance together, wherever we are, this is what we'll remember. ... God, your body is so sweet."

The music ended and their dance concluded with a long kiss. Then Alpha Lee turned away from Jan quickly and hurried to put her scanty pajamas on. But he pulled her down beside him on the bed and held her close. "Honey, I want you again," he told her.

"Mmmm ... yes," she whispered. But she pulled away from him. "Not yet, love, please. Later ... yes. Now I have an idea," she said. "Not as crazy as yours! ... Not quite as sweet and exciting, either! Mmmm ... *so* exciting ... Jan, it's early still. The clock says six thirty. It'll be light for hours yet. Will you take me for a drive, up into the mountains? Can you find that place where we parked above the river?"

He sat up on the edge of the bed. "Sure, we could do that. You mean that place with the great view of Mount Rainier?"

"That would be perfect, Jan. I'll go and get dressed, and we can take some Coke and snacks along. And my charcoals."

It took Alpha Lee only a few minutes to put on a pair of white shorts and a dark blue sleeveless shirt, and to tie her hair back with Susan's scarf. She put Ritz crackers and cheese and some fruit into a paper bag, and wrapped two bottles of Coke in a towel with ice cubes. "We're ready!" she said with an enthusiastic smile when Jan appeared in his tee shirt and tan work pants.

"Wow! Look at you! Honey, you're almost as pretty in that outfit as you were in *no* outfit just a minute ago!"

She turned away in embarrassment. "Jan ... stop it. Don't you *dare* ever tell anyone about that dance. Not Fred -- not any of your army buddies. I'll die." Jan just laughed at her blush and, wrapping his arm around her waist, led her to the car.

The holiday traffic was heavy as they drove along the highway; it seemed that everyone was hurrying to the city to watch fireworks, or hurrying home from camp or beach or park. It was after seven when they reached the high overlook, but the sun was bright and far above the horizon. Alpha Lee had decided this was the vista she would draw for Dr. Sparks.

She quickly drew the basic lines and some of the textures; the remaining areas could be added at home. She drew in the important details and noted the color values she would need to complete the picture. The brilliance of Rainier's snow-covered summit would be difficult to render in charcoal; she might need to use touches of chalk to brighten it against the less-than-blue sky. The composition, she decided, was very artistic from this perspective; she was glad she had been at this place before to view the mountain from this closer aspect than at the lodge.

Alpha Lee spoke little while she worked, concentrating on her drawing. Jan strolled around the area, even climbing down the slope for some distance to take pictures of the river below. He had taken several shots of the mountain from the "scenic view" where Alpha Lee worked. He called to her to come if she could, to see something ... and she put aside her charcoal sticks and hurried over to him.

"Look down here, honey," he said, pointing down the steep craggy slope. She saw dozens of tiny animals, something like the ground squirrels common to West Virginia, but smaller and with different markings. They scurried around the rocks, disappearing and reappearing.

"What are they, Jan?" she asked. "What are they eating?", because she could see that they were scavenging some kind of small fruits or seeds that were scattered among the rocks.

"I don't know, Alpha Lee ... we'll have to 'look it up', as my mom always says. I think they're eating some kind of little berries from those bushes. Maybe huckleberries?"

"Maybe, but I don't think so. Did you take pictures of them, Jan?

"Yeah but they may not show up on the print. They may just disappear among the rocks and we'll wonder what the picture is supposed to show." He climbed back up to her. "Are you finished with your picture, honey?"

"Yes, I think so. There's some more 'fill' to put in, but I can do that at home. This picture is for Dr. Sparks, Jan ... the nice lady doctor who examined me. This is what she asked for as payment. I couldn't believe it. I want it to be especially nice for her, to hang beside the charcoal of the lodge. She asked for one to be a sort of a companion or pair"

"Well, honey, she should really be pleased, it's beautiful! That mountain is really spectacular."

They sat on a bench and ate their crackers and cheese and drank their Cokes. The sun had finally fallen below the horizon. The sky was cloudless, for a change; a perfect night for fire-works. The full moon was rising, its leading edge just visible in the east. There was soft sweet music playing on the car radio: "Blue moon ... You saw me standing alone ... without a dream in my heart; without a love of my own." Jan took Alpha Lee's hand and pulled her to her feet. "Dance with me, sweet lady," he said, and they held each other close and danced on the sparse grass. A passing car sounded its horn in approval, and they smiled at each other. "What are you thinking of, honey?" Jan asked.

"Probably the same thing you're thinking," Alpha Lee replied. "Just as you promised, I'm remembering our dance back at the lodge. You're right, Jan, how could I ever forget that?"

The music ended, and Alpha Lee picked up her drawing supplies and the picnic leavings. Now the moon was fully visible, flanked by a brilliant star. She made a secret wish. Star light, Star bright, first star I see tonight .

They headed down the highway toward Tacoma, where the city lights made a sparkling pattern across the landscape below. Occasionally they could see in the distance a skyrocket exploding against the darkening sky. As they approached the city, Jan saw a sign: FIREWORKS it said. He stopped at the small stand and bought some sparklers and fountain cones. "Now we can have some of our own!" he told Alpha Lee.

They stopped again to buy ice cream cones, and Jan followed a street that led down to a small beach. He parked there, and when they finished their ice cream, he set off the fountain cones and they enjoyed the brief display of sparks showering into the air, reflecting brightly from the little wavelets. Alpha Lee clapped with delight. "I love it," she said. "It's just like we used to have at home, before the war. Daddy always got fireworks for the Fourth of July. Roman candles and skyrockets, and tiny little firecrackers in a string that went off, rapid-fire ... it sounded like popcorn! And pinwheels ... he nailed them to a tree and they whizzed around throwing sparks in all directions... I wonder what our families are doing tonight, back home," she said, suddenly pensive.

"They might be in bed by now, Alpha Lee. The fireworks at the athletic field in Brick City would be over by now, in real time." He looked at his watch. "It's half past nine, after midnight in West Virginia," The fountains were all spent now; the full moon was shining on the water, its companion star still nearby. They walked back to the car arm in arm. "Do you want to go to Williamsons' to watch the big fireworks show, Alpha Lee?" She didn't answer, but turned to look deeply into his eyes. "Honey," he said softly, "do you want to go back to the lodge?"

She touched his face, and then she kissed his lips very tenderly. "Yes," she murmured.

They stood very close, facing each other beside Jan's bed. He unbuttoned her shirt, and she unclasped the buckle on his belt. The slow ritual of undressing awakened desire in both of them, and when they slipped under the wolf blanket, they came together easily. Taking his cue from Alpha Lee's impassioned response, Jan abandoned the slow and tentative moves of their first lovemaking earlier in the evening; this time the foreplay was short and intense, and their shared climax came in synchrony with the distant booming of skyrockets over the water. It was as if the excitement of the fireworks entered into their own passion, and magnified it.

They were reluctant to let go of each other, kissing and fondling urgently, unwilling to relinquish the intensity of their pleasure. At last Jan withdrew and rolled away from her with a sigh of satisfaction. "Oh Alpha Lee ... just when I think it can't get any better, ... it gets better."

He propped himself up on one elbow and looked down at her. "Are you *sure* you haven't had years of experience at this?"

She lay with her eyes closed, the yellow sheet pulled up to cover her breasts. Her only response was, "Mmmm-m-m."

The distant booming ended; the dim faraway flashes in the sky were over. Alpha Lee retrieved her clothes and hastily dressed. "Susan and Roddy will be here before long," she said. "We'd better get ready to face the real world again, Jan, my darling ..." But as she turned to him, he pulled her down on top of him and held her for another moment, another kiss, before releasing her and getting out of bed himself.

"What a way to celebrate," he said, stretching. "Hey, honey ... let's make this our tradition. Let's do this every Fourth of July! We can make our own fireworks!"

She laughed. "Yes! I love that idea. As long as we don't have to wait a whole year to celebrate this way again! We could celebrate lots of things, couldn't we? Fridays ... sunshiny days " Secretly she was thrilled at Jan's casual reference to the future -- a future of being together.

They heard Roddy's car coming down the driveway just before midnight. By that time, they were sharing coffee and popcorn while

Jan's radio (moved to the living room) was playing patriotic band music. Jan opened the door and invited Roddy to come in.

"Where were you two?" Susan asked. "We thought you'd come into town and watch the fire-works with us. Don't tell me you missed the fireworks!"

"We had a really nice evening," Alpha Lee said. "We went for a drive up into the mountains to have a picnic, and we watched the moon rise over Mount Rainier. And we had fireworks ourselves ... Jan bought some on the way back." From Roddy's knowing glance, Alpha Lee discerned that he probably had ideas about what kind of "fireworks" she and Jan had enjoyed. But she just smiled at him sweetly. I don't even care if he knows, she thought. "Have a cup of coffee with us, and a bowl of popcorn, Roddy."

"Oh, gee, thanks, Alpha Lee ... it's too late. This has been a really busy day. I want to get home and hit the sack. ... Susan, are you up for a rehearsal tomorrow evening? I can come out to pick you up after dinner."

"I can drive her to your house tomorrow, Rod," Jan said. "I'll be going back to T. E. after we eat. About seven?"

"Fine," he responded. "Okay ... see you then, Suz," and he bent to kiss her cheek, his arm comfortably around her waist.

"Bye," she said. "Thanks for a great evening, Roddy." Susan was blushing, self-conscious at Roddy's easy familiarity. With a final wave, Roddy left them.

"Hey, Suz," Jan said, "Looks to me like you and Rod are getting pretty friendly."

Too quickly she retorted, "Friendly, that's right, Jan. We're just friends."

Alpha Lee rolled her eyes and shook her head. "Yeah ... right. You're gonna break his heart, Susan," and she picked up the cups and empty bowls to rinse at the sink. Then with a mischievous backward glance, she hurried toward the bedroom.... Last one in bed is a rotten egg!"

Chapter 22

'Hurry up and wait': It was one of those days. Jan spent long intervals between runs in the big six-by-six waiting while the supplies for the mess hall were being loaded and unloaded. He wished he had a book or a magazine with him. He rummaged through the glove compartment and found a tablet of report forms, and decided he'd "waste" a couple of them writing a letter on the back. He hadn't written to his brother Willis for a couple months, and there was plenty of news to share.

Willis was in summer school at the University, trying to accelerate the pace so he could earn his degree in less than the usual four full years. He was working nights driving a taxi cab; the pay wasn't great, but with tips he made enough so that he had some spending money. When there was time, he could take Gail out to dinner or a movie, which had been next to impossible previously, when he had been living like a pauper.

"Ft. Lewis, Wash. July 5, 1949

Dear Willis,

"I suppose you will be back in summer school by the time you get this, but I hope you had a nice holiday, with a respite from studies, and somewhere you were able to see a nice fireworks display. Did you actually end up going to Charleston? I understand the fireworks by the river there can be really spectacular, but I've never seen them, only the Brick City ones, which are pretty good, on the high school field. I'm glad to hear you are still dating the pretty Miss Gail. I've seen pictures of her. Wow ! She is a knockout!

"My 4th of July celebration sure was different this year from the "old days" when we used to set off firecrackers and go someplace for a picnic. I wound up driving a bus to a parade in downtown Tacoma, hauling the 2nd Division Band, a durn good outfit, with a Bagpipe Corps, believe it or not, kilts, fancy drummers and all, they were the centerpiece of a pretty big parade that lasted over an hour. There were fireworks over the Tacoma harbor after dark, which I've heard are really worth seeing, but Alpha Lee and I got involved in something else and we didn't make it. We did have a little private picnic earlier, up on a high scenic overlook where there was a great view of Mount Rainier. Alpha Lee made a charcoal drawing of the mountain while we were there. Wow! What a day it was!

"I'm sure Mom has told you that I'm living in a rustic old log fishing lodge right on Puget Sound now, sharing its two-bedroom/one bath accommodations and fishing pier with *two* beautiful women, and I do mean beautiful. I had a chance to rent this place for a year at a below- the-market price, completely furnished (such as it is) with a wood cooking range with a coil built- in for heating water. I'd love to buy this place after I get my discharge, and I may be able to swing it.

"The girls you may have met, but maybe not. They are both from Brick City, and graduated this spring. Alpha Lee Evans was in my math class last year, and is a truly talented artist, and we have been corresponding since about Christmas. She copied a postcard scene of this lodge using charcoals, enlarging it to about 10" X 12" ... and sent it to me. A lady who runs an art shop saw it, and put it in her shop window, and a rush of people wanted to buy copies. I invited Alpha Lee to come out here for the summer and stay with me to do her art ...

and the orders just keep coming in for this, and she is working on other things, too, oil paintings and such.

"In her spare time she also cooks (Boy, does she ever cook!), and sews for herself, and costumes for Susan, and dances like a dream when I can take her to the club Saturday nights.

The other girl, Susan Remagen, is a talented singer, a really beautiful blonde, and Alpha Lee's best friend, who has found work at the Art Shop, and also is singing with a dance band that plays at the service clubs at Fort Lewis and the air base nearby. Alpha Lee's parents wouldn't have let her come out here without a companion, and she probably would have been pretty lonely and bored even if they had, since I'm away from the lodge all day, every day, except Sundays. I think both of the girls are enjoying their little adventure out here, making money and learning new things, and making friends.

"I have felt fortunate to have them living here, and frankly, brudder, I think Alpha Lee is the gal I want to marry, when it is possible. I'd say we're pretty much in love with each other. Time will tell. This fall she will be back in West Virginia, at Wesleyan, where she has a grant as an art assistant. And I, of course, will be staying here working full-time and taking night classes again. Hopefully, I'll be able to get a degree here in four or five years, and so far the company is paying the tuition for me. Here I go again, Willis, with a long-distance love relationship. I hope it'll work out better this time, and I believe it will.

"The army is treating me pretty well. Basically I'm just teaching new drivers how to use the big tank haulers. Two of us teach, and we get eight or ten students for four days every other week. Some of these students have no experience at all with big trailers, and sometimes we keep them an extra day. On the off weeks we still drive the usual army vehicles, and practice on the tank haulers. I think you could say we get special treatment by the Captain and first sergeant and I think we're doing a good job of teaching.

"A couple weeks ago the company where I work part time asked me to take 3 days of leave and fly down to Burbank, California, to visit with the buyer and engineer at Lockheed, sorta make a sales call, I guess. I had a fun trip, and I came away with a good feeling that our equipment will be on the next airliner down there. I am amazed at flying, these airliners are so fast ... 200 mph, and so comfortable. Even in some pretty bad weather I felt safe. As you can guess, I enjoyed the sight-seeing, and having all expenses paid on a great trip like that was special, too.

"I'm now pretty much involved in designing new equipment for them, and making the first models to test, and doing package design. Willis, these are good people, with a real willingness to work with their customers, and I think they have an excellent future. I can't believe how well they have treated me.

"Have a good second summer term. I'll see you early in September. I'll be home for two weeks.

"Best wishes, Jan"

Alpha Lee sat at the kitchen table in the quiet lodge. It was mid-morning and she was alone with Sunshine, the little kitten, who was chasing a ball of crumpled paper around on the floor. Alpha Lee was making a list. I have so many unfinished projects, she had said to herself. I must tie up some loose ends. She had taken out her notepad and a pencil, and she had written:

1. Make appointment with Dr. Sparks. Deliver charcoal when I see her.
2. Talk with Naomi about Nisqually Princess.
3. "Girl with Guitar" (Susan's portrait): Put on final touches if needed; Take to Arte Schacke for framing.
4. FINISH Fred and Ronnie's wedding portrait!
5. Write to parents about 4th of July; Enclose money for deposit.
6. Write to James.
7. Cut out blue velvet.

   There, that gives me some objectives, she thought. I have lots of things to do. ... I'll write the letters first. Oh, one more thing...
8. Do last three charcoals.

"The Fishing Lodge on Puget Sound "July 6, 1949

" Dear Mother and Daddy,

"We celebrated the Fourth of July by watching a parade in town. Jan and his friends Fred and Sgt. Herndon drove busloads of the Second Division Band to their staging area, and then they came to stand in the street outside the "Arte Shacke" and watched with us and we all snacked on smoked salmon and crackers and fruit. Did you ever taste smoked salmon? It is *delicious.* The band includes a unit of bagpipers in full regalia ... even kilts! They were spectacular. Bagpipe music is eerie ... haunting and strange, but I love it.

"Jan and I drove up into the mountains after his duty was finished so I could do a charcoal drawing of Mount Rainier for a lady I met recently. She had bought one of the other charcoals, (the picture of the lodge) and she wanted a 'companion piece'. The view from up where we stopped is just wonderful, so it made a nice picture. The mountain is huge, and snow-covered all the time. Jan took pictures ... I'll send you one when we get them printed.

"On the way back, Jan stopped and bought some fountain cones and sparklers, and we had fun with those. There was a big fireworks show over the water in town, and we were invited back to Williamsons' to watch that. They are really nice people. ..."

(The truth, she thought ... nothing but the truth. But not quite the whole truth. There were some aspects of her Fourth of July celebration that were private and precious ...) "When we went to Seattle a couple of weeks ago, Mrs. Williamson took us to a remnant shop, and I spent the money you sent for my birthday for a beautiful piece of deep blue velvet to make myself a dress. (I hope Jan will want to go to the special services dance sometime this summer!) It was flawed, so the price was reduced, and I'm going to have to cut it carefully to avoid that. Thank you for making that possible for me! Speaking of money ... I'm going to go to town tomorrow and get a money order to enclose. I have made another $375 from my charcoals and other things since the last time I sent you money to deposit, and there will be more. I think I'll have a painting to sell to the Seattle Art Museum; the curator made me a very generous offer. And Mrs. Williamson is making prints of the charcoal drawing which she is selling for ten dollars apiece. I'll get five dollars for each of those. I have a real career going on here! It's wonderful, I feel so good about it.

"It's raining again today. It rains about every other day, no, probably even more often than that. Our garden is thriving. We've had green onions, and our first tomatoes will be ripe in a week, I think. The green beans are blooming, and the squash have big fat buds. How do you cook squash, Mother? The seeds Naomi gave us are called 'zukini', a small summer squash. She says they're good; I've never even heard of them.

"It's almost lunch time. I think I'll just have some crackers and cheese and an apple; I'm here alone for the whole day (except for Sunshine, the little black kitten Jan gave me for my birthday). Tonight is Jan's class night (M-W-F), and so he'll eat at the base and come home late after class. Susan is working, but she'll be home to eat supper with me. I'm going to make vegetable soup. Please write soon. I wonder how the fireworks at the Athletic Field were this year? Was there a parade in Brick City? I miss you all. Love, Alpha Lee

She wrote to James about the various military vehicles Jan drove, and about his assignment, training other GI's to drive the big tank haulers . She wrote about the many sea birds she saw daily, as well as seals and otters occasionally. She described to him the "floating concrete bridge" in Seattle, how she had expected it to sink into the waters of Lake Washington when they drove on it (... well, not really, but it made a good story). And she made a quick sketch of Mount Rainier, a small depiction of the charcoal she had drawn from the scenic view along the highway, where she and Jan had danced in the grass ...

With the letters finished, she made a neat check mark beside items five and six, and then she went to the bedroom and took the checks for her artwork from the dresser drawer and put them in her purse. Now, about those last three charcoals. No, not now. Maybe the light will be better this afternoon, she thought. I'll work on Susan's picture now, I can work with the oils if I use the lamp. The picture was almost finished; only some of the background needed to be filled in, a dark shade of burnt umber that set off the blonde hair, the warm skin tones and the ivory dress with its highlights and shaded folds to best effect. I think Nancy and the doctor will like this, Alpha Lee said to herself with satisfaction. And Jane, too ...

Wednesday would be a long day. Jan had left at seven; Susan stayed until half past eight, and then walked up the driveway and on to the bus stop to catch the bus into town. She had a short walk to the Arte Schacke from the next stop, arriving at about 9:15. She would meet Naomi at five for the ride home. But the evening would pass slowly without Jan. Alpha Lee walked out onto the pier. The morning mist had evaporated and there was some pale blue sky showing, but in the west massive clouds were approaching rapidly. She brought her charcoals outside, hoping to finish all three copies while the light held. Sunshine peered cautiously over the edge of the planking, interested in the moving water below but instinctively apprehensive. Alpha Lee worked quickly, but she was able to finish only two by late after-noon, just before the rain started. From the window she watched the heavy drops pelting the water's surface like bullets, and making half-dollar-sized dark circles on the gray wood of the pier. There would be no walk, and no bike ride today to stretch her muscles. I wish I had a telephone, she thought; I'd call Ronnie. And Dr. Sparks, too.

When Susan returned, Alpha Lee had the blue velvet material spread on the table and was trying to fit the pattern pieces on it, mindful of the flaw along one edge that made the fabric narrower than the pattern required. She was finding it challenging to make the pieces fit, and she was glad she had bought an extra half-yard; she'd need every bit of it.

"Mmmm" Susan said as she walked into the room. "What's cooking, Alpha Lee? Smells good."

"Just some vegetable soup, Suz," she answered. "I thought soup would be good for this rainy day. Did Naomi bring you all the way down?" It was still raining.

"Yeah. It's miserable out there. But we had a pretty good day at the shop. Jane's going to do one of those shows this weekend, introducing an artist with lots of new pieces, and she wants me to play my guitar during the daytime while the visitors are coming in. She's having catered refreshments and everything. You should come, too."

"I'd love to. Sounds interesting. I need to go into town tomorrow, Susan, so I can take you in *if* Jan doesn't need the car. I have some things to mail and I do have to see Jane, anyway. ... Are you ready for supper?"

Jan came home at a quarter past ten, looking for a cup of coffee 'and some sugar from my sweet lady', he said as he took her in his arms, lifting her off her feet, and kissed her hard. "Sugar for you, sugar for me," she said with a bright smile. "Nice how it sweetens both ways." She poured a cup of coffee for him and one for herself, and brought them to the table. "Do you want some ice cream, Jan? Or anything?"

"Well, the 'anything' sounds exciting," he said. "No, I don't need anything to eat. I have something to show you, honey." He pulled a rolled-up pamphlet out of his back pocket. "Remember the drawing you made for Charles?"

Jan had delivered Alpha Lee's drawing of the V-2 box to Charles the day after she finished it, over a month ago. Charles was still at his desk when Jan arrived at T. E. after dinner at the lodge. He propped the drawing up on the top of the filing cabinet.

Charles looked up from his ledger. "Hi, Jan. ... Oh, look what we've got here!" he said. "Your girlfriend isn't just good ... she's *fast*. See, Jan, how much classier this looks than a plain old photograph would? I like it. Yes, that's exactly the look we want. ... Can I give you a check for her, Jan?"

"Yes, sir," Jan replied.

"What do you think ... thirty dollars?"

"I think she'd be very pleased with that, Mr. Williamson."

"Well, I'm pleased, too. You tell her that, will you? We might want her to do other illustrations for us from time to time. ... Did you see the sheets on the new amplifiers, Jan?"

"Yes, sir ... those temperature ratings look great, don't they? I wrote for more samples last week. We'll model something up to put on life test."

Jan had delivered the check and Charles's thanks when he returned home that Tuesday evening. Alpha Lee was amazed at the amount. "Thirty dollars! My goodness, Jan, that much for one simple little drawing? I'm only getting twenty for the lodge drawings. This one didn't take me an hour to do. I'll write him a thank-you note." The payment was her first earnings since she arrived, and was part of the first money order she had sent home for her parents to deposit in her savings account. "I'd almost forgotten about this, Jan." The drawing had been reduced by half from her original, which sharpened the detail, and the lettering identifying the instrument on the cover was printed in stately Roman style. "Quarterly Report to Stockholders - Second Quarter 1949" was the title discreetly printed in small letters across the top of the cover. She opened the booklet to find information that meant nothing to her: a report featuring a technical description of the V-2 unit, and an itemized accounting of the company's financial status. "Well ... it looks okay, don't you think?" she asked, scrutinizing the cover picture again.

"You betcha, honey. Charles liked it so much he had the original framed! He has it on the wall above his desk. ... I'm sorry it took so long to get you a copy. There was a hitch some-where along the line, and the printing didn't get done when they expected it. Then ... I have to admit it, I forgot to ask for a copy to bring you, and there went another week or more. ... This little box has been very successful, Alpha Lee, and profitable, too. I'm proud that I had a hand in designing it. These men, Professor Heiden and Charles, and there's some other guys involved, too ... they are real visionaries. They have some pretty exciting ideas. Takoma Elektroniks may be a big name in the field before long. And Yours Truly hopes to be part of the company!"

"Well. I'd like it better if they'd open a branch in Brick City, or Harrison ...," she said with a wistful smile.

"Is that where you expect to be, Alpha Lee, after you've completed your education? Are you planning to settle down in the old hometown? Is there a future for you there?"

She pushed back her empty cup, rose and walked around to stand before him. "I hope my future is wherever you are, Jan," and she bent to kiss him tenderly.

By the end of the week Alpha Lee had most of the items on her list checked off. The final copy of the charcoal was finished and ready to deliver to Jane with the others. Her appointment with Dr. Sparks was set for the thirteenth, Wednesday of the next week. Alpha Lee had signed the charcoal of Mount Rainier; she would take it with her on Wednesday. The portrait of Susan was at the Arte Schacke waiting to be framed; Jane was so busy with preparations for the special showing on Saturday and Sunday that she had to lay it aside until next week.

But she was deeply affected by the painting, and asked to make a print to keep for herself.

"Could you make a print for me, too, Jane?" Alpha Lee asked. "Just a small one would do. I'd like to have it as a momento of this wonderful summer. The summer I learned to paint with oils. The summer of our visit to the northwest." The summer I fell in love with Jan, she thought, but did not mention.

"Yes, of course," Jane said, dabbing at her eyes. "It has been a wonderful summer, Alpha Lee. I wish both of you girls could stay here with us. ... Maybe I'll make several prints. Roddy will want one, too, and there might even be a market for such a sensitive and beautiful portrait, if you and Susan would allow me to sell it." The painting would be securely packed and shipped to Brick City later; Jane would display it, marked "Not for Sale", at the Schacke for the next month.

The 'Nisqually Princess' would remain at the Seattle Art Museum. Alpha Lee visited Naomi at home on Thursday evening and gave her the enlarged photograph Darius Arthur had made of the painting. "He offered $500 for the painting, Alpha Lee?" Naomi asked, incredulous. "I can't believe it. Oh, don't get me wrong, you did a really beautiful job, honey. You made this old squaw look ... well gorgeous! My grandmother would be so proud. I guess I just didn't have any idea that anybody would pay that much for a painting. Well ...," she said hesitantly, "I think you should take the money, Alpha Lee. What's the sense of me having a treasure like that hanging here on the wall in this little old house, when it could be seen by hundreds of people if it's at the art museum? Go ahead and tell the man to keep it. ... That's my decision, Alpha Lee."

"Naomi, thank you! I think that's the right thing to do. Of course you'll get half of the money and a copy, as I promised. I'll tell Jane Williamson to call Mr. Arthur right away. .. But, Naomi, I want you to promise me you'll go to Seattle and see the exhibit of the work of artists from this area. You said you'd never been there ... you really should see the totem poles, and the beautiful work done by the Indian artists. My picture of your grandfather's fishing lodge is on display there, too."

"It sounds really great, Alpha Lee! If Frank won't take me, I'll find somebody else to go along. I have some cousins who'd be interested,

I'm sure. ... D'you have to leave so soon?" she asked as Alpha Lee rose. "How's your garden doing, honey?"

"It's doing great, Naomi! We're having onions, and there'll be beans and tomatoes soon. And there's some of those squash beginning to develop, too. Tell me, Naomi ... how do you cook 'zukini'? I've never eaten those before, or Jan either."

Chapter 23

"Frankly, Alpha Lee, I thought that so-called 'art' was a bunch of junk," Jan said as soon as they got into the car. They had gone to the Sunday morning service at the base chapel and then, after lunch at Jan's favorite diner, to the Arte Schacke to see the exhibit of the work of one Cecily Martinka, an artist from Chicago whose work was currently popular. Susan was ensconced prominently in the center of the room in one of Jane's big upholstered chairs moved from her house to the Schacke for the occasion. She strummed her guitar and sang softly as the visitors circulated about the showroom, sipping coffee or wine and sampling dainty tea cakes. Miss Martinka was there, her lank black hair hanging below her shoulders, heavy black-rimmed glasses framing her dark eyes. She was dressed in an ankle-length black skirt and a black pull-over with a massive metal chain around her neck, and she smoked a cigarette in a long fancy holder.

"Well ... I guess an artist has the right to do the work he or she is inspired to do," she replied, "but I could never do that kind of stuff. My inspiration just doesn't lead me in that direction. I just don't 'get it'."

"I don't either. I wouldn't hang those paintings on my wall even if she gave me one. Most of 'em are flat-out ugly, and some of 'em look like she was just using up leftover paint ... smearing it around like when you clean paint brushes. ... D'you think Jane really likes that kind of stuff?"

"I don't know, Jan. She has all kinds of things on display there, to appeal to all kinds of people. That artist is making a big impression in the cities, so I guess there's a huge market for it. Look at Picasso ... he's the greatest thing to come down the pike, you know? I don't like his work, either."

"That woman looks like a witch," Jan added, "and she is so put-on! What a fake. Butter wouldn't melt in her mouth." The smell of chicken simmering in a pot with celery and onion greeted them as they opened the door at the lodge. "Wow ... it smells like Sunday in here! Honey, does this ever take me back. At home, Mom used to put on chicken to cook before we went to church, and when we got home, the house smelled just like this ... Mmmm, good."

Alpha Lee looked into the pot and pricked the chicken pieces with a fork. "It's done," she said. "The fire's not quite out, which is fine. I was a little afraid it would go out before the meat was done." She took the pieces out of the broth to cool. Chicken potpie was the menu for dinner; they were expecting Fred and Ronnie at six, and Susan would be back by that time, too, unless she stayed with the Williamsons for dinner.

"I'm going to change clothes," Alpha Lee said, "and then when the chicken is cool enough, I'll take the meat off the bones and mix up the biscuit dough."

"Can I help you change clothes, sweet?" Jan whispered, standing close behind her. He unzipped her dress down the back and slipped his hands inside, feeling the bare warm skin. Her answer was to turn to him and kiss him passionately. "Is that a 'yes'?" he asked as he unhooked her bra.

An hour later, Alpha Lee did change her clothes; leaving Jan sleeping peacefully, she borrowed his bathrobe and walked into her own bedroom to hang up the dress she'd worn to church and to the art show. She dressed in a more casual skirt and a cool blouse and returned to the kitchen to prepare the potpie. Her hands were greasy from the chicken when Jan walked in, wearing only his shorts, and embraced her from behind. "Hmmmm ... I think this is the way it all started, isn't it?" He pulled her hips close against him, enjoying again the pleasurable sensation of arousal.

"Ohhh Jan, Jan." she breathed, "it feels so good to be close to you like that, even with my hands too greasy to touch you!" She laughed. "We can't be alone in this place for five minutes without, well ,you know."

"Well, honey, we waited a long time. We paid our dues, don't you think? We didn't rush into anything, did we?" He snitched a bite of chicken meat from the bowl and licked his fingers.

"I guess not, but it was best this way, I think. We really know each other now. And I was right from the start: You are *the best*, love! The *best* person I've ever known! ... Now, love, we should make some effort to get ready for our guests. Maybe if you would just put some clothes on, it would be a good way to begin! We wouldn't want Fred and Ronnie to arrive and suspect that we've been up to something, would we?"

"I don't think we're fooling anybody, Alpha Lee. But I will get dressed, if you insist."

Alpha Lee had invited Fred and Veronica to come for dinner to provide an occasion to give them their late wedding gift: The wedding portrait she had painted was finally finished, framed and wrapped. Alpha Lee had used the photographs Jan had taken at the wedding, choosing views of Fred and Veronica from different pictures and combining them to paint a dual portrait that flattered them both. The result was not the typical formally posed wedding picture that usually appeared on the society page of the newspaper, but a more spontaneous depiction that conveyed the emotion and joy of the occasion.

She presented it to them after they had finished their dessert and coffee. "I feel bad that this is so late," she said as she brought the large gift to them, wrapped in festive white and silver paper, and adorned with the silver bow she had saved from her birthday gift from Jane.

Veronica was surprised. "Oh, Alpha Lee! We didn't expect a gift from you guys! How sweet you are!" She gave the package to Fred to unwrap. As he tore off the tissue, she squealed with delight. "Ohhh Fred, *look!* It's just so beautiful!" Her eyes sparkled with tears.

"Well ... I'll be damned," Fred said. "Alpha Lee, this is really nice. Really nice," and he reached to pull Ronnie close to him to hide his own emotion.

"Fred, you said it a long time ago, when you looked at my valentine, remember?" Jan asked. "You said, 'Your girlfriend's an artist.' Isn't she ever?"

Veronica got up from her place beside Fred on the couch and rushed to hug Alpha Lee. "I just love it, Alpha Lee! Thank you so much! I can't wait to show it to Mom. I want Grandma and Grandpa Stone to see it, too, someday."

Susan arrived with Roddy just as Fred and Veronica were leaving. "Hi, Ronnie! Hello, Sergeant Harris!" Susan said. "How'd you like that picture? Isn't it sweet? ... Roddy, you remember the bride and groom, don't you? ... What a great wedding that was! ... *So* romantic."

"Did you feel that too, Susan? I sure thought it was," Veronica said. "I've been to several of my friends' weddings, but I think my own was the best of all! And your beautiful song helped make it that way." She smiled brilliantly and turned to kiss Fred on the cheek. Then they turned to go. "Please call me, Alpha Lee ... we could go to a movie or something."

"I'd love that! I promise, I will, Ronnie," and the girls waved goodbye.

Roddy was offered a piece of chocolate sponge roll, and he hesitated only a moment. "Well ... maybe just a little piece." and Alpha Lee went to fix it for him, with a big dollop of whipped cream on top and a cup of coffee to accompany it.

"We had a little private rehearsal," Susan explained, "after dinner. Do you know that song, 'With My Eyes Wide Open, I'm Dreaming', by Patti Page? I just love it. She recorded all four parts, Roddy told me, and they were combined into perfect harmony! Isn't that amazing? Well, I'm gonna sing it, but with only one voice," Susan said, laughing.

"Suzie, with you, one voice is enough," Roddy said gallantly. "It's a great romantic song. All of those guys are gonna fall in love with you."

"Oooooohhh ... wouldn't that be nice!" Susan said, rolling her eyes.

On Wednesday Alpha Lee again caught a bus from the stop near the Arte Schacke and went to Dr. Sparks' clinic, carrying with her the unframed charcoal drawing of Mount Rainier, hoping it would please the doctor. She had shown the picture to Jane, and had told her about her examination. "You aren't pregnant, are you, Alpha Lee?" Jane asked, her voice full of concern. They were in the workshop while Susan watched the front.

"Oh, no," she answered. "Jan and I weren't ... umm ... we didn't... "

"Well, I'm glad you aren't, anyway. That would complicate your life tremendously, Alpha Lee. Please don't let that happen!"

"No, no, no!" she agreed. "I just had some pain ... and Dr. Sparks said I should have an examination anyway, so .... And she told me all she wanted in payment was another charcoal to make sort of a pair with the other one. But I promised her this one would be hers alone, no prints, no duplicates for anybody else." She looked at Jane for approval.

"That just makes it more valuable," Jane said. "You certainly have the right to make that kind of a deal. Actually I think it's a very good deal," and she smiled warmly. "It's a beautiful picture, Alpha Lee. I'd love to see it painted, to see the colors."

"Yes ... it was evening when I painted it, and the pink sunset light tinted the snow so beautifully. Maybe sometime I will go back, when the weather is perfect, and try to capture it in color. ... Now I must go. It's almost time for the bus."

Dr. Sparks was pleased. "Oh, Alpha Lee, I love this," she said. "And I'll bet I know where you went to make this drawing. Is this the view from that pull-off above the river, way up on the mountain? I've been there myself, many times. We used to take a picnic lunch and eat there."

"Yes, yes!" Alpha Lee agreed. "We had a picnic there, too, Jan and I. It was on the Fourth of July. Do you remember what a pretty day it was?"

"It was, certainly. How nice not to have rain for the fireworks that night. Instead, we had a beautiful full moon, didn't we? ... Now let's get down to business, Alpha Lee. Have you had pain during intercourse?"

The directness of the question startled Alpha Lee. "Ummm ... no," she murmured, looking at the floor.

"Fine," the doctor said with a smile. "Marjorie will help you get ready, and I'll be right in to check you."

Again the hard examination table and the stirrups; again the acute embarrassment. But Dr. Sparks was so cool, so matter-of-fact, that Alpha Lee was able to relax a little. "Looks like you're healed and perfectly normal," she said. "Have you had a period since you were here last?"

"No," Alpha Lee answered. "That should happen next week."

"Well, I hope your cramps will be a thing of the past. ... Now I want to talk to you about a diaphragm," the doctor said. She explained the use and care of the device, urging Alpha Lee to become familiar with it so she could be protected against becoming pregnant until she was ready to have a baby. Alpha Lee listened, fascinated in spite of her self-consciousness. "You must be responsible for your own body, Alpha Lee. Don't expect your lover to take care of this important matter."

'Your lover' Alpha Lee blushed at the words. How sweet it sounded.

In a half hour it was over. Alpha Lee dressed and the nurse escorted her out of the examination room to Dr. Sparks' office. "Thank you again, Alpha Lee, for the lovely drawing. It's just exactly what I wanted." Dr. Sparks smiled and grasped Alpha Lee's cold hand in both of her own warm ones. "If you should need a doctor while you're here, you know where I am, Alpha Lee. Don't hesitate to call."

"I'm so glad you like the picture, Dr. Sparks. And I'm so grateful for what you've done for me," she said. "I do hope I'll see you again before we have to go back home," Alpha Lee told her.

"We'll have lunch, Alpha Lee ... I'll get in touch with Jane, and we'll just plan to do that," and she waved as Alpha Lee left the office. I am *so* lucky, she said to herself as the bus pulled away.

Alpha Lee was hand-hemming the blue velvet dress when Jan arrived from class on Friday evening. There were only a few finishing touches of handsewing to do before it would be finished. She had tried it on yesterday and Susan had pinned up the hem; the dress was beautiful, fitting snugly around the bust and waist, with a sweeping skirt that fell several inches below the knee, in accordance with Dior's "New Look" ... not so new after a year, but still the preferred style. The lustre of the velvet accentuated every curve and fold with deep shadow and luminous highlights. The sleeves were short, and the "sweetheart" neckline plunged to a deep V between "cupid's bow" curves over her breasts. As she had cut the bodice in this style, Alpha Lee couldn't help but remember the formal gown she had made with this same neckline to wear to the All- State Chorus last spring... and how, after the Valentine Dance, Mark had bent to kiss her just where a hint of cleavage showed. "Tempting innocence". She hoped Jan would be tempted this time.

But Jan didn't need a sexy dress to be tempted. Even though she was dressed in a casual pull- over top and a full cotton skirt, when he held her close she could sense from his touch how much he was enjoying the feel of her body close to him. She felt a sense of wonder that both of them found such intense pleasure in being close like this ... Love: it sweetens both ways, she thought again. After a long embrace, Jan released her. "God, it's so good to come home to you, sweetheart. It's the best part of my day," he told her with a grin. " Hey, there's good news ... sort of . Today was the last class of the semester. I'll be getting my grade by mail next week. Should be an A ... mechanical drawing is boring as hell, but I'm sure I did pretty well. The final test was Wednesday, and I know I aced it. The not-so-good news is ... Monday starts a new semester, and so my schedule stays the same. And so does the subject ... only this time it's *Advanced Drafting.* so I guess I'll get *Advanced* boredom."

Alpha Lee laughed. "Maybe boring is better than *hard*," she ventured. "Well, you should get all the credits you can, I guess. Summer classes aren't so bad, are they? The semester is shorter, the weather's nice.. When will you finish the second semester, Jan?"

"August 26 ... just a few days before I finish my army hitch. Then I'll be free as a bird, for a couple of weeks. We'll fly back home right away for a little vacation, and you'll get ready to go to college."

Alpha Lee set a cup of coffee on the table for him, and a plate of cookies. "I have a surprise for you, Jan," she said, handing him a long envelope. "I rode the bike up to Naomi's this evening, and she had some mail for us."

Jan helped himself to a cookie and took the letter from her hand. "Thanks, honey. ... Hey, a letter from me big brudder! Now that's a rare treat! Let's see what's goin' on in the old home town." and he slashed open the letter with his pocket knife.

"Morgantown, July 11 Dear Jan,

Thanks for your letter. You made my day. I sat through three boring lectures in subjects I didn't want to take, but am forced to take anyway because they're required for my chosen degree. No, I hadn't heard about you having any young ladies living with you ... you know Mom wouldn't tell me anything like that.

I think I vaguely remember Alpha Lee ... I think she came around after your graduation ceremony. I remember the unusual name (sounds like maybe she was named after her grandma or somethin) ... she was the "well endowed" little gal with the red hair. I remember thinking that you had attracted some *nice* looking ladies to you in high school ... more than I ever did. So tell me, how did you con *both* of them to come out there for the summer? You are some operator, brudder !

Speaking of nice looking ladies, I did go to Charleston over the 4th with Gail Morris ... and I think she is one of the prettiest *and* nicest girls I have ever dated ... and happily for me, she thinks I am special, too. If I ever get finished with this degree and get a decent job, I'm going to think seriously about popping the question. She is a very bright and talented person. She even gets along well with our folks.

Jan, we stopped in on the folks for a couple hours on the way back from Charleston, and I really think this has been a hard year on both of them. Mom doesn't look or act very well ... and Dad is pretty lethargic. The hot and dry weather we had in June may be the cause, but I wonder. They've had to haul a lot of water from the big creek just to keep the garden alive. They've been working too hard for folks their age. We'll go back down there this weekend to see if we just caught them in a bad moment.

As we were eating some of Mom's famous blackberry pie, Gail asked what news they had had from you, and Mom almost burst into tears. She could hardly control her voice when she told Gail that you were firm in your decision to stay out there ... that they had gotten a postcard from you when you were down in Los Angeles "on business" ... and that you had "taken up" with a girl from Brick City. She whimpered something about a "rebound romance". You know she really liked Mona Dee and expected you'd marry her when you finished your hitch. Funny how things turn out. Dunno if you heard ... Dee and that Jack fella from Pgh. were married last month."

....

.... Dee was dressed in a cloud of white lace and satin ... the beautiful "big" wedding dress she had dreamed of wearing years ago. It had cost a lot ... over two hundred dollars; ... the only time she had ever shopped at Benedetta's exclusive formal salon in Harrison, where the rich girls bought their prom gowns and wedding dresses. The money she spent was part of the insurance settlement after the wreck that had broken her leg and caused other serious damage. She had high-heeled white slippers and white silk stockings, and a veil that trailed behind her, falling from a crown of little satin rosebuds. Jack had given her a beautiful string of pearls and matching earrings. She had posed for a portrait by a photographer friend of Jack's in Pittsburgh, and the picture would appear in the Harrison paper (the Pittsburgh Press, too) after the wedding.

But on the day of her wedding ... with her home church decorated with flowers and candles ... Dee felt strangely less than happy. She loved Jack; she had occasionally spent the night with him in his apartment in Morgantown. He was a gentle lover, very considerate and sweet. So what was missing? She tried not to remember ...

When she had told her parents and Linda that she was going to marry Jack, that she had broken off her relationship with Jan, there were shocked reactions all around. May cried, while Burl shook his head and went outside in the January chill with a cigarette and a beer to escape the female theatrics. Linda was hysterical, screaming at Dee, who could do no more than sit with her head in her hands, her eyes filled with tears. Finally, between sobs, she had yelled back at Linda, "Jack was there for me when I needed someone ... he even came to see me in the hospital ... and JAN didn't come ... dammit, he didn't even answer my letter." But she couldn't keep the tears from falling.

Linda retorted "Dee, you dummy! How the hell could Jan come from way out there? And whaddaya mean, he didn't answer your letter? He wrote to you all the time, you dumb cluck! He always wrote to you! He even sent you a ring with a fake diamond for Christmas, for God's sake! You were engaged to him! " I know why you dumped Jan ... 'cause Jack is rich, that's why! You dumped the best guy you'll ever know in this world ... a guy who worshipped the ground you walked on, just so you could marry a rich guy! You're gonna be sorry, dammit!" And Linda rushed up the stairs, slamming her bedroom door with a crash. ....

"Aunt" Budge had been silent, staring at the floor with unseeing eyes. Her hubby Toby tried to be neutral, but he came across as simply dumbfounded, at a loss for words, unable to come up with a wisecrack to break the tension. "Aunt Budge ...," Mona said, her throat tight with the effort not to cry, "don't you think I made the right decision?" There was no answer. "How could I stay here with Jan way across the country, thousands of miles away, for maybe *YEARS*? I didn't know what to do! And Jack is so good to me. He loves me ... he's asked me to marry him over and over." Still the silence. Mona could not hold back any longer. She hobbled to Budge and threw her arms around her and sobbed against her shoulder. "Please, don't be mad at me, Aunt Budge. I'm so confused"

Finally Budge was moved to pat Mona lovingly on the back. She, too, was close to tears. "Dee -- You know how I feel about Jan. He's the best young man I've ever met since Toby was his age. It breaks my heart to think you'll never ..." They cried together. Then Budge pulled herself away, wiping her face with a handkerchief she pulled from her pocket. She dabbed at Mona's wet cheeks. "Honey," she said, "you made the decision. Things will work out. You're right ... Jack does love you, and he's a good person. You can't look back." She smiled a weak, sad smile at Dee. "You have a wedding to plan, honey. ...Let's go shopping for that beautiful dress you dreamed of ." Her throat tightened again, recalling the time when Dee, just sixteen, had described the fabulous dress she wanted to wear when she and her sweet Jan were married ... But she swallowed hard and spoke firmly. "And there are so many things to do, decisions to be made. We must get organized, Dee. The past is past, and the future is exciting. It's *your* life, honey ... you must make it the best possible. Thank God you've got this nice young man to love you and take care of you." And she was able to actually smile at Dee, and quiet her sobbing. And Toby, once again so proud of his wife, walked over and put his arms around both of them. ...

And so Mona walked down the aisle of the Church on her father's arm to the familiar strains of the wedding march ... played not by Elise Short, or by her own sister Linda, but by a woman from Harrison who had been hired for the occasion. Gail Morris, dressed in a lovely pastel yellow dress of her own design, was maid of honor; Elsie Fleisher and Betsy Arnold, another Salt Lick classmate, were Mona's attendants in frilly summer pastels.

And as Mona Dee walked down the aisle, a beautiful bride, with everyone's eyes on her, she felt a sense of unreality ... Why am I here? she asked herself. I shouldn't be doing this ... it's all wrong ... But there was Jack, waiting for her up ahead with the best man and the minister. There was no turning back. There never had been. ... So she lifted her chin, deliberately smiled the dazzling smile that had so enchanted Jan, and became the bride she was expected to be ... a picture of loveliness and joy and anticipation.

Willis's letter continued: "Mom and Dad are looking forward to your visit in September ... I hope you won't have to disappoint them for some reason. I have a hunch that part of their problem is that they don't have their little boy around any more. The old farm is a pretty dull and lonesome place, I'd guess.

But enough of that. I'll try to keep watch on the folks, and let you know if some cooler weather, and a bit of rain, will make them both feel better. With luck, I'll have 3 years of credits worked off by football season, and then only one more to go.

My best to you, and Gail sends her good wishes, too, Ur brudder, Willis"

Jan was silent for a long moment when he finished reading; concern about his parents, and some kind of nameless emotion from reading about Mona's wedding left him subdued. Alpha Lee came to stand beside him, touching his face tenderly. "Bad news, love?" she asked softly.

Her question brought Jan back to the here-and-now, as he offered her the letter. "A little. Will says Mom and Dad seem to be kind of under the weather." A long pause. "He says Dee was married last month. Honey, I don't mind if you read this. You'll meet Willis in September, and I think you'll like him ... and Gail. I haven't met her either, but Willis and I have always been pretty close." He sipped his coffee as he gave her time to read the letter.

She looked at him with pain in her eyes as she finished the letter. "Oh, Jan, I'm sorry. It still hurts, doesn't it?"

He got up from his chair, encircled her with his arm and pulled her close. "Not really, Alpha Lee. ... Just a bit of nostalgia, I guess, and concern about Mom and Dad. ... How can I complain? She's married to her new love, and I have you. Come on over here, sweet thing, let's neck," and he led her to the sofa where they sat close and snuggled until they both were thoroughly aroused. "Do we have time, honey?" he whispered in her ear.

"It's eleven fifteen," she answered breathlessly, stealing a glance at her watch. "Susan won't be home until ...."

He didn't let her finish, smothering her mouth with his. "Let's go into my room," he said, pulling her to her feet. "There's time."

Chapter 24

Alpha Lee was hoeing between the rows of beans when Susan came down the driveway. "I got a letter from Ben!" she cried out.

Alpha Lee straightened and stretched. "Great! It's been a long time since you heard from him, hasn't it? ... Look, Susan ... we have two tomatoes that are almost ripe!"

"Good. I'm looking forward to tomato sandwiches ... BLT's. ... Ben says he's doing okay in summer school ... he's taking chemistry, you know. He'll start the second semester on the eighteenth. Hmm ... that was yesterday, wasn't it? ... What a dismal way to spend a summer! But it's only half a day; then he works with his dad the rest of the time. ... And he says Miss Booker is leaving Brick City High to teach at the University this fall. And Tim and Ginny Samuels had a baby boy, so our principal is a grandpa now," she said with a happy smile. "And, Alpha Lee, they're planning to build a new gym for the High School! I hope that happens ... it's about time."

"That's wonderful news!" Alpha Lee said. "Isn't it fun to get news from home? I wish I'd get a letter. It's been almost two weeks since I wrote to Mother and Daddy ... they owe me a letter. And James, too." She picked up the hoe and took it to the shed. "Oooohh, I'm hot. I need to take a shower before Jan comes home. I made a little fire, which I hate to do, because it'll heat the house so much. ...I know!" she said with sudden enthusiasm. "Let's have our supper out on the pier! At least there'll be a breeze out there."

Alpha Lee hadn't let the fire go to waste; she took a pan of brownies out of the oven to cool. "Let's see ... I'll make some ham sandwiches, and we'll have potato chips and a can of pork and beans. I wish I'd thought of this sooner ... I could've made deviled eggs. Would you cut up vegetables for a salad, Susan, while I shower? There's iced tea in the fridge. If you have time before I get finished, I'd love it if you'd sweep off the pier, too." Susan nodded and went to change into shorts and a cool blouse before attending to her assignments. By the time Jan arrived, Susan had spread a tablecloth on the pier and had placed the sofa cushions around it for them to sit on. She was carrying out the bowl of chips and a plate of pickles when he came in the door.

"Hi, ladies!" Jan sang out. "Whatcha doin', Suz ... are you gonna feed the fish tater chips?"

"We're having a picnic, Jan!" Alpha Lee told him. "I made the house so hot, heating water for a shower, that I thought we'd enjoy the breeze off the sound with our supper. We'll just eat out tonight." He interrupted her sandwich making with a hearty hug.

"Sounds like a good idea to me, this kind of eating out doesn't cost a lot. ... A shower sounds good, too. Can I pop in there and take one before we eat? The souffle won't fall if I delay our meal for a few minutes?" "Gee, I've never even tried a souffle before, just brownies today, and they won't fall. Go ahead, Jan. You can take the fastest showers of anybody I know," she said with a suggestive smile.

"Yeah, I can when I'm motivated," and he winked at her as he headed for his room, unbuttoning his shirt as he went.

The sea breeze with its exhilarating saltwater tang was a relief from the summer heat; the nearby pines provided some shade on the pier by early evening. As they ate their picnic, they watched a pelican sail low over the water and dive to scoop up a fish in its huge beak. "'A peculiar bird is the pelican'," Jan observed, and Alpha Lee provided the second line: "'His beak can hold more than his bellican.'" Together they recited, "'He can store in his beak ... Enough food for a week ...'" and Jan turned to Susan to supply the final line of the limerick.

But Susan just looked puzzled. "What?" she asked.

So Jan finished it for her: "'And I don't know how in the hellican!'"

Susan laughed, and they joined in. "Ogden Nash," Jan explained. "My favorite poet."

"Okay ... is everybody ready for brownies?" Alpha Lee picked up the plates and went into the kitchen to get the dessert. "Ice cream, too, if you want?" she suggested. "It's strawberry," and Jan voted for the ice cream as well. "Tell us what you did today, Jan," she said when she returned with a plate of brownies, still warm from the oven, and Jan's bowl of ice cream. "You're doing the driving classes this week, aren't you? I hope there weren't any accidents or anything this time."

"No, we've got a pretty sharp group this time ... most of 'em can actually walk and chew gum at the same time. Makes our job easier. Actually, Alpha Lee, you may not like what I did today." She looked up in surprise. "The duty roster for next week came down for sign-ups, and I had a choice between taking a six-by-six to Yakima for four days" (Alpha Lee grimaced at that) *or* a band bus to Portland for four... and I took the Portland trip. We'll leave Sunday afternoon and be back Wednesday afternoon. The band is scheduled to do concerts at three high schools and a parade and concert in Jantzen Park on Tuesday night. I guess this is some kind of recruiting tour."

"So you'll be away for a while. ... Jan, how far is Portland? That's in Oregon, on the coast, isn't it? I don't have a clear idea about where it is. Is it an all-day drive? Where will you stay? Will you have to camp out somewhere?"

"Not that far, Alpha Lee. But really, honey, Portland is about a hundred miles from the ocean. It's only about a half day down there for our military vehicles, not all day. They told us we'll be sleeping at an old army barracks in Vancouver, that's in Washington, not British Columbia ... just this side of the Columbia River from Portland. And the good Sergeant Kras will be taking a kitchen crew along, so we'll probably eat like kings."

Alpha Lee sighed resignedly. "Well, Jan, you are in the army ... 'Duty first,' and all that. We don't have to like it, that you're away, but we'll be just fine, and thankful that when you go away, it's just for something easy like this, instead of something dangerous. Susan and I will surely survive ... won't we, Suz? ... But you'll miss your Monday class, won't you? Will you be back in time for the class on Wednesday night?"

"I doubt it, Alpha Lee. By the time we get everything loaded after the concert and stop for lunch somewhere, we'll probably not get back here and unloaded before late. Fred and I'll have to take our books along and do some studying while the band plays on. And then we may have some make-up work to do when we get back."

Susan spoke up. "Jan, you said 'Jantzen Park' ... that sounds like the swimsuit name. Is there a connection?" She smirked: "Is your GI band gonna play for a parade of models in bathing suits?"

"I don't know, Suz ,there might be a connection. They spelled it J-A-N-T-Z-E-N, like the bathing suit company. Maybe they have a factory in Portland. I doubt if we'll see any models in swimsuits, though, but I'll keep my eyes open!" he said with a leering grin. "Maybe you should go along, Suz, maybe you could get a job as a part-time model down there. You've got all the right stuff."

Susan blushed as only blondes can. "Jan, you *are* incorrigible," and she turned and strutted away in her best "Nisqually" style.

Picnic weather ended overnight; the weather front rolled in from the Pacific during the night, and the rains came, with thunder and bright flashes of lightning. Sunshine sought shelter under the girls' bed, and the windows on the west side had to be closed, even though the fresh cool wind was welcome to chase away the heat indoors. Jan and Alpha Lee shared a cup of coffee before he left at a quarter to seven for breakfast at the base. They held each other for a long moment at the door; it would be another long day, with Jan at class until after nine.

"What are you gonna do today, hon?" he asked her.

"I have one more piece of material to make up for Susan," she replied, "now that my blue velvet dress is done. Jan, will we ever be able to go to one of the dances? You haven't had a night off since Fred's wedding."

"That was a month ago, wasn't it? I guess it *is* about time for a break. I'll see if we can do that this weekend, before I leave for Portland. Maybe Ronnie and Fred would take an evening off, too, and we could double date with them. Yeah ... I'll work on that. Bye, I'll see you tonight." and with a lingering kiss, he turned away and dashed out to the car.

"Alpha Lee, I really love that maroon sheath dress you made for me," Susan said over breakfast. She had worn the dress for her Saturday performance at McChord, with the full bell-shaped overskirt Alpha Lee had made from the sheer material of the same color. "There's just one problem: When I dance with those guys, they don't look me in the eye ... they just stare down at my neckline. They're trying to see my breasts, Alpha Lee! It's so low-cut. I can't wear a bra with it because the straps would show ... I guess I should buy a strapless. That would be another eight bucks."

Alpha Lee laughed. "Well, can you blame those guys? A lot of them left their girlfriends back home, and haven't seen a woman close up for months! But I have an idea that might help."

After Susan had left under her umbrella to walk up the driveway to catch the bus, Alpha Lee found the remnants of the maroon sheer fabric, and, folding it in a long narrow bias strip, she twisted and wound it into a large rosette. She secured the lower edges to keep it in shape, and then she sewed two pieces of the matching taffeta to look like rose leaves; which were attached underneath. Susan could pin this big "rose" at the center front of her dress, and the view down her cleavage would be hidden. That should solve the problem, Alpha Lee thought with satisfaction. It's kind of pretty, too.

That project finished, she began cutting on a silky pale green rayon print. This would be another sleeveless summer dress for Susan to wear for her performance, with a flaring skirt that would be perfect for dancing. No problem with the neckline here; it would be a wide "boat" style, exposing some shoulder and upper neck area, but cut high enough not to be so revealing. Sorry, fellas, Alpha Lee thought with a smile.

Alpha Lee was relieved that she was not experiencing cramps on this day, or yesterday. Thank you, Doctor, she thought. My life has changed for the better! Maybe I'll never have to miss school again on my first day. ... I mean, classes at Wesleyan. Her thoughts wandered to the device Dr. Sparks had demonstrated for her ... the contrivance that she could use to prevent pregnancy. Alpha Lee felt some strange combination of emotions ... excitement, guilt, sexual quickening, embarrassment, anticipation. She left her cutting table as it was and went to the bedroom to find the small package. She read again all of the material that was enclosed with the diaphragm, and examined it carefully. The next time ... if there is one, she thought. ... Of course there will be a next time! ... I will 'take responsibility for my own sexual activity', she thought, echoing Dr. Sparks' words. I am an adult woman, she thought; I will do it. .. An 'adult woman'? she asked herself. Sometimes I feel like I'm still just a dumb kid. But when I'm with Jan ...

On Saturday night Susan put on her new pale green dress and thanked Alpha Lee with a hug for making it for her. "This is a pretty color, isn't it?" she asked, looking into the mirror. "I haven't had anything in light green for ages, Alpha Lee." She whirled around to watch the skirt ripple into a wide circle that exposed her slim legs. "I think this one will be a big hit with those guys," she said with a giggle. "They do love to look at legs. And other things," she added with a wink.

"Well, I guess that proves they're just normal males," Alpha Lee replied. She was carefully pulling on her sheer nylon stockings, brand new; while they were beautiful, they were, she had found, very delicate. Inevitably there would be a runner that would ruin them. Tonight she would wear the blue velvet. "I'll be overdressed, I suppose," she said to Susan. "Everybody else will probably wear something more casual. But I don't care! I want to wear this ... I love it." She pulled it over her head and adjusted it, and Susan zipped it up the back. Now it was Alpha Lee's turn to admire herself in the mirror. "Oooohhh, I *do* love it!" she said, smoothing the soft fabric close to her body. The play of light on the velvet created a luxurious sheen and deep shadowed folds, and accentuated the curves of her body.

"Alpha Lee, that is just gorgeous," Susan said softly. "That is the most beautiful dress I've ever seen. It is your perfect color ... your hair just sparkles against that blue. Wow! You are a knockout."

Alpha Lee smiled rapturously. "Thank you," she said demurely. "I've waited a long time, dreaming of hearing somebody say those words. 'Course, it would be nicer if a certain someone said it."

"He will, never fear," Susan assured her.

The girls spent five minutes on the final perfecting of hair and make-up. Tonight, at last, Susan had her hair in the "upswept" do that was so popular in the movies. Jane had insisted that she would take Susan to her own hairdresser, and they had left the Schacke in Marsha Burks' care for an hour that afternoon to get the job done. They were both pleased with the effect; Susan did indeed look very glamourous.

The girls emerged from their bedroom to find Jan waiting out on the pier, watching a mother loon paddle across the water, followed by five young ducklings, almost fully grown. He was dressed in a fresh uniform, sharply pressed at the military laundry facility. He turned to face the girls and feigned shock at their striking appearance.

"Wow! Look at this!" he exclaimed. "The prettiest pair of dolls in the whole world, right here within my reach!" And he did reach to pull them close, one on each side. "Lucky me. ... Hey, stay right here ... I'm gonna get the camera," and he went inside to find it.

When they reached the club at McChord Field, Susan insisted that she would enter through the side door. "If you walk in between both of us, Jan, there'll be a big fuss ... really. Every time I go in through the main entrance, these guys, who know me, carry on, whistling and clapping.

It's better if I sneak in the back way. Alpha Lee looks so gorgeous she's gonna make a big stir anyway. They get so excited about a pretty woman and a new face. I'm warning you, Alpha Lee, these guys are gonna want to dance with you. Better be prepared."

Alpha Lee did indeed turn heads as she walked with Jan through the crowd. When Jan saw Fred and Veronica seated at a table near the bandstand, he led her quickly to sit with them. Ronnie stood to hug her. "Alpha Lee! You look so beautiful!" Alpha Lee smiled and nodded her thanks. "I suppose you made that yourself, you couldn't possibly find anything that fits so well just on a rack somewhere. ... Hi, Jan," she exclaimed. "It's good to see you. ... Where's Susan?"

Jan seated Alpha Lee and smiled at Ronnie. "Hi, Ronnie ... Fred. She snuck in the back way to try to avoid the grand entrance thing, with a bunch of noise from the flyboys. I guess she can't stand the attention," he said with a wink.

"These guys love her, that's for sure," Fred said. "Hey, did you see the picture?" and he gestured toward the far side of the stage, where Alpha Lee's portrait of Susan was displayed on an easel, with a large sign in Jane's own calligraphy beside it. Jane and Charles were seated at a table close by. Alpha Lee was surprised. "Oh, Jan, I want to go over and speak to Jane. Be back in a minute," and she walked across the room. "I'll get us some Cokes," Jan said, and rose to go to the counter .

"Oh, Alpha Lee ... Hello!" Jane said in her deep voice. "How pretty you look, dear! That dress is lovely. I remember when you bought that velvet, when we shopped in Seattle. It's your perfect color. I must say, dear, you're getting some mileage from my old sewing machine! Your skill and your designs are outstanding."

"Thank you so much, Jane. I love using your machine. When I get back home, I'm going to get one for myself, as near like it as I can. It makes the work go so fast. Have you seen Susan? I just finished the dress she's wearing."

"Alpha Lee, I hope you don't mind us using the portrait of Susan here tonight. Roddy just insisted ... and of course I couldn't reach you at the lodge to ask your permission. And Charles insisted that it be framed and protected behind glass before we brought it. I'll keep a close eye on it. It's so lovely. And Roddy loves it. He wants it in the worst way."

Charles motioned to Alpha Lee to sit with them. "I have another request for some artwork, Alpha Lee. Are you available? We want to make up a brochure describing our newest product, that Jan helped dream up ... a double amplifier in a case, to send out to prospective buyers. Could you come to Tak Elek to talk about it with me?"

"Sure I can, Mr. Williamson. I'll drive in on Monday morning ... if that's okay with you. Jan has to go to Portland for a three-day excursion with the band, so I'll have the car." He agreed that they could meet at that time, and Alpha Lee smiled and left them to return to Jan.

When the dance band struck up its first tune, Jan led Alpha Lee to the floor and they danced very close. "Honey, I'm so proud of you! I feel like the luckiest guy in the room," he whispered in her ear. "You look so beautiful."

"Jan, thank you. Honestly ... there was a long time when I thought no man would ever say that to me." Her eyes were shining, the deep blue that he had noticed the first time he ever saw her, so long ago.

Suddenly Jan turned her in a different direction, and whispered: "Look, Alpha Lee ... see that girl over there in the red dress ... good looking, with long hair? ... That's Louise Schaffter! The woman you thought I'd have living in the lodge with me while you did the cooking and cleaning." He chuckled. "Crazy idea! D'you want to meet her?"

"No!" Alpha Lee answered vehemently. "Why would I want to meet her? Now *there's* a crazy idea! We don't have much to talk about, do we?" Alpha Lee discreetly watched as Louise danced with a tall airman. "She *is* pretty ... isn't she?"

"Yeah, I guess so. Not as pretty as you ... and she's not my type." The music ended and the dancers applauded, and they returned to the table. Fred and Ronnie were not there; they had stayed on the dance floor to wait for the next set. "Look at 'em, Alpha Lee," Jan said. "Don't they look like a happy couple? God, I'm so glad they got back together."

"Yes ... it's so romantic. Ronnie is so nice, Jan. She's gonna come out to the lodge next week while you're gone, and I'll help her learn to sew." Alpha Lee's face lit up in a bright smile of anticipation. "We'll have such fun!"

They were sipping their Cokes when a big corporal approached the table. "Hello," he said. "I'm Corporal Calvin Moneypenny, from West Virginia. D'you remember me? We sang together when you guys were here last time."

"Sure ... How are you, Corporal?" Jan said, and he rose to shake the corporal's hand. "Good to see you again. Sit down and visit a spell. It's good to see a West Virginia face ... not many of 'em around."

"You're not kiddin' ... us hillbilllies are scarce way out here," the corporal said with a grin. "Hey ... I just wondered if Miss ... ummm ... Miss Alpa Lee, is it? ... I just wondered if you'd dance with me, Miss.

Miss Suzie said you might. ... With your permission, Private, that is ..."

Alpha Lee looked quizzically at Jan and then at Corporal Moneypenny. "Well ... I guess so ... Jan?" She hoped he would make the decision

"Sure, honey. Who could resist a flyboy from back home? ... Just watch yourself, Corporal. This is *my* girl, y'know." Jan grinned at him as Alpha Lee slowly rose and allowed the Corporal to lead her to the dance floor. "Alpha Lee, I'm gonna go over and talk with Charles and Jane for a minute."

Corporal Moneypenny, Alpha Lee discovered, was not a gifted dancer, but she followed his lead as best she could, and made conversation that, she hoped, would distract him from his fascinated stare down the front of her dress. Now I know how Susan feels, she thought. "Did you say you're from Flatwoods, Corporal Moneypenny?" she asked. "I've just been through there a couple of times on the way to Charleston. Where did you go to high school?"

"Well, Flatwoods isn't much more'n a wide spot in the road," he admitted with a grin. "I graduated from Sutton in 1947."

"Did you play football? You look like a football player."

"Oh, yeah. Where're you from, Miss?"

"Brick City, in Hacker County," she replied. "I've lived there all my life. Did you ever go to Jackson's Mill, Corporal? I worked there one summer. Actually I met a guy from Sutton High School. He was a football player, too. Maybe you know him ... Nick Sizemore?"

"Oh, hell, yes, Ma'am!" he exclaimed. "'Scuse me, ma'am. Sure... Nick was our quarterback. He's tossed me a few passes. Boy, they say it's a small world ... ain't it the truth!" By now the corporal was fully engaged and was looking into her eyes, not down her front, and Alpha Lee felt more at ease. Yes, he had attended FFA camp at Jackson's Mill, he told her; it was a nice place. His family raised cattle, he said; they owned a hundred and sixty-five acres of land in Braxton County. Pretty country. Good deer huntin' there, too ...

When the music stopped, he took her back to the table. Jan had finished a dance with Jane and was just returning. "Thank you, ma'am

... I enjoyed talkin' with you. ... Private, you're lucky, you got a nice girlfriend. Real pretty, too."

"You betcha, Corporal. See you around." Jan shook his hand again and, with a nod to Alpha Lee, the corporal walked back to his table with the loose-limbed farmer-boy walk that Alpha Lee and Jan had seen so often back home.

"He's nice, Jan," she said. "I think he's a little homesick. He enjoyed telling me about his family's farm in Braxton County." She sipped her Coke. "Oh, Jan ... do you think they'd give me some more ice? This isn't cold at all."

Susan took her place in front of the microphone, smiled and waved her acknowledgment of the welcoming applause, and, after a short intro by the band, she sang:

"And now the purple hush of twilight time
Falls across the meadows of my heart
High up in the sky, the little stars climb,
Always reminding me that we're apart"

"Stardust," Jan whispered as they swayed to the slow dreamy rhythm of the seldom-heard verse of the popular song. "What a piece of work it is. And what a piece of work *SHE* is. I think Suz has the prettiest voice I've ever heard, outside of the pro's you hear on the radio."

"Sometimes I wonder why I spend the lonely night
Dreaming of a song ... the melody haunts my reverie,
And I am once again with you ..."

"You know, Alpha Lee ... that song takes me back. I sang that at Waters, in an assembly the last year I was there. It wasa different world."

"It *was* a different world, Jan," Alpha Lee agreed. "Everything has changed so much in just a year's time. You know ... high school is such a sheltered environment. I never realized until now how safe and protected we were; all those years in our own little controlled world. How different it is now. Oh! Listen to me. Let's just be quiet and listen to Susan sing this sweet song," and she closed her eyes as Jan bent to touch her face with his own, kissing her cheek gently. They listened with new awareness to the romantic lyrics ...

"My stardust melody --

The memory of love's refrain."

Alpha Lee's eyes were filled with tears when she looked up at Jan at the end of the song. "I hadn't realized how sad that song is," she said softly. "Funny how you can hear a song a hundred times, and never really understand the words until you really listen."

"Yeah, it is kind of sad. But, Alpha Lee, *we* aren't sad! Hey, I'm one happy soldier. Dry your pretty blue tears, sweetheart, and smile!" He gave her a quick hug right in front of everybody, and they returned to their table.

"Private, that kind of flagrant behavior is out of line for a member of America's armed forces! You've gotta save that stuff for the bedroom!" Fred said in his best "sergeant" tone of voice.

"Okay, Sarge," Jan replied, "we'll just head on home then," and he made a move toward the door . "No, no, don't leave yet!" Ronnie cried, grabbing his hand. "I haven't even danced with you yet ... and Fred, you can dance with Alpha Lee. Let's change partners for this one. Maybe *I'll* get a hug," and she winked at Alpha Lee. So they took a quick sip of Coke and returned to the floor.

Susan had swung into a livelier rhythm as Roddy moved to the piano for the lead in a familiar arrangement of "Near You":

"There's just one place for me ... Near you
It's like heaven to be ...Near you ..."

Several of the dancers were into the jitterbug routine, which wasn't Jan's strong suit, so he and Veronica just stepped smartly in the familiar style he was used to. Fred was leading Alpha Lee in the intricate moves of the jitterbug, and she was gamely following, and, from what Jan could see, she was enjoying herself immensely. When the piece ended, she was happy to sit for a while to catch her breath. "Thank you, Fred ... that was fun! Jan, you MUST learn to jitterbug ... What's to learn?" she asked. "Just do it!"

"I will!" Jan vowed. "Heck, if Fred can do it, I know for sure I can! We'll just try a few steps on the pier, Alpha Lee."

Alpha Lee laughed. "Whooo! That could end in a big splash! ... But we'll do it, won't we, Jan? We'll find the time somehow."

"Yeah, we will! So let's get going! " and he rose and turned again to go.

"NO, no, no! Jan, what's the matter with you?" Ronnie asked, laughing. "The evening is just beginning. *Sit down* a minute. Alpha Lee, don't you have any control over this guy?"

"No," Alpha Lee admitted, with a tender smile for Jan.

Alpha Lee was asked twice to dance by servicemen she'd never even met, introduced by Susan during breaks. "Alpha Lee, this is Sergeant Howard Hillerman, from Melbourne, Florida. I guarantee he's a nice guy, and a great dancer. Make his day, sweet sister," and Alpha Lee followed him to the dance floor, with a backward glance of trepidation at Jan. The second was a tall, tanned corporal from Minot, North Dakota, who told her about his home on the windy plains, and his family of seven sisters and brothers, and the life of a sheep herder. "Kinda boring," he said. "The air corps looked good to me. One of my brothers was in the war, stationed in England. He was a navigator on one of them Flying Fortresses, y'know? ..." These men seemed to welcome the chance to talk, and Alpha Lee was a good listener, fascinated with the various stories these strangers had to tell.

Jan claimed her again when Susan began to sing another sweet slow ballad, and he held her very close, so that every move was as if they were one. "Honey, this velvet is so nice and soft ... You know, you feel like the baby chicks my dad used to get every spring ... soft and warm. I liked to cuddle them in my hands when I was a kid, although Dad didn't want us to do that, they were so delicate. Now I get to cuddle you ... it feels so good."

"Mmmm ..." she replied with a dreamy smile. "I love to be cuddled. Your hands are strong and so gentle ... they give me much pleasure, love."

"Alpha Lee," he said suddenly, "I want to go home."

Susan wouldn't be finished until after midnight; it was only ten. "Yes," she whispered. "Let's leave after this dance."

This time when they told Fred and Ronnie they were leaving, there was no protest. Their need to be alone was understood and unquestioned. "See you Monday, Ronnie," Alpha Lee promised. "'Night, Fred. It was fun being with you folks. I hope we can do it again."

As soon as they were in the car, Jan took her in his arms, stroking her body, enjoying the luxurious soft velvet that covered her. Their kiss was the beginning of lovemaking. Jan drove slowly with one hand on the wheel, his right hand in her lap, clasped in hers. At the lodge, there was no pretense or hesitation; the blue velvet dress was laid carefully across the bed in Alpha Lee's bedroom, with the nylon stockings on top. Underneath she was wearing the pale blue satin bra and panties, frosted with white lace, that had been hidden away since that night last March when she had been with someone else ...

Then Alpha Lee told him, "Jan ... please, no rubber tonight. I have my own way to keep from getting pregnant. Please." let me be 'responsible for my own sexual activity,' as Dr. Sparks said. "I want to do this."

Jan was dubious. "Honey, I've never had intercourse without using a rubber," he said. "Are you sure ...?"

"Yes, I'm sure. I couldn't get pregnant anyway at this time, so... don't worry, love. Trust me. And trust the doctor." She kissed him passionately and he lifted her onto the bed and climbed in beside her.

"I almost wish you could have left the dress on in bed," he said. "I've never touched anything so sexy. You looked so beautiful tonight, honey."

"Just for you, my darling Jan," she whispered. Her every word and every move invited him, and when he thrust inside her, the feeling was so intensely pleasurable that they both came to climax quickly, breathlessly, and they lay a long time, lost in the sweet afterglow.

Chapter 25

Jan awakened to sweet music from the clock radio. The early morning sun had turned the cloud strata on the eastern horizon to fiery orange, and the day creatures began to stir and to assert their identities and territorial claims; he heard gulls screaming even before he could get the radio turned off so as not to awaken Alpha Lee and Susan.

He brushed his teeth and shaved quickly, then put his kit of toilet articles into his pre-packed overnight bag and carried it to the front door. His watch said 5:10, so he knew it would only be minutes before Fred and Ronnie would drive down the lane. He reviewed the "drill" in his mind: Fred would pick him up, drive on to pick up Sgt. Herndon, and they should be at the mess hall by 6:00 for a quick breakfast before manning their vehicles to pick up the band for an 8:00 departure for Portland.

When they returned from the four-day trip, with a scheduled arrival back in the motor pool at four o'clock on Wednesday afternoon, Alpha Lee would have the car at the base, and Jan would drive Fred and Bob Herndon home. That would leave cars available for Alpha Lee if she needed it for errands, for Ronnie to get to her work at the hospital, and for Sally Herndon to take Cheryl to day camp at their church. A very good arrangement, Jan thought. They had even developed a back-up plan, in case of a delay or break-down coming back: Sgt. Herndon could call his wife, and Alpha Lee would stop there before she drove out to the base.

Alpha Lee had heard Jan stirring, and had come in barefooted to stand beside him at the door, with her arm circling his waist, as they watched for Fred's car in the lane. "Honey, you'll be all right while I'm gone, won't you?" Jan asked.

She looked up at him with those pretty blue eyes he loved, and said, "Don't you worry about a thing, Private Short. Just enjoy your trip, and take lots of pictures of the flowers and mountains, so I can see what's down in Oregon too. Someday, Jan, maybe we can go to Portland together."

"I hope so, honey. It's more fun to SHARE seeing new sights with someone you love."

They saw the headlights turn off the street by Naomi and Frank's, and Jan turned around for a parting kiss. "Keep the home fires burning, love."

She reached up with both hands to hold his face tenderly. "I'll be waiting for you here in our little summer nest. Drive safely ... I don't need to tell you that! I'll see you Wednesday, love."

Sgt. Herndon was in charge of the "small convoy", although the Bandmaster riding in Jan's big bus outranked him, since he was a Warrant Officer. But just as surely as Sgt. Herndon wouldn't tell the band what to play, neither would the Bandmaster attempt to direct the convoy. Herndon asked Jan to take the lead bus ... following an MP escort Jeep. Then came Fred's bus and two others, three six-by-six trucks with short tank trailers, and the big wrecker with Sgt. Herndon.

The weather was absolutely perfect, Jan thought ... morning temperature in the high 60's, and the forecast high was eighty degrees with bright sunshine and light winds from the west. As they drove, several members of the band sitting near the back of Jan's bus were playing pleasant dance music as a group. The Bandmaster asked Jan if he minded, and Jan told him he didn't, as long as the players didn't mind him singing along.

Their route took them along Highway 99 through Olympia, with a view of ships in the harbor at the southern tip of Puget Sound, and the state capitol building, then south on the nicest highway Jan had ever driven... for much of this road was four lanes wide, with a median strip, even out in the open countryside, away from towns. He was seeing this part of Washington for the first time; even though his troop train had rolled along on the track beside the highway almost a year ago, it had been at night.

Through Centralia they traveled, and after Chehalis they enjoyed the view of Mount Deschutes; as they approached Kelso, they sighted Mount St. Helens, and finally the lead Jeep pulled into a large parking area where the men could have lunch. After lunch, through Kelso, Jan got his first look at the Columbia River, and was amazed at how wide the river was... wide and blue, and dotted with pleasure boats and barges. He recalled the West Fork back home, never blue; the water was always olive drab, although he had never heard of such a color in those days. The highway ran along the river closely enough that they could often see it as they continued southeastward toward Vancouver. Finally they were able to see the majestic Mt. Hood in the distance beyond Portland ... perhaps the most beautiful of all the peaks in the Cascade range.

Jan noted the farming country they were passing through. Fruit orchards, nut trees, large fields of blueberry bushes set in neat grids and mulched with straw, and always trees, trees, and more trees ... evergreen forests that seemed endless. He was amazed at the loaded log trucks he saw moving along the highway in both directions ... huge trailer rigs, sometimes carrying only one or two logs, but such logs! He guessed that some might be as much as a hundred feet long, and of huge girth; possibly they were redwood, or giant Douglas firs, on their way to the mills.

Finally, after nearly five hours of driving, the lead Jeep turned in to the old Vancouver Barracks, an army camp that had been used only by the National Guard since the end of World War II. They disembarked near a pine barracks building with peeling white paint, and the men were assigned a bunk area and issued clean bedding out of the back of a six-by-six. Sgt. Herndon bunked in an open bay near Fred and Jan, although he could have insisted on a small two-man room. After their beds were made, Herndon asked Fred to supervise the fueling of the vehicles, while Jan was assigned to accompany Sgt. John Edwards of the MP's (who had driven the lead Jeep) to scout out the route to the schools they would visit, and be sure there was adequate parking for the vehicles they would need. The other drivers were given duties helping the cooks set up the field kitchen, and stoking the coal-fired water heaters so showers could be available for all.

Sgt. Edwards had been a recruiter in Portland, and was a native Oregonian, so he knew the city well. They drove across the long bridge into downtown, and followed the route the sergeant had picked, with Jan enjoying the ride, seeing nothing that would cause problems for the buses or the truck that would carry some of the instruments. At last they arrived at Jantzen Park, where the band was scheduled to perform. There were spectacular rose gardens at the park, and Jan made a note to be sure and bring his camera along when the band played here.

Sergeant Edwards loved history, and he told Jan many stories about the early settlers of the rich and beautiful Willamette Valley, and the tradesmen and manufacturers of that time, who also had flourished when the Alaska gold rush lured thousands to Oregon on their way north to the gold fields. As they drove back toward the bridge, he detoured to show Jan the shipyards and commercial docks, full of ocean-going freighters of all types.

When they returned, the band was set up as a concert orchestra, and was having a final practice session. Jan was delighted at some of the music he was hearing ... selections from Gershwin's "Porgy and Bess", and the "Atlantis Suite," which he was not so familiar with. The finale was the stirring "Stars and Stripes Forever," arguably America's favorite march.

At six o'clock sharp a mess sergeant Jan didn't recognize walked into the practice room, and pointed his long-handled spoon at the bandmaster, who waved his baton to stop the music ... and the cook yelled, "Chow's on *NOW* ... and I'll only hold it for thirty minutes, sir ... better come and get it while it's hot." The bandmaster's face pinked, but he recognized the gravity of the situation: this man controlled the food for his band, and therefore the band schedule had to conform to that of the mess hall; it was fair and just. He said immediately, "Dismissed."

After supper, Fred and Jan spent an hour reviewing their Mechanical Drawing text, and, satisfied that they had covered the material, decided to go with Sgt. Herndon to see a movie in Vancouver. A bus had been scheduled to make continuous trips to the downtown area where there were theaters and clubs, leaving the barracks every half hour until midnight. During the short trip downtown, Jan heard a discussion among several band members about their discharge dates, and he discerned that many of these young men, like he himself, had enlisted for the twelve month hitch, and would be going on to college when they were released, just as he had planned to do. I'm *so* lucky, he thought ... *my* college training has already started, and I'm working for a company that *wants* me to get a degree. He grinned so broadly at the thought that one of the bandsmen asked what was so funny; and he replied, "I'm a twelve monther too ... and I'm already picking up college credits at COP. *And* my part-time job in Tacoma will be full-time starting August 30. I really got lucky."

"You're gonna stay out here, Jan ?" Asher Fazzari of Milwaukee asked. Asher and the Gloster twins from Minneapolis had ridden down to Vancouver on Jan's bus ... and Jan had learned that Asher had played his cello with the symphonic orchestra back home. Jim Gloster played clarinet in the orchestra, and bagpipes with the marching band, while his brother Jack played the marimba and tympani, and was a show to be watched with the special Scottish drums when he wore kilts with the pipers. On the trip south, Jack had sat on the front seat across the aisle from Jan, and with a pad and pencil was busy sketching the scenery.

During the lunch stop at Kelso, he had pulled off a sheet and handed it to Jan ... a caricature of Jan holding the steering wheel easily and whistling ... he had drawn musical notes floating above Jan's pursed lips. Jan laughed and then mentioned that his girlfriend was an artist, selling her art in Tacoma, and Jack immediately asked if she was *the* Alpha Lee Evans who had been written up in the newspaper, which Jan acknowledged.

"Yeah, she's been sort of sponsored by Jane Williamson, the lady who runs the Arte Schacke. Have you ever been in there? It's over on

Oceana Road." When Jack answered in the negative, Jan added, "Hey, you oughta go over there when you have some time to kill. Alpha Lee's there sometimes, and her best friend works there during the day. Interesting place." Then he remembered he hadn't answered Asher's question. "Yeah, Ash, I'm gonna stay out here ... I've got a good job and I like the area. I'll take a two - week leave to go back and see my folks, and then come back here to work and get some more college. I'm lucky that my hobby electronics has turned into a sort of profession."

Jack Gloster said, "I thought the newspaper said Miss Evans was from West Virginia. Is that where you're from, Jan?"

"You betcha, Jack ... I'm a mountaineer too ... that's why my left leg is shorter than the right one!" The men groaned at Jan's old joke. "When I get out, I have to take Alpha Lee back home to start college ... she has a grant at West Virginia Wesleyan, to be an assistant."

The crowds at the schools amazed Jan. The Portland Parks Commission had advertised the concerts on the radio and in the newspapers, and even though the schools were closed for the summer, the auditoriums were filled. The applause was generous as the curtains were opened to a seated orchestra on stage; then the audience was thrilled as they heard the bagpipers playing "Scotland the Brave" as they marched down the aisles from the rear to join their comrades on the stage. Each concert lasted just an hour, and included some light, popular music for the younger folks in the audience ... in some cases the songs were performed by a vocal group of band members... and they also played some more sophisticated near-classical orchestral music as well.

But the biggest crowd was at Jantzen Park. A free evening concert had been scheduled to accommodate working adults, with the band seated in a huge outdoor band shell in the midst of beautiful beds of roses, and near the largest swimming pool and dance pavilion Jan had ever seen. Just at eight o'clock the drums rolled in the parking lot, and the haunting wail of the bag-pipes filled the evening air as the pipers marched in stately cadence down the aisles to the stage, to massive applause. Jack Gloster twirled his thickly padded drumsticks with practiced skill as he thumped the big drum that set the marching rhythm. A one-hour schedule was planned, but the audience demanded several encores, and the program actually lasted nearly two hours.

Finally the Bandmaster called for his band to play "The Stars and Stripes Forever", and in spite of thunderous and insistent applause, the band members started folding their music stands and putting away their instruments. Jan felt a thrill of pride in the Second Division Band's performance. These folks just can't get enough of it, he thought. The tour had been a great success.

The trip back was uneventful. Preparations started early after breakfast; a dozen bandsmen had been assigned to help Sgt. Kraskovic clean up the kitchen and make box lunches. Jan and Fred had refueled all the vehicles, and checked the engine oil levels, and thumped all the tires. The buses were swept out, and the loading of the gear and bedding was accomplished by nine. An early morning fog had dissipated, and the convoy rolled northward in perfect weather.

Alpha Lee had watched until Fred's car disappeared at the top of the driveway. Already the lodge felt a bit lonely. It was still early... not even six o'clock yet. She stole back into the bedroom for another short nap before time to get up for breakfast. Susan had not awakened when Alpha Lee got up to see Jan off, and she was still fast asleep.

The girls attended Sunday services at the base chapel, and they met Veronica there. They were seated in their accustomed place when Sally Herndon arrived with little Cheryl, who caught sight of them and begged to sit next to "the bride". Ronnie was glad to see her, and she gave her a quick hug before the little girl sat down, snuggling close to Ronnie. Sally was carrying a big bouquet of summer flowers for the altar, and she excused herself to take them up and arrange them in a large vase beside the candlesticks. Captain Durbin thanked her with a warm smile.

After the service, Sally Herndon invited all of the girls to have lunch at her house, and Alpha Lee and Ronnie followed her in their cars back to the little house with the pink roses blooming out front. The women enjoyed each other's company and the fellowship that came from being left behind when their men were away. After lunch Sally showed them her flower garden. She had an artfully arranged grouping of many kinds of flowers in addition to the rose garden.

"Sally, I think you have a green thumb," Alpha Lee said. "I've never even seen some of these flowers before. What is this?" she asked, indicating a tall bushy plant with odd greenish ball- shaped flowers that looked prickly.

"Those are globe thistles," Sally told her. "I wasn't familiar with them, either, but I thought I'd order some seeds and try them. They are good in dried arrangements, too. I like to make arrangements and wreaths from so-called 'everlastings' for fall," she explained. "This is a wonderful climate for growing things. I'm from Sierra Blanca, Texas, and there's a lot of things that won't do well there, because it's so hot and dry. But the northwest has such great light, and plenty of rain ... It's fun to grow things here."

Susan had a guitar lesson scheduled for two o'clock; she asked if she could call Roddy to tell him she was still in town. He told her he'd pick her up in a few minutes, and they'd do the lesson on his guitar; he would take her home later, he promised. Ronnie and Alpha Lee said their good- byes to Sally and Cheryl, thanking Sally for her hospitality. They were planning to see a movie, "On the Town", that afternoon. "I hate to miss it," Susan said. "I love Gene Kelley musicals, and Frank Sinatra's in it, too! It'll be great. Maybe I'll suggest to Roddy that we should go too."

Alpha Lee grinned. "Sounds like a sure thing to me," she said.

On Monday morning Alpha Lee drove to Takoma Elektroniks to keep her appointment with Charles Williamson; Susan stayed home to do the hand washing and to practice the music Roddy had given her the day before. Alpha Lee chatted with Naomi, telling Naomi about Sally Herndon's garden when Charles came in.

. "Good morning, Alpha Lee," he greeted her. "Nice to see you. Will you come into my office, please?" Charles showed her a small piece of equipment which, he said, he wanted combined with a picture of an airliner in the background. "This will be an informational brochure describing our new development," he explained. "I'd like another charcoal rendering, like the one you did before. Do you think you can do this?"

"Oh, I'm sure it won't be difficult," she replied. "But I'd better do it here, so I'll have the ... the *device* to model. Also I'll need a good picture of an airplane. I'm not familiar enough with airliners to be able to draw one just from memory," she said.

"Fine," Charles answered. "I'm sure we can find something for you. The plane just needs to be a representation ... we'll try to sell it to several companies, so we don't want it to look like any recognizable plane.... Now, Alpha Lee, I have another project I'd like you to do for me personally. I'd like you to paint a portrait of Jane. Her birthday is Septembe first, could you do that before you leave for home?"

The suggestion elicited much more enthusiasm from Alpha Lee than the prospect of doing a charcoal of an inanimate object. "Oh, I'd love to do that, Mr. Williamson! Do you want it to be a surprise? It could be done from a photograph, although a painting from life might be better."

"I'd like it done from life, Alpha Lee. It could be done at the shop, I think. There are days when there's not much going on. And with Susan there, I'd think it would be possible for Jane to pose for you. When could you start?"

Alpha Lee thought a moment. "Well ... I've promised to spend some time with Fred's wife while he and Jan are gone to Portland. ...I'm going to teach her how to sew. But maybe next week? Maybe I could come in on Tuesday, a week from tomorrow, and start. I would guess it might take me a week or two to finish, because she'll only be able to sit a little while at a time, with people coming in all the time. Now, about the charcoal ... Jan will be coming back on Wednesday; I could come here with Jan the next day, when he comes in to work after supper. Would that be soon enough? And do you think you can find a picture of an airplane for me?"

After Alpha Lee left T. E., she drove to Veronica and Fred's apartment, carefully following the directions she had written down the day before. From there the girls drove to a shop Alpha Lee had discovered where she had bought notions for her sewing projects. They looked through the limited amount of fabrics stacked in bolts on the tables, and Alpha Lee suggested a piece of sturdy striped Indian Head cotton for the skirt Ronnie wanted to make as her first project. "The stripes will give you an understanding of how to cut fabric on the straight grain and on the bias," Alpha Lee had told her, "and also how to match the stripes at the seamline. This fabric is strong and easy to work with, and has good body." They picked up a pattern, a zipper and buttons; Alpha Lee had thread on hand that would match.

When they reached the lodge, Alpha Lee found a note on the table: "Jane asked me to come in and help her do some cleaning and rearrange some of the stuff at the shop. I probably won't get back till late afternoon. See you then .. Susan."

"Well, it looks like we have the place to ourselves, Ronnie. Susan's at the Schacke today, after all. They're closed on Mondays, but I guess Mrs. Williamson wants to do some work, she's taken Suz back to town to help her. She's so attached to Susan ... I'm afraid she's gonna miss her a lot when we leave."

Sunshine darted out from under the couch, and Veronica couldn't resist picking her up and cuddling her. "Ronnie," Alpha Lee said hesitantly, "do you think you could keep Sunshine for a while when we go back to West Virginia? We'll be leaving in late August, when Jan finishes his hitch. He says he'll take her back when he returns. He'll continue to live here, I think."

"Oh, Alpha Lee, you know I will! I'd love to. Fred tried to get me a kitten, but all of Millie's were gone by that time.... Don't worry about a thing, we'll enjoy having her."

"Well, that's a relief! I was afraid that maybe Fred was one of those guys who hate cats! A few of them do."

"Cats are a part of life on a farm, Alpha Lee. There were always cats in the barn both at Fred's dad's farm and ours. Otherwise the mice would overrun the place."

"Yes, I grew up on a farm, too, Ronnie," Alpha Lee said as she shook out the length of fabric to spread it on the table. "Daddy had this thing he did: when he was milking, he'd squirt milk right from the cow toward the cats, and they just caught it in their mouths! Then they'd have to do a major clean-up job, licking their fur and whatever was spilled on the floor. We thought that was the funniest thing we'd ever seen."

Veronica laughed, and then became very serious. "Gee, Alpha Lee... you and Jan are going to be separated for a long time ... Are you planning to get married this summer, or ..."

"We don't have any plans, Ronnie, although I do think he loves me and wants to be with me; he's said little things that make me think we'll be married someday. I don't know how we'll manage being apart for so long." She saw the look on Veronica's face that said more than words. "Yes ... I know how much risk there is. Jan's girlfriend, that he expected to marry after his discharge, dumped him when he told her he wanted to stay with T. E. instead of coming back to West Virginia. She met somebody else in college, and he just heard that they were married in June. He was just crushed last winter when he got her letter. That's when we started writing to each other." She paused, and there was silence between them for a long moment.

"I know you and Fred sort of lost each other for a while, and I know it could happen to us, too. I *am* afraid of that, Ronnie. That's why I just want to enjoy our relationship while it's happening, and not look too far ahead. I *do* love him. I am just not interested in anybody else. Nobody could measure up to Jan, he's the *BEST* person I've ever known."

Ronnie saw tears sparkling in Alpha Lee's eyes, and she grasped her hand. "I know how you feel. I felt that way about Fred, too. I couldn't give up on him. He was the one I wanted ... and I'm so glad I went out on a limb and let him know I still cared. ... You and Jan seem so perfect for each other ... I hope you'll always be together."

"Thank you, Ronnie. I'll just have faith that it'll turn out that way for us. Now ... let's dry our tears and get serious about this sewing business!"

Alpha Lee showed Ronnie how to place the pattern on the straight grain, and to line up the seams so that the stripes would match when the two pieces were stitched together. "This makes your skirt look much more professional. If the stripes are mismatched, it just doesn't look right.

Sometimes you even see store-bought clothes with mismatched stripes. They look cheap."

The girls ate grilled cheese sandwiches for lunch, with pickles and chips on the side and fresh peaches for dessert, and then they quickly went back to their sewing project. Alpha Lee mimicked her Home Economics teacher, giving Ronnie the how-and-why each step of the way. "This little electric sewing machine is wonderful, Alpha Lee," Veronica said as she hummed along on the front seam, the stripes matched carefully and held in place with pins. "I had to use a treadle machine in school, and I had a terrible time trying to keep it going. I think I ripped out as many seams as I stitched. I felt like a complete idiot. I guess that's why I never did any sewing after I finished that class. I had bad feelings about it."

"Well, Ronnie, I hope we can change all that! This skirt is really easy and quick to put together. You could make another one in a different material later on. When we finish, we'll start on the blouse ... that's a bit more complicated, but you'll catch on in no time."

It was almost five o'clock when Jane brought Susan home. "Well, hello, girls!" she said. "What are you up to? Oh, a sewing lesson, I think. Very nice, Veronica." Ronnie was standing on a chair, with Alpha Lee pinning up the hem, measuring with a yardstick from the floor to make sure it was perfectly even.

"Nice skirt, Ronnie!" Susan exclaimed. "Are you gonna make a blouse to go with it?"

"Thanks, Susan. Yes, I want to but I'll have to work tomorrow ."

Alpha Lee inserted the last pin and Veronica climbed down from the chair. "Excuse me," she said. "I'll be right back," and she went into the girls' bedroom to change into her slacks. Susan followed, eager to get into her cool shorts.

As Alpha Lee began to straighten up the sewing mess, Jane approached and laid her hand on Alpha Lee's shoulder. "Alpha Lee, Charles told me that I'm to have a birthday surprise! I am so thrilled at the prospect of having my portrait painted! I'm in a tizzy, trying to decide what I should wear, and so on. When can we start?"

Alpha Lee smiled. "I'm excited, too! I'm glad I can do it. I told him maybe we could start next week ... Tuesday, maybe? Or I could come in on Monday, if you'd like. You decide on what you want to wear, and your hairdo, and maybe jewelry ... and let me know."

After a minimum of persuasion, Veronica decided to stay overnight, so she could finish the skirt, and Alpha Lee could show her how to cut out the blouse the next morning. She helped Alpha Lee fix hamburgers and canned baked beans, and the girls had a pleasant evening that included a sing-along with Susan playing guitar accompaniment, and lots of laughing. Ronnie and Alpha Lee took turns hemming, and the skirt was finished by bedtime. They put clean sheets on the girl's bed, and Alpha Lee slept in Jan's room.

The next morning, after Susan left to go to work, Alpha Lee and Ronnie worked quickly to get as much done as possible on the blouse before Veronica had to leave for her two o'clock shift at the hospital. "Can you come back out here tomorrow morning, Ronnie? If we can get it finished, you could surprise Fred with a new look when he gets back! Making the buttonholes and sewing on the buttons will take a little time, but the buttonhole maker on this machine makes it much faster than doing them by hand."

The girls worked as quickly as possible, and by noon they were well along on the blouse, and Veronica was delighted, both with the way her outfit was coming together and with what she had learned. She left immediately after lunch to give herself time to get home and shower and change clothes before going to work. Suddenly the lodge was quiet and a bit lonely for Alpha Lee; but she felt satisfied with her time with Veronica and grateful that she could help her learn and to get a pretty new outfit made to show off what she had learned. I wonder what Jan and Fred and the band are doing, she thought as she picked up the sewing debris and put the machine away. Then she gave herself a moment to sit on the pier in the sun, her bare feet dangling, just to enjoy the silence. There was, as always, the music of the birds and the water, as the wavelets splashed against the pebbled shore. She felt a sense of peace; Oh God, she prayed, I am so thankful for my life. If this is a dream may I never wake up. She went to get her charcoals and drew just what she could see from her place on the pier, and she hoped the picture would capture some of the quiet joy she felt.

Veronica was back early on Wednesday morning, and the finishing work on the blouse began. It was made of soft semi-sheer white cotton with small navy blue buttons down the front, and the job of carefully spacing the buttonholes and then stitching them on the machine was the most challenging technique Veronica had to learn. Alpha Lee made the first one, demonstrating the method; then Ronnie made one on a folded scrap, for practice. In a while the row of six were finished, and ready for the buttons to be sewed in place under the buttonholes.

While Veronica sewed the buttons, Alpha Lee set up the ironing board for a final pressing of the finished pieces. "Alpha Lee, I can't believe we got these done so fast!" she said. "It's a lot simpler than I remembered. Maybe I didn't pay as much attention when I was in school. I was only fourteen, I think, and not much interested anyway. But this outfit just went together so easily and quickly. I'm anxious to try something else!" Veronica laughed. "If my mother could see me now. She won't believe this. ... Now the big question: How am I gonna get a sewing machine?" She frowned, perplexed.

"Maybe you could find a second-hand one ... I'll bet there's lots of women who have machines they don't use ... just like Jane. She might even sell this one to you, she said she never uses it. A second-hand machine would be so much less expensive than a new one."

When Ronnie tried on the finished blouse and skirt together, she posed in front of the long mirror in Alpha Lee's bedroom and smiled happily. The narrow white stripes on a navy blue background met in perfect inverted V's along the front seam of the skirt, and the blouse looked cool and fetching. "Do I ever feel smart!" she said. "Fred will be impressed. I wish I could go with you to meet them, Alpha Lee, but I have to work again. In fact, I have to leave immediately ... I'm due at the hospital at two again. I won't see Fred until after eight o'clock." Veronica folded her new clothes carefully and put them on the back seat of the car; then she hugged Alpha Lee. "Thank you so much, Alpha Lee. It was lots of fun working with you. Do you think we could do it again sometime? You have a whole month before you have to leave?"

"Sure, we could. Think about what you'd like to make next. It would be fun to make some-thing really pretty, to wear to the USO, wouldn't it? We'll go shopping again, and look at patterns and material. I'd love to. See you soon, Ronnie."

It was almost time to leave for the motor pool. Alpha Lee dressed with Jan in mind, and touched her pulse points with the lilac cologne. She looked in the mirror and saw reflected her own eagerness. Oh, Jan, she thought, it'll be so good to have you home again!

She parked outside the motor pool in an area where she could see the gate, and while she was waiting, she was reading a book Susan had given her about Italian Renaissance artists. She admired the many colored illustrations that had been included depicting the works of Raphael, Leonardo da Vinci, Michelangelo ....

At last, there they were, the convoy of four big olive drab buses, followed by the six-by-sixes and the wrecker. Alpha Lee smiled and waved as she saw Jan's bus roll into the compound, within fifteen minutes of his estimate of their return. She quickly got out of the car, waving at him, and he acknowledged her greeting ... as did Fred and Sgt. Herndon as they passed.

The mail clerk handed out letters to the drivers who had been away, and finally Fred and Sgt. Herndon and Jan walked toward the car where Alpha Lee waited. She was wearing a light summer dress she knew Jan liked, and their embrace was long and lusty, while Fred and the sergeant looked on and grinned knowingly.

Chapter 26

As usual, there was a large crowd at the USO club at McChord Field on the first Saturday night in August. It was a warm, balmy evening with the promise of rain in the air, and it was stuffy inside the ballroom. Ventilation was provided by a large roof-mounted exhaust fan that pulled air through the open front door and removed some of the cigarette smoke, but it did little to cool the place when it was filled to capacity as it was tonight.

Susan finished her second solo, and quickly, before anyone could ask her to dance, picked up her purse and headed for the ladies' restroom. She could not explain the moodiness she felt on this night. She wished Alpha Lee and Jan were there; she always felt happier when they were in the audience. She looked at her watch ... ten minutes to nine. Jan would be home in a half-hour or so; why couldn't they just drive on out for a while? I suppose he's tired from his long day, she thought.

Susan checked her reflection in the mirror, touched up her lipstick and dabbed on a bit of cooling cologne. She was wearing the flowered full skirt Alpha Lee had made, worn this night with a sheer pink blouse she had found on sale ... a pretty combination, she thought. It was really too hot for the sweaters, even though they were short-sleeved. Susan became aware of an unpleasant odor ... Smoke, she thought. Something's burning somewhere. Trash? Must be someone burning something nearby, she thought. It didn't smell like cigarette smoke; she was quite used to that, since most of the men smoked. She dismissed it from her mind and returned to the hall, where Roddy and the band were playing a fast instrumental number and several couples were jitterbugging.

She bought a Coke and sat down at Jane's table. "Oh, Susan ... I'm glad you're back. I'm going to leave at the next intermission. Do you mind? Of course Roddy will take you home."

"Okay, Jane." She laughed. "'Home' ... this place feels almost like home to me, I've spent so much time here." She took a long sip of her drink. "But I sure wish Jan and Alpha Lee were here."

"Is there no chance they'll come by late?"

"I don't think so. By the time Jan gets home on the nights he works, he's usually pretty tired. I'm sure they didn't plan to come tonight. Alpha Lee said she was going to do some garden work and then take a shower. No ... I don't look for them. But they'd better be there for me on my last performance. That's only three weeks from tonight."

"Oh, Susan, I don't even want to think about that," Jane said with a wistful smile. "How are we going to get along without you? ... I wonder if Roddy will try to find another girl vocalist. The men have enjoyed you so much."

Susan smiled and thanked Jane. Then she frowned. "Jane ... do you notice that smoky smell? I noticed it when I was in the rest room. It's getting strong, even in here with the cigarette smoke. I don't blame you for leaving ... I'll bet other people will leave, too."

The music ended and the audience applauded, and Roddy started his verbal countdown for the next number. But he was suddenly interrupted by the harsh clanging of the fire alarm. The Master Sergeant who managed the club walked briskly to the stage and, with a glance at Roddy, he grabbed the microphone. "*ATTENTION PLEASE*, ladies and gentlemen," he said loudly, "we have a problem. We must ask you to vacate the building *NOW!* There seems to be a small fire somewhere in the ventilating system." Even as he spoke, there was the sound of sirens, faraway at first but coming nearer. Everyone stood quickly, their chairs scraping the floor noisily. The sergeant held up his hands for attention. "Let's have an orderly evacuation, people. Men, get your partners and form a line, and exit from the nearest door in good order. *No panic, No running -- No screaming!.* Everything's under control."

He turned to Roddy and said something, and Roddy spoke to the band and they struck up a fast march tempo. The sergeant nodded and again spoke to the moving crowd. "That's right, folks. Just be calm and leave the building as rapidly as possible. Give way to the firemen ... they'll be here soon. Thank you for your cooperation." The sergeant's voice was overwhelmed by the sirens as the big trucks pulled in, just outside the front door. Two firemen rushed in, their faces dripping with sweat from the exertion of running in their rubber jackets and heavy boots.

The hall was emptied in less than four minutes, as the smoke thickened. Roddy quickly picked up his guitar and music folders, directing the band to take their instruments and music and leave immediately. Jon was carrying his drums to the big car where Jane waited; Susan picked up her guitar and another of Jon's drums and hurried outside, and started to return for another load.. "Suzie, we've got all we can take," Roddy told her. "The piano stays. They'll get this thing taken care of in a little while, I'm sure. Let's go, honey." With his arm around her waist, he propelled her out the front entrance. The look on her face was stricken. "Don't worry, Suzie. It'll be okay."

The parking lot was filled with people, unwilling to leave, unable to resist watching the firemen at work. No flames were visible anywhere, yet there was a lot of smoke pouring from the roof near the big exhaust fan. The firemen had rushed back outside and erected long ladders, then they moved up quickly to the roof and ran to the big metal cage that held the fan, pulling a heavy fire hose with them. Over the noise the watchers heard the lead fireman on the roof yell: "Electrical fire! Bring up the CO2 units!", and soon another fireman carried one up the ladder.

Master Sergeant Portman approached Roddy and Susan. "Sorry this happened, Mr. Williamson. We'll have everything fixed up by next weekend ... so plan on being here again, with your beautiful singer," he said, with a smile in Susan's direction. "Sounds like just a fan motor on fire. I've never seen that happen before. Have to replace that, I guess, but there won't be much damage inside." He nodded to them both and hurried off to attend to the business of dispersing the crowd.

Roddy drove slowly, navigating through the crowd and the traffic, while Susan sat silent beside him, staring straight ahead, her hands clenched in her lap. When finally they were out of the congestion, he reached for her hand. "Sorry this had to happen, Suzie ... it sure messes up our evening, doesn't it? D'you want to go to a late movie or something? That'd take your mind off of it."

"No," she said in a small sad voice. After a long pause she added, "I hated to leave the piano. Do you think it'll be ruined?"

"Oh, I don't think so, Suzie. I don't think there'll be ANY water damage. You heard the sarge ... he didn't seem to think it was as serious as it appeared to be, with all that smoke. It'll be business as usual next week, I think. We'll concentrate on practicing for our next gig." Roddy was not driving toward the lodge; he had taken the beach road, and now he parked as close to the water as possible. "Let's walk down to the shore, Suzie, for just a little while. I think we need to sorta calm down, don't you?"

"I can't walk on sand in these shoes!" she said impatiently. "I just want to go home, Roddy. I want to tell Alpha Lee about the fire."

"Take off those high heels, honey. We'll head for the lodge in just a few minutes. I'd just like to talk a little while. Okay?"

"Oh, I suppose so, Roddy. Just a little while. I'm tired," and she took off her high heeled sandals, and then, turning her back to Roddy, she unfastened her stockings and removed them, too. I can't walk on the beach in my good stockings, she thought. They'd be ruined.

Roddy opened her door and took her hand, and they walked down to the water. The vast expanse of the sound stretched on forever toward the western horizon. The moon in its waning quarter floated in a sea of clouds, now visible, now hidden, and reflected its bright silver on the waves. "This is nice, Roddy," Susan said. She looked up at him and smiled. "Thanks for bringing me here ... it's so calm and beautiful ... it makes me feel better."

They sat on a huge rock, and Susan dangled her feet in the water. Roddy asked about her plans for the future, and about the college she would be attending. Classes would begin, she told him, the Monday after Labor Day; she and Alpha Lee would move into the dorm on the weekend before. He told her his teaching job would begin on that day, too, after a two-day orientation for all teachers. He would continue with the week-end performances at the clubs, but with a significant difference: His beautiful singer wouldn't be with them. "The troops are gonna miss you like the dickens, honey."

She looked up at him with a sad smile. "I'll miss them like the dickens, too, Roddy," she said tremulously.

They walked slowly back to the car, Roddy's arm around her waist. Susan tried to rub the sand from her bare feet before she got into the car. As soon as they were seated, Roddy turned to her. "Suzie, we've only got three weeks left. I'm hurting already. I hate to see you go."

"You can find someone else, can't you, Roddy? Surely there must be girls around here who could sing with the Outlaws."

"I suppose there are ... but I'm not just talking about that, Suzie." He hesitated, and, turning to face her, he grasped her hand and kissed the palm. "Don't you know, Suzie, I'm in love with you. I don't want you to leave." He tried to pull her close, but she resisted.

"Please, Roddy, you know I have someone back home --"

"Suzie, I don't think I believe that. I think this 'Ben' is just an excuse to put me off. Besides, in this game, 'someone back home' means nothing. We're together, and I love you, and I can't believe that you don't have some feelings for me." When she didn't answer, he took her in his arms. "'No more Mister Nice Guy', Suzie." and he kissed her lips as he had never done before ... hard and hungrily.

Susan was torn; Roddy's kiss felt like coming home; she could not resist responding to him, and yet she was terrified, as though she were wading into an ocean, turbulent and huge and dangerous. After a long moment, she pulled away from him. "Roddy ... please take me home now! I don't want to do this."

"Suzie ... please give me some kind of hope. Please tell me you'll come back next summer. Won't you just think about it? Jan will be here, working for T. E. and living in the lodge, just like now; he and

Alpha Lee will surely get married before long, and she'll come back, won't she? I know she will. I want you, Suzie. I want you to be here with me." He stroked her hair and her cheek and pulled her close again. "We've had such a great summer. Please don't tell me we'll never be together again." And he kissed her again, deeply and passionately. "I love you, Suzie," he whispered.

"Ohhh, Roddy ... " She began to cry softly. "You've been so good to me ... so sweet ... such a dear friend." He kissed her eyes, tasting the salt of her tears. "Being friends has been so easy, so nice and comfortable. This other stuff is so ... so scary and complicated." She looked at him pleadingly. "Roddy ... please don't push me. I do care for you, a lot, you know ... but I just can't get too involved ... or something. I don't know what I want. I'm afraid," and the tears came again. Roddy handed her his handkerchief, since she didn't appear to have one of her own.

"Okay, honey. I don't want to cause you any pain. ... We'll just go on as we have been, okay? We'll get together on Wednesday evening for rehearsal, and we'll be 'friends', if that's what you want for now. But you know how I feel. I love you, Suzie," and this time he just held her close in his arms until he could feel her relax a little. "Let's go home, honey," he said, kissing her on the forehead. She smiled at him gratefully.

Roddy drifted slowly down the driveway and stopped near the porch. Susan reached quickly to open the door, but he stopped her. "Suzie, can I come in for a few minutes?"

"Oh, Roddy ... please just let me go. I'm so tired."

"Okay, okay ... I'll go. But I'll be out tomorrow afternoon for your lesson, just like always." He got out of the car and came to open her door, and they walked together to the door. Before she could go inside, he pulled her close again and kissed her hard on the lips. She did not pull away from him. "Good night, Suzie."

"'Night, Roddy," she replied, unable to find words. "I'm sorry." He squeezed her hand and smiled down at her troubled face.

"It's okay, honey. I'll see you tomorrow," and he turned with a wave.

There was a dim light in Jan's room, and in the kitchen, and Susan could hear music; Jan had his radio playing. She wondered if Alpha Lee was already asleep. Still in her bare feet with the pretty high heeled shoes dangling from her fingers, she padded into the lodge and closed the door. She became aware of strange sounds ... a rhythmic moaning that awakened both curiosity and ... something else. The door to Jan's room was ajar. She tiptoed close to the doorway, and ignoring a warning voice in her mind that said, *DON'T OPEN THAT DOOR!*, she pushed it open. There in the shadowy lamplight, she saw Jan's naked body, moving in a slow rhythm, and Alpha Lee's legs extended ... The moaning grew in intensity and urgency ... and Susan could hear, could *feel*, in her mind her own voice making those same sounds, with a hard hand pressed over her mouth to muffle her ... Suppressed memories flooded her mind, and she felt, to her horror, her own sexual response awaken in reaction to the sight and sound ... and as she stood unable to move, she heard the unmistakable sounds of orgasmic ecstasy ... both voices crying out in a duet of sexual climax. Susan clapped her own hand over her mouth, and turned to run like a terrified animal to the front door and out to the porch. She screamed "*RODDY! ROD-EEEE!*" but it was too late ... she saw the taillights of his car just pulling out of the driveway at the top of the hill. She collapsed in a heap on the porch, clutching herself and sobbing hysterically, as she experienced the sexual reaction she had hoped she would never feel again...

For Jan and Alpha Lee, there was this time no sweet afterglow to complete their lovemaking. They jolted apart ... Alpha Lee grabbed her robe and threw it on as she rushed from the room crying, "*Susan! SUSAN!*" And Jan dragged himself out of the bed in a state of groggy confusion to search for his shorts.

Alpha Lee followed the sound of Susan's wailing to the porch. She found her curled in a fetal position, her hand pressed between her legs. "*SUSAN*" she cried. "What happened? Susan ... are you hurt? What ..."

"*STAY AWAY FROM ME, YOU FILTHY WHORE!*" she screamed, repeating the word: "You're a *whore! A fornicator! I HATE YOU!*"

Alpha Lee felt as though her blood had drained from her body, stunned and uncertain of what was happening. She approached Susan and knelt beside her. She could hardly speak. "Susan," she said in a choked voice, "... what's wrong? Are you all right? What ..."

Susan's reaction was swift and violent. She struck at Alpha Lee with both hands, slapping and pushing. "Don't you dare touch me! Get away from me, you filthy harlot!"

Alpha Lee was knocked off balance and fell backward, almost falling off the edge of the porch. She scrabbled at the rough floorboards and regained her balance, and turned angrily to face Susan. "*SUSAN, SHUT UP!* Her voice was so uncharacteristically loud and harsh that Susan was taken aback, staring at her in bewilderment.

Jan, in nothing more than his shorts, had come as far as the front door; he waited, bewildered and anxious, uncertain whether to intervene or to stand by to see how this bitter interchange would work out. Alpha Lee took advantage of Susan's momentary shock. *STOP CALLING ME THOSE NAMES, SUSAN!* she shouted. "Just listen to yourself! You sound like your father, using those hateful Bible words!"

"*NO NO NO!!*" Susan screamed, falling face down on the porch in a fit of hysterical crying. "Don't say that! *I HATE HIM!* Don't talk about him! I wish he would *DIE!* I wish I could *KILL HIM!*"

Alpha Lee was stunned. She had a feeling that something enormous was happening in the dark places of Susan's mind. She ventured close enough to touch Susan's heaving shoulder, and her voice returned to its customary softness. "Susan ... don't worry about that now ... you're safe here. He can't hurt you any more."

Susan sat up in a sudden move, and Alpha Lee flinched, expecting another onslaught. She was astonished at the look on Susan's face: Her eyes were unfocused, her cheeks flushed, her teeth clenched. "*DAMN HIM!* she screamed, pounding furiously on the porch floor. "I wish he would *DIE!* He hurt me ... he ruined me ... he did *BAD THINGS* to me! He ..." Her voice dropped to a whisper: "He had *CARNAL KNOWLEDGE* of me, Alpha Lee! He did that ... lots of times ... He *ruined me forever.* Damn him! Ooohhhhh!" Her cry was like she had physical pain.

Alpha Lee stood, turning to the doorway where Jan waited, shocked. He came out, and together they lifted Susan to her feet. She struggled violently against them at first, cursing at Jan shrilly. "*You son of a bitch! You raped Alpha Lee. You ... you ... screwed my friend.* You're just like *ALL MEN!* ... all you want is ..." Susan could not say the gutter words.

She beat against Jan's chest and sobbed, her face contorted with rage. And then she seemed to run out of strength, sagging against him as though she couldn't stand alone. Jan encircled both girls in his arms. Susan was still sobbing, and Alpha Lee was crying, too. He hugged them strongly; Susan had lost the strength to resist.

"Poor Suz," he murmured into her ear. "Don't be afraid, honey. You're safe ... you're always gonna be safe. Don't cry."

"My goddamned so-called father!" Susan wailed. "He did it to me, lots of times! He told me it was God's will ... He told me it was what he was supposed to do ... Oooohhhh ... I wish I could die... I am so wicked and filthy ... I'm ruined forever." She was trembling violently, and her face was a ruin, swollen and flushed, her make-up washed away with tears. ".I heard you two having sex! I saw you ... I didn't mean to ... I heard you, and I opened the door, and ..." She struggled against him. "I'm sorry. ... Oohhh, God, I wish I hadn't done that!" Her tears started again, the violent sobs shaking her body and stopping her breath. When she could speak again, the words came in a confused tumble. "It made *me* have those ... feelings ... again... too! No, No! I don't want to think about ... *NO ... I won't!* It didn't happen ... I'm not ... I didn't do it, I didn't!" Again she fought against Jan's tight embrace as though trying to escape a demon. "I'm gonna go to hell! God will punish me for ... Let me go!"

But Jan held her firmly, afraid to release her in her frenzied agony. He spoke calmly to her as he held her. "Suzie ... you are safe. We love you, honey. God loves you, too ... Don't worry ... you haven't done anything wrong ..."

"You don't know ... I've sinned terribly. You just ... don't know," she mumbled brokenly between sobs. "I'm gonna burn in hell ... I know it!"

Suddenly Alpha Lee spoke, her voice steady and normal. "Susan, why did you come home early? Are you sick? Did they call off the dance?"

And to Jan's surprise, the return to everyday concerns seemed to cool Susan's hysterical frenzy. She swallowed hard and answered, "Yes... there was a fire. The club was full of smoke ... the sergeant made everybody leave. The guys just grabbed their instruments and went out ... but we had to leave the piano ..." Her tears began afresh, but more quietly. "I hated to leave that beautiful piano ... but Roddy said it probably wouldn't be damaged ... the fire was on the roof ... Everybody had to leave ..."

Jan seized the moment of Susan's more relaxed state. "Let's go inside and have a coke, or something. Come on, girls ... my sweet ladies ... you can tell us more about the fire, Suzie ... ", and he gently propelled them inside. He almost fell over Susan's discarded high heels as he stepped into the darkened room.

Jan brought glasses of coke while Alpha Lee sat with her arm around Susan's trembling shoulders. "Alpha Lee, I'm sorry I said those things to you ...," Susan said mournfully. "I didn't mean it ... I'm just so darned mixed up ... I feel so ba-a-a-ad ..." She found her purse where she had dropped it when she had first come home, and under the balled-up stockings, she found a handkerchief and wiped her face. "I didn't do it," she mumbled to herself. "No. I didn't do it. I dreamed it ...it was a bad dream..." Her voice was resolute in denial.

Alpha Lee was dazed by the horror of Susan's confession, but she knew there was more that would have to be told. In spite of her own dread, she turned to Jan. "Why don't you go back to bed, Jan ... Susan and I will talk a while, maybe ... and we'll go to bed, too."

"Sounds like a good idea to me," he said wearily. "Are you sure everything's okay? Suz, will you be all right?" he asked her, and he stood and laid his hand gently on her shoulder.

"Yes," she answered shortly.

"Good night, then, honey ... please get some rest." He bent and kissed her wet cheek. "You're safe here. We all love you."

Alpha Lee rose to join him and they held each other for a moment. He whispered in her ear, "I love you, sweetheart," and gave her a quick kiss before turning to go to his room. Susan pushed away her glass, her drink unfinished. Alpha Lee sat down beside her at the table and waited for her to speak.

"Alpha Lee ... you and Jan were ... umm ... '*DOING IT* '... I saw you. Have you been having sex every time I'm not here? Have you been doing it all summer?" Her voice was constricted, full of pain. "You and Jan are so beautiful together ... but I didn't want to think about *that!* ..."

She hesitated. "Susan, I don't want to talk about this. It's sort of personal ... you know. Jan and I love each other ... and when a man and a woman love each other, this is the natural thing that happens... otherwise it would never be complete."

"How does it feel, Alpha Lee?" Susan asked, her face turned away.

"It feels wonderful. I want to be with him forever. I wanted that before we came out here,...well, you remember, I told you how I felt when we were on the plane. I loved him before we ever ... even before he ever kissed me. ... Susan, I'm not ashamed. You called me a lot of stupid things a while ago ... but I don't feel sinful. I feel like this is the way my life is supposed to go."

Susan's eyes filled with tears again. "It'll never be that way with me," she said, her throat tightening. "I'm the one who is a harlot. I am so ... so damned. I am ruined, Alpha Lee. Ben, or Roddy, or whoever thinks he loves me, will never know the truth. I won't tell them, and I won't fall in love with anybody, and I won't let them love me. It just wouldn't be right."

Alpha Lee reached for Susan's hand. "I'm sure you're wrong, Susan. What *IS* the truth? Can you tell me why you feel so guilty? If your dad hurt you, you're the *victim*, not the guilty one. *HE* is guilty."

"Yes, the *SON OF A BITCH*, my own father, the Reverend Remagen" her voice was filled with bitter sarcasm ... "is guilty as hell. But I am, too. ... Okay, Alpha Lee ... you want to hear the truth? You won't be my friend any more." She sniffled and dabbed at her eyes with the already-damp handkerchief. "You won't want to sleep with me ever again. But I'll tell you a little bit. Enough to make you retch! ... My father 'knew' me carnally. He did those things to me. He touched me, and he made me think it was okay. ... It started when I was twelve, when I just started ... umm ...developing, you know. After I started having my period. Mother Geraldine was gone for the afternoon, and he came into my room with his Bible, Alpha Lee. He talked to me about 'becoming a woman' ..."

"You are becoming a woman, Susan," Reverend Marshall Remagen told his daughter gently as he closed the bedroom door behind him. "There are important things you must be taught now, and it is my duty as your father and a man of God to help you understand your role in life as an adult woman." He sat down in a small chair, crossed his legs and indicated that she should sit on the bed. "As you must know, God has blessed the union of a man and a woman, and the first man in your life experience is, of course, your father. The time has come in your life when I must teach you your womanly responsibilities." He opened his handsome leather- bound Bible to the place marked with a white satin ribbon. "Let us share the Word, Susan."

"This is from the The Song of Solomon, daughter. ... Behold, thou art fair, my love ... My beloved spake, and said unto me, Rise up, my love, my fair one, and come away. For, lo, the winter is past, the rain is over and gone; The flowers appear on the earth; the time of the singing of birds is come, and he voice of the turtle is heard in our land; ... Thy two breasts are like two young roes that are twins, that feed among the lilies ... Thou are all fair, my love; there is no spot in thee..." Marshall Remagen laid the Bible beside Susan on the bed. "You are my beloved, Susan ... my beloved daughter, and you, too, are fair and spotless. Through Solomon ... that wise patriarch who spoke the Proverbs ... the Lord has sanctified physical love between man and woman, and through these words has described the beauty of a woman's body." He embraced her, and his hands lingered on her breasts. "Susan, take off your dress, my beloved child, and reveal the beauty the Lord hath delighted in."

Susan hesitated; it didn't seem right to her to take off her clothes ... But this was her father, after all; and besides that, he was God's servant; it *must* be okay, she thought. She took off her blouse and skirt. "Now your brassiere and your panties, my sweet child. Your body must be pure and uncovered before the Lord."

Susan looked at the floor and stood unmoving. "I don't want to, Dad. Please don't make me do that ... I feel embarrassed ..."

"Your embarrassment is because of vanity, Susan, or what the Bible calls pride. Pride is one of the Seven Deadly Sins." As he spoke, he began to push down her panties. Susan was miserable and afraid; but she did as he told her, and stood naked before him.

He reached into his pocket and withdrew a small bottle of baby oil. "Now, my dear child, I will anoint thee, to initiate thee into thy new status as a woman," and, pouring a small pool of the oil into his palm, he began stroking her shoulders, her neck, her breasts. Susan was over- come with the strange sensation that flooded through her body. His hands moved down to her stomach and groin; his fingers probed between her legs. She felt weak; she could hardly breathe. "Lie down on the bed, Susan," he told her, and slowly, confused by conflicting emotions and overwhelmed by powerful physical reactions, she did so. She felt dreadfully exposed and vulnerable. "Lie on your back, Susan," he said. Reluctantly she obeyed, and he poured more oil into his hand and stroked her thighs and down her legs. He took off her shoes and rubbed oil on the soles of her feet.

Then he bent over her and kissed her on the lips, on her breasts and her pubic mound. She felt paralyzed and horrified; and something more ... a stirring of something she had never felt before.

He helped her get to her feet. "That will do for today, Susan. We'll have more orientation sessions from time to time. Just remember: You are a child of God, spotless and pure. You belong to the Lord ... and I am his representative." He smiled benignly and turned to leave. "Now, get dressed as quickly as possible. You'll feel much better as time goes by ... this process will make you feel sanctified and serene. Bless you, my child.

... "That was just the first time," Susan said, her eyes downcast, her voice tight. "Every time my stepmother was gone, shopping or to a Ladies Auxiliary meeting or anything, he came to my room for a 'lesson', as he called them. He told me our sessions were to be kept secret ... even though, he said, he had told Geraldine what he was doing, which I know for sure now wasn't true. ... Oooohhh, Alpha Lee ... I can't tell you how awful I felt! I was just positive it was wrong, wicked, sinful, what we were doing; but he kept talking about God's will, and him being an instrument of the Lord, and that kind of stuff. I didn't know ... did I? How could I stand up to him, to defy him? I was just a dumb kid ..."

... "You have never seen the male member, Susan," he said to her in a matter-of-fact tone one winter afternoon some weeks later. ("It was like he was teaching a class," Susan told Alpha Lee bitterly.) He exposed himself and placed her hand on his penis. He demonstrated how a condom was put on; she wondered why he had done this, but was too mesmerized to speak, to ask the question. He placed his hand over hers, closing it firmly over himself, and moved it rhythmically under his own. In minutes he grunted and moved jerkily as she felt a spasmodic movement and a sudden hotness under her hand. He was breathing quickly, his eyes closed, and he made strange guttural sounds. She was terrified, both by his odd actions and by her own physical reaction, as though things were happening to her body that she had no control over. When she made small whimpering sounds, he clamped his hand hard over her mouth. "Hush!" he hissed. ...

"One day he told me to kneel before him," Susan said. "I thought he wanted me to pray ... but that wasn't it! He pushed that big thing into my mouth, Alpha Lee!" Susan again shook with violent sobbing. Almost unable to speak, her voice continued as though she must rid herself of words that she could no longer bear to hold inside her. "He held my head against his hairy smelly body and pushed it into my mouth! I gagged and tried to pull away, but he kept holding me and talking like a ... like a teacher, or a policeman, or something ... like I *had* to do this!"

Alpha Lee was sickened. She remembered Mark, and the condom covered with her own blood She embraced Susan and wept with her. "One time when Mama Geraldine and I were alone, I tried to tell her about the things he was doing to me. I was afraid, but I was desperate for someone to talk to, to help me! D'you know what she did, Alpha Lee? She took me into the bathroom and she got the half-used-up cake of Ivory soap that everybody had been using when we took our baths, and she shoved it into my *mouth*, Alpha Lee! It was soft and melted, and it made me gag." Susan was almost screaming, gagging again with the pain of the recollection. "She said, 'Such filthy lies to come out of your mouth! *If I ever hear such smut again. I'll REALLY scrub your mouth out with soap.* so you'll never forget it!' ... I'll never forgot it, Alpha Lee. I still remember the taste of that soap ... it was in my teeth and down my throat. I had to brush and brush to get rid of it. I thought I was going to throw up." She was quiet for a moment, wiping her face with her ruined handkerchief. Alpha Lee rushed to find another one for her. "That's when I knew I had *NO* help, *NO* escape. I knew what was happening would never end ...

"There was *no one* I could talk to. So ... I just obeyed him. I accepted my fate: I would never have a real boyfriend. No one would ever want to marry me. I belonged to my dad ..."

"Susan," Marshall Remagen said softly to his daughter after he had brought her to orgasm with his fingers during one of their "lessons", "you must beware of these young boys at school who want only to use your body for their own pleasure. You are too young and innocent to be violated by these boys. At this point in your life, you legally *belong* to me, so I can protect you. You must *never* allow those boys to touch you! Even if they just put their arm around you, or try to hold your hand, you must be aware that this is the first step in seduction. What they are aiming for eventually is to rape you, to *HURT* you, Susan, in the back seat of their dad's car! *DO NOT* give them any encouragement! If you permit this kind of wickedness, I will be forced to punish you, and that would cause me great pain."

"I *belonged*' to my dad! As long as I 'behaved', and did as he told me God expected me to do, he was very loving to me. ... It makes me retch to think about how '*LOVING* ' he was! ... Ooohhh, Alpha Lee!" She broke down into a paroxysm of sobbing, writhing and twisting as if to escape from the torture of her memories. Alpha Lee hugged her and spoke softly as to a child in pain.

Susan took a deep breath and spoke the appalling words in a tightly controlled voice. "After a long time ... after he made me feel a sexual climax many times ... I ... I began to *enjoy* it. The feeling it gave me was so powerful ... so exciting, so thrilling ... that I actually looked forward to it!" She turned to face Alpha Lee. "*YOU* know! I asked you how it felt, a while ago ... but I *KNEW* how it felt! Oh, God ... I wish I could forget. I don't want to remember ... Now do you understand? *I AM GUILTY TOO!* I actually *WANTED* it to happen! I *LOVED* that thrill, Alpha Lee! Don't you understand? Don't *YOU* love it? .... Well? Answer me, dammit! Don't you love it when Jan does that?"

Alpha Lee could not speak. God, help me! she prayed. I don't know what she wants from me! I don't know what to say ... Finally, she murmured, "Yes, Susan, I love it. But Jan is my lover ... our relationship is not ..."

"Dammit, Alpha Lee, I know that! It's okay for you ... that's what you're telling me! Sinful for *me*, but *okay* for you!" She smirked bitterly.

"He's the *BEST,* isn't he? ... Oh, Alpha Lee! I wish I had a boyfriend like that. I never will. Never. No one will want to touch me ... I am damned. I had sex with my own father, lots of times! And I actually *ENJOYED* it! That has to be the worst sin of all!"

... After months and years of sexual episodes between Susan and her father, all pretense of "training in womanly responsibilities" was abandoned. Whenever they were alone in the house for an hour or two, it was understood by both of them that there would be 'love' -- there was not even a need to talk about it. Susan's emotions were so conflicted that she was torn and tormented. She came to her father as a lover, and yet she hated him (and herself) for what she knew instinctively was unspeakably immoral.

She cringed and cowered; she couldn't look at herself in a mirror. If her stepmother suspected, or even knew, what was happening, she said nothing. The only thing that helped Susan escape from her self-hate was music. Nancy McAllister encouraged her and gave her what little training she was able to provide, and Susan warmed to Nancy's kindness. And when Ben Humboldt began to show an interest in her, Susan was again torn. She secretly enjoyed Ben's adoration, but she was deathly afraid of what would happen if her father found out about it.

By the time Susan was eighteen, he had become suspicious, domineering and abusive. Some-times he slapped her hard if he believed that she was consorting with any of her male class-mates. He watched from the window when she walked home from school, her head bent, her eyes downcast,... always alone.

And on the day when Susan threw caution to the winds because she was feeling so safe and happy in the warmth of Ben's affection, and she walked home smiling up at him, unsuspecting of her father's surveillance, she was taken by surprise when she opened the door and her father struck her brutally, repeatedly, while Ben stood by, incredulous and incapable of stopping the attack.

"It was *MY FAULT* when he beat up on me. He tried to hit Ben, too, but Ben fended him off. Ben tried to help me, but Dad kicked the door shut in his face and just kept hitting me till I fell down on the floor." Susan began to whimper again, sniffling into her handkerchief. "He was waiting for me to come home, I suppose," she moaned. "He expected me to ... to go to bed with him, I guess. He called me a *WHORE* ... he said I was tempting other men to fornicate with me. He told me I was going to go to hell, that I was filthy and sinful ..." She looked up at Alpha Lee hopelessly. "Oh, Alpha Lee ... I *AM* sinful. What am I gonna *DO*?"

"Susan--" Alpha Lee began, not knowing what to say. "Susan ... I don't think you are sinful!" She pulled Susan's cold hand into both of her own. "You're a *victim!* I think your father has committed terrible things against you. I think he has hurt your mind even more than your body." Alpha Lee had no doubt about that. How could Susan reconcile these horrific memories, and her corrosive guilt, so that she could go on enjoying the happy life she had been experiencing during this summer? The question drummed in Alpha Lee's mind ...

And some answers began to form, the beginnings of vague inspiration. Prayer, of course ... if Susan could believe in its power. Something else: Alpha Lee remembered someone who had reassured her non-judgmental, comforting, matter-of-fact ... someone who had calmed her agitation and made her feel comfortable, confident ... and *not guilty*: Dr. Sparks. She would call Dr. Sparks and see if ...

"Susan," she said, "I know it's been terribly hard for you to talk about this stuff. I didn't really want to hear this awful stuff, to tell you the truth ... it's like a nightmare ... scary and almost unreal. But, Susan ... Gee ... you're just exactly the same person that you were yesterday. You're still my best friend. I still love you like a sister, and Jan does, too. And all of those GI's ... they'll be looking for you next weekend ... they love you. Jane loves you. And Roddy, Susan, you know darned well Roddy does ."

Susan looked stricken. "Oh, Alpha Lee ... what am I gonna DO? I think he does."

"Susan, I don't know. I am *so tired..* It's past two o'clock, Susan... I can't even think straight any more. You must be worn out completely! Let's go to bed. We'll both feel better tomorrow, I just know it. ... Susan, you're still my best friend. Please remember that. We are *not* harlots and *fornicators* and *whores*. We're *FRIENDS*. Can't we just leave it at that, and go to bed?"

They slipped under the covers and Alpha Lee embraced Susan and whispered, "Good night, sweet sister. ... Hey ... let's say 'Now I lay me down to sleep' together ...?" And they did, like children; Susan sniffed only a little, and was asleep in minutes.

Exhausted as she was, Alpha Lee could not fall asleep; her mind was in turmoil from the terrible, incredible revelations she had heard. She yearned to tiptoe into Jan's room and climb into bed with him, to feel his warm arms around her, to sleep peacefully beside him. But she stayed with Susan, who needed her even more than she needed Jan.

Chapter 27

"But, Alpha Lee, I'm not a psychiatrist ... I'm not sure I could be of much help to your friend -"

"Dr. Sparks, you were a great help to *me*, when I was feeling upset. Susan is much more seriously disturbed than I was, certainly ... but I just think it would be helpful to her to talk with you. You have a way of putting things in perspective. She just needs to talk with someone with a calm, professional manner ... and I thought of you right away. Could you possibly find time for her ... just a half-hour or so? I know you're busy ..."

"Well ... let me see." There was a pause; Alpha Lee could visualize Dr. Sparks looking through her appointment book. I have *some* nerve, she thought, calling her to ask her to talk to Susan. Maybe this is a crazy idea; but I just have faith in Dr. Sparks' calm manner and good sense to help Susan get over her guilt ...

"Could you bring her to the clinic tonight, Alpha Lee? It isn't open in the evenings, but I could come in for a while ... would seven be possible for you?"

"I think so ... Yes, I think that would be perfect. Jan will be in class tonight; I'll ask for the car and we can come in after supper. I'm glad you can see her so soon ... this big blow-up happened on Saturday night, and I think it's best that she talk with you as soon as possible. She's still very emotional and depressed."

"Okay ... I'll see you at the clinic tonight at seven."

Susan had slept late on Sunday, after the exhausting turmoil of the previous night. Jan and Alpha Lee went to the chapel and said some earnest prayers for her. She was just getting up when they returned to the lodge. She was unnaturally subdued; the "Nisqually" posture was forgotten as she slumped in her former demeanor, her eyes focused on the floor.

"Is Roddy coming this afternoon, Suz?" Jan asked.

"I think so," she muttered.

"Honey, don't let him see you like this," Jan said, his arm around her shoulder. "He won't understand what's happened to you ... and I don't think you want to tell him about it." She jerked away from him as though his touch burned her skin. Jan looked at Alpha Lee for help.

Alpha Lee shook her head slightly and moved close to Jan. "Jan's right, Susan," she said. "Don't forget: *Nisqually*. Please be yourself, sweet sister."

Susan reluctantly straightened, and smiled a blatantly artificial smile. "Hmmm ... that's a little better," Jan said, "but I hope you can be more convincing by the time he gets here."

Alpha Lee engaged Susan in helping fix lunch. Focusing on the real and practical seemed to help her put aside her misery, and soon she was able to smile at Jan's gentle teasing. After Alpha Lee had removed the lunch dishes and placed a plate of cookies on the table, Jan said, "You know, girls, we've got to start winding up this operation. Three weeks from today we'll be packing and getting ready to make the flight back home. There's a bunch of things we have to finish up here. Alpha Lee, can you make one of your famous lists, so you can be thinking of the loose ends you need to tie up? Like taking Sunshine over to Fred and Ronnie's? And ... what's the status of Jane's birthday portrait?"

"I've already started, Jan," she replied. "The portrait is on schedule. Another item: We'll have to send a box of Susan's clothes separately ... she has a lot more to take home than she brought out here. It sure won't fit in the suitcase.

"And my portrait, too," Susan added. "Can we take that on the plane, or should it be shipped somehow? Maybe I should ask Jane.

"Yes, do that, Susan. ... And there's the garden," Alpha Lee said. "How I do hate to leave it behind, now that the tomatoes are coming on so well, and those great beans! But Naomi will probably be willing to pick whatever's ready and maybe sell the extra, or just give it away to some of the 'old ones' who need food."

"And when I get back, I'll be happy to take it over again," Jan said. "Those tomatoes taste like home. I'll bet Mom is busy canning."

Susan was disinclined at first to talk with Dr. Sparks about her private shame. In the light of day she even regretted her frankness with Alpha Lee, and she tried her best to re-bury her disturbing memories and pretend that the entire episode never happened, but Alpha Lee would not let her. "Dr. Sparks is so realistic, so sensible, Susan," she told her. "I'm sure she can help you to get rid of this terrible guilt, so you can have a normal life and make better decisions about your relation-ship with Roddy. And Ben ... and whoever else comes along."

"I hope *NOBODY* else comes along," Susan responded gloomily. "I already have too much to think about, and I don't know what to do."

Susan's session with Dr. Sparks on Monday evening lasted much longer than a half-hour. Alpha Lee sat in the waiting room, having decided, against Susan's wishes, that it would be better for her to talk with the doctor alone. She had brought along a book to read, although it was hard to concentrate. I'm glad it's lasting so long, she thought. That can only mean they're doing some serious talking, and Susan hasn't panicked and walked out.

"... Susan," Dr. Sparks said, after listening to a long, harrowing recital of humiliation and guilt, "are you willing to allow your father to reach out from wherever he is, to control your life far into the future ... to keep you from living a normal life ... marrying and having a family, and all that?"

"*NO! Of course not.* Of course not," Susan sniffled, dabbing at her face. She had brought along plenty of hankies this time.

"*OKAY!* Then you must take control of your own life, Susan. This long, horrible enslavement is over; do you agree?"

"Yes ... I know that. My foster mother, Nancy, and Dr. John, will adopt me, and I won't have to even see my dad, ever again ... I hope."

"You are an *ADULT* woman, Susan. You can make your own decisions. You are surrounded by people who love you. You are blessed with a unique talent. You have been saved, Susan, by FACING your demon and acknowledging it. But that salvation will only work if *YOU* are convinced that you no longer owe your father anything ... not even *hatred* or resentment. You are *FREE* ... and whatever you felt in the past, Susan, is *PAST.* It can only impact your life, and your future ... if you choose to let it do so. *LET IT GO*, Susan." She reached out to clasp Susan's cold damp hands in her own. "I want you to walk out of here with your head high, remembering that you are the captain of your soul, the master of your fate. Open yourself to love, Susan ... whatever happened between you and your father has been faced and passed by. It has nothing to do with your future relationships. You are *FREE!*. You are *FREE!*"

Susan looked up to face the doctor with a strange expression. 'You are free.' It was a revelation. Susan actually seemed to feel a burden fall away. She returned Dr. Sparks' smile and murmured, "Thank you, Doctor. I'M GONNA BE OKAY."

When she came out of the examination room, Alpha Lee could tell instantly that something icy cold in Susan had begun to melt. She was walking tall again and, with just the ghost of a smile, she said, "Let's go *home*, Alpha Lee. *HOME.*"

Chapter 28

Wednesday afternoon; rain. The oppressive humid heat of the preceding days had been cooled by the big storms that had rolled in from the Pacific. Alpha Lee had surrounded her easel with whatever lamps she could find to augment the weak overhead bulb. She was doing the finishing work on the portrait of Jane Williamson. This was the largest canvas she had ever done; Charles wanted a big picture, almost life-size.

There had been several sessions at the Schacke, with Jane posing for ten minutes at a time, between customers. She had chosen a deep green cock-tail dress of lustrous taffeta, which Alpha Lee found easy to capture in oil. More difficult was the emerald and diamond necklace she wore, a gift from Charles on their twenty-fifth anniversary. Can you paint the sparkle of a diamond? Alpha Lee asked herself. Tiny points of white against the skin tones was the best she could do.

Actually Jane was very pleased with the portrait; she accused Alpha Lee of flattering her, which was true, albeit very discreetly. She had rounded the sharp contours of Jane's face and arms, and deleted some of the wrinkles in her neck and face. The dark hair shot with gray was pulled back in Jane's customary French twist, and Alpha Lee had enhanced slightly the smooth highlights this severe hair style revealed.

Jane wore a long smock to protect her silk dress while she worked between the sittings. Alpha Lee thought it might have been more realistic to paint her in the smock! That would be the perfect illustration of her work and lifestyle. But Jane looked regal in the luminous deep green, with her diamonds at her throat; this portrait would be treasured, Alpha Lee thought, and she determined to give it her best.

Now it was finished; the last of the dark background was drying slowly in the damp air. By the week's end, Alpha Lee thought, I can take it to Charles to be framed. He had something very special in mind for a frame, he had told her; he had bought a beautiful antique frame, teakwood inlaid with ivory. Alpha Lee hadn't seen the frame yet, and Jane didn't even know about it. It must be really special, Alpha Lee thought. Teakwood, I'll have to go to the library and look that up. She was familiar with the hardwoods that grew plentifully back home, maple, oak, walnut.

"That's really gorgeous, Alpha Lee!" Susan exclaimed when she came home from work. "Jane'll love it. How much are you gonna charge Charles for it?"

"He offered me two hundred, without even seeing it completed," Alpha Lee answered, "since it's so *big*. But of course I can't accept that much money. This has been a labor of love ... just like painting your portrait was." She was fixing tomato sandwiches for supper, with cheese and sweet onion slices, and there was lemonade for a change from iced tea and coke. A small bowl of potato chips completed the meal. There would be strawberry ice cream cones for dessert.

"I'm hungry," Susan said, "and this sure looks good. Alpha Lee, you are so good at fixing meals. ... and making clothes, and painting ...,"she added. "I just have to say *thank you* ... for lots of things. Thank you for being such a friend ... and for forgiving me. ... and for taking me to see Dr. Sparks. Oooh, I'm getting misty ..." she said with a twisted smile.

Alpha Lee laughed as Susan hugged her. "What an emotional response to a tomato-cheese- and-onion sandwich! I'll have to try one on Jan," she said mischievously.

The painting, carefully draped in a sheet, was delivered to Charles on Saturday, with Jan driving. Charles cleared his desk and the two of them were able to install the painting into the heavy antique frame. Charles was very pleased. "This is way beyond my expectations," he said exultantly. "Wow, it looks beautiful in that frame, doesn't it, Jan? ...What a good-lookin' woman!"

Jan agreed, refraining from voicing his thoughts: Skinny old Jane never looked quite *that* good! But, then again ... maybe she did, a long time ago when Charles fell in love with her ...

The portrait would be delivered to the Arte Schacke the following Saturday. Charles had invited Darius Arthur to be there for the presentation, and Jon would be on hand with his camera to take his mother's picture for the newspaper's Arts section.

Alpha Lee declined Jane's request that she appear in the news photo. She felt that the emphasis should be on Jane herself. "And," she explained, "I'll be gone from here in a couple of weeks. It won't matter who painted Jane's portrait; just some stranger from the east."

But Jane did insist that the girls be her guests at lunch, along with Frances Sparks. And so, on Monday they drove again to Seattle, and had lunch at the little tea house near the Art Museum. Dr. Sparks was privately gratified to observe that Susan seemed animated and congenial; from all appearances she seemed to be handling her new-found "freedom" well. Susan had given her a "daughter-to-mother" hug when she had come into the Arte Schacke, and as if she could read the doctor's thoughts, Susan had turned to her a few times with a smile in her eyes that spoke many words.

On the same Monday afternoon, Jan found a note tacked beside his name on the bulletin board: 'SEE THE FIRST SERGEANT'. After he had washed the truck he had been driving that morning, he walked to the Orderly Room. Corporal Dunmyer greeted him. "Hey, short-timer ... the first soldier told me to give you these clearance papers and explain them to you. Sit down here a minute," he said, indicating a chair beside his desk. Jan sat and waited while the corporal dug through a stack of papers in his tray. "Here it is, Jan," he said, handing him a file folder full of forms. "Your discharge date is next Monday, Jan, but you'll be clear *only* if you get all of these forms signed. Now, you may think some of this stuff is not very important; but this is the ARMY, and if you want to get out on time, and get your final pay and your travel money, you *will* report to all of these various offices and get a signature on each and every page.

"A couple of your destinations are on the main fort, and the Captain says you can take a Jeep, if you wish ... in fact, he almost insisted that you do that, so you'll be more available for duty. You can start first thing in the morning, and when you get this all finished, you will report back to Sarge Herndon ... but right now this is your number one job. *If* you're lucky, you'll be done in two days, maybe less. Any questions?"

Jan leafed through the pages, which were fastened inside the folder with a metal clip, reading the names of the places he would have to go: the laundry, the library, the Chaplain, the Special Services Club, the Mess Officer; the medical facility and the dental offices. He didn't see any problem. He did have questions as to the requirement to report to some of these facilities; but he remembered, as Corporal Dunmyer had stated, this is the Army ... so he just shook his head. "Nosir, Corporal ... no questions. I'll hit it first thing in the morning."

When Jan returned from class that evening, he sat at the table sharing a last cup of coffee with Alpha Lee. She told him excitedly about the trip to Seattle, where she and Susan had had lunch with Jane and Dr. Sparks, and showed him the gift Jane had given her: a beautiful basket woven of the long needles of the huge pines, made by a local Indian craftsman. It was decorated with quills and abalone shell and obsidian beads, in the traditional fashion. "Jane told me this is to keep my sewing things in," Alpha Lee said, "and there is a silver thimble inside, with my initials engraved ... see?" She excitedly showed him her gifts. "She gave Susan a heavy bracelet, silver with copper inlays. She was thrilled."

"Jane is one classy lady, honey," Jan said. "Both of the Williamsons have really been nice to us. ... Did you ever settle with Charles on the price of the portrait?"

"Yes. I asked him for fifty dollars."

"You're kidding!" Jan replied. "I thought he offered you two hundred."

"He did ... but I refused the offer. I told him I was glad I could do this for Jane, who has done so much for me, and for Susan. How could I possibly have accepted such a huge payment? Anyway, he wrote the check for a hundred. Fifty dollars would have been plenty. That money, plus the thirty he paid me for the charcoal cover drawing for the brochure, will pay for most of my plane fare back home.

"Speaking of that ... the Army has set things in motion for me to terminate my association with them. I got my papers today, and tomorrow I'll start what they call 'clearing the base'. That means I have to report to a whole bunch of facilities and make sure they're willing to let me go. Cut the strings, so to speak," he said, draining his cup. "Is there any more coffee, honey?"

She brought the coffee pot and refilled his cup, emptying the last gritty bit into her own cup. "I wondered if there would be any kind of termination ceremony or anything," she said.

"No ceremony ... just a lot of runnin' around gettin' signatures on a bunch of papers. They'll not waste a ceremony on a 'short-timer'. As a matter of fact, I'll bet the Army discontinues this one-year hitch deal ... there's no pay-off for them. Just a bunch of guys like me, getting the bare minimum of military duty out of the way so we can go to college without fear of being drafted for a longer hitch. No ... this is just the Army's way of letting everyone know that a soldier will be leaving the base. They call it a 'PCS' ...'permanent change of station'. Can you believe they have a special nomenclature for *leaving*? I have to get all of my medical and dental records that becomes part of my permanent file in the Pentagon. There's a record there for every member of the armed forces, past and present, which is kept probably forever, and probably in triplicate." Jan grinned. "First thing you know, they'll have so much paper in that place that maybe they'll have to remodel it into a *hexagon* ... or maybe even a dodecahedron!"

Alpha Lee giggled. "I remember 'dodecahedron'," she said, "from Miss Booker's geometry class: a twelve-sided figure. Yeah ... that'd be good... it would hold lots more file cabinets than a Pentagon! ... But, Jan, why would you have to go to the library, and the Chaplain?" she asked. "Why would they care who comes and goes?"

"Well, Alpha Lee ... I suppose maybe there might be some guy who has an overdue book that they want back ... hey, it belongs to the United States of America, doesn't it? They won't let you out of the Army with a library book fine overdue! And I suppose the Chaplain needs to know in case of an emergency at the soldier's home, or something like that. The Red Cross would maybe try to arrange an emergency leave, granted by the Chaplain. ... I dunno why, honey ... but this is the Army, and don't you forget it. Everything is done *their way* ... sometimes even for a reason, and PROBABLY always in TRIPLICATE."

"Jan, I've been thinking, and meaning to ask you: After you get your discharge, or transfer to the reserves, or whatever ... and when you come back out here to work full-time at T. E. ... will you ever be back on the base?"

"I don't think so, Alpha Lee," he answered. "I won't have a sticker on my windshield, I'm sure, so I'd have to register as a visitor to get on the base. I wouldn't be able to buy at the PX or any-thing like that... unless my reserve assignment is here. But that doesn't mean I won't see Fred from time to time, or Sarge Herndon."

"Well, that's good. You and Fred are more than just army buddies, aren't you? I knew you'd want to keep in touch with him and Ronnie. Ronnie and I plan to write to each other. We've become good friends, Jan. She is so funny, and so sweet. I'll miss her a lot." Then she asked, "Jan ... will you get to keep your uniforms?"

"Just one set to go home in. Why would I want to keep my uniforms? I don't *want* to be a soldier, Alpha Lee!" He laughed. "I couldn't wear it to work ... they'll expect me to dress like a civilian. The reserve outfit I'll be in will probably issue me a new set for summer camp."

"Well-l-l," she said softly, "you look so beautiful in it, Jan. *All* guys look great in a uniform ... but *you* look better than anybody else!" She kissed her fingertip and then reached across the table to touch it to his lips.

"Maybe I could get a job driving a Greyhound bus ... those guys wear nice uniforms," he said with a wink, catching her hand in his own and retrieving the fingertip kiss.

"Well ... you could, couldn't you? You've had lots of experience driving buses ... "

"More than I ever wanted," he agreed. "I can get along just fine if I never have to drive one more bus or big truck for the rest of my life. Alpha Lee ... the next big machine I learn to drive is gonna have *wings*. That's a promise." He stood and stretched, and reached to pull her close for a long kiss before bedtime.

Early on Tuesday Jan walked to the Orderly Room to check if Captain Ross could see him. He knew what the Commanding Officer's form was for; the mandatory re-enlistment speech that was given to all soldiers whose enlistments were ending, if the unit wanted to retain them. The Captain was at a meeting and was not available, so First Sergeant Berkowicz aptly took his place. "Short, you've been a credit to this little part of the Army, and we'd be more than happy to see you re-up for three years and stay right here. I'm sure there would be another stripe on your sleeve if you should decide to stay, and an appropriate raise in pay. Don't forget the free medical care and all of the other benefits military service confers... including retirement after only twenty years, if you choose. You couldn't get a deal like that anywhere else, you know." He took out the Captain's signature stamp and put the mark on the bottom line of the form as he talked. "Short, if the new job in Tacoma doesn't look as good after a few weeks, you've got sixty days to reconsider. All you have to do is call us." Sergeant Berkowicz stood and offered his hand, and Jan grasped it in a strong handshake. "Good luck, Short ... we'll miss you, and we'll be looking forward to hearing from you. By the way, the Captain said you're to have a Jeep to do all the rest of the running around so you might as well sign one out right now."

With the Jeep available, Jan made short work of most of the destinations on his list, and by the end of the day he lacked only two stops, which were on the main base. He would have gone on to take care of those, but he knew the offices would be closed at five o'clock, so he turned in the Jeep and rode back to town with Fred and Herndon. Sergeant Herndon was happy; Jan would be available the next afternoon, and he needed him to drive a bus. The other drivers didn't like to drive "Old Number 7." because of it's different shift pattern.

On the Sunday after the fire at the McChord service club, and Susan's discovery of Jan and Alpha Lee in bed together, Roddy did come out to the lodge as he had promised, to work with Susan on the classical guitar music. This was more of a pretext than serious instruction; both of them knew it. But at that time, after her exhausting emotional outburst and lack of sleep, she begged off, telling Roddy she wasn't feeling well. He stayed for a half hour, visiting with Jan and Alpha Lee, and told Susan he hoped he'd see her for rehearsal on Wednesday evening. She listlessly agreed.

When he saw her that evening, she was subdued, but she worked well with the band and the rehearsal was successful. After the other players had gone, she told Roddy and Jon that she had some ideas for her final performances ... some songs she would like to sing, she said, to say goodbye. Could they find the music for "Sentimental Journey", and "Thanks for the Memories"?

Roddy was pleased and relieved to see her showing more interest and animation. "Sure, Suzie. I think I have 'Sentimental Journey' ... that's a great song. It's often done in harmony; what would you think of singing part of it with Kenny?"

He saw a spark of excitement in Susan's eyes. "Oh, yes, that'd be great! But, Roddy ... couldn't *you* sing harmony with me? I'd like that better ..."

Roddy was surprised at her suggestion; but, why not? "Well ... Yeah... I think I'd like that, too, honey. Let's do it!"

Jan and Fred's final Mech Drawing class was on Friday, ... this would be the session at which they would get their final grade; it had been announced that class would be short. This was also Susan's final performance at the Fort Lewis club. Veronica suggested that she and Alpha Lee go together, and Jan and Fred could join them there as soon as their class was dismissed. Susan had decided to wear the gold-striped dress from Kaufman's, the costume she had worn for her first performance. She topped it with the maroon bolero for a different look. Jane had given her the gold leather sandals to keep. "I'm too old to wear them anyway," she said, "and they do go so well with that dress, Susan." Jane was having trouble keeping her voice steady.

While Susan dressed for her gig at Fort Lewis, Alpha Lee watched her admiringly. "Susan ... do you realize that you couldn't have even walked in those shoes three months ago ... before we started our

'Nisqually' program... you would have lost your balance. It makes such a difference."

Susan turned from the mirror to face Alpha Lee. "This has been the best summer of my life, Alpha Lee," she said earnestly, "*All* of it. I feel so thankful to so many people ... *you* and Jan most of all, but Jane, and Roddy, too , and Dr. Sparks, and all of those great guys at the clubs ..."

...She tried to express her gratitude to "all of those great guys" in the audience at Fort Lewis. She sang with passion, making straight-on eye contact with as many as she could. She took the mike and circulated among the tables, singing personally to the members of her audience; Roddy had given her a quick course on how to manage a hand mike, to be mindful of the trailing cord, to avoid tangling it or tripping over it.

"What'll I do, when you are far away,
And I am blue ... What'll I do?"

She had asked for an exaggerated slow tempo for this song, and she sang so intimately that there was no doubt she meant every word. And when she and Roddy sang their close-harmony duet, it brought whistles and cheers.

"Gonna take a sentimental journey,
Gonna set my heart at ease.
Gonna take a sentimental journey,
To renew old memories ..."

As they finished the final vocal chorus, Roddy circled her waist and held her close and they danced the final instrumental chorus together in front of the bandstand. The audience applauded and whistled their approval. Alpha Lee and Veronica watched as Suzie Remagen and the Band of Outlaws performed. "She is *so good*," Ronnie said wonderingly. "Why would she need to go to college, Alpha Lee? You know she could get a job without any trouble at all, doing just this very thing, for *big* money. She's such a natural. Her connection with the audience is just amazing."

"I know, Ronnie. Actually, she may be having second thoughts. The original plan was for her to get formal voice training for a concert or operatic career ... but she loves this kind of per-forming so much, I'm not sure she'll want to bother with that classical stuff."

When Jan and Fred arrived, they tried to convince the girls that they had failed their finals. "Damn ...," Fred said with a long face, "we're gonna have to take Remedial Mech Drawing. Can you beat that?"

Veronica shook her head in mock exasperation. "No, I can't," she said, "and I can't believe it, either. C'm'ere and dance with me, soldier," and she moved into Fred's arms, smiling enticingly.

"Ronnie's looking especially pretty tonight," Jan observed. "She looks good in your color, Alpha Lee. ... Not as good as you do, of course. ... Hey, do you wanna dance?"

"Let's just wait till the next number, Jan ... I want to just sit here with you and watch for a while. ... Yes ... that dress was our last sewing project. Light blue is a good color for blondes," she answered. "But then, what isn't?" she asked with a wry smile. "Ronnie's going to buy Jane's sewing machine ... she's really enjoying making her own clothes. ... Jan, I told her we'd bring Sunshine over to their place tomorrow."

"Okay, we can do that tomorrow afternoon. Fred's gonna drive us to the airport in the new company station wagon, Alpha Lee," he told her. "Charles just got a new one for T. E. a few days ago ... it's maroon, with real wood trim on the outside, state of the art, and bigger than the one I've been driving. We're gonna travel in style."

"I think I'll need something to cheer me, Jan. Talk about sentimental journeys .. I sure do have mixed feelings about leaving this place. Oh, Jan, I'm forgetting, Susan brought this to us this evening," and she handed him a small expensive-looking envelope with "Jan and Alpha Lee" written in Jane's elegant calligraphy. The card inside read, "You are invited to a Midnight Supper and Going-Away Party for Susan Remagen at the Tacoma Yacht Club .. hosted by Roddy Williamson and the Band of Outlaws, and sponsored by Charles and Jane Williamson, Saturday night, August 27, after the performance at McChord Service Club."

Jan was amazed. "Wow! They sure are giving her a fancy send-off, aren't they? The Tacoma Yacht Club, no less! Boy, Alpha Lee, we sure know how to pick high-class friends, don't we? ... Well, we'll go, of course. But, dammit, honey," he said, squeezing her hand, "I was hoping we could have some time to ourselves tomorrow night It'll may be our last chance to be together."

"Oh, Jan, I'd rather be with you at the lodge than anywhere else! I wish we didn't have to go, but I think we'll have to be there. We couldn't just not show up."

"Well ... tell you what, sweetheart, we'll go, and we'll socialize for a while, and then we'll just thank our hosts and say good night, way before the party's over. I'm positive Roddy knows the score; and now Susan does, too. D'you think it would upset her?"

"No, not for long, Jan. I think she's able by now to understand, and to allow us to be alone. She'll be surrounded by all those people, having the time of her life. I think she'll be able to let us go without getting upset, or anything. ... Maybe she won't even notice we're gone." She was silent just a moment. She looked up at him with her eyes full of passion. "Jan, I want to be with you again! Maybe it'll be the last time until ... next summer, or ... or maybe *EVER!*"

"*NO*, Alpha Lee, no! That won't happen. Don't think such things, honey. ... Come on, let's dance, Alpha Lee. I want to hold you ..." And so when the music began again, they joined the dancers, holding each other close while Susan sang ...

"Watch the sunset on a tropic isle;
See the pyramids along the Nile;
Just remember, darling, all the while,
You belong to me ... "

"'You belong to me', Alpha Lee," Jan sang softly into her ear. "Don't you ever forget it."

Chapter 29

Saturday morning; a day of tying up loose ends, Alpha Lee thought as she combed her hair. She could hear Jan in the kitchen, making a fire in the stove and filling the coffee pot. He greeted her with a broad smile as she came to stand beside him, and he pulled her close for a kiss. "Good morning, sweet lady," he said. "What's on your breakfast menu today?"

"French toast, I think," she said, "with bacon and applesauce. Do you approve?"

"Yum! Sure do." He put plates and silverware on the table. "Alpha Lee, I'm gonna go in to TE. this morning and work a couple hours ... there's a project I want to finish before we leave. Maybe I'll come home for lunch, if there's no big problem with that, and then we'll take little Sunshine over to Ronnie in the afternoon. Is there some laundry to pick up, or anything?"

"Yes, there is, we'll need to do that. I'll do the final hand washing this morning. I'm glad it's not raining."

Susan appeared while they were eating breakfast, ready to ride into town with Jan for her last day of work at the Schacke. "Good morning," she said with a yawn. "Mmmm ... French toast with bacon," she said. "Did you save any for me?" She found two slices in the frypan on the back of the stove and filled her plate. "Of course you did. Thanks, Alpha Lee. This is my favorite breakfast."

Alpha Lee watched Jan's station wagon climb the driveway and disappear onto the highway beyond Masseys' cottage. Ignoring the breakfast dishes, she walked out onto the pier to drink in the sweetness of early morning ... to savor this quiet moment in the awareness that it would soon be only a memory. The silence of the pine woods was only enhanced by the soft lapping of the waves against the shore. Sunshine meandered around and around her feet, rubbing against her ankles in a cat caress. Alpha Lee bent to pick her up. "Today we'll take you to your new home," she said. "I'll miss you, li'l friend."

After doing the hand washing and hanging bras and panties and stockings on the line, Alpha Lee studied her to-do list; most of the items bore bright red check marks to indicate they had been taken care of. Susan's portrait had been expertly packed at the Schacke, and shipped off (with great reluctance on Jane's part) to Doctor John and Nancy McAllister. Alpha Lee had been hesitant to disassemble and pack her easel, hoping to make one more small "farewell" painting to celebrate the bittersweet occasion. ... I'll do it now, she said to herself, and then I'll pack my oils and take the easel apart. There'll be plenty of time for it to dry before we have to leave on Monday evening ... and she brought out paints, easel, turpentine and wiping rags, and set to work on a morning view of the mountain, the pine woods, and the pier. A few shore birds invaded her scene and were duly rendered in shades of gray, black, white, profiled against the rocks.

.Will I ever come back here? she wondered, feeling a tightening in her throat. Will Jan and I ever be together again, after he comes back to this place, alone? 'You belong to me,' he had said last night. Was he only singing the words of Susan's song? ... She determined to shake off her doubts and fears. Concentrating instead on the painting, she finished it before Jan came home, and she closed the paints tightly and packed them away in their metal box, leaving the rest of the turpentine in the shed.

Sunshine was curious, her eyes wide and anxious, as she felt the moving car carrying her along. Alpha Lee held her tightly to make her feel secure. Once they arrived at Fred and Veronica's apartment, the kitten was so fascinated with her new surroundings that she busily went exploring through every room, and when Alpha Lee picked her up for a final emotional good-bye, she was impatient to get down on the floor to continue her investigations, and she totally ignored Alpha Lee and Jan's departure. "Cats are so fickle," she lamented to Jan. "She didn't even say goodbye to me."

"Nope," Jan agreed. "She didn't shed a single tear ... after everyting we've done for her. All that milk, a special litter box, a pretty blanket."

"You're teasing me!" Alpha Lee accused, and Jan turned to her with a wink, his lips mimicking a kiss.

After supper Susan dressed for her final performance at McChord; she had insisted that Jan and Alpha Lee come to this one, too. She would wear the maroon taffeta sheath dress ... her most provocative costume, with her shoulders bare and the skirt slit to permit easy movement. Her hair fell free to her shoulders; no beauty-parlor hairdo tonight. "Wow, Suz," Jan commented. "You sure do look fetching. Those flyboys are gonna hate to see you go."

"I wish I could just stay here and do this job forever," she replied. "This has been the best summer of my life, Jan."

Alpha Lee appeared in her blue velvet dress; Jan had asked her to wear it again. "Lucky me!" he crowed. "I've got the two prettiest gals in town to go to the dance with. *My* summer's been pretty darned good, too, Suz!"

The Special Services dance hall at McChord Field was filled to overflowing. Even the many girls who had come by bus from Tacoma and Olympia to dance with the troops were excited; some had seen Susan's last performance at Fort Lewis the night before, and wanted to see her perform one final time.

Susan repeated some of the special songs she had chosen for her farewell, and she and Roddy again sang "Sentimental Journey". After their final turn around the dance floor as the chorus ended, Roddy touched her lips with a quick kiss, and the audience reacted with noisy approval.

Then she sang :

"Comin' in on a wing and a prayer –

Look below, there's our field over there!

Though there's one engine gone,

We will still carry on ..

Comin' in on a wing and a prayer!"

And she invited the men to sing along on the chorus of the popular song from World War II. When she sang "What'll I Do?" in the very slow, and intimate style she had chosen, she walked through the room, stopping for a moment to sing directly to Corporal Calvin Moneypenny from Braxton County, West Virginia, and to Private Michael Cochrane, who had been the guard at the gate the first time she had performed at McChord; having met her before anyone else at the base, the private claimed a special privilege and had made a habit of asking her to dance every time she per-formed there. When she touched the bristly blond hair of a very young private with a buzz-cut, he reached up to grab her hand for a moment and their eyes met in a private glance. I think this guy loves me, she thought, and she smiled at him tenderly.

Roddy announced an intermission for the band, but Susan stayed on stage. "As you folks know," he said, "tonight is the final performance for our sweet singer Suzie Remagen. She'll be returning to West Virginia to attend college in a few days. ... Suzie, honey, you're on."

Susan seated herself on the tall stool with her guitar, and in a pensive mood, very slowly, she crooned, "It's West Virginia ... It's West Virginia ...The pride of every mountaineer ..." The University marching song, always played in a very fast march tempo, was rendered as a romantic, homesick ballad. But not for long. "Come up and sing with me, Calvin!" she called, and Corporal Moneypenny sauntered toward the stage with his self-conscious grin. "Anyone else here from the Mountain State? Come on up, Jan!" she insisted, and three more men, including Jan, rose and approached as she beckoned them. The tempo of her chording had changed to a more spirited beat, and now she dropped the guitar and clapped in time, inviting the audience to clap, too. After two choruses, she urged the audience to sing along, and the sound filled the room. By the time Roddy and the band returned to their places, there was loud applause and Suzie was all smiles. "Wasn't that fun?" Susan asked over the mike, and there was more applause.

The band resumed playing with a conga, and Jon and Ricky switched to some appropriate rhythm instruments to define the irrepressible beat, while Roddy's guitar carried the syncopated Latin melody. A very tall sergeant with curly red hair reached Susan first to lead her in the conga line. The twisting line moved through the room until almost everyone had joined the parade, laughing and swaying to the irresistible rhythm.

It was almost ten o'clock when Roddy signaled Jon for a drum roll, and he held up his hands for attention. "Ladies and gentlemen ... at this time I have been asked to call Miss Suzie up to the stage again. I believe Sergeant Ed Gillis has a special presentation to make ... Sergeant ?" and the tall red-headed sergeant hopped up to the mike.

"Folks," he said, his voice rich with a Texas drawl, "we've all enjoyed Miss Suzie's great performances this summer, and we hate to see her go." He turned to Susan. "Miss Suzie, for givin' so much pleasure to the airmen of McChord Field for the past three months, we would like to present you with these one-of-a-kind special hostess wings," and he opened a small black box and removed the pin to show her. A skilled artisan had transformed a pair of silver bombardier wings by working the center motif of a bomb shape into a tiny guitar; even the strings were articulated in the silver. "Ma'am, these wings flew over Guadalcanal and Tokyo, and the guy who wore them was proud to do his job. Now we're happy to present them to you.. May I pin them on you, Ma'am?"

Susan smiled brilliantly at him, blushing, and murmured, "Please do, Sergeant."

His fingers slipped under the cloth of her neckline, while he held the pin far lower down on her breast than she had expected, and he attached the back to the pin and stepped away so everyone could see. "Don't that look beautiful?" he asked, and the crowd cheered. Susan reached up to kiss his cheek. But that wasn't quite what the sergeant had in mind: He quickly took her in his arms and bent her so far backward that she would have fallen on the floor had he not held her securely, and he kissed her soundly. She struggled for balance for a moment, and then relaxed in his arms. The audience loved it, whistling and clapping thunderously. When he lifted her to her feet again, Susan looked into the crowd, rolled her eyes and, grabbing the mike, she cried, "Whooo-eee!" and then she, too, applauded. The sergeant grinned broadly as he strutted back to his table while his comrades roared their approval.

Jan was laughing and clapping with the best of them. "What a show!" he said to Alpha Lee. "God, she is so good!"

Susan held up her hands to quiet the crowd. "Thank you! I'm very proud to wear these wings ... it's a huge honor. We can never forget the bravery of the men who flew our planes in the war." She turned to Roddy. "Can you tell me who made these wings for me? They're so beautiful."

Roddy took the mike and gestured to where Sergeant Gillis was sitting. "The sergeant made them himself, Suzie. Those were his own wings."

"Ohhh ... Sergeant, thank you very, very much! I can't tell you how much this means to me! ... Will you dance with me, Sergeant, the next time Roddy plays a fast tune? I've seen you jitterbug You've given me wings, Sergeant ... now teach me to fly!" More applause; and then Roddy obligingly cued the Outlaws and they struck up the familiar chords of "Take the 'A' Train", and Sergeant Gillis met Susan on the floor where she did indeed "fly" in some of the more flamboyant jitterbug routines. Only a few other couples took the floor to compete; the others, including Jan and Alpha Lee, were happy to sit at their tables and watch the "floor show".

Susan joined them at their table as Jan pulled another chair close for her. She was breathless after her exertion, but she was elated and glowing. "What fun!" she exclaimed. "Ed is wonderful! ... See my wings? Aren't they beautiful?" Her smile was radiant.

Susan had asked Roddy to give her a solo spot just a half-hour before closing. The band retired outside for cokes and cigarettes and she took her place on the tall stool again. "Guys and gals," she said, "I want to do something different right now." Then she laughed and said, "This whole evening has been pretty different, hasn't it? Our next caper will fit right in!" She played a few strong chords and then continued. "I want to sing something special that you all probably know. Jan, Alpha Lee, please come up here with me." They looked at each other, wondering what Susan had in mind, and then Jan led Alpha Lee up to the bandstand. Susan smiled brightly at them and continued speaking. "My friends from Brick City High School and I sang this song for assembly once, I think it's appropriate for tonight. Jan, Alpha Lee, let's do 'America the Beautiful' like we did it back home. We'll each sing a verse, and then we'll repeat the first verse ... *EVERYBODY* knows that ... and I want *EVERYBODY* to sing along on the finale." Susan sang the first verse, and cued Jan for the second.

He was relieved that the words came back to him so easily. Alpha Lee sang the third verse as Susan changed to a lower key, and then she lifted her arms in invitation, and the airmen of McChord Field joined them in the familiar words of the classic patriotic hymn. Susan repeated the final chorus: "America, America, God shed his grace on thee ...", gesturing for full participation, and the room rang with the volume of strong young voices, and the applause was deafening.

Roddy called his Outlaws back inside and they played a popular instrumental. Susan made her way through the crowd and found the young private with the crew cut, and asked him to dance with her. He was astonished, and not a very good dancer, she found; but it didn't matter. Susan's chatter helped him get over his extreme shyness, and he told her his name was Robert Olson; he was from Dana, Indiana, home of the famous war correspondent, Ernie Pyle, he told her. He'd only been in the air force for eight months, but he was in for the long term; he was going to be a pilot, he said. ... When the music ended, he reluctantly let her go. "Will you be back next summer, Miss Suzie?" he asked with great seriousness.

"Oh, Bobby, I just don't know," Susan replied. After a pause she added, "I hope so," for the first time admitting to herself something she had tried to deny. "I've enjoyed singing for you guys so much," and she smiled at him, and with her hands on his shoulders, she kissed his cheek lightly. "It was great dancing with you, Bobby. Good luck with the pilot training," and she shook his hand and returned to the stage. She turned to look back at him; he was still standing where she left him, watching her, and on impulse, she threw him a kiss. He grinned, waved and returned to his table.

Jan and Alpha Lee had been dancing, too, to the sweet strains of "Moonlight and Roses," the first part of an instrumental medley of "moonlight" songs, and Jan hummed the easy refrain close to Alpha Lee's ear. He sang softly, "Moonlight and *lilacs* ... Remind me of you!", and he smiled at her. "Honey, you're the prettiest girl in this room! And Suzie is the next prettiest.

This is her night to shine, isn't it?" The music ended with the final strains of "Moonglow", and they watched Susan walk away from the blond private and turn to blow him a kiss. "She's really a star. She has these guys eating out of her hand."

"Jan, this job has been the greatest thing that could have happened to her! She is so self- confident, and so happy! I think she's really gonna be all right. Thank God." Alpha Lee herself looked exultant and overjoyed. "Oh, Jan," she whispered, "I can't believe how well things have turned out. For both of us."

At last it was time for the final set. Susan took the mike from the stand, and again she walked among the tables, softly singing, "I'll be seeing you ... In all the old familiar places ..." and then the band segue'ed into "Thanks for the Memories", for which Roddy and Susan had written some new lyrics to express her own personal feelings. When she returned to the stage, she whispered to Roddy, and he accompanied her on the piano, with only Jon's softest percussion brushes to accent the rhythm, and she crooned "Always"; then she invited the crowd to sing along with her on the short chorus. After long applause, Roddy started the band on their usual ending theme, and then he escorted her to the main exit where she shook hands and accepted the occasional hug or kiss from the patrons as they left. "Bye, Bobby," she murmured as Private Olson clasped her hand. "Maybe I'll see you next summer. Bye, Calvin ... I'm so glad we met ... it was fun singing together. Look me up in Brick City next time you come home!" And then there was Sergeant Gillis. He got another hug, this one more restrained than the previous one. "Thank you so much, Sergeant! I love my wings. I'll never forget you!"

In spite of her exhausting performance, Susan was full of excitement and enthusiasm. "I'll see you at the yacht club!" she said to Jan and Alpha Lee. "You *will* be there, won't you? You just have to be!"

"Yeah, Suz, we'll be there for a while. ... You were great tonight, honey, absolutely great!" Jan said. "I wouldn't have missed it. ... See you later."

Alpha Lee hugged Susan; both of them had tears in their eyes, but smiles on their faces. "See you in a little while, Susan. It was a wonderful performance."

"It was, wasn't it?" Susan replied. "It was so much fun! Alpha Lee, I think *this* is what I want to do for a career! How could I possibly have this much fun singing opera or classical stuff? I feel like I'm really touching these guys."

"Isn't *that* the truth!" Jan said, chuckling. "And some of 'em are getting a big kick out of touching *you* ... like Sergeant Gillis. What a show you two put on! I'll bet you wouldn't let me pin anything on you like he did." Susan just stuck her tongue out at him and walked away.

Chapter 30

The drive to the yacht club took under a half hour. The big white two-story building was close to the water, with piers extending far out, lined with boats large and small. "One of those big white boats belongs to Charles," Jan said. "He showed me a picture when he ordered it. Alpha Lee, sometimes I think those folks don't know what to do with all their money."

"I never guessed that rich folks could be so nice," she said, laughing, "since I've never known any really rich people back east, except maybe Doc and Nancy, and they weren't *that* rich. Jane has been so nice to us. Roddy's given Susan such great opportunities."

"Wouldn't it be something if she and Roddy would get married, Alpha Lee? The guy's really taken with her. I mean really starry eyed, gaa gaa over her. And he has his degree, and a teaching job. I'll bet he proposes to her before she leaves. Do you think they've been in bed?"

"I don't think so, Jan. Susan's been so over-sensitive about that kind of thing. I think she *was* really afraid and even revolted by the idea of sex ... at least until after that *showdown* when she walked in on us, and then had the talk with Dr. Sparks. I *hope* that was a turning point for her. She had all of those *terrible* memories to get over. I can't tell you *all* of it Jan."

"Well, I think she seems to be more relaxed than she was before ... don't you think? ... Well, honey ... let's go in and see what this party is all about. We don't have to stay very long."

The ballroom was decorated with the typical nautical motif: bright semaphore and weather flags adorned the walls, and large maritime paintings of clipper ships running before gale winds and other heroic scenes. There were ship's-lantern lights in sconces that illuminated the room in soft subdued light, and large models of racing yachts and windjammers in brass bound cases. Dance music played on a jukebox. Several friends were seated at the tables, some were dancing.

Jane was at her station, ready to greet the guests as they arrived. She clasped Alpha Lee's hand and welcomed them. "Hello, Alpha Lee, Jan! Wasn't tonight's gig fun! I hate to think that Susan's leaving, just when she seems to be hitting her stride. The boys will miss her so. Jan, Charles has something important to tell you, I think he and Joe Nutter walked out to see our new boat ... maybe you two could catch them out there."

"Well Jane, Rod may have to try to find another girl singer, cause I think Susie *is* gona go back east with us.. But he'll have to look a long time to find one like Suz. She has a gift."

"Yes, she has, Jan. But what will I do? There's no way I can find anyone to replace Susan. She's been very special to me. I wish ..." But she let her thought go unfinished.

"Honey, .lets see what Charles wants, come on, lets go see his new yacht." They stepped through the pier-side door and found themselves on a long, flood-lighted pier, with perhaps a hundred craft tied securely in their berths, bobbing up and down with the minute waves that seem to be always rippling the surface. They walked along the pier nearly a hundred yards before Alpha Lee spotted the pattern she recognized, and she pointed ... "Jan there it is, just look."

On her bow in flowing letters was the name "VEE THREE - TACOMA", framed in a box shape that Alpha Lee had recognized as the subject of the charcoal depiction for Charles' brochure which she had made soon after she had come to Washington. "There she is. Isn't she a beauty?"

Charles and another gentleman were sitting on the luxurious divans inside the cabin as they walked up. "Well, Jan, Alpha Lee, come aboard and look around." Alpha Lee was uncertain, she had never been on any boat before, and tonight she was wearing pumps with two-inch heels, so was unsure if she wanted this adventure. Jan assured her that he would steady her, so they walked across the boarding ramp, holding on to the rope side rails, and went aboard for a look. Charles introduced them to Joe Nutter, a new face to Alpha Lee, but a man who Jan had seen at TE a few times, without knowing why he was there. Alpha Lee was astonished with the luxury of the cabin furnishings, wood inlays and carpets and curtains, and was even more surprised by the furnishings in the cabin ... the beds and dressers, even a small restroom. Jan was pleasantly surprised to see all the engine room gauges, which were duplicated by another set by the large wheel at the helm.

After a short tour, Charles said "Jan we have some things to discuss, if you will join us at the table inside in a few minutes ... there are some papers to sign. I think Joe wants to discuss a couple things with you as well." Joe nodded in assent.

When Roddy and Susan arrived, there was clapping and whistles. Susan smiled radiantly and waved. She was still wearing her "guitar wings" on her breast, her trophy of her success as an entertainer. The crowd was small ... just close friends and the band members with their wives and girlfriends. Veronica waved from across the room, and Fred gestured for Jan and Alpha Lee to join them and the Herndons at their table beside a window that looked out over the sound. "Oh, Alpha Lee! You're wearing that gorgeous blue velvet again!" Veronica gushed. "I do love that dress. I think I'll make myself a velvet dress, too .. what color should I choose, d'you think?"

"Black," Alpha Lee said without hesitation. "With your blonde coloring, it would be *so* flattering, Ronnie. *So* elegant. ... But I have to warn you, sewing on black velvet would not be easy. You should have help from an expert. ... Sally, do you sew?"

In a few minutes, Charles and Joe walked in, and Charles motioned for them to come to a table, where Jan had noticed two briefcases. Charles said: "Folks, Joe Nutter is our banker at TE, and a long time friend, also a stockholder. Jan, I asked him for a quicker than normal review of your loan application, since you will be going back east next week. But before he gives you his news, I'd like for you to review, and hopefully sign, this non-compete and non-disclosure contract that is part of your acceptance of your new job. Jan, it's just a pretty standard clause that says you won't take any job with somebody else who might compete with us, or give away our secrets, for three years. You might want to notice your new job description before you sign. We'll discuss all the new duties when you get back. Of course your promised raise will happen, too, effective immediately." Alpha Lee looked wide-eyed at the long piece of type-written paper he handed Jan ... the job description was penned in, in triple height calligraphy letters – it said *"Assistant Engineering Sales Manager."*

Jan scanned the contract, believing that Charles was presenting him with a necessary and legitimate agreement. Charles continued as he looked at it, "Jan, while you are back east, we'd like for you to make a side trip for us, perhaps a day or two, to visit the Lockheed plant in Marietta, near Atlanta. We've wanted to get somebody down there, but haven't had the time. We'll cover your expenses, and buy your plane ticket round trip ... via Pittsburgh, of course. We've already made the reservations, leaving you on the same east-bound flight with your friends.

"I didn't tell Millie it wasn't a "done deal" so she went ahead and made them; she said all she could find out of Harrison was a puddle jumper that made several stops before Washington, where you'll catch a non-stop to Atlanta. So, I hope you *will* agree to do this. Now, Joe, its your turn."

"Jan, I did review your loan application, which our loan officer had already acted on, and the money from your Brick City bank was transferred by wire this week. It didn't quite cover the slightly increased down payment, but Charles said they would fold in a bonus they wanted to give you. A few details needed to be haggled over ... our policy is to *not* issue a loan on a house without a modern water heater, range, or furnace, so we talked your seller, Naomi and her husband, into adding those to their offer. The estimate is that a small gas wall heater will suffice, and since you are so far from any natural gas line, these units will be propane types.

"We needed to adjust the selling price accordingly, *as well as the down payment,* which you also need to agree to, since it will increase your monthly payments slightly. By the way, you *will* be buying it *"furnished as-is,"* which means all the furniture and the refrigerator will stay. All you need to do is sign right down here, and we'll set up the closing for when you get back in three weeks or so."

Alpha Lee had a *big* smile on her face. She was *so* happy that Jan was going to buy the lodge... there were so many wonderful memories there for her. Now *if* only ... did she dare to *dream?*

...She restrained herself from screaming with joy as she said. "Jan! That's *wonderful!* ... Oh, I'm just too happy. I'm so glad! When I'm lonely this winter, I can think of you in that cabin ... I can remember ... I'll visualize you sleeping under the wolf blanket ... " ... she almost said ... and I'll pretend I'm there beside you!

Mr. Nutter continued, "Of course we require all buyers to have fire insurance to protect both of us, so we've included the premiums for your "Homeowner's Policy" in your monthly payment, and you can sign the line down here to agree to that. If you find that our rates are not fully competitive, you can choose another plan after six months.

"The final thing is an offering that we make, a life insurance policy on the lender, so that if you are disabled and can't make the payments they will be automatically paid; and if you should die before the mortgage is paid off, your widow would own the house, free and clear. If you agree with this, just sign on the last line."

"Thank you, Mr. Nutter, and Charles. I'll sign both of these contracts happily, *and* make that trip for you, Charles. Sir, what you have done for me at TE has been so *wonderful,* so good for *me* ... I just don't know how to thank you enough." He was near tears as he spoke.

"Jan, it has been a two-way street, we're happy to have you as a valued employee of TE, and we look forward to a *long* association."

Susan and Roddy walked back in after a tour of the new yacht, and Alpha Lee left the table to tell Susan her wonderful news, and they hugged each other tightly after Susan heard.

"Jan, there's something else, Charles continued, ... the handsome Sergeant Gillis gave me something for you tonight. He said he had done this for his sister-in-law, Naomi, and had wanted to give it to you himself, but didn't catch you before you left. There's some history about this that you might want to know. He held a silver ring in his hand ... with a dime-size piece of turquoise set like an emerald. It was the rarest form of very hard turquoise, with a rope-twist of gold surrounding the oval stone, and there were gold threads worked into the stone itself, and an ornate silver setting and band.

"Turquoise isn't common in this area, Jan ... it's usually found in the southwest. I'd guess this is quite old. Turquoise was occasionally traded by the Zuni tribe in New Mexico to the Northwestern tribes in exchange for wooden craft products, hides and the like. It was highly prized around here ... there was something about it being a piece of the sky, I think. It was considered a very lucky commodity. The sergeant told me Naomi had found the stone in her grandfather's garden by your fishing lodge years ago. He said he had coated it with a special jeweler's shellac to reduce the tendency of turquoise to dissolve in water, but I doubt it should be used to wash lots of dishes. And, the sergeant gave me a riddle. He said Naomi had told him that if you were half as smart as she thought you were, you would know exactly what to do with it."

Jan smiled as he took the beautiful ring, and looked at for a couple minutes before he slid it into his pocket. "Charles, thank you for bringing it here tonight. I know *EXACTLY* what I'm going to do with it, when the time is right, and I really think that is what Naomi had in mind.

Jan saw Alpha Lee sitting by Veronica, and went to find Susan, who was dancing with Jon while Roddy danced with a pretty girl Jon had escorted to the party. He went to the jukebox and dropped in a coin, and chose a song. When the dance was over, he asked Susan to come over to sit with Alpha Lee. . "Alpha Lee, if you would slide over, and let Susan sit just here," he asked.. Alpha Lee wondered what he meant, but did as she was asked, sitting in a seat between Susan and Veronica.

Charles had watched the seating rearrangement, and waved to Jane to come and stand where she could see this action.

In a minute Jan heard the jukebox begin to play the song he had selected, "You Belong To Me." He knelt before Alpha Lee on one knee and clasped both her hands in both of his. "My sweet Alpha Lee, I love you with all my heart, as you surely know. Will you marry me, a poor country boy, and live with me for the rest of our lives? We can plan a June wedding, if you choose, I think Charles will give me a week off to fly back to get you."

Alpha Lee stared at him wonderingly; and then her face was transformed by a radiant smile and her eyes filled with tears. "Oh Jan," she whispered, "*YES, Yes,* I will! I'll love you forever ... my wonderful 'country boy'!" He slipped the turquoise ring on her ring finger, and she looked at it in amazement. Then she held his face between her hands and kissed his lips passionately.

The huge clock in the foyer was striking midnight as their kiss ended, to much applause from the onlookers. Susan and Veronica were ecstatic, Susan jumped up and down for joy, then turned and gave Jan a huge emotional hug and kiss on the cheek. "Thank you Jan," she said. "That almost makes my summer complete, too."

The waitresses began pouring champagne in a beautiful glass for each of the revelers. Jane tapped her glass with a spoon as Roddy raised his hands for attention. "Does everybody have a drink? Okay, folks ... I want to propose a toast: Here's to health and success to the beautiful girl singer who's given us so much sweet music .. and even a few laughs now and then. Here's to our own sweet Sue, as she leaves us for her home in West Virginia. Suzie ... we love you!" He held his glass high, touching Jane's and Charles's with a barely audible 'clink', and the guests followed suit; and after sipping the drink, there was applause and cheers.

When she could be heard, Susan flashed a happy smile around the room and acknowledged the accolade. "Thank you ... thank you so much!" she trilled. "Roddy ... you've given me a chance to do something I'll never forget. I've loved singing with the Outlaws ... I've loved entertaining the troops. I'm gonna say it again: This has been the best summer of my life. Thank you all so much!" She sipped her champagne tentatively, and then she tipped her glass toward Jan and

Alpha Lee, saying "And here's a toast to the newly engaged Alpha Lee and Jan," and drained her glass. "Hear! Hear!" was heard from Charles and followed by many similar toasts.

As the jukebox played "Sweet Sue" Roddy led Susan onto the floor for a joyous dance .When the music ended, Jan and Alpha Lee said their good-night to Fred and Veronica, and to Jane and Charles. "You will be at our house for dinner tomorrow, won't you?" Jane asked. "We'll expect you about seven."

"Thank you, Jane ... Charles," Jan replied. "We'll be there. Nice of you to ask us." Jane hugged Alpha Lee for a moment, and then they turned away to find Roddy and Susan, who were still on the dance floor. "Rod, we're gonna leave. Nice party ... nice of you to do this for our sweet Sue. Havin' fun, Suz?"

She giggled. "Oh, *YES* It's wonderful!" Then her expression changed. "... But I hate that you're leaving." Then her eyes met Alpha Lee's, and she understood. "Okay," she murmured. "Bye."

"We'll be breaking up here before two, Jan," Roddy told him. "I'll bring her home safe, sound and happy by two-thirty."

"Thanks, Rod ... Bye, Suz," and they turned to go. As they left the club, he said to Alpha Lee, "Did you hear that, honey? Rod deliberately gave us a couple of hours alone ... letting us know when they'll be home."

When Jan stopped the car in front of the lodge, he turned to Alpha Lee and pulled her close for a long kiss, as was his habit before getting out of the car. As he held her, he stroked her back, her shoulders, her hips. "The only thing I love to touch more than this baby-kitten velvet, Alpha Lee, is your bare skin! C'm'on, sweetheart ...let's go inside.

"Ohhhh, Jan ," she breathed, "Yes, I want you close to me tonight."

After their long and intense climax, Alpha Lee rolled over beside him and lay close to him, breathing hard, and caressing his naked body. "Jan, I love you so," she whispered. "I love you forever, no matter what." In a very short time, both of them were sleeping ... the sweet and peaceful sleep that follows sexual fulfillment.

The last guests had left the yacht club by ten minutes before two; Jane and Charles spoke to the club manager for a few minutes, and then walked over to the table where Susan and Roddy were enjoying a final glass of champagne together. Susan grasped Jane's hand, then stood and kissed her cheek. "Thank you for everything, Jane." Then she whispered close to her ear, "I really do love you." Jane smiled, her eyes glittering with tears. Charles put his arm around her and gently moved her away.

"So, now, Suzie ... it's just the two of us. One last private dance?"

Susan drained her glass, the third drink she'd had, she had found the champagne exhilarating. "Roddy, you are the most romantic person I've ever known! That would be so sweet. Let me pick the song," and she looked over the selection, and with a giggle, she punched the numbers for "Save the Last Dance for Me." While the yacht club clean-up crew wiped tables and stacked chairs, they danced with abandon, enjoying the open space of the empty dance floor. After the music stopped, they hugged each other for a moment, and then Susan headed for the rest room, and Roddy gave the manager a nice tip and thanked him for the special treatment for his party.

Roddy drove slowly in the direction of the lodge, with soft music playing on the radio. His watch glowed to indicate the time: 2:30. Susan hummed along with the music. "Did you have fun this evening, Suzie?" he asked; a rhetorical question, since her mood was euphoric.

"Oh, Roddy ," she murmured as she leaned her head against his shoulder, "it was just so wonderful! I don't think I've *ever* had such a wonderful evening! I feel like I could fly to the moon! Everybody has been so nice to me ... especially *YOU*," and she stretched over to kiss his cheek. He squeezed her hand in acknowledgment.

When they reached the pebbled area beside the lodge, he parked and walked around to open her door. The lodge door was unlocked, and when Susan went inside, he followed her, not even waiting for an invitation this time. She took off her high heels as she always did, and walked noiselessly across the room. There were no lights on except for the porch light; nothing showed beneath Jan's bedroom door, which tonight was firmly closed, but moonlight poured in through the windows, illuminat-ing the silent lodge. Susan looked into her own bedroom; it was empty. "They're in Jan's room, together," she whispered.

"Of course they are," Roddy said very softly. "They love each other. They should be together. And we should, too, Suzie." He took her in his arms and held her very close; this time she did not resist. His hands moved down to cradle her buttocks, holding her hard against him. Susan felt the rush of arousal that signaled the old conflicting emotions of desire and revulsion; but now she heard in her mind Dr. Sparks' voice, reassuring and liberating: You are *free*, and she consciously dismissed the instinctive guilt that had always tainted her response. Roddy's touch, so tender and passionate, became exciting and intensely pleasurable. His hands moved to cup her breasts, and he lifted them high and kissed the soft rounded swells that rose above the low neckline of her dress. "I love you, Suzie. Do you love me?"

And breathlessly she whispered, "Oh Roddy ... I think I do!"

His hands explored her body and found the zipper of her dress under her left arm, and he pulled it open down to her hip; but then he was stymied. "Help me, honey ... I don't know how to take this off ...," and she reached down and lifted the dress over her head, and stood exposed to him. There was no bra; Susan had never gotten around to buying the expensive strap-less bra she would have needed only with this dress. He looked at her, naked in the moonlight except for her panties and garter belt and stock-ings. "Oh, Suzie ... you're the most beautiful thing I've ever seen!" He pulled down the lacy panties, his hands moving smoothly down her legs.

She unfastened his bow tie, unbuttoned his shirt and unbuckled his belt. "Roddy,you won't make me pregnant, will you?"

"Of course not, sweetheart." They stood for one more moment, skin against skin, and then he lifted her onto the bed and climbed in beside her. He stroked the golden hair between her legs, and she cried out in an ecstasy of desire. Somewhere far away there was a voice: *Harlot ... whore ... fornicator.* But they were only empty words, meaningless, no longer relevant to her. The only reality was Roddy's touch, awakening a new extreme of sensation. When he penetrated her, it was very slowly, gently, tentatively, until her hands pulled him down to thrust more deeply. There was no maidenhead to be breached, no resistance. But for Susan it was truly a "first time" ... sexual pleasure without the poison of shame. She screamed softly, and no rough hand clamped down over her mouth to smother her. She was overcome with escalating pleasure that finally burst in a climax, and she cried out his name aloud, over and over.

In Jan's room, Alpha Lee awakened, hearing the sounds from the other room. She recalled that other night when she had heard Susan screaming Roddy's name; she sat up quickly and reached for her robe at the foot of Jan's bed. But he caught her arm to stop her. "It's okay, Alpha Lee. Don't get up, honey," and she realized what he meant and lay down beside him again. As they listened to the sounds of passion, they felt a new surge of arousal, too, and Jan pulled her close and stroked her body, kissing her lips and breasts. In a moment they were together again in lovemaking.

In the other bedroom, Roddy finally pulled reluctantly away from Susan. "Honey, I have to go home."

"Oh, please, Roddy -- don't leave me. Please stay here tonight --." She reached for him, to pull him back, but he sat up and bent to kiss her as he held her face between his hands.

"I'd love to stay right here till morning, sweetheart -- but I must go. Mother'll be calling the police -- she'll think I had a wreck somewhere. I have to go, Suzie. I'll come back tomorrow, I swear." He put on his pants and shoes. "I'll come back tomorrow afternoon -- I promise. We still have a day to be together. ... Now, sweetheart, sleep, get some rest. I love you, Suzie -- Oh, God, how I love you." He kissed her again as she sat up on the bed, and he stroked her breasts, reluctant to leave.

Picking up his tie and jacket, he pulled away. "Bye, Suzie," and he walked out the door, closing it soundlessly behind him. Susan lay down in the warm bed, stretched luxuriously and smiled in the darkness. She could smell the fragrance of his shaving lotion on the pillow, and the odor of his masculine sweat on her skin. She had never been so happy.

As Roddy tiptoed through the dark lodge, he could hear soft sounds from Jan's room. "Go for it, buddy," he whispered. When he got to his car, he could see the beginning of dawn in the eastern sky.

Chapter 31

Jan awakened first on Sunday morning. For only a moment he was startled to find a bedmate lying beside him, for Alpha Lee had stayed the night and was still breathing softly, evenly, still sound asleep with her hair streaming over the pillow. He stared at her for a long moment, not wanting to awaken her; but he couldn't resist touching her, stroking her body under the covers, and she moved and stretched, her eyes still closed, and rolled over close to him, her arm around his waist.

"Good morning, my love," he said softly, and when he gently kissed her mouth, she awakened and responded to his kiss not so gently. "What a way to wake up in the morning!" he said. "I could get used to this in no time."

She opened her eyes and smiled at him. "Oh, Jan -- I feel like a -- a 'lady of the night' -- is that what they're called? I should feel ashamed, but -- somehow it just isn't there. ... What time is it?"

Jan looked at his watch. "Eight thirty- five," he said. "We really slept in, didn't we? ... I have to get up, honey," and he sat up, pulled on his shorts and walked to the door. "Don't move," he said. "Stay right where you are. I'll be back in a minute."

But Alpha Lee didn't stay; she put on her robe, picked up her clothes and hurried to her own room, hoping Susan was alone by now. She peeked inside and saw her, sound asleep still. She quickly dressed and combed her hair, and when she left the bedroom, she ran into Jan on his way from the bathroom. "What're you doing up?" he asked. "Couldn't we just spend all day in bed?"

"No, no no," she said, and started the morning routine of making a fire, filling the coffee pot. Jan took over the fire building while Alpha Lee took plates and coffee cups from the cupboard. She turned to watch him, and then came close behind him and hugged him. "I just love the way you look in nothin' but your shorts, Jan," she said. "How about posing for me? I want to do you nude in charcoal -- since my oils are already packed for the trip."

"No no no," he answered, mimicking her. "I'm not in the nude model business, love." He turned around and kissed her, holding her close against his bare body. "I want to do YOU nude in bed," he whispered into her ear. "That's my kind of art."

"And you're very talented in that field, sir," she told him, laughing. They had coffee and cold biscuits with apple butter for breakfast, and while Jan showered and dressed, Alpha Lee cleared away the dishes with as little noise as possible, then returned to the bedroom to do her make-up and put on her stockings and shoes; they would go to chapel one last time. Susan was still sleeping deeply.

Sally Herndon was there, with little Cheryl, but not the sergeant, and not Fred and Veronica. "I think some folks slept in after their night of celebrating," Jan whispered. "Suzie's not the only one."

After the service Jan and Alpha Lee said their goodbyes to Sally and Cheryl and to Chaplain Durbin. "You'll be coming back here after the trip home, Private Short?" he asked. "Yes sir, but I'm getting my discharge tomorrow, so it won't be as easy.to get to your chapel." "Well, have a pleasant visit with your family. You've been gone a long time -- they'll be so happy to see you. ... And Miss Evans -- will you be returning, as well?"

"No, sir, I'll be going to college in West Virginia. But I've loved my summer in Washington. I hope I can come back next summer." Jan tightened his arm around her waist at her words as if in affirmation. When they returned to the car and started back to the lodge it was just past noon.

"Alpha Lee, I have a suggestion," Jan said. "Let's drive up on the mountain again, to that little roadside park where you made the picture for Dr. Sparks. I thought we could take a picnic lunch along -- What do you think?"

"Sure we could, Jan! I'd love that." She giggled. "I can make 'leftover sandwiches', to use up some of what's left in the fridge. I'll take the rest of the perishables up to Naomi tomorrow. ... Yes, that would be fun. What about Susan?"

"You know, Alpha Lee, I'll bet she and Roddy have their own plans for today. We can invite her, but I kinda hope it'll just be the two of us. We have some business to take care of." His glance was mischievous.

"'Business'? What do you mean?" But he would say no more; just a teasing grin.

When they arrived at the lodge, Alpha Lee found Susan still in bed, but stirring. Her shoulders were bare; she was still as Roddy had left her – no pajamas, her clothes casually laid aside where she had put them the night before. "Morning, Alpha Lee," she mumbled. "Is there hot water? I want a shower."

"Probably -- but we can build up the fire a little to make sure. ... Susan -- umm -- How are you this morning? Are you rested? Did you have a good evening?"

Susan smiled happily. "Alpha Lee, I feel wonderful! If you're asking about Roddy and me -- Yes, he was here last night. HERE, Alpha Lee, as in right here --" and she patted the pillow. "I think I love him," and she rolled over on the pillow she had just indicated and squeezed it tight to her face. "Mmmm -- smells so nice," she murmured.

"Susan -- you were okay? You didn't have flashbacks, or anything?" Alpha Lee sat on the other side of the bed. "You weren't afraid, or – disgusted, or anything?"

Susan laughed. "NO! ... Oh, Alpha Lee -- Roddy is so sweet. He's been so gentle, so careful not to hurt me or upset me or anything.

How could I not love him?" And then she laughed again. "Alpha Lee, Roddy is the BEST person I've ever known! NOW I understand what you mean!" Alpha Lee reached over to hug her. "Alpha Lee -- just like Dr. Sparks told me: I'm FREE! FREE! It's wonderful!" Their hug was long and meaningful.

While Susan showered, Alpha Lee made sandwiches with the last of the meat loaf, and she put a half-bag of potato chips in the grocery bag with two apples and some cookies. She had filled a jar with ice cubes and poured tea over them. Then she went out and found a ripe tomato to take along; Don't forget a salt shaker, she reminded herself, and a sharp knife. Jan contributed a Hershey bar to share.

"Roddy's coming by this afternoon to get Susan," Alpha Lee told him with a smile. "They have their own plans, just as you guessed."

"Probably another guitar lesson," Jan suggested with a wink, and he picked up the picnic food and took it out to the car.

They found a shady spot close to the tall pines for their picnic. Alpha Lee held up her ring to sine in the sunlight. "Jan -- this ring is just SO beautiful! I've never seen anything like it. It looks -- precious. ... Oh, thank you, my darling Jan!" and she fell into his arms, pushing him over, and they laughed together on the grass. "Jan -- where did you find this? It's different from any-thing I've seen. Turquoise combined with silver AND gold? – That's really unusual --"

"It really is one of a kind, honey," he said. "That ring has an interesting history. The stone itself was found in the garden at the lodge by Naomi's grandfather -- she kept it for many years, and then offered it to me when I told her I wanted to marry you someday. She wanted you to have it, she said, because she felt so grateful to you for the portrait you painted of her, and the other picture you made from the sketch of the totem poles at the Seattle Art Museum. They have that one on the wall at the place where they have their tribal meetings, framed in old wood salvaged from a canoe used by tribesmen long ago."

"Gee, Jan -- I wish I could see it. ... That IS an interesting story. Well, I will treasure this ring, love. It'll be a little token of YOU and all this summer has meant to us."

"But that's not all, Alpha Lee. You'll never guess who crafted this ring." He paused while she looked at him expectantly. "McChord Air Base's own resident jeweler -- Sergeant Ed Gillis. He's Naomi's brother-in-law. Charles told me that normally turquoise will dissolve in water, but Sgt. Gillis has coated the stone with a special shellac so it won't dissolve so fast, but he said it would probably be better to not wear it when you do dishes.

Her face lit up. "Really? REALLY, Jan? That's incredible!" She laughed with delight. "Oh, that's so good! The man's really a genius, isn't he? What's he doing in the air force? ... I wish I could thank him, too. Oh, I can't wait to tell Susan about it!" She grasped his hand and kissed the palm. "Jan, my dear love, thank you so much for NOT giving me just a little old diamond, like everybody else gets when they're engaged. AND which costs too much anyway. How boring that would be!" She laughed again. "This ring is so special -- so different, so precious. I love it, Jan. Thank you!" She hugged him again, pushing him down on the warm grass, and they lay together under the hot sunshine. "Jan, I'm so happy you're buying the lodge. That's just won- derful! ... Oh, I'm just too happy. I'm so glad! When I'm lonely this winter, I can think of you in that cabin -- I can remember -- I'll visualize you sleeping under the wolf blanket -- and I'll pretend I'm there beside you!"

"Hey -- we could go back there right now and make that come true!"

She laughed. "We could ... but not yet. Let's explore a little while."

The peak of Mount Rainier glowed brilliant white in the afternoon sun; the snow had receded somewhat in the nearly two months since they had seen it last. "Jan," Alpha Lee said, "I decided to give the painting I made at the lodge yesterday to Dr. Sparks. I really made it for myself, as a keep-sake of this summer -- but I must give it to her. She never asked for any payment for the full hour of counseling she did for Susan, and that was so helpful. I did call and ask her receptionist about a bill, but she told me the doctor said we didn't owe her anything. Actually I think we owe her more than we could ever pay -- but maybe she'll accept the painting as a gift. I'll have to leave it with Jane to be framed."

"I'd think she'd be pleased with it, honey. It's really a pretty scene. I kinda wish we could keep it, too, but I understand your feeling, and I think you're right. I don't know what she did for Susan. That night she came home early she had me really worried. I had thoughts we might have to find a looney bin to put her in! But in an hour of talking she had her pretty much cured -- it's almost like she hypnotized her and told her when she snapped her fingers she would NEVER REMEMBER what her father had done." She is some kind of MIRACLE WORKER.

Alpha Lee shook her head yes, thinking, Jan, you'll never know how much of a Godsend the good Dr Sparks HAS been.

They walked to the edge of the cliff above the river; the tiny voles were nowhere to be seen. The berries they had been harvesting in July were gone long since. Then they walked through a grove of pines that grew so close together that there was no undergrowth, and the light was dim and dusky. The ground was so deeply covered with decades of fallen needles that their footfalls were utterly soundless. The silence in the grove was eerily profound; the only sound was their breathing. They did not speak until they were back out in the sunshine. "I don't ever want to forget that, Jan," Alpha Lee said. "That's the first time I've ever experienced such quiet. It was sort of -- unearthly, I think."

"Me, too, Alpha Lee. I'm glad we went in there -- the pine woods must be the quietest places on earth. We'll go there again someday."

When they returned to the lodge, Susan was gone; there was a note: "Roddy's taking me to see his dad's boat -- maybe we'll go on a cruise. See you at dinner at Williamsons'. 7:00 PM."

They arrived at Williamsons' a little before seven. Alpha Lee proudly flaunted her ring. "Look at this, Susan! -- you'll never guess who made this ring -- your friend Sergeant Gillis! And the turquoise was actually found in our garden by Naomi's grandfather a long time ago! My ring has a history."

"Maybe more so than you know, Alpha Lee," Charles said as he examined it closely. "Turquoise isn't normally fond in this area -- it's usually found in the southwest, and it does dissolve slowly in water, so it doesn't last long outdoors here. I'd guess this is quite old. Turquoise was occasionally traded by the Zuni tribe in New Mexico to the North-western tribes in exchange for wooden craft products, hides and the like. It was highly prized around here -- there was something about it being a piece of the sky, I think. It was considered a very lucky commodity."

He grinned at Alpha Lee. "That's a good sign, isn't it? Maybe it'll bring you good fortune in your marriage. By the way, when will that be?"

"We can't be married until after my first year at college," Alpha Lee told him. "My grant specifies that it's for an unmarried student, and I have to live on campus, in the dorm. ... So --" she looked at Jan, blushing, "maybe next summer."

"It's gonna be a long winter, Charles," Jan said with a grin.

Jane served the smoked salmon they loved as an appetizer with crackers and crisp vegetables, and then there was steak grilled by Charles on a brazier outside, with side dishes served by a Japanese woman Jan recognized as the lady who had catered the food at The Arte Schacke on the fourth of July. Dessert was tarts filled with cultivated blackberries and rich cream.

"Oh, Jane, this surely is good," Jan said. "Makes me think of Mom's blackberry pie. My brother Willis and I used to pick berries up on the hill behind our house. ... I suppose the blackberry season's about over back home -- don't you think, Alpha Lee?"

"I would think so. But they grow a lot of berries as crops up here, don't they, Jane?"

"Oh, yes -- Washington grows all kinds of fruit for shipping all over the country – strawberries, cherries, blueberries, apples, pears, plums – the climate is ideal for fruit crops. Flowers, too."

"It's a big change from Minnesota, where we came from," Charles said. "It's the same latitude, but the ocean current makes the climate here much more moderate. You'll like making your home here, Jan."

After dinner Alpha Lee showed Jane the painting she wanted to give to Dr. Sparks. "Would you frame this suitably for me, Jane? I'll leave some money –Dr. Sparks did both me and Susan a huge favor, and I really want her to have this to pay part of what I feel I owe her. "

"No, no, Alpha Lee. If you really want Fran to have this I'll have her come in and choose a frame, and I'll take care of it. It's a beautiful picture. Did you paint it to keep yourself?"

Alpha Lee laughed. "How did you guess? I intended it to be a keepsake of my time here. I just did it yesterday."

"It shows. It just looks like you invested a lot of yourself in it. It has an emotional quality -- a kind of nostalgic feel. ... Let me make you a print to keep, Alpha Lee. I'll ship it to you."

"Oh, Jane -- you're still being the fairy godmother! Thank you – that would be wonderful. ... I'll tell you what, Jane -- I'll paint a West Virginia scene for you in return. I'll make a picture when the autumn leaves have turned, and our mountains are covered with bright colors – Yes! I'll paint a picture of Hacker County in October, and send it."

They left Williamsons' house at ten o'clock; Roddy insisted that he wanted to bring Susan home later. So there were tearful goodbyes, hugs and handshakes, and Jan and Alpha Lee drove away. Alpha Lee dabbed at her eyes. "They are the nicest people, aren't they, Jan?"

"The BEST," he agreed. "I'm looking forward to working for Charles and Professor Heiden full-time. The work's just exactly what I want to do, and they have some pretty exciting ideas for new developments. I can learn as much from them as I'll learn from my classes at C.O.P." Jan unlocked the door and they walked into the silent lodge. "Our last night," he said. "Tomorrow at this time we'll be winging our way toward West Virginia. Are we about ready?"

"I think so -- Susan and I have to pack the rest of our clothes, and I have to clean out the fridge, and I'll wash the sheets if it doesn't rain. I'll take the rest of the food up to Naomi when she gets home from work. Maybe you could go up there with me and say goodbye to Frank and Naomi – and I want to tell her how much I love the turquoise ring."

"Oh, Alpha Lee --- I forgot to tell you: Frank's gonna install the water heater and a wall furnace and a gas cookstove while we're gone. That's part of the purchase agreement the bank wanted. When you come back," (Alpha Lee noted he had said "when", not "if") "you'll have a REAL stove to cook on. No more building fires."

"That'll be just great, Jan," she said, "And hot water for showers any time at all! ... But it's been fun learning to cook on the big old wood stove. I wish we could keep it. I feel sort of sentimental about that old stove --"

Jan laughed. "Alpha Lee, I think you're sentimental about everything!" He hugged her close, and his mood changed. "Sweetheart, every time I hold you close like this, it's like it's the first time-- at the airport, in the drizzle? You felt so good -- and you still do."

Monday morning Jan had to report to Fort Lewis one final time to turn in his GI bedding and pick up his last paycheck and his discharge papers. First Sergeant Berkowicz shook his hand when he checked into the orderly room. "Don't disregard the advantages of reenlistment, Jan. Give it some thought -- we'll save a place for you. The captain's not here today, but he asked me to tell you he was very pleased with the training you and Corporal Harris conducted for the tank transport drivers. ... I understand you plan to return here to work for Takoma Elektroniks?... Good, good. Looks like they have a bright future. Good luck, Short."

The girls worked furiously, getting their clothes packed, the bed clothes washed (by hand), even though Jan had told them not to bother with that job; he could take them to the laundry when he got back. There was a stiff breeze that dried the sheets in a short time, and the beds were freshly re-made before the rain came in early afternoon.

Supper was a hodgepodge of what was left in the refrigerator and a last harvest from the garden. By eight o'clock the suitcases, packed to capacity, were waiting beside the front door, along with Susan's guitar case and Alpha Lee's easel, disassembled, strapped and labeled, and the metal box of paints. Darkness was deepening; a fine mist was falling. Fred was expected soon to take them to the airport. But when they heard a car coming down the driveway, it was Roddy; he had insisted on taking Susan to meet the plane himself.

"Hi, Rod -- Before you go, Suz, we need a final ticket check. Are all our plane tickets handy so we can check in quickly?" Jan asked, patting his uniform shirt pocket where his own ticket was stowed. Susan and Alpha Lee retrieved their tickets from their purses and waved them at him, and he nodded approval. ... Dollars Alpha Lee had earned from her art and Jan from his soldiering had been combined to exchange for tickets on the late eastbound mail plane; Susan was using the return portion of her round-trip ticket the McAllisters had purchased for her three months ago. Jan had not abandoned his life-long habit of frugality: he had chosen the night flight because it was all he could afford. He was grateful for Alpha Lee's insistence on buying her own ticket; he had needed the extra cash to give Frank for the down payment on the lodge.

"We'll meet you at SeaTac at 9:30," Roddy said, and he picked up Susan's suitcase as she took the guitar case and waved briefly.

Jan and Alpha Lee walked to the back door and looked out over the sound while they waited for Fred. The sky was light in spite of the rain, illuminated by the glow of a full moon above the overcast. They could hear the lonely cry of a loon far away .... And then there was the crunch of tires on the pebbles. "That's Fred," Jan said. "Are we ready, Alpha Lee?"

No, she thought, I'm not ready! I don't want to leave this place! ... But: "Yes, I guess so," she answered, and reluctantly turned away as Jan closed and locked the back door.

Fred appeared at the open front door. "Cab's here," he called, and Jan grabbed the suitcases to carry to the station wagon. "Hey, Alpha Lee -- you look like you've lost your last friend. Aren't you thrilled to be goin' home to the Hillbilly State?"

Alpha Lee merely gave him what she hoped was a withering glare. "No, I'm not, Sergeant Harris. ... Here -- will you take this out, please?" and she handed him the easel and picked up the paint box herself.

When she climbed into the back seat of the station wagon, she found Veronica holding Sunshine in her lap. "I thought maybe you'd like to say goodbye to her, so I brought her along for the ride," she explained.

Alpha Lee took the kitten and held her close to her cheek. "Thanks, Ronnie. Is she behaving herself? I sure have missed her the these past two days. Oh, Ronnie -- the next time I see her, she'll be a full-grown cat! " and Alpha Lee had to find her hankie again. "How I hate to leave," she sniffled.

"I'll miss you so much," Veronica responded. Promise you'll come back just as soon as classes are out next summer! We can make some more clothes! ... Maybe maternity clothes," she whispered.

The trip to SeaTac Airport took an hour as Fred drove slowly in the drizzle. Jan and Fred unloaded the luggage and hurried it into the terminal. "Thanks for the ride, Fred," Jan said. "I'll see you in about three weeks."

"You're comin' back on the sixteenth, right?"

"Yeah, I'll leave Atlanta at 0700 and get back here around 2200 if all the fights are on time. 'I'll have changes in St Louis and Denver.

"Okay, Jan -- I'll check with Williamson, and if he can't pick you up, I will. Your car will be at the lodge so you can get to work the next day. Have a great vacation, buddy," and Fred clapped Jan on the back.

Hugs and handshakes -- tears and promises and well-wishes ... and then the sleek maroon station wagon rolled out onto the driveway and was gone into the darkness. Jan turned to Alpha Lee, who was dabbing her eyes with a handkerchief that was already too damp. "Hey, pretty lady -- cheer up! We're homeward bound! C'mon, let's go get this baggage checked in. ... Look, here come Roddy and Suz. I was afraid they'd get sidetracked somewhere along the way."

The goodbye kiss between Roddy and Susan was quite different from the friendly pecks that had characterized their relationship during the summer. Alpha Lee could not help but wonder: When will be the next time that Jan and I can hold each other like that? And then she remembered Jan's promise as they had been together the night before: "I don't know how right now, Alpha Lee, but I swear, I WILL find a way for us to be together while we're back home. I can't spend two weeks without loving you, and then leave. I'll find a way ..."

Jan stacked the suitcases and the other items on the scale beside the baggage desk. "Three for Pittsburgh," he told the agent.

Three for Pittsburgh ... The phrase rang in Alpha Lee's ears as the plane bored through the night sky. Susan was asleep in the seat behind Jan and Alpha Lee, stretched as far as possible across the empty seat beside her own, with her guitar case propped beside her. "Comfortable, honey?" Jan asked softly. They had skimpy pillows at their backs and were sharing a thin blanket.

She snuggled against him. "I'm fine, Jan." She was silent for a moment. She looked out the window; nothing there but darkness since they left the cities behind. "Jan, it feels strange, going back home. I feel like I'm a different person from the girl who left Brick City in May. Don't you have that feeling, too?"

"Sure I do, honey," he replied. "I've been gone a whole year -- and yes, I am a different person. You grow up a lot after you leave home. The folks we left behind will notice it, too, and maybe it'll make them a little sad, because -- in a sense, they've lost forever the children they've known all those years. You know, honey, you can't really ever go all the way 'back home'. Because things won't ever be quite the same. Because WE won't ever be the same. ... Does it scare you, Alpha Lee? Are you afraid of the future?"

She pulled away to look up into his eyes. "Oh, no, Jan. I felt a little bit afraid when I graduated, and when I got on the plane in Pittsburgh to start off to -- whatever was going to happen out here. But not now. I feel confident -- I'm excited about what's ahead. I'm not afraid." She kissed his cheek, and she touched the turquoise ring. "And now I have you, and your promise, to take with me into whatever I do. Why would I be afraid?" Her smile was radiant.

"Well, then--" he replied. "'Three to Pittsburgh' it is, Alpha Lee – and then two to Brick City, and one to Waters -- and from there, who knows? But whatever it is, you and I are ready, aren't we?"

She squeezed his hand. "YOU BETCHA!" she agreed..

LaVergne, TN USA
03 August 2010
191897LV00003B/6/P

9 781449 049935